Mary Brock Jones lives in New Zealand but loves nothing more than to escape into the other worlds in her head, to write science fiction and historical romances. Sedate office worker by day; frantic scribbler by night.

Her parents introduced her to libraries and gave her a farm to play on, where trees became rocket ships and rocky outcrops were ancient fortresses. She grew up writing, filling pages of notebooks and filling her head with stories but took a number of detours on the pathway to her dream job. Four grown sons, more than one house renovated and various jobs later, her wish came true.

To keep up to date with her latest news and releases, sign up to her newsletter here:
subscribepage.io/mbj-landing-page

Or find Mary here:
http://www.marybrockjones.com/
https://www.facebook.com/MaryBrockJonesAuthor

Also By Mary Brock Jones:

A Heart Divided
Swift Runs the Heart

Hathe Series

Resistance: Hathe Book One
Pay the Piper: Hathe Book Two
Toil and Strife: Hathe Book One and Two

Arcadia Series

Torn

AFTERMATH

Hathe Book Three

Mary Brock Jones

Mary Brock Jones

Auckland, New Zealand

DEDICATION

To my sons who grew up with Hathe, and whose gift allowed me to finish
it

CONTENTS

CHARACTER LIST AND GUIDE TO HATHE

Hathian names use the format: [First name] [prefix] [Patrilineal family name]

Further to this, family genealogy and marital status are very important on Hathe. The name prefix shows the marital status for each Hathian: for example, see the difference in names of the two asn Castre twins at the time of this book:

Bendin asn Castre—deceased before he ever married, therefore permanently known by the single form.

Marthe an Castre—Married to the Terran Hamon Radcliff (known as Hamon an Radcliff in the Hathian format).

GOVERNMENT

The Hathian system of government has three main branches:

Council: The supreme branch of the Hathian government. The members are appointed by the individual family lines and the rules of appointment vary between lines. Every Hathian 'looks to' both a matrilineal and patrilineal councilor, as well as having connections to the councilors of other lines depending on their individual family connections. Democracy is based on a fluid and well understood system of personal contacts through family connections. For this reason, the accuracy and integrity of the family genealogical records are fiercely protected.

Senate: Each region has a Senator elected by all the inhabitants of that region, who deals solely with regional issues.

Local bodies: These vary in name and rules, but deal with all the day-to-day issues of each local community such as provision of community facilities, school buildings, water and sewage etc.

CHARACTER LIST

Jacquel des Trurain: Resistance hero, historian, colonel in the Security Department.

Rheia asn Forvrad (aka asn Postrova): Interplanetary relations analyst with the Department of Interplanetary Affairs (DIA).

Marthe an Castre: Resistance heroine, physician and an old childhood friend of Jacquel. Married to Major Hamon Radcliff of Earth, ex-head of the Terran Security Service during the Terran occupation of Hathe.

Bendin asn Castre: Marthe's twin and Jacquel's other closest friend. Pilot who died in the original battle to delay the Terran invasion of Hathe.

Gauvan de Trurains: Jacquel's father, A university academic and specialist in political strategies.

Anhuilla deln Vestros: Jacquel's stepmother and sister to Marthe's deceased mother.

Dougan: des Trurains family butler/factotum.

Manny: des Trurains family housekeeper.

Master an Pientos: Rheia's great grandfather's name. Her mother was a daughter of his youngest son.

Marisa an Postrova: Samarkan trader's daughter, married into the an Pientos family. Rheia's great grandmother.

Garin an Forvrad: Rheia's father.

Marya an Pientos: Rheia's mother.

Bucephalis asn Forvrad (nickname Bupha): Rheia's younger brother.

<u>JACQUEL'S SQUAD</u>

Raz den Koprorth: Jacquel's sergeant and right-hand man.

Joshan an Thanis: Ranger and a tracker.

Trooper Dreya an Vathin: the senior female trooper on the Plateau and the field medic.

Trooper Anton der Phebasin: the troop Third.

<u>PLATEAU MISSION</u>

Katrin den Phadros: hazardous waste expert (environmental engineer).

Kaya deln Trannis: pilot.

Phillipos athns Kronkist: geotech engineer, dirtsider extremist rebel.

Varda an Tarkst: chemical engineer.

Maria asn Rostrum: ecologist, born on the edge of the plains.

Braken das Shondreth: hydrogeologist specializing in water containment and prevention of waste chemical leaching.

COUNCIL

Councilor Gilda an Rathman: senior councilor with close links to the Security and DIA and pro-dirtsider. Closely involved with the Resistance during the occupation.

Councilor Sylvan an Castre: father of Bendin and Marthe, and good friend to Jacquel. Senior councilor and pro-dirtsider, heavily involved with the Resistance during the occupation.

Councilor Philos der Greystan: Prominent moonie-favoring Councilor.

Councilor frey Radkish: ally of Councilor der Greystan.

Councilor Trundain an Delsin - councilor and computer comptroller (in charge of genealogical records, births, deaths, and marriages).

Councilor an Heurain: moderate councilor, in the undecided group.

Councilor an Baktish: The oldest member of Council. Third cousin by marriage of Marthe an Castre's grandmother.

Councilor an Jordan: influential member of the undecided group.

Councilor Aaron deln James.

CITY - OTHER

Gof deln Crantz: commander of the Security Department and a senior member of the Resistance.

Myron ven Raden: Director of the Department of Interplanetary Affairs (DIA).

Advocate Generals Justice Maritsa ven Bradden and Ventnor deln Croasch: Senior prosecutors with the Planetary Prosecutions Service.

Graia - Jaca's original assistant.

Dr an Mathson: senior doctor with the Resistance and now with the Security Department

Senator an Kroth; Moonsider senator opposed to increasing dirtsider power.

Narvin asn Chrostic - cousin of Rom der Greystan and advisor in Councilor der Greystan's office. Pro-moonie.

Caya der Greystan: daughter of Councilor der Greystan.

Rom der Greystan - son of councilor der Greystan and a land developer.

<u>AVENUE CAMP</u>

Madame Julianna da Festran: Organizer of supplies and logistics.

Karven: resistance strategist and ex-math teacher.

Phaedra: a maid during the occupation.

Yurin an Begum: dirtsider lawyer who defended Marthe asn Castre.

Mathis an Begum: lawyer.

HATHIAN TERMS AND PLACE NAMES

Aerion: family of predatory flying animals now found only on the plateau.

Kryptark: thorny bush.

Snipkit - tiny insect.

Gnur - ground dwelling herbivore. Favourite prey of aerions.

Dynat: small scavenger found only on the plateau. Unofficial Resistance mascot.

Nystat: urban species of vermin, related to dynats. A term of derision.

Metrin: drug that gives impression of being drunk/drugged while staying sober. Dangerous if used long term or to excess.

The City: Hathe's capital.

Hyrvettin: Rheia's home village.

Dromorne: the larger of Hathe's two moons.

Mathe: the small, less easily seen moon. Visible more often in the early morning when Dromorne begins to fade. Secret home to those Hathians who took refuge in hidden bases there during the Terran occupation of Hathe.

Pillars of Mathe: Legendary and ancient arc of stone pillars placed on Mathe by unknown species. The Zenith of the Pillars of Mathe occurs when Hathe sits directly over the central pillar and marks the alignment of the solar system that causes disruption to Terran designed technological devices.

Cloughtarch: city on Islandia, one of the lesser continents.

INTRODUCTION

The stars beckoned and man went, spreading out to populate the new worlds with new ideas and new ways. Shining among those worlds was Hathe. It had peace, stability and wealth, all in sufficient abundance to bring forth a world in which there was a blossoming of the arts, the sciences and sheer curiosity.

Particularly, it had wealth.

Wealth yes; a well-trained and equipped military, no. Why bother when surely no Alliance planet would invade another. Too difficult, too costly and far too damaging for intergalactic trade.

A pity no one told Earth. Traditional home of mankind and still the most populous planet, it saw no need to look outwards to the newer colonial worlds to solve its problems. What could raw, new worlds teach a planet that was home to all the accumulated knowledge of human history? But Earth did not have urgonium, the most efficient source of energy known. Only Hathe had that, and Earth desperately needed it.

Yes, Hathe was a world blessed by nature. But that was before the Terran ships appeared in Hathian space, before a raw and untried Hathian fleet flew out in futile battle against the invaders.

Before the Terrans stole the most precious jewel in the Hathian treasury:

Freedom.

Now Hathe has won it back. But freedom is a treasure needing to be guarded constantly.

PROLOGUE

Jacquel des Trurains brought his flyer down in the courtyard of his home. He had raced down those steps and climbed that far wall, played in this courtyard with his friends. Childhood memories, lost in some half-remembered time before the war. He peered through his viz screen, trying to make the past match the present, but failed. Whatever it was that had made this place home no longer lived here. Gone, waiting to be restored like everything else on Hathe.

What did he expect? Five years of abandonment. Five years living under Terran rule since any had set foot here. The fake radiation signals had kept the Terrans out of the City, but not even Resistance tricks could stop the erosions of time.

"Let me go in first," he'd told his superior. "The parents don't need to see the worst of it."

"Do you?"

"No, but better than some unknown cleaning crew."

Now, Jacquel wasn't so sure. He opened the flyer's hatch but couldn't move. Not yet.

Weeds grew through the pavers, a wild vine sprawled over the upper colonnade roof and the air was filled with the skittering sounds of small animals frightened by his flyer, while a drunken mass of greenery over the entrance door warned of a buzzers' nest.

At last, something he could fix. He threw himself down the steps, grabbed a broken bract from the hanging creepers and knocked down the old nest.

"My home now," he said to the abandoned greenery. "My home."

If he repeated it often enough, he might just believe it.

Up the steps and slam a hand against the door control on the massive front doors. A sickening pause, as if the house system needed to be shocked into life again, then the door opened to his palm print, still swinging smoothly on command. Inside was almost as he remembered, but overlaid with the stale whiff of emptiness. He coughed as a cloud of dust hit his face, scuffed up by his first step in the door. His step-mama was due to arrive in two days, back from her refuge on Mathe. She mustn't see this. He called up central control and ordered a crew of cleaning bots.

"Please complete details of work required," said the automated form.

"I've only just walked in the door."

"Full analysis of most urgent work required before the order can be processed."

Stupid anachronism. "Fine then. I'll get back to you."

He kicked at the rug, releasing another cloud of dust, then turned and flung wide the big doors, the front reception windows, any window within reach, letting in the sun and free air of Hathe.

"Make it better."

There was a falafaux flowering in the garden and the faint scent of it whispered through the windows. He drew in a deep breath of the outside air and, for the first time, began to feel at home.

"Right. No point putting it off," he said, his voice battering against the answering silence of the house.

He was a professional. This was a mission, a job that must be completed and in proper order. He made himself look at walls and structures, scanning and recording physical details, rather than memories and heartaches.

The main house systems had kept working throughout the long silence. There was dust, stale air, but no damage or water entry, no signs in here of the wildlife living in the garden. He checked each room, counting down his list. Reception rooms, main hall, living and dining areas, the great kitchen, staff quarters, his parents' bedroom and offices. The staff quarters and kitchen would need to be restored before he let Manny, their old housekeeper, see them again. She would either read him a huge lecture or burst into tears, and neither could he bear.

Lastly, he came to a door at the end of a hallway. His own quarters. He stopped, laid a hand on the familiar whorls etched into the surface, then palmed the lock and pushed the door open. He could do this.

The outer room looked as if he'd just left. An antique book of poetry lay open beside his favorite chair, a sweater draped carelessly over the back of it, and his collection of book cubes on Alliance history sprawled untidily over the shelves above his desk. A drawer sat partly open and a broken stylus hung drunkenly over the lip. The room of a history student, forced to leave hurriedly.

He'd thought himself so clever when he'd put together the montage. He pushed open the bedroom door and saw the same carefully contrived scenario, untouched since the day he'd left. He pulled the bed covering straight, lined up the rare Antoni light on the bedside table with its opposite on the far side and set all to rights in the carefully ordered tidiness that he preferred in his private rooms. Only when the last piece was resting in its proper place did he approach the painting on the far wall. An interactive collage by asn Lucino, so expensive that surely even the Terrans would leave it untouched if they braved the radiation signals protecting this place. His fingers traced a whorl in the upper left corner, pushed a flower just so, then tapped on the lower frame panel. Beside it, a space appeared in the wall. A small cavity no wider than a hand's breadth.

He pulled out the pack of info slivers and cubes and counted each one. All present; all still there. His personal files, research notes, and the cube of precious holo-vids. His family, his first day at school, a holiday on Phoebus. Then he reached right to the back, and his hand clenched tight around one more cube. He pulled it out and set it on the table beside his bed. Then touched it and stood back as the holo-image sprang to life.

Three figures, caught forever in perfect miniature. Two young men and a woman, standing on a hilltop in an eerie half-light. He and his two best friends, Bendin and Marthe asn Castre, on the night of their graduation, the miniature faces alive with the excitement and expectation of that day.

Bendin was at the front as always, big, strong and tall with shoulders already showing the promise of size to come. Head high and filled with the magic of his personality. Jacquel looked at his own figure, slightly back and to one side. Sun and moon, they'd been dubbed by the public, thanks mostly to Bendin's golden hair and his own silver gilt. Bendin, the laughing golden god of them all, and Jacquel, the slimmer echo at his side. But not sad, never that. He was laughing in this holo-pic; they all were. His figure looked across at his friends, and he saw exasperation mingling in with the laughter. That wasn't unusual in those days either.

Between them stood Marthe—so tiny, so vital, her dark hair touched with a shimmer of sunlight and wearing a smile that sat halfway between anger and glee. Now he understood the look on his figure's face: he'd been caught in another of the asn Castre twins' feuds. Something about a banged foot and Bendin teasing Marthe; but also a protective hand Bendin had shot out to his twin and the strength in the arm that pulled her up to the final summit.

Where were they now, those bright youths of yesterday? Those three laughing faces?

Jacquel couldn't stop the twist of his mouth. Not here, and no longer laughing. Bendin's grave lay far from here, a hasty wartime resting place. Plans were in place to rebury him with full honors in the memorial avenue of the main city cemetery. As for Marthe? Heartsick and hiding, her doctors and family all desperately trying to get her to fight back. Fight for her own life and that of her half-Terran child.

Only he had survived unscathed.

"I'm sorry," he whispered to Bendin, and to all the other bright-eyed youths who could not come home. "I couldn't protect her, and I couldn't save you…but I did protect Hathe. We won our freedom back. Isn't that enough?"

Suddenly the images were too much. He crashed the cube and slammed the holo to the floor. The three youthful images sprawled on the mat, lying drunkenly to one side.

Still they laughed up at him.

CHAPTER ONE

"Hello boys. Planning a party?"

Jacquel des Trurains grinned at the group of budding conspirators huddled around the beat-up table and pawing through their haul of antiquated weaponry. He gestured to his troops silently filing in through the tavern doors and pointing decidedly more dangerous weapons.

The conspirators froze in place, half-standing, and scowled back at him. All except one who stood straight and held the biggest and ugliest weapon square in front of him.

"If it isn't the mad captain. Playing away from home tonight, *sir?*"

Jacquel could feel his temper rising, and saw his second frowning and vainly shaking his head.

Too late, my friend.

He plastered on an even wider grin, set his legs apart and slowly scanned the brave idiot in front of him. The boy's stance said he was untrained, his clenched fist said he was angry, and the too clean jacket and the way he held the very nasty piece of weaponry in his hand said he had no idea what he held or what it could do.

Ras would like him to go slowly, coax the stuff out of this civilian's hand and bring to bear all those vaunted diplomatic skills of his.

He let his hand drift down to the holster on his hip and heard Ras groan.

"Now, what do you plan to do with that?" Jaquel said. "Has no one warned you about playing with fire?"

The young man scowled back, the only one of the group still standing. The rest had carefully sat back down and were keeping their hands in full view of his troopers. Unlike the hothead who thought he led them.

But then, the hothead was the only moonie among them. The rest had been honed by a youth spent under the heels of the Terrans and could recognize real danger when it stood right in front of them. While he'd been moaning about homework assignments up on his safe haven on Mathe, the rest of these young men had been running Terran security posts as Resistance couriers or lumped into rough and dirty work patrols.

These boys knew exactly who faced them. No longer a mere captain, though he doubted his troopers would ever refer to him as anything other than 'the Cap', Jacquel was now a senior colonel in Hathe's Security Department. He reviewed the file on these boys he'd read before coming here, glanced at his troops with a brief nod and then at each one of the seated boys.

"Home. Now," Jacquel said softly.

They really had heard of him. One looked like a ghost, he'd turned so white. But that one had watched his father collapse under a load in the mines and been beaten to death because of it. That this moonie cub should expose such a boy to any more danger made Jacquel even angrier.

The moonie cub now dared to put out a hand to stop the boy leaving.

This time, Jacquel made no attempt to hide his feelings. "Let go of him."

"Why? You gonna stop me?" Jacquel wasn't too many years older, but he was lean, wiry, and a trained ex-Resistance agent who'd been in situations this boy couldn't dream of. This *boy* clearly only saw the lean part. He stared back at Jacquel. Big for his age, the moonie seemed to think them a match.

Ras moved closer, put out a hand. "Cap?"

He shrugged it off and plastered on a grin that made Ras's face even longer.

"This boy has asked me a question. It's only courtesy to answer him." He switched his gaze back to the wannabe rebel. "Am I going to stop you? Oh yes, most definitely. You think I can't?" It was a juvenile taunt, added to by the sharp bite edging his voice. He was beginning to enjoy himself. He outright grinned when the cub launched himself forward.

Yes, he could have finished it quickly. A step here, a touch there, and the boy would be hog-tied and led away to face the justice system.

He probably ought to do it like that. He sidestepped, flicked out a tap, let the boy land a blow that did nothing.

Ten minutes later, the room was clear and Jacquel was feeling much better.

"Cap, time to end it," said Ras.

Jacquel looked at the boy. He had guts at least, but Ras was right. A quick clip to the back of his head, a pinch on a critical nerve and the young man collapsed in a heap. Jacquel stepped back and the squad medic rushed forward.

"The senator's not going to be pleased."

"You mean the one who refused to agree to fund that rescue team last year, the one who said it hadn't been so bad down here."

Ras grinned back. "Yeah, that senator."

His squad had powered off their weapons long ago. They marched the boy out to a hearty cheer from the bar's patrons straggling back inside, and soon life went back to normal.

Unfortunately, when Jacquel returned home soon after, life there was also back to normal. Doughan, the factotum who'd run his family home as long as Jacquel could remember, caught him as he came in the side door.

"Your father would like to see you in the study, young sir."

Jacquel gauged the look on Doughan's face. "Senator an Kroth been to visit him already?"

"As to that, no sir. But the professor has been on the com link for the last hour."

Doughan could be stonier faced than any Hathian Resistance agent, but Jacquel had grown up with him. "That bad, huh?"

A slight grimace and a twist upwards of his lips, with a discreet glance at Jacquel's bruised knuckles. Jacquel shoved them in his pockets.

When the doors opened, his father's face confirmed it; the look on it the one he used when speaking to a particularly annoying junior.

"Senator an Kroth tells me you arrested his son this afternoon. To do which, he also claims, you used less than conventional means."

The devil rode Jacquel still. He kept his hands in his pocket but shrugged his lack of concern.

"Are you deliberately trying to sabotage me?" said his father.

"As you do what? Try to pretend the occupation never happened?" Jacquel hitched himself on the edge of the only other chair in the room and raised an eyebrow.

"No. Restore Hathe and bring its inhabitants back to civilization."

"Like you had on the moon?"

His father opened his mouth, then shut it again and Jacquel felt his anger rise, despite all his intentions.

"Where I should have stayed," Jacquel said, propping one leg carelessly across the other, "instead of playing hero down here?"

His father's mouth tightened. "We have had this discussion. You will act in a manner suited to your position."

"My position—or yours? *My* position is colonel in the Hathian Security forces, and we answer to the Council, not to a pack of jumped up senators who have forgotten who truly rules Hathe. My job is to make this world safe again for every single Hathian. Particularly those of us who endured those five years down here, so you could return to your nice homes, safe and untroubled."

His father rose. "Do not—"

Jacquel thrust up a hand. "I have work to do," he said, and marched out of the room, all his good mood banished. But work didn't help, and he finally took refuge in the small library near his own rooms. Yet not even his favorite retreat was safe today.

"You have a visitor asking to see you, sir."

It was Doughan, standing patiently at the library door in a way that said he wasn't going anywhere until 'sir' did something about the latest intruder. Jacquel sighed and put down the book he'd just opened.

"Show them into my sitting room, please, Doughan."

He allowed himself a bare glance at his book. Genuine late isolationist period from Earth, the fragile pages composed of real paper. The diary of a general-turned-politician involved in the rehabilitation of the area known as Europe after a catastrophic war. It had seemed appropriate today. It had taken him months to track down a copy and had been delivered just days before his own world's disaster; when the Terrans had invaded and conquered Hathe. Months after his people had overcome the Terrans and thrown them out, he had only just found time to unearth his special files from storage and restore them.

Actually reading them was going to take longer, it seemed.

The sun shone into the sitting room, making cheerful play with the flowers the housekeeper insisted on placing there. A sad contrast to the face of the man sitting waiting for him, two small children tucked close either side of him and peering warily out from behind their father's arms. Worse, he knew the face of the man.

"Bareth, I haven't seen you since that last mission together."

A tight smile, the man's body held too rigid, too ready to meet humiliation. Jacquel had learned the hard way not to bluntly ask what a man needed.

"So, what are you up to these days?" he said instead.

Doughan came in before the man was forced to answer, carrying a tea tray laden with goodies, and Manny following close behind bearing some of the toys Jacquel kept for these meetings.

Manny had once been his nurse and was long wise in the ways of managing the most scared of children. In quick time she had lured out these two, a boy of about eight and a small tot of a girl no more than six. A fearful look at their father, a quiet nod in reply from the man after he glanced at Jacquel's carefully blank face, and the children nervously moved out from the man's sheltering arms. But no further than an arm's stretch away.

It was enough.

"A dram, Doughan," Jacquel said, having dredged up a lost memory of a campfire and this man chuckling openly after a successful mission.

Jacquel was a past master of social ease. A born charmer, as his stepmother was prone to remark dryly, but it took him half an hour of careful gossip before he could bring the man to the point of his visit.

"I need a job," he said baldly.

"What kind?"

Bareth looked awkwardly around and his gaze fastened on the flowers in the vase. "I was a gardener—during the occupation."

As well as a first-class engineer and brave undercover Resistance agent. Resourceful, courageous, a man who had faced down danger and resolutely kept the secret of Hathe's people right to the end.

"Have you tried the re-start programs?"

The man nodded slowly. "But…"

"You didn't fit," guessed Jacquel, when he didn't finish.

A slow shake of the head, a humiliated frown. That look of shame and defeat.

It was the look Jacquel hated the most. "Not many do."

The man said nothing.

"What about your old job? The one you had before the invasion?"

The man shrugged. "Already taken."

Jacquel didn't bother asking by whom. Too many dirtsiders had come to his door. Five years of occupation, five years of pretending to be no more than simple, defeated peasants couldn't be thrown off readily.

The dirtsiders and the moon-based. A sharp division that was tearing apart his once splendid world. On one side, those Hathians who had lived through the occupation on the hidden bases on Hathe's smallest moon, Mathe. The politicians, the technical staff, the support staff and all the other Hathians not needed to keep up the outrageous facade that was the peasant society Hathians portrayed to their Terran occupiers. On Mathe, the Hathians could still enjoy to the full the advanced technology of their home world, kept safe from Terran invasion by the illusory screens concealing them from Terran eyes, and by the courage of the Hathian population remaining on the home planet.

On the other side, his dirtsiders; those incredibly brave and stoic Hathians left behind on the home world and tasked with fooling their Terran invaders. Those who created and maintained the outrageous hoax to keep Hathe safe until the day when their solar system came together in a unique configuration of moon and sun, creating a surge of solar energy that killed dead all the Terrans' technology, including their hated arsenal of repression. Hathians had long learned to live with the periodic disruption and adapted their technology to withstand it. On that day, when Hathe rose high in the sky to stand above the center of the ancient pillars on Mathe, the Resistance threw off their invaders in one swift reversal of power and took back their home.

It should have brought the shining future they had been promised, but too many had found the future as this man had: their old jobs taken by returning moonies and their confidence long eroded by constant subservience to their Terran conquerors.

Breaking out of that servitude was proving far harder than the Hathian Council had expected. First, you had to give a man back his self-esteem. Only then could you give him back his life.

Jacquel racked his brains. "My step-cousin has a small house on the high plateau. She cannot live there now but it needs caring for. Moonies refuse to go to the plateau—too wild, they say. You interested?"

"Your step-cousin's name? Sir?" added the man nervously. Wary also, as if already guessing the answer.

"Marthe an Castre. She lives off-world now," Jacquel said blandly. Exiled by the Council and married to a Terran, he refrained from adding.

He didn't have to. This man knew Marthe's name. All dirtsiders did.

His reaction was mixed: half, the respect Marthe still inspired; half, a bitter smile.

"You've met her?" said Jacquel.

The man shook his head, "But I wish I had," he then surprised him with.

Jacquel waited, saw the grief-ridden glance at his too quiet children, playing on the floor beside him. "My wife…"

"Yes?"

"We were taken in a work gang."

By the Terrans. Too many dirtsiders had been through the same.

"She was seven months gone," the man said now. "They *allowed* her to work one hour less a day."

"And her delivery?"

The man's hands clamped tightly together. "Too early. The baby came early." He looked up. "It was after Madame an Castre left the mines, after she stopped her doctoring."

A look of such anguish on the man's face. "She saved so many mothers and babies, but she was gone. My Beth, she had no one. Just me."

Jacquel kept the muscles of his face tightly controlled. "You lost them both."

All the man could do was nod. A deep breath. "If the Council had let Marthe stay…My Beth…"

Jacquel made no attempt to deny it. But this man hadn't seen Marthe by the end of her time in the mines, hadn't heard the despair in her voice.

Marthe was a good agent, one of their best. As a doctor, by the end of that first year in the mines, she was at the point of breaking. The Council had no choice—it was pull her out or watch her be destroyed by grief at all those she couldn't save.

The man agreed to his offer, of course. What else could he do? Another to add to Jacquel's growing list of pensioners, said the look on Doughan's face as he showed them out, but the relief on the man's more than made up for it.

Heartsick, Jacquel set out for the Security headquarters building in town, setting his flitter to automatic. He usually opted to dodge through the traffic layers using the manual mode, but not in his present frame of mind. Far too dangerous. It was no better when he got there. Cursing the inevitable security screens at the building's entrance, he slammed through the protocols and marched straight to his office, saying nothing to the usual chorus of morning greetings. His chair moved out to his favored position and waited for him to sit, but instead he stared at the clean surface of his desk. Pristine and untouched by the nightmare reports spilling across it. He slammed a fist down, smashing it into the shiny veneer. Not even a scrape showed on the hard top. No hint of a mark or scratch, nothing to match the pain shooting up his hand.

A stupid moment of weakness. It achieved nothing, changed nothing for all the unending ranks wanting justice and silently demanding he fix Hathe for them. He laughed bitterly and touched the com unit patch on his arm to pull up his schedule, waiting as the air shimmered and the projection settled into his preferred scheme of stacked up drawers, each blazoned with the priority level of the jobs inside waiting to be cleared. So many, and each filled to the brim with waiting files. He swept the projection aside with a wave of his hand and pulled up the top ranked ones only. Then thrust that drawer aside as well, to stare unseeing out the window.

The capital city of Hathe was a beautiful place. Called simply "the City" by the first settlers, the plain name gave no hint of the elegance of design that marked the central buildings. The Security Department headquarters was located on the main avenue, right in the heart of the government sector. From his upper floor office, he could look out to the university where his father lectured. A strategist during the war, the professor had for years before that taught a course on the principles underlying political and civic interactions in a democracy. A course urgently restored and made compulsory for all senior departmental heads, to remind them they were no longer working in a war environment.

Says who, thought Jacquel sardonically. The current Hathe bore little in common with the dreams that had sustained the dirtsiders' resistance.

He twisted in his chair to see the most beautiful building on the avenue; the one where his stepmother held power. The Hathian Central Library, restored to almost its full glory. All the precious files, all the ancient relics and genuine Earth books had been packed up and moved off-planet before the Terran invasion, the one department wholly evacuated. Knowledge; the only real weapon Hathe possessed. The library was more revered now than ever, a precious symbol of the heart of his people.

He had been a schoolboy still when the plans for a new library were accepted. He still remembered her glee that day, and the absolute joy on her face when they all walked in the front door for the first time. How his dour and constrained father had ended up with a woman so full of bubbling laughter had always bemused Jacquel. He had no memory of or regrets over his own mother, dead in an accident when he was no more than a toddler. Anhuilla deln Vestros was Mama to him, the only mother he remembered, and had given him two precious sisters.

A family. His family. It was one of the few things he thanked his father for in his growing up years.

Anhuilla had worked so hard, loved them all so much.

It wasn't her fault he couldn't feel like he belonged. Without the asn Castre twins, he dreaded to think of the loneliness that would have been his lot.

Like the loneliness that assailed him now.

A ping, and his latest assignment banged into his inbox. He glanced at the message bot hovering above the desk surface, in no mood for more meaningless demands, then saw the ranking against it and groaned. The Council had marked this top priority, so he couldn't escape. He opened the file and groaned even louder.

Garbage patrol!

All right, they'd given it a fancy name. "Identification of energy dense deposits, evaluation of the risk and securing said deposits from random incursions." What it meant was garbage patrol. The Terrans had come here for urgonium, the mineral that was still the most efficient known source of energy. But the Terrans had no idea how to use it properly. Had wasted much of it and shoveled the byproducts into crudely built pits near every Terran settlement, leaving dangerously emitting piles of corroded minerals scattered in a cluster of environmental time bombs that must be identified and eradicated. So this assignment was essential, could even use some of his old Resistance agent skills.

It was still garbage duty.

He glanced at the holo cube of Bendin asn Castre in the cluster of family images on the shelf by his desk. *This is your specialty. You should be here still.*

His eyes scrolled down, looking over the assigned team. His own squad; men and women who had been with him on one mission or other throughout the occupation. The rest made up of technical staff: geotech and chemical engineers, an ecologist and various other associated specialists and support staff. Men and women with whom he'd have to find some kind of common ground. At least they all looked to be dirtsiders, from the names. Some recognized only from Resistance reports and others more familiar. He'd been at school with Varda an Tarkst, a skilled chemical engineer. He didn't know the geotech,

Phillipos athns Kronkist, but had heard of him. He was a second cousin of a distant friend. The ecologist's name was less familiar, and he quickly scrolled through her file. Maria asn Rostrum would be critical to the mission's success. At first glance, she appeared competent but reserved. He'd have to make sure she got the help she needed to do her job.

Then he came to the last name, one he had never seen before.

Rheia asn Postrova. Specialist with the Department of Interplanetary Affairs, previously based on Mathe.

Every muscle went rigid. A desk-bound, Mathe-based infiltrator from the DIA, the one department that near equaled his Security Department in devious trickery and was least trusted by Security. Too much like Resistance agents, every one of them.

A moonie diplomat.

He'd been assigned to babysit a family-unknown, job-unknown, purpose-unknown and no doubt heavy-on-theory *moonie*. She could be one of those causing so many brave dirtsiders to knock on his door for help. His boss had a fair bit of explaining to do.

Jacquel marched down the halls of Security's headquarters, filled with righteous anger and demanding to see his commander, the newly appointed head of Security, Gof deln Crantz. The man charged with keeping some kind of control over all the grasping, self-serving, disparate factions on the planet Hathe. Too many differences, too many competing interests, and a population still too traumatized to handle any conflict—the dirtsiders, in particular.

Jacquel had only come under deln Crantz's direct command toward the end of the Terran occupation and was still trying to figure out the man. Not that it stopped him today. He barged in the door and thrust his com screen at his boss, finger thrusting at that last name. "She's a moonie. What use is she to me?"

Gof merely tented his hands and gazed calmly back. "Are you telling me all those speeches of yours meant nothing? All your talk of finding ways to reintegrate those who stayed on Hathe with those returning from exile? How better to find a way to make the new Hathe work than having a Mathian seconded to you?"

Jacquel wanted to hit someone, preferably the man in front of him. Except that Gof deln Crantz was thirty years his senior and a third his height. He was also a whole lot wilier then he let on. "The woman probably spent the war safely ensconced in the Interplanetary offices on Mathe, no doubt polishing up her credentials so she could slot into *a cushy number* once we won the war back here."

A smile on Gof's face; one that Jacquel had learned to thoroughly distrust. "I wouldn't call working with you *a cushy number*. Not the way you attract trouble," he said. "She is assigned to this mission, and I expect your full cooperation. The agreed purpose is listed in your mission notes." With which Gof turned back to his com screen and waved Jacquel out, leaving him no option but to make as dignified an exit as possible.

A DIA specialist. A moonie woman shadowing him for the undefined future. Just great.

Back in his office, he called up the woman's record. The council wasn't above setting a minder onto him, courtesy of his father, and there was a limit to what even Gof could stop. There was also a very set limit to what Jacquel would tolerate.

Madame Moonie asn Postrova was in for a well-earned education.

CHAPTER TWO

Jacquel stood at the head of the room, his troops clustered to one side and the tech staff ranged along the benches. He noted carefully who sat where: who took a prominent front seat and who slid into a back row as if wishing to be anywhere but here. Preferably back in their lab.

He waited till quiet fell, then checked his list.

"Someone's missing," he said to his second in command. Ras raised an eyebrow in query and Jacquel lit up the missing name on his screen. Rheia asn Postrova, of the Mathian arm of the DIA.

"The one who's going to teach us dirtsiders how to get on with moonies?" Ras's lips quirked upwards and his look mirrored Jacquel's thoughts.

A sound as the door slid open and a woman stepped into the room, stopped to survey the rest of them, then marched straight up to the front.

Ras's face wore a grin as wide as the plateau. "You sure get some tough assignments, Cap."

Jacquel shut his mouth, suddenly realizing it was hanging wide open. She was magnificent. That was the only word his addled brain could find.

Tall, coming up to near his own height, willowy and with a natural grace in every step as she stalked up the aisle to stand in front of him. She looked him straight in the eyes, and he was caught in the magic of pure molten bronze staring back at him. A breath, and he blinked to escape her spell but then saw the rest of her. Dressed in a quietly elegant business tunic that only served to enhance her unique beauty, her face was the pale cream of someone having spent too long in artificial habitats and would waken to warmth under Hathe's sun while his hands itched to tug at the formal braid binding her hair. Rich and dark with a hint of a curl in the one loose strand, a treasure he would very much delight in exploring. Her mouth twitched then curved into a smile, one as precisely composed as he suspected the rest of her appearance to be.

"Colonel des Trurains? Rheia asn Postrova, interplanetary relations specialist. I've been told we're to work together for the immediate future."

His orders said she'd been seconded to him, but now didn't seem the time or place to point that out. She gave him the brisk nod of equals, then took a seat at the front of the room, right in the middle of everyone. A quick look around, a brisk nod and a smile to the rest. Then she settled those long, long legs of hers under her chair and took out her comtab before giving him a smile that left him reeling.

"We can start now," she said.

Ras was all but belly laughing, his face bright red. For Jacquel, his world had just taken one extraordinary step sideways. He had to struggle to regain control, to force himself into full Resistance agent mode. He may have been known for his playacting ability during the war, but right now he had to call on every last thread of it.

"Quite ready, asn Postrova?" he said with a semblance of cool detachment.

She tipped her head and graciously nodded her assent, with a sudden twitch of her mouth that suggested she was laughing. He refused to give any sign he recognized the fact.

"Introductions then. Names and jobs, starting from your left."

His troopers first. Soldiers who had served with him from the start of the conflict and who surrounded him always these days. From her front row seat, their moonie specialist watched each one closely as they stated their name and details. Her eyes fastened on every face, as if fixing it in mind and filing it away for later.

Then the tech staff. Next to last one to speak was a stern-faced woman; their chemical engineer. The one responsible for recognizing and organizing disposal of the Terran's waste urgonium byproducts. After that, the ecologist, who had to be urged to say anything. Her file's summary had been dead right. She glanced up at him now with the look of a hunted gnur, and he forced himself to patience as he nodded encouragement. She cleared her throat.

"Maria asn Rostrum; ecologist. Specialist in the environmental degradation of Hathe during the Terran occupation."

Her voice disappeared into a whisper by the end, and he was forced to glare markedly at his troops to stop them echoing the smothered cracks of laughter from the other tech staff. The first of his own people to copy them would be stuck on whatever passed for babysitting duty on this mission, and every one of them knew it.

Then his new moonie leaned over to the ecologist. Jacquel began to step forward nervously.

"Doctor asn Rostrum. I've heard of your work. It's a pleasure to meet you." The drekking DIA woman gave a new kind of smile, the kind that said all was well, taking the hand of the ecologist in a light clasp, then released it and turned back to face Jacquel, at the same time effortlessly bringing all eyes in the room onto her face.

The ecologist looked like she'd been released from a trap.

"And me, Colonel," said Rheia asn Postrova. "Shall I introduce myself again and give my reasons for being here?"

He had to swallow, half of him admiring the skill of her intervention and the other half on sudden high alert.

"That would be very kind of you, madame."

"As I said when I entered, it's Rheia asn Postrova, interplanetary relations specialist, assigned here from the Department of Interplanetary Affairs to observe and report on matters relating to the restoration of Hathian internal relations."

"Which means what, exactly, madame?" Ras, coming to his rescue at long last. Except his second was no match for their newest recruit.

"That I will be working with the colonel, of course, trying to find ways to prevent the unfortunate disruptions between those Hathian citizens who were Hathe-based, and those who were Mathe-based."

She'd said it. Placed the unspoken divide between her and the rest of the room out in the open. Moonies and dirtsiders; those evacuated during the war, and those who'd stayed to endure the full horror of living under Terran rule. He could hear the gasps from his troopers and the caustic titters of the techs. It wasn't the kind type. They were definitely laughing *at* her.

"And you know all about that from your cozy nest up on Mathe?" said Ras, with no hint of a smile remaining.

"So how do you plan to manage the Hathian divide?" she shot back.

"Did you ever set foot on Hathe during the occupation?" jeered one of his troopers from the side of the room. His senior tracker and a native of the plateau. The rangers who made their home there had been badly hit by the occupation.

"Of course not. I was far too busy."

Did the woman have a death wish?

"Enough. Madame asn Postrova has her orders, which concern her and me only. Right now, we have a mission to organize."

He glared at Ras and the rest of his troops, and their suddenly rigid attention must have got through to the technical staff because the room fell silent. Not a comfortable silence but at least it let him get on with the real business of the meeting. By mid-afternoon they were well and truly finished and it was with a sense of relief that he dismissed them. A salute to Ras and his troops as they marched out, a brief farewell to the technical staff.

"Madame asn Postrova. A minute, if you please."

She raised an eyebrow at him, then sat down again, rearranging her body with the grace of a hunting aerion. Then leaned back in her seat and looked him square in the eye, and he suddenly realized that for the first time he was talking to the person behind the persona.

"You want to know what I'm doing here and how we're going to make this work," she said. "You need to know I'm here because my superiors ordered me to be here."

She looked as happy about it as he was, and as unsure of the wisdom of their collective bosses.

"How long have you been back on Hathe?"

"A few days. I had just returned from a mission to Samarkan. We've been working to ensure they would stay out of the change of power and reassure them that their supplies of urgonium would be uninterrupted."

"Samarkan?" A planet at the very center of interplanetary trade, the saying went that all natives of Samarkan were born with credits in their blood vessels and their first words were *let me make you an offer.*

She waved off his query. "I've been part of the diplomatic branch since the invasion. This was a routine visit to pass on our thanks and tidy up some loose ends."

But Jacquel knew the importance of those loose ends, of the danger of the other Alliance planets siding with Earth. If even one of them had broken the secret of the huge hoax the Hathians had wrought on the Terrans, the Hathians would have lost everything. To have been a part of that throughout the occupation said that Rheia asn Postrova was good at what she did. Right now, she should have been helping in the very critical task of working with the other Alliance worlds to restore Earth. The Terrans had only invaded Hathe because they saw no other way of staving off the mass starvation and destruction of their people. All the Alliance planets were agreed on one thing: the home world of humanity must never again be backed into such a corner.

"Now you're here. Any idea why?"

Another smile, tight and not amused. "Your fault, I understand. You've made enough noise with the council about the fate of your dirtsiders and the growing divide on Hathe."

"You don't think it's real?"

She shook her head. "It's real—but I have yet to see what putting us together can do about it."

"Then, Madame asn Postrova, we can agree on one thing it seems. Unfortunately, our joint superiors have decided otherwise. They've seconded you to me, and I don't have the time or energy to prove them wrong. Can I have your word you'll do nothing to hinder me at least?"

He could see her hackles rising and couldn't resist prodding to see if he could add to that spark of fire in her eyes. "My work is important, and I am not going to see any of my people sacrificed to a spoilt Mathian's uninformed misconceptions. My people have lost enough; I will not let anyone steal one more grain of self-respect from them. What they have been through, what they've lost…It's not something you can understand."

She shot up at that, and suddenly Jacquel wasn't so sure of himself. That thoroughly gorgeous burst of fire shot through her eyes, bronze flaring to brightest gold, but a dark shadow touched that fire, a shadow that said she knew more of loss than she was telling. He straightened, ready to call her back as she marched up the aisle. But then she halted at the doorway and turned to face him.

"I will do as ordered by my superiors. I will come on this garbage collection mission of yours, make my reports and work with you as professionally as I can. But outside that…"

It was as if she'd reached the end of her forbearance. She shook her head and slammed out the door, leaving Jacquel feeling as small as if he'd just slapped down something rare and precious.

Rheia had never been so mad. She'd had to bite her tongue so often these last few years it was lucky she could talk at all with the mangled mess it should be. But that man. That upstart, dirtsider, blood and glory *hero* had deliberately riled her up, and for no good reason. She'd been mad enough coming into their meeting. Last she checked, her jobs-pending file was way out of control with more pouring in. She didn't have *time* for this babysitting nonsense. She'd read her new partner's file— seconded, hah! His bosses might have sold it as that to him, but her own senior had more sense. *Her* boss had told her she was here as a co-leader. Which Jacquel des Trurains should have been able to work out too. He was too damned smart to play their stupid games, and she was too damn smart to let him.

She slammed a hand against the security panel at the exit and rudely flipped a finger at the too-smooth-for-itself, disembodied voice of the control program as it took her through what seemed an entirely superfluous series of verification checks.

"I got in here, didn't I? Of course I'm who I say I am," she muttered as the scanner read her retina and she stabbed her thumb against the light panel for her DNA check. This place had tighter security than the main council offices down the road. You'd think the Security branch were the ones really running Hathe.

But they are.

A shuddering chill, and harshly drawn breaths. So she didn't like this situation, didn't know if she could work with Colonel— "the Cap"—Jacquel des Trurains, the man even more compelling in person than on the news-vids with his silver bright hair and long, lean body but that divide between dirtsiders and returning Mathians? That was real enough, thanks to the actions of a callous few and the indifference of too many others, and it directly threatened the peace her home world had bought so dearly. As for standing back while a bunch of lowlife scum tried to steal control of her home world? Never, not while she had breath in her body. Moonies they may be, but these cowardly upstarts were nothing like the hardworking patriots she had worked with on Mathe.

As for the dirtsiders wallowing in their self-imposed victimhood, this world needed their skills, needed that courage and determination they had used so valiantly during the occupation, and it was past time they got over their fit of the sullens and got back to being the citizens Hathe deserved.

Still simmering, but with her hard-won control restored, she walked as sedately as she could manage out the main lobby. She may have lost this round by losing her temper, but that was the last time. There was too much at stake here for her to indulge in tantrums. She would go on this trip—go back and face the plateau again—and find out just what she needed to do to cut short this assignment. She had real work to do, work she was far better suited to, in a world where officials spoke the familiar language of diplomacy—and didn't threaten to slash open all her old wounds.

She wished for a quick ending to the trip even harder as their flyer hovered over the plateau. Her seat was by the last window, where she could hide her face as she caught her first sight of the vast inland wilderness that was the central plateau country. Her first view of it in too many years—not since that day of the rushed evacuation and the compulsory order for her to join those who were leaving.

Some reward that had been for all those years of study, of going without to make sure she could meet the costs of it. All that struggle, and for what? Her grades and expertise meant she'd been ordered to board a transporter after the barest of farewells to her family and leave behind all she held dear. Everyone had to play their part in that gigantic battle for freedom: her family back here on Hathe, she in the stratified comfort and hard bargaining of the salons and offices of so many other planets, so many interstellar flights, so many strange beds and awkward meetings.

And now she was back, and alone. She stared out the window, nose pushed to the plasmax.

It looked the same. Gray clouds chased across a sky in battle mode and a bleak land faced it below, with grasses stubbornly rooted in soil that was more rock than dirt. Grasses stirred to constant motion by the endless wind of the uplands.

A cold wind it was, an unforgiving wind, a wind that challenged your very life.

How she'd missed it.

She set her hands against the port, bracketing her face as if focusing on the scene below. No one must see what this land did to her.

They landed at the base camp and she hung back, needing to be on her own as she set foot on the ground. She fiddled with her pack, waiting for the rest to disembark.

"You coming, Madame asn Postrova?"

Her new partner, stopping at the door to check on her as a good mission leader should. She nodded. "Be along in a minute. No need to wait for me."

She shook her bag, reopened it as if checking for one last thing, and he shrugged and stepped out. Only then did she stand, lift up her pack and step toward the hatch.

Then she was out, and the smell, the sounds, the glorious winds of home snatched at her hair and tugged her onward. She'd meant to act as if the place was nothing special, but had to stop, had to lift her head, shut her eyes and let the land fill the lost places inside. High in the air above, the eerie skreeeeaaak of a soaring aerion gave a clarion call of welcome, mixing with the shoosh of the grasses, the skittering of stones, the whip of hair against cheek and the wonderful bite of a late summer's blast warning of the winter to come.

Home.

Slowly, slowly, she opened her eyes and let the unique light of the plateau bathe her face—clear, untrammeled by city dust and human seepages. Light that highlighted each precious plant, each thorny shrub and broken ridgeline. A snikket buzzed against her cheek, the tiny bug sensing new prey, and she waved it off with the practiced whisk of childhood. "Not here, little one. Go feed on those others."

She wanted to smile, to laugh out loud—and to weep great buckets of tears. Instead she ducked her head and walked across the landing pad. Breathe, steady, in and out, one, two, one two. Anything to bring herself under control, to look like someone seeing this country as an outsider.

Then she realized that Jacquel des Trurains stood by the door of a newly built set of barracks, watching her. She shoved back her shoulders and stared back at him.

"The plateau country isn't for everyone," he said. "You all right?"

She gave a bit of a shiver. "A mite colder than I'm used to, and emptier. But making do is normal for me." She kept on walking toward the door.

"You haven't been here before?"

"Long ago," she conceded to the touch of suspicion in his voice. "Don't worry, I spent a considerable time studying your survival manual. I can survive here."

"Maybe." He moved aside to let her pass. "But don't take it for granted. The plateau has a way of biting those who don't respect it."

And so do cynical heroes of the Resistance, said his tone of voice. She ignored it and tugged at the outer door of the barracks. Inside was a simple layout. Entrance hall for storing boots and equipment, then through to a large common room— dining, meeting, and general dogs body room by the looks of it. A plain, utilitarian space badly needing the frazzled clutter of just-unloaded gear to bring it to life. A chaos of orders, chatter, and laughter ratcheted through the room as the team made themselves at home. But silence fell when she entered. She refused to acknowledge it, walking head high to check the plan on the common room wall and then marching off to her quarters. The only saving grace, she had a room of her own. For part of each day she would be free to be herself, free of pretense.

For the rest, she must take care. No one must discover how well she knew this country—especially not Colonel, *the Cap,* Jacquel des Trurains.

The next morning, she was up early. Everyone else was still asleep as far as she could tell, recovering from settling in late last night and a prolonged first camp night of laughter and old

Resistance stories. She'd heard the noise of it through the thin walls of her quarters but had used the food dispenser in her room to order up a meal there and left the dirtsiders to it.

But this morning she was free and alone. No one cluttered up the common room and a clunking of mugs from the kitchen said the trooper on duty was safely ensconced there, rustling up an early morning drink. She looked around in satisfaction then soundlessly donned her gear and left the building.

The piercing "skree skree" of an aerion on the hunt filled the air. She searched the skies, and at last found it. A dark, pointed shape riding effortlessly on the up currents over the next ridge. Then tucking its wings close and plummeting arrow-like straight down.

A ruffle in the waving grasses, an awkward waddle to the nearest rock ledge, and the aerion fell off the edge into its natural home, great wings spread as it spiraled upwards with a limp bundle suspended below. A successful hunt.

The vicious predator had always been her favorite animal on the plateau. Deadly, focused, cutting cleanly through the air to its chosen kill. So much simpler than the world she inhabited.

She swung her pack onto her shoulder, slapped her pockets to check she had her emergency rations and equipment, and tapped a locator sequence into her com unit with a message for the colonel, sending it to the general station com point.

Never venture onto the plateau without leaving a message. That was the first rule her father had taught her.

She stamped down twice on each boot, settling them firmly into place and stirring up a puff of dirt in the ritual she always followed before starting out, then headed toward the ridge, her feet automatically settling into the rough rhythm of the land. A strange bubble fizzed up inside her gut, one she had not felt in a long, long time. One she barely recognized.

Happiness, she suddenly realized.

Many hours passed before she returned. She glanced at the sun and guiltily discovered it was near noon. Entranced back into childhood rambles, she'd plain missed the passing of time. So many old friends to meet again: the dainty astelia flowers, far tougher than their appearance suggested; the extraordinary tussock-like grasses that thrived here and controlled the water balance of this whole region with their capacity for drawing moisture out of little more than a damp mist; the thorny, lethally-tipped kryptark bush that paradoxically told of fertile hollows, like some schoolyard bully defending its prime share of the candy jar; and the tiny buzzing snikkets that fertilized the hidden flowers of the kryptark. All beloved, all so much more alive here than in the synthetic gardens on Mathe. It was like slotting back into place all those missing pieces of herself.

Her boss had been reluctant to let her come on this mission, fearing what a return to the plateau could do to her. He had good reason, but the mission had been too important, he'd told her. Someone had to start trying to find a way to bridge the gap between dirtsiders and moonies, and she was recognized for her ability to observe and analyze difficult situations.

Right now, she was suddenly and fiercely glad she'd come. This was her home, and it was long past time she claimed it back. Head in the clouds, a smile on her face, she marched over the last ridge and into the camp.

To be faced with a scowling Colonel Jacquel des Trurains, flanked by two equally angry team members.

"Nice of you to join us, asn Postrova. Where in Mathe have you been?"

She shrugged. "Out and about."

"If I had any choice…" He looked about to explode. "Except I don't. You're here, and I'm stuck with you. I can't even bawl you out like any other newbie under my command, and, by the Pillars, I need to yell at you. Do you have any idea of the trouble you caused?"

"I left a message."

He lifted his wrist, activated the message. "This one?"

Back rigid, she cast it no more than a glance, then registered what she'd left and could have cursed.

"Next time, try leaving one in proper Harmish," said her nemesis.

At least he didn't recognize it and couldn't know she'd automatically left a coded tag from her childhood, using the locator sequence of her old ranger comtabs. He was too busy yelling at her. "Have you ever set foot on the plateau?"

She'd already answered that one yesterday. "Yeah," she said briefly.

"A field trip in college, I bet." It was the woman on his left, the chemical engineer Varda an Tarkst, looking at Rheia as if she was something crawled up from the earth.

"Is she right, asn Postrova? How well do you know these lands?"

His eyes tracked her, from her worn boots to the beaten up old pack on her back, friend of so many rambles. Then up to meet her eyes. She refused to give him the satisfaction of backing down.

"A bit more than that," she conceded.

The colonel still held her gaze, still waited for her to answer.

For a long time it lay in the balance, neither of them prepared to give way. Till finally the techs had had enough.

"Come on, we're wasting time," cut in the man on the colonel's right. Phillipos athns Kronkist, the geotech engineer.

Jacquel des Trurains held her gaze as he barked an order into his com unit—to the rest of the squad, all out looking for her she realized now but refused to feel guilty. She'd known what she was doing, knew how to stay safe on her rambles. Not that she was about to explain why that was to their precious colonel.

"Yes, there's work to do," she said.

He had no choice but to growl agreement, his eyes glaring at her. The other two gave in readily, only too pleased to get back to whatever they'd been doing. She shrugged off her pack to enter the barracks.

Jacquel des Trurains stood in place, blocking her entry. "You and I need to talk, asn Postrova," he said softly. "Not today, I've got damage control to run after you pulling this stunt. But we will talk."

It had the air of a threat. One she should challenge. But, this threat, it was real and very personal. The kind that could smash through all the precious guards she had built up so carefully during the war.

And that must not happen.

CHAPTER THREE

Jacquel lifted his face and let the harsh winds tear at his hair. It was good to be back.

Once, he couldn't wait to get away from here. Cold, hard slogging across the unforgiving ground, long nights and little sleep. That's what the plateau had meant to him. Yet now it almost felt like coming home. No room here for subtleties and misleading complexities. This land gave only one choice. Do what's needed to survive; nothing else mattered.

In the hollow below, the rest of the team scurried about their duties. The technicians busy with their measuring and analysis. His troop on guard, huddling into their thermal tunics and looking as miserable as he had expected to feel at being back here. His eyes roamed over them all, matching each figure with their portfolio file. Each one settling to their work according to their unique skills.

Or maybe not. At one side stood his Mathian, Rheia asn Postrova. She was shadowing the ecologist, the timid asn Rostrum. No, they were talking. Asn Rostrum pointed out something, asn Postrova listened, replied, then her hand encompassed an arc as if describing something as they both peered closely down at the ground. For once, the moonie woman looked at ease.

Why should that be?

He shook his head. The woman invaded his thoughts too drekking often, and never comfortably. At least whatever had caught her attention kept her away from him and out of his orbit. He swung around and marched over the top of the ridge, desperate for a break from thinking, worrying, the constant nagging of *what now*. Over the top, down the other side and to a rocky outcrop; one among the many that littered this region. Except this one had deep gouges in the side, the kind he'd seen too many times when undercover. The kind made by dirtsiders building roads for their Terran overlords. Then he looked again, and a heavy kick jolted his heart down in one mighty stroke. He'd seen this rock, this stone-mantled track before.

An angry Terran soldier standing over a frightened Hathian—a boy no more than fifteen, new to hard labor and striving desperately to hack out the rock face. Jacquel put out a hand to trace the chisel lines on the boulder, the ineffectual chippings of a boy forced to wield a heavy jackhammer he couldn't control.

Nor should he have had to. The Terrans did have modern construction tools, including laser-guided rock-sculpting equipment. But forcing Hathians into primitive drudgery was a prime weapon they'd used to control his people, keeping them exhausted, battered and too frightened to rebel.

That boy. A heavy pounding began in Jacquel's head. So young, yet just the previous night he had single-handedly broken into the Terran stores and liberated scarce medical supplies and high-energy rations to keep their troop going just one more day. Jacquel stared down at the hard ground, remembering. Then saw the slight mound to one side, with a hardily struggling small astelia plant coating the dirt. His grave, Jacquel realized in shock, and swung around to march blindly out into the grasslands.

No one said a word when he returned. They all had too many memories of their own. Too many years of occupation, of living hard and poor while keeping up a constant veil of pretense. Until too many of them believed deep in their souls they were as low, as mean, as *worthless* as the Terrans treated them. A belief he would root out, if he did nothing else. Somehow, one day, he would give his people back their spirit. Return them to their true selves. He nodded brusquely at the troops on guard by the flyer but said nothing, the memories too raw.

Earth had sent the worst of its military here, hardened men and women with nothing to lose, who reveled in a world where they were all-powerful and the scarcities of Earth no longer troubled them. They had enjoyed exercising their control of Hathe, the boy in the grave only one of many who had suffered the full force of their bullying.

Yet a handful of Terrans had questioned the dirtsiders' charade. He frowned, thinking of Marthe's husband. Hamon Radcliff, head of the Terran security forces during the occupation, and a major thorn in the side of the Resistance. One of the few who had seen the threat to Terran control coming.

Also one of the few Terrans who had tried to stop the worst of the conquerors' brutality—"inefficient," the man had termed that kind of treatment when challenged why, but even Jacquel had to concede that his actions had saved the lives of many Hathians.

He frowned and the pounding in his head tripled in intensity. Conceding anything about Marthe's husband did that to him. Especially having to concede he was a good husband to Marthe, that the Terran loved her deeply and truly. He swung around to march out into the wild again, a familiar rage tearing at him. One more thing he could not fix. He could not give his oldest friend back her home, could not bring back her twin brother. Bendin was dead and Marthe banished to exile.

Only he was left.

He kicked at the dirt, hugging himself tight as he lifted his eyes to the far horizon. What was it about the plateau that broke down his usual defenses against the past?

That was when he noticed her. His moonie, as useless here as he. No longer with the ecologist, she stood alone on the brow of a small hill across from him, head back, face raised to the open sky and a strange mixture of grief, fear, and joy etched into the taut lines of her body.

His moonie had secrets.

He squatted down as if checking something on the ground, but his eyes never left her. Not while she thought she was unobserved, but then she turned her head. He quickly looked down, fingers pulling at the dirt and tracing the rocks that liberally sprinkled the ground here, as if busy with something. When he looked up again, she had gone. He pulled out his com to track her and found her heading around the far side of the hill and then turning back to the ecologist.

Safely returned to the fold and behaving as if nothing had happened. He stayed where he was, scanning the team at work but focusing on the moonie. She knew he was monitoring her; an occasional glance up the hill at him a giveaway, but it was the only one. Her behavior other than that was professional, engaged, exactly what he would expect of someone with her training.

After a while, she drifted off from the ecologist and wandered over to one of the guards on duty. Not that she'd have any luck getting anything out of his people. His squad were among the best trained of the security forces. Jacquel grinned when she tried the soft approach, her whole body bending and hands fluttering as she looked up at his trooper. No doubt treating him to that truly dangerous smile of hers. Despite all her presumably flattering chatter, the man did not once give way, steadfastly refusing to engage. After a while, she moved on, leaving Jacquel free to com the trooper.

"What was she after?"

"Nothing obvious. Small talk, a comment on the view. Had I been stationed out here before."

They all had, and Rheia asn Postrova would have known it. So it was as he'd thought: She was sounding out the squad, trying to get a fix on who they were as people. Moving them from figures in a scheme to living, breathing people with a background and opinions of their own.

She was good, but he was better when it came to dirtsiders. She hadn't spent those hellish years down here and could never understand what it had done to them. Nor was he about to let any moonie add to it, no matter how beautiful. Mathe knew he'd tried hard enough to get his own father to understand what it had been like.

He wandered around the site for a while, helping where he could. Having little formal scientific training, he understood the broad parameters of what the experts did but the details and the jargon were beyond him. *Hold this, stand there, pass me that.* All his years of study, and no more use here than the simplest child.

He chuckled inside. What would his father say if he saw him now?

He continued on, following a random path to his target. She'd been watching him as she worked alongside Varda an Tarkst. His spirits rose a bit higher. Good luck to her trying to get the chemical engineer to open up. Varda was as grim inside as out and liked very few people. A moonie had no chance with her.

He strolled up, casually taking the instrument Varda passed him as she squatted down to dig at something in the ground. At least, that's all it looked like to him but he knew better than to ask what she was up to. "Nice day for it," he said pleasantly, glancing up at the broken fragments of blue breaking through the clouds. Varda ignored him and Rheia only gave him a glance before steadfastly looking down at the scanner, holding the probe exactly as ordered by the martinet chemical engineer.

Fortunately, within a very short time, Varda's natural surliness took over. She snatched at his device. "Not that way. Go take yourself off somewhere you can be of real use. You too, Madame asn Postrova. I don't need you here anymore."

Jacquel made no effort to hide his grin. He held out a hand to Rheia. "The troops have set up a table in the shelter of that bluff. Time for lunch."

She looked at the hand. Would she accept? He held his breath, turning on his most charming and least challenging smile. Those gorgeous eyes lifted up to his as if seeking…what? He kept his hand out, waiting tensely.

"Hmmph." She lifted her hand, took his outstretched grasp, and jerked her chin up. Her palm was so soft, and something inside him settled as those long, clever fingers curled around his.

Not that he pushed it further, no matter how tempted. He held her lightly, helping her over the rough rocks so that to anyone else he would appear to be offering the merest of courtesies to their untrained newcomer.

Unfortunately, it was only a short distance to the table where he would have to relinquish his hold and hand her to her seat. His moonie said nothing as he released her, gave no sign of shaking him off, or of wishing his hold back.

His own hand felt empty.

But it was a gain, and her eagerness to launch into the kind of meaningless small talk both were so well-trained in had him feeling suddenly better. Cover, that's what such talk meant. A way of hiding what you felt.

The rest of his squad wandered over in spurts and grabbed a place at the table. He wondered if she noticed their glance her way before his nod had them taking a seat. As for the technical staff, they all clustered at the far end of the long board, for which he was heartily grateful. It saved him having to listen to their endless exclaimings over their findings. He didn't need their screeds of data to tell him the plants of the plateau were struggling. He could see the dying grasses, and the thorny kryptark bushes were far too few in this sheltered hollow.

The talk in his troops soon drifted to the times they'd spent in this territory during the war. They had served together so long that the stories came out in a kind of shorthand. Snippets of *remember when*, never fully completed. Beside him, Rheia listened politely and few of the troops would have picked up the tension in her.

But his hand had brushed hers when passing a dish and his body felt the tight wall of hers. Nothing like reminiscences to make someone feel like an outsider, and their moonie was definitely that. Yet if she was going to be any use in breaking this moonie-dirtsider divide as their superiors had ordered, she had to face the reality of what the others here had been through during the occupation, then find a way to break through the wall cutting her off from them.

And he suddenly knew just how to make a start for her. He sat back, staring languidly down his nose at his troops.

"That was nothing," he said with an airy wave of his hand and an accent straight from the most exclusive clubs in the City university. The shock on her face drove away all that annoying detachment. He redoubled his efforts. "A simple matter of peasant doggedness," he drawled, letting his lip curl in aloof displeasure. "What else would you expect?" A flung piece of dirt landed square on his chest. He looked down, picked it daintily off his tunic and flicked it to the side, all the time completely ignoring the shrieks of laughter around him.

"Meet his mightiness, Master Jacquel des Trurains," bowed Ras amid chokes of laughter. "Haut Liege lord of all he commands. And how may we serve your exulted supremeness today?"

"Haut Liege?" said Rheia.

Ras stepped in with a glint in his eyes. "Aristo, high faluting lord of all of us, spoilt offspring of the mighty Hathian elite that fled this fair planet, leaving us ignorant yokels to face the conquering Terrans."

"He means you, my lady asn Postrova. And all the other Hathians skulking up on Mathe." A thoroughly untrustworthy grin lit Trooper Dreya's face.

"The haut lieges were a fabrication, and we did not skulk. I was ordered to leave."

"Of course you were," said Jacquel haughtily, trying to regain control of the game. But his team were enjoying themselves far too much, and for once including Rheia in the laughter. "I forgot entirely. But it was pleasant there. Whereas here…"

"He had to soil his precious lieger fingers with honest graft and hard toil," finished Ras, amid the shrieks of the rest of them and some pointed looks from the technical staff.

Suddenly, a light dawned on her face. "*That's* the character you inflicted on the Terrans when you were captured? You're lucky they didn't execute you out of sheer aggravation."

Jacquel smiled, restored to himself. "Radcliff was tempted, believe me."

"Nah, you just had the man coddled green with jealousy," said Trooper Dreya an Vathin.

Rheia looked at the woman, who looked nothing like a senior trooper as she grinned cheerily back. "Between him and Marthe, and their very *affectionate* blatherings, they twisted that poor man so tight he didn't know what to believe."

"Yeah, he actually thought Marthe mad enough to want to marry the Cap here," put in Anton der Phebasin, the Troop Third.

"She did occasionally act like a woman of sense," said Jacquel plaintively.

"Cap." Ras shook his head in mock horror. "She always acted like a woman of sense, except when you and that twin of hers stirred her up to no good."

"Now that is a total falsehood." Jacquel sprang out of his chair, giving in once more to his masquerade. "The asn Castre twins are the main reason for my father's gray hair. They got me into more trouble as children than anything I ever did."

Trooper der Phebasin turned to Rheia and nodded sagely. "Probably true. I was at the same university. The asn Castre twins turned the hair gray of *every* tutor they had, and Marthe was as bad as her brother."

"Whereas I was a model of scholarly rectitude."

His solemn pronouncement finished off the rest of them, and it was some time before the howls of laughter died down.

"I think we need a walk," said Jacquel. "Time to get you away from these reprobates before they corrupt you completely."

That just set them off again. He gave them one pained look, then took their moonie's hand and had her out of the chair and off up a near slope before she could say otherwise.

Not that she was fooled by his carefully managed exit, moving away from his touch as soon as they were out of sight of the troopers and techies, but she kept walking with him. Over the hump and down a nearby hollow to the small stream that gurgled its way through the rocks and shrubs. He led them to a couple of larger boulders tossed up on a bank by one of the sudden floods that characterized all creeks in this area, and dropped the laughing face. Time to talk. He propped himself against one boulder and gestured to her to take the other.

She looked at the rock, then at him, before seating herself as if at a gala dinner, with hands folded in her lap, and turned to face him with a fire in her eyes totally at odds with the demure pose.

"What have I done now, according to your dirtsider code?"

The tone of her voice was designed to insult, *dirtsider* made to sound like something crawling out of a primeval swamp, and all of it very precisely calculated.

"Yes, we are dirtsiders, which means that every single person here is still in recovery mode from the kind of treatment you cannot comprehend."

Her hands gripped tight together. "It wasn't a picnic off Hathe either."

He raised an eyebrow at that, and a ripple of irritation skimmed over her face. Subtle, but he was watching her very closely and for some reason ruffling the facade of this moonie satisfied some deep need in him. She could shut out the rest of the world, but he wasn't about to let her shut him out.

"I do respect the importance of what you in the diplomatic branch did to keep the rest of the Alliance out of this mess, but your life was never at risk. Nor did you have to stoop to the Terrans."

"You think I don't know what it cost you and the rest to stay behind? You really think I was one of those running to catch the first transporters up to Mathe?"

"No." This woman would run from nothing. "But nor do I think you understand how fragile those left behind are—and how hard they must fight every day to recover what they lost of themselves. Which isn't helped one bit by all the moonies flocking back and taking over the jobs that should have been theirs."

She crossed her arms as if defending herself against his words, and that felt all kinds of wrong. Not that she showed any intention of backing down. "I didn't ask for this job. Councilor an Rathman ordered me here."

"Aah." Gilda an Rathman was a good friend of Sylvan an Castre, Marthe and Bendin's father. This was personal then. Jacquel had been there when Marthe asked Gilda to help the dirtsiders. It was Marthe's last action before going into exile, and a promise was made that day that Gilda would not break. "Then we're stuck with each other. Which doesn't mean I'm about to let you hurt one single member of this team. Varda is tough enough, but not Maria asn Rostrum. Be careful there."

Rheia jumped up, eyes flashing magnificently, and it was all Jacquel could do not to say whatever it took to keep that fire alive. Or kiss her. But it changed little. She could break asn Rostrum.

"If you want to get to know my team, ask me how to go about it. Do not manipulate any of them, and yes that is a warning. This team is under my care."

After which, he wasn't surprised when she swung around and marched off. His eyes followed her as she stalked back to the others. He spoke into his com, warning Ras to keep an eye on her, and refused to acknowledge a niggle of guilt. Not when the rear view was even more delicious than those flashing eyes.

The man had some nerve. Rheia could feel the rage surging through her, driving her to walk, to march, to *run* as fast she could away from here. A coward's reaction, yes, except it wasn't rage alone coursing through her. The man had hurt her. There was just something about him and when he'd taken her hand she'd felt a rare moment of belonging, that firm hand a special kind of promise.

Only a fantasy, a stupid moment of wishfulness. He didn't trust her, none of them did, and maybe never would.

Did he truly think only dirtsiders had lost family in the war?

As for telling her to keep away from Maria, did the man ever look below the surface? Shy and timid she may be, but Maria asn Rostrum faced every day with more courage in her little finger than the likes of Varda an Tarkst ever brought to bear. Rheia spent time with Maria because she plain liked the girl.

Not so Varda. A cruel streak ran through the chemical engineer. Ambitious, and with a scary lack of empathy that meant she'd trample over anyone in her way; right now, that was Maria asn Rostrum. Varda an Tarkst had clearly assumed she would be lead technical expert on this mission. A short hop on her way back to that cushy university position she lusted after. Yes, the chemical engineer had fought with the Resistance, but Rheia strongly suspected Varda's main motivation had been the glory she assumed would come with it. Glory that should have secured her place in the new Hathe.

Only nothing about the new Hathe had turned out as any of them had assumed, and Varda was stuck with playing second fiddle to a "scared little widget." The engineer's words.

As for Maria asn Rostrum, the ecologist's specialist knowledge of this region made her the one vital cog in the mission. Maria truly loved the high plateau, and that alone would have gained her Rheia's support. The gentlest of interrogations revealed that the girl had grown up in a region just south of the plateau country, spending childhood holidays exploring these wild lands. She became an ecologist because of it, and loved each plant, each small and large animal that lived here. Maria was hell-bent on saving the plateau; Varda was equally hell-bent on saving Varda, and if Colonel Jacquel des Trurains didn't realize that, it was about time he was made to.

That day set the pattern for the ones following. Rheia went out with the team, helping where she could, trying anything to find a way through to these weary, battle-hardened victims of the occupation.

Too many days, she despaired of it ever happening. All of them spoke in only the most flippant of terms of the years under the Terrans. Jokes, repartee and a dry cynicism that covered what she was sure were harsh truths. At night, she retreated to a quiet corner of the common room. The tech staff spent the evenings around the middle tables, poring over the day's findings, while the troopers had taken over the end of the big room for their training. Fierce and uncompromising, they threw and pounded bodies, jumped and twisted in a series of quick-fire moves that had her heart in her mouth, yet at the end ragged each other with a dry wit that had them all choking with laughter. Most nights, their leader joined his troopers, his face alight with something she rarely saw. Relaxation, maybe, or just at home in a way he could be with very few others. But then he would retreat to his office, with the door firmly closed.

Then one night he finished his work early, coming back into the main room before she could make her usual retreat to the peace of her quarters. She pulled up her com screen and scanned it closely as he wandered through the room passing a comment here and there, then throwing up his hands with a chuckle.

"Too much information, doc. I'm no scientist." With a grin over his shoulder, he left the techs to their talk and sauntered over to her corner.

"Mind if I take a seat? I need a jargon-free space."

She had no choice but to move over on the bench, curling up her legs between her and the space left to him. His lips twitched, but he settled down, opened his own com screen and propped his legs on the small table in front of them.

Silence, unnerving her. Pulling her away from her reports. She tried, told her eyes to focus on the details of the work piling up on her home log. Try as she might, she could not ignore the long body beside her. She finally gave up.

"A cup of khrova?"

He looked up slowly, as if disturbed from deep concentration, gave her a quick smile and nod of thanks. Why, she couldn't say, but something about his response set her on edge, something about the touch of that smile looked too careful, as if he had some purpose. Yet that night all he did was accept the drink with his usual courtesy, ask casually about what she was reading, then settle back to his com. He barely appeared to notice when she judged she'd spent enough time in the room to be able to retire without comment.

Over that next week, he made a habit of joining her in her corner at the end of the evening. Slowly, she began to relax, even got used to his presence, and had to take herself to task the night he stayed late in his office. She *would not* admit to missing his company.

The next night he was back again with that easy smile of his, a bit earlier than usual, the long plateau twilight still lighting up the plains outside. She'd been gazing out the window as he sat down, and quickly switched back to her com screen. He said nothing, taking up his reader and settling to his com screen as usual.

"You're not a gym lover," he said after a while, when a triumphant shout from one of his troopers had her looking up.

"I do what's needed," she said. Taking part in exercise periods was a required activity in the close confinement of the bases on Mathe and on her numerous interplanetary voyages.

"So, what do you like?" He looked her over, and she tried desperately to stop the blush warming her cheeks. She kept fit, but there was a warmth in those eyes that said he noticed more than the tone of her muscles.

"Walking," she muttered. "I like to walk. It's how I get to know new places."

"Aah." He looked out the window. "That first day…"

She shrugged.

"The plateau is no place to venture on your own. But…," he looked out the window again. "There's still a few hours of daylight, and it's safe enough if I go with you. What do you say?"

Yes, said her heart. Don't be stupid, said her mind. This man was too acute.

Yes, far too acute to accept some half-baked excuse. "Thank you, that would be lovely." And saw again that quick-fire twitch of amusement at her formal politeness. But all he did when she joined him outside was give a quick nod of approval at her protective gear and check she had her com alarm set, before letting her set the pace and direction.

Surprisingly, after a time, she began to relax, breathing in the twilight air and basking in the freedom from the constant tension of being under watch. Jacquel des Trurains was an undemanding companion, talking of people and places they both knew. Safe, relaxing, and surprisingly enjoyable. She hadn't realized how much she missed talking to someone who understood her world of politics and diplomacy. He had been raised in the heart of the Hathian government sector and brought both an acute grasp and a wicked dissection of the central players familiar to them both with their all too human foibles.

"Thank you," she said when they arrived back. "I needed that."

"It was mutual, madame." And the warmth of his smile gave the proof of it. "Any time."

And so began another part of the daily web of her new life. On any evening the plateau's moods allowed, Jacquel escaped with her to the wild open air. Two of his troopers always followed them, but kept a discreet distance back, and she could mostly forget they were there.

"Ras read me the riot act that first night for going out without backup," explained Jacquel the next evening with that quick smile of his.

He didn't say who he needed protection from, and she didn't feel able to ask. Not yet.

She also insisted he called her Rheia. Madame asn Postrova belonged in the corridors of diplomacy, not in this wild place of her heart. His answering smile was wide and genuine.

"And my name's Jacquel. Not colonel, not the Cap. Just Jacquel."

She smiled back. Jacquel. She could do that. His family and close childhood friends called him Jaca, said the deeper layers of his profile, and being asked to call him that would have raised all kinds of alarms in her. Jacquel was the name of a friend, but with enough distance to feel safe.

Or that's what she told herself. Until the night he caught her hand as he said goodnight at her door, lifted it and touched his lips to her palm. She couldn't sleep for a long time after, the memory of that touch echoing in her head and the tingle of it alive on her skin.

He made no mention of that touch the next day, or the one after that, and she began to relax again. Until the evening he brought her to laughter, belly-deep chuckles which had her grinning maniacally at him and throwing her arms around him in a moment of sheer glee. But then he leaned forward wearing that wicked smile of his, took her face in his hands and kissed her. His lips were warm, sensitive and ripe with a promise sanity said she shouldn't return. But she did, losing herself in her response, until memory came crashing back and she pulled sharply away from him, forcing herself to ignore the sense of loss as his body no longer touched hers in a dangerous promise.

A moment of madness? It had to be; she couldn't dare consider it meant more and resolved there would be no repeats. She only hoped she could keep to it. The man was just too attractive for comfort and belonged to a world barred to her— by birth, connections and history. He was too observant, too quick to recognize any attempts to hide the truth of her background—and that was one thing Jacquel des Trurains must not learn.

The guards had already gone inside when they returned and didn't see them thankfully. What would happen if they knew the effect their leader had on her? As for what the rest of the mission thought of their rambles, she couldn't say. His squad were slowly thawing towards her, but a distance remained.

Moonie and dirtsider; a divide she still had no idea how to bridge. Out on site a few days later, she came upon the geotech engineer, Phillipos athns Kronkist, without a shirt and glimpsed the dark, bloody slash of a scar crossing his back. It was a hot day and he'd been working on his own, off to one side. She hadn't known he was there when she stepped away from the rest, needing a time of solace, a time with just Rheia and the plateau.

He saw her rounding the bluff and swiveled sharply away, muttering angrily as he jerked on his tunic, even as she hastily backed off.

No point asking where he'd got that scar. The pain and humiliation on his face said it all. She added the incident to her report that night but wondered if it would change anything. Would she ever find a way through to these dirtsiders. The past must always stand between them and the rest of Hathe.

The next day their search took her near the one place she'd dreaded visiting, yet yearned to see. A wild place at the heart of this territory. The worksite lay in a natural hollow, with a hill just to the south. A hill she remembered clambering up, then standing stock still at the top as she took in the view opening on the far side. It felt like you could see the whole plateau from that ridgeline. Her father had been with her, crouching down beside her, his strong arm holding her safe.

"Take a look, Rye. This is your home, the place you belong. It's here, right here," he had tapped gently on her heart, "and no one can ever take it away from you."

She *had* to climb that hill.

Her first attempt was blocked by a too watchful guard. Trooper an Vathin caught up with her as she strolled in a random fashion toward the small hollow that would hide her from sight as she made her escape.

"Best not to stray out of sight. The plateau can be a dangerous place for those unfamiliar with it," said the young woman.

Such as a moonie bureaucrat, thought Rheia wryly.

She had to let it go that day. The trooper may have been lightly built, but Rheia wasn't stupid enough to underestimate her. She wouldn't have been in this squad if she wasn't among the best of the Resistance troops. They were due back here the next day, and this time Rheia was not going to be thwarted.

It started out well. After the cold shoulder she'd come to expect from the more surly of the team and the usual jostling when they settled into the transporters, arrival at the site was like all the other days. Rheia followed her usual routine, taking time to breathe in the fresh air, finding a place to watch the rest set up, then began her rounds of the technical staff. Always drifting closer to that ridgeline.

Nothing in the site marked it out. Wind-scarred land, small hillocks gouged out on one side into dangerous overhangs and water-scoured channels running down the open faces. Tussocks and the lichen-like sponges best suited to survive this country, with here and there one of the precious astelias clinging to a cleft in the rocks, flowering outrageously in the face of nature's worst assaults.

She concentrated on her work, helping collect specimens for Maria. The ecologist had given Rheia a table with detailed sketches of each plant type and she followed it closely, wandering along her designated track, peering closely at the ground and checking back frequently with her table on her com. Again and again she stopped, crouched down and rifled through the dirt and grasses as if trying to find something. After a while, the prickle on the back of her neck that said she was being watched began to fade. The late summer sun staged a fight back, bathing the plateau in a rare warmth that had many drooping in their work. She was nearly at her target, crouching, peering and wandering purposefully as she ambled closer, ignoring the ridgeline till she could work her way around to a small dip in the ground.

A creek tumbled riotously along the bottom of the hollow, taking a sharp turn under a small bank. She stood, stretched upwards as if working out the kinks from all that bending and crouching, then walked down to the creek, kneeling down and dabbling her hand in the cool water to bring up a handful to splash on the back of her neck.

She stayed kneeling, stayed playing with the water, till a cautious glimpse said the closest trooper had turned away.

Kneel again, crouch down further, then a quick side step and she was around the corner. From there, it was easy enough to work through the higher tussocks to the base of the slope, then up again using grasses, scrubby bushes, whatever she could find to hide her passing. It was as if the years had melted away and she was back in the favorite game of her childhood, slipping unseen through the sparse cover up to the top and over.

Then she came to what she sought. A small patch of astelias clinging to the rocks covering a barely noticeable mound near the top of that far slope. Rheia had only seen holograms of it; she had begged, but never been allowed to come here until now. In the images sent to her, it was raw dirt to match the raw pain in her heart. She had tried for months to get permission to return to Hathe, even resorting to emotional blackmail. The powers owed her on this one. But always they refused. They were at war and too many others shared a similar pain to hers. She was needed elsewhere.

There were other mounds somewhere, but she'd never found even a hint of their location. One day she would find them—or so she made herself believe, the alternative too sickening. Reports from the first days of the occupation told of Terrans roughly tossing bodies into great piles to be vaporized, and the remaining traces of sediment left to vanish into the soil or drift away on the wind.

She had visited some of the memorial cairns. That had been one of the first priorities for the returning Hathians: to honor their dead as they had not been able to do for five gut-wrenching years.

None had held the names she sought.

But today she could honor one, honor him as no one else would. Few knew the real story; for most, his end was covered in the slime of ignominy.

She knelt beside the astelia clump. Her favorite flower, so fragile and beautiful in appearance, yet a true survivor that smiled fiercely in the face of the worst thrown at it by the plateau. It had seemed right to ask for it to be planted here.

She leaned back, half-closing her eyes and turning her head towards the mound.

"Hey Da." A soft murmur only, the barest moving of her lips as she kept a careful ear open for the troopers.

None must know of this place. The council had promised to wipe its location from the files and the mound was undisturbed, one with the land. They had kept their word. Her father would be at peace here. He'd earned it. She placed one hand on the gritty dirt and closed her eyes. If she ignored the faint sounds of the team, concentrated hard on the song of the wind and grass, she could almost feel his big sturdy hand holding her firm as they wandered these slopes.

Then a heavy footfall, a scratching in the dirt coming up the slope behind her.

"Asn Postrova, the troopers are asking where you've got to."

It was the geotech with the scar. He watched her now with nothing friendly in his eyes. She stood, trying to look unbothered, slowly dusting off her work gear. "Just coming," she said. "I needed a break and it looked like you'd get a good view up here."

He scowled, waiting for her to move. She nodded thanks, and walked with him up the slope, over the ridgeline and down the other side. Back to her duty.

Not long after that, Jacquel announced it was time to go, and it was with relief that she headed toward the ship. Then noticed the timid ecologist, desperately reading scans and shoveling equipment into her bag. The rest of the team were already packed and starting to load up the transporters. Maria looked petrified, as if all hell's fury would pour down on her if she failed to be ready on time.

"Need a hand?"

When there was no answer, Rheia grabbed hold of the girl's bag and began to pack the overflowing contents properly into it. Maria stared in panic mode at the scanner screen, even as her free hand kept trying to shovel what Rheia was sure was expensive and fragile equipment on top of Rheia's neatly packed contents. She grabbed at Maria's hands, gently disentangling the device.

"Leave the scanner reading to me. You get everything else ready and into the flyer."

Hands clenched, the girl stammered as if apologizing for doing her job. "The reading. It's not finished. I need those figures."

"I may not know much about your work, but I can see when a scan is complete and send the log in. That's a standard operation."

Poor Maria was near to tears—thanks to a day of bullying by Varda an Tarkst, no doubt. Rheia had checked the engineer's Resistance file. It looked good, but strangely the woman had avoided any real danger. Rheia had a strong streak of cynicism, thanks to the years negotiating the treacherous currents of interplanetary relations, and she would bet the chemical engineer had only one, true loyalty. To herself.

Maria finished packing her bag and was literally hopping from foot to foot.

"Go, get seated. I'll wait for this to finish and follow you. They're not going to leave without me, and I can't get much lower in everyone's opinion anyway," Rheia said.

"Th-thank you." The girl gulped, shouldered her bag and went to leave. Then stopped and half-twisted back. "It's not true, you know. You…you're not what they say."

Then she was gone, before Rheia could utter an astonished "Thank you."

She sighed and bent back to the scanner. Not long after, she heard the first transporter leaving. *Come on, scanner. Time to go.* She would have liked to shake the thing but suspected that would just make it take longer.

A sound, from over the slope. It sounded like a transporter starting up. No, not possible. She carefully placed down the scanner, then scrambled up the slope.

Dust, and a shape disappearing.

"Hey, wait up. Hey, hey!"

Nothing. The transporter kept on going. What happened to those guards keeping watch on her? The ones she'd expect to *check if she was on board before taking off?* It was a good day's hike back to base from here.

She stared at the vanishing cloud of dirt for some time, but it made no difference. She really had been left behind.

Finally, finally, when all sign of the transporter had completely vanished, she turned back down the slope and picked up the scanner again.

"Oh, nice, now you decide to finish."

She logged in the results, sent them back to base, then carefully packed up the scanner and pulled out her supplies from her pack. She stowed the energy bars in the pocket carrying her emergency kit, then put the rest back in. A quick glance at the sun. She had a few hours yet before nightfall. She'd set off the locater function on her com but wasn't hopeful anyone would be listening. Someone had made sure she was left behind, and they'd got away with it because no one had cared to check on her. Which meant no one was coming back for her. Time to get a move on.

She was right at the heart of the cold temperate desert that made up much of the inland plateau. Short on rainfall, moisture came fitfully in hellish storms that swept across the rumpled land, followed by gusting barrels of desiccating winds. The result: only the toughest plants and animals survived here, in a landscape dominated by a barren, leached-out ground strata of rocks, clay, and gritty, coarse gravels. No sand, not in this desert, but the soil offered little more sustenance than the hot deserts of warmer regions.

And whoever arranged for her to be left behind believed she could make her way across it, could survive in the rugged country that lay between here and base?

No, she didn't think so.

She set out, one foot in front of the other, her gear carefully packed for the tough hike. She had about four hours of daylight left.

At least she knew the area. She also had the emergency kit she always carried in her pocket out here. It included a knife, ranger survival capsules and an antique Terran compass, handed down through generations of her family. With it, she could find her way back to base no matter what anyone tracking her might do to her com unit link. Even on Hathe, the compass could be adjusted to show true north as well as any com. Best of all, it was off the com grid, totally undetectable.

For the first couple of hours her journey was like enough to the field trips of her childhood that she didn't miss the company of others. She had enough gear with her to keep her safe and years of training in how to manage in this country. She sipped sparingly at her water and chewed a few mouthfuls from the high-energy bar in her pocket.

It was in the second couple of hours the truth of what she faced hit home. The first transporter would be back at base, and the second one not far away. Someone should be questioning where she was.

The dark streaks of evening were spreading across the folded hills. Time to look for a safe refuge for the night. She reached deep into her tunic pocket to finger the ranger capsules she kept hidden there. Then drew her knife, tugged out an energy bar to keep her going, and stopped at the peak of a hill. One of the capsules held a tent, but it would be little protection if the weather cut up rough. A small cave lay not far from here, if she remembered rightly, one of the many that pocked the barren landscape.

There, a dark shadow tucked into the hillside. Not much protection, but better than the tent and a fire in the entrance would keep away the creatures that prowled the plains at night and stop the bite of the night winds.

At the same time, she set the beacon on her com unit to broadcast, on the chance that the colonel might just notice her absence and see through the lies he'd no doubt been told.

Who was it who'd organized this, she wondered yet again? Varda an Tarkst seemed too obvious an answer, or maybe the geotech, Phillipos? Then she shook herself.

Right now, it didn't matter. What mattered was surviving.

An hour later and she was at the cave entrance. Fuel for a fire was no real problem here, the ground littered with old twigs, scrub and dried grasses, so she had soon cleared a circle, marked it out with stones to stop it spreading and set her material. A few strikes of the blade of her knife against a firestone—a particularly hard rock easily found here. They littered the plains, as long as you knew what to look for, and Rheia knew exactly what to look for. It was the first lesson in geology her father taught her.

"This may save your life one day, Rye," he'd told her, and it had been proven right on too many occasions of her naive teenage treks. Or would have, she'd discovered later, if she'd been in any real danger. Her parents had inserted a locater sliver into all her trekking boots. Rheia had been a wanderer since she was born, her mother had complained one day.

With the fire going and another energy bar to munch on, the night didn't seem so bad. Soon she would open the ranger capsule holding a thermal sheet for her bed, but not yet. It had been too many years since she had last sat before a fire on the plains, dream-gazing out into the restless night and getting lost in the endless patterns of the waving grasses. The winds rifling through the dry stalks made a familiar song with the krik-uk of a night aerion. Smaller than its day cousins, sleek and with inbuilt sonar senses, it was a deadly predator but was so beautiful that Rheia never begrudged it the lethal efficiency of its killing dives. Not much bigger than her hand, the night aerion had the soft fur-like covering of all aerions, thicker on the large, and multijointed wings with their small, retractable claws at the point. Sleek and long, yet in structure the fur was closest to the wool on the sheep of old Earth. A tube-like fiber, hollow inside and flattened into a blade on the outer surface, each small clump of fibers could be moved individually, giving aerions a precision in flight unmatched among the fauna of the known planets. It was also the reason they were found only on the plateau now. The larger species had been viewed as too dangerous by the first settlers, and the plateau was their last bastion.

Dangerous, yes, but only if you provoked them or looked too much like their prey. Since most of them ate only small ground-dwelling creatures, Rheia had never understood that early fear. She loved the aerions, as she loved the high plateau. Too her, they embodied the harsh risks that made this place special.

Lost in dreaming and trying hard to spot the night aerion, she almost missed hearing the small flyer until it was on top of her. A gust of wind, a flurry of gritty dirt that left her coughing and quenched her fire, and it landed.

Someone had come for her.

CHAPTER FOUR

Jacquel stepped out of the flyer and heard a hacking cough. Something eased inside him, something that had been riding him ever since he'd checked the second transporter and his trooper said they'd been told Rheia was on the first transporter.

Who had told him that, the trooper couldn't remember. A comment passed in the flurry of packing up, the source not worthy of note. Now, that harried coughing throttled down the beast raging within him. She'd turned on her com's alarm beacon to guide them here; the only thing keeping him sane as he flew out in search. A figure appeared through the dust clouds and into the light from his flitter. He strode toward her.

"Do you know how many people under my command I've lost in the last five years?"

She jerked up, a hand over her mouth to stifle a last spasm of coughs, and stood facing him, back rigid and face bleached of welcome. A straight stare, a slight shrug and an offhand, "Sorry, must have been a misunderstanding."

She was doing that thing again, staring past him. That, combined with the crack of a voice break she couldn't hide, was all it took to slice straight into the churned-up mess of emotions swirling through him.

He'd so badly needed proof she was okay, that she was alive. Yet all he'd done was choke her up with the filthy wash from his craft. He passed over a container of water, then realized she already had one and was lifting it to those stern, beckoning lips of hers.

She's a moonie. An off-planet bureaucrat and academic. And good at working out the strands of power in his team with a subtlety and intuition he had to admire. He watched edgily as she cleared away all signs of her fire and packed up.

Then realized something. She worked as if on autopilot. This was something she'd done many times before.

"Where did you grow up, Madame asn Postrova?"

Something scurried across her face, something that looked drekking like nerves. Something totally alien to what he knew of her so far. She waved a hand vaguely south.

"Aways over there," she said.

"Your family, they still there?"

She shook her head, looking like he'd asked her to reveal the most intimate details of her personal log. He couldn't do that, but he sure as hell meant to access her records as soon as he got back to the city. Right now, he had to get her home to base camp, so they could both get a proper sleep. He'd had more than enough of garbage patrol; more than enough of seeing places with too many memories attached. The news Rheia had failed to return tonight had plunged him right back into the worst of the occupation. He was not going to lose one more person on his watch. Especially not this one. Not this tough, steel-backed and far too acute woman.

When he'd first seen her name on the mission list, he'd thought her a plant from his father, sent along to keep an eye on him, but he'd quickly discarded that thought on meeting her. One of his father's protegees would never be so obviously unhappy at being sent here. He'd watched her from the first, one more brick in the growing wall of tension he could never ignore but had soon realized she was more than capable of looking after herself here. The others labelled her moonie—*as do you*— but she had a name, and that had made her real. A name that scared all the Pillars out of him. Or more to the point, the woman behind the name.

She never complained at the tasks given her, never pointed out that she wasn't here as a general dogs body—the only role most of the techs allowed her. With no scientific or security training, they reasoned, it's all she could do. Except that she wasn't here to help the team in their work. She'd been sent here to start the healing Hathe needed, and if it meant working like a drudge, it seemed their senior moonie diplomat had decided to put up with it.

Nor did she complain during their evening chats. He'd come to value that time when he'd finished his day's work and could join her on their walks or in that quiet corner of the main room. "Checking on the day's work," she would always tell him. He rather thought it was more that she preferred her corner to the awkwardness of joining in with the others in the common room, seizing this time and place for her own small place of sanctuary. Her barriers never fully came down, but in those evening talks he found a kind of sanctuary of his own. Debating back and forth, ideas tossed out with consequences and options, like in his old days at the university.

On one of their walks, he'd even got her to laugh. She was telling him of her first off-world mission.

"Theonis delns Casteron was the nominal head," she said, and that gorgeous face of hers tilted up at his hastily smothered chuckle.

"I was in higher college with him," he said in explanation, and those mobile eyebrows lifted. He had to grin. "His father is very senior in his region's affairs…"

"And Cractus Minor is a very well-endowed region indeed," she said dryly.

"Yes." He chuckled. "Where would Hathe's building industry be without Cractus mud? And Theonis…"

"Is a true son of his homeland," she shot back. "A solid brick."

He grinned at the sparkle in her eyes, and she grinned back. "It was quite a mission."

And suddenly the laughter sang from her. Not the practiced, purposeful chortle of her public face, but a deep-throated, full-bellied laugh that had him grinning madly along with her. He couldn't help it. He had to kiss her.

He reached to hold her, paused to let her refuse, then he held that precious face in his hands and leaned down, gently kissing cheeks, foreheads, then mouth as his lips and tongue teased hers.

And for a moment she returned it, for a precious space her mouth opened and welcomed him in, until suddenly the walls shot up again and she carefully stepped back, the smile returned to polite again, her cool voice denying the rosy blush washing her cheeks.

"Yes, a memorable mission, and one that helped my progress in the department," she said as if nothing had happened.

There was so much he wanted to say to her, so much he wanted to be when she was ready. One day, he hoped, wished, promised himself. One day, he would find what drove that huge wall of reserve.

Her actions weren't those of someone with a grudge against dirtsiders. No, her wall was defensive, almost as if she was hiding something. But he hadn't had time to find out what, and selfishly hadn't wanted to disturb those few grasped hours in their evenings with turmoil, hoping against hope she would welcome him in her own time, this woman with whom he could be himself in a way he hadn't found in a long time.

Those brief moments of refuge were no excuse for his failings today. He'd taken his eye off her, too busy with the mission and the news from the City. So much left to settle after liberation, so many disparate groups all trying to figure out where they fit in this new Hathe, while he was stuck out here. Isolated and too far from the ignition points.

He'd taken his eye off Rheia and look at what happened. The plateau country was no place to be caught out at night if you didn't know it.

"Time to get back. Night's closing in fast."

She nodded, shouldering her backpack and walking toward his flyer without a word. He opened the hatch and she climbed in and strapped down.

But as they were lifting, he caught the slightest of backward glances from her. Barely perceptible, a slight turn of head only, but that look on her face? As if saying goodbye to something very precious, and suddenly he found himself wondering whether she had welcomed his rescue or cursed it.

She said little on the way back. Meaningless small talk, with adroit sidesteps every time he tried to ask something too personal. Avoidance that was too subtle to be other than practiced, and his curiosity peaked. After the occupation, his superiors had a terminal case of caution, so she was no threat. Everyone working for him was closely vetted by high command. So what had been left out of her mission profile? And did he have the right to ask, he suddenly found himself wondering for the first time in too many years.

The occupation had made him a first-rate spy, one of the leading undercover agents in the Resistance, and he had spent five years prying into anything and everything that had looked even slightly useful to the Hathians' cause. It had left him with a decidedly battered conscience. He would check her open files, he amended, and find out if she had anything blocked from view.

And if she does?

Luckily the bustle of their arrival at base meant he had to stop thinking about it. He looked across at his passenger.

She had that straight back and distant stare again, the one he really did not like.

And that made him sound like a spoilt moonie. Her cool stare did silence any attempt at exclamations of concern. Including from those he suspected to be as false as their smiles of welcome, and he watched the faces closely, the most obvious suspects and the least. But none gave him any hint, and he was forced to give up.

It was late, he was hungry and his rescued moonie needed looking after.

"Any dinner left?"

Ras nodded. "Kept some for you both, Cap. It's ready as soon as you've washed up and got out of that work gear."

"Good. Madame asn Postrova…ten minutes enough?"

She muttered something.

"You're not hungry? Or you want to sit down to eat in those?" he couldn't resist adding. Anything to disrupt that cool mask of a face.

And couldn't stop the grin twitching at his mouth as her teeth clenched, all the while pretending to ignore the grime coating her clothing.

"We'll *both* be ready in ten minutes," he said, then marched off to his quarters before his contrary moonie could argue otherwise.

It was definitely past time he had a good long look at his beautiful Mathian. Too many secrets. He was well trained in the art of subterfuge—*but so was she.*

Any such plans had to be forgotten. He was woken early next day by a message from Central, typically choosing that morning to interfere.

Meeting notification for Jacquel des Trurains. Time: today at post-meridian three hours. For security reasons, your physical presence is required.

It came direct from Gof deln Crantz and couldn't be refused. As well as being his boss, the man was one of the few people Jacquel bowed to, a man who understood the tensions threatening to split giant wedges through post-occupation Hathe. Nothing for it, he'd have to leave immediately.

"Keep an eye on Madame asn Postrova," he said to Ras. "Not sure what's going on there, but I'm not convinced she was accidentally left behind yesterday."

The look in Ras's eye said he'd been thinking the same. One problem less then. He still felt an unexpected reluctance at leaving and took one last look back as he lifted off from the plateau camp. That unmistakable cramp in his neck, a warning. Of what, he couldn't say, or why. A feeling that couldn't be shaken, as if he'd left some important detail unfinished.

Rheia fell into bed after her rescue, worn out and exhausted. And that night, she dreamed of the plateau of her childhood. So real was it that waking next morning to the stark walls of her room and the sounds of the other women through the thin walls felt like waking from reality and into a bad dream. She lay still, making no sound at all, in no mood for the usual morning confrontation with the dirtsider women.

Footsteps, stopping outside her door.

"Time to wake her up." Varda's voice, with its usual overlay of anger and scorn.

"No. Cap's orders. She's to be left to sleep today." Dreya an Vathin, one of Jacquel's troopers. None of the troopers ever talked to Rheia, other than to issue orders, but she had come to have a degree of trust in them. They were professionals, and "the Cap" had their whole loyalty.

"We don't need her anyway. I reckon Central only sent her along as a sop to the moonies." The speaker was another of the tech staff: Katrin den Phadros, the hazardous waste expert. Not a friend, but not quite as vindictive as Varda—and Rheia had to agree with her. So far, she'd seen little sign she could make a difference here. Though part of her would love to put the likes of Varda in their place by letting the techs know just how familiar she was with this country. No one knew this land like her father had and she'd grown up rambling over it with him. She could have found all their dumps in no time, just by the changes in the plants and wildlife.

Still, she kept her eyes closed and gave a huffed breath, half-snore, just loud enough to be heard.

"Cap's order is to leave her to rest today. She needs it after last night. He also says she belongs on this trip."

The trooper's words made it final, and they soon left. Rheia could finally, really relax. Apart from the couple of troops on guard duty and the base cook, she was alone. A day off.

She used it to the full, getting up at her leisure and wandering out to the kitchen only after a proper session in the cleansing unit, pulling out her viewscreen at the end to set her face to rights—casual and in control was the look she programmed in—and taking the time to sort through and do her own laundry.

After yesterday, it seemed safer.

The rest of the day, she spent in her own corner of the common room. Her space, her blocked out area where none of the others intruded. None except Jacquel of course, and she hadn't yet decided how she felt about that. She leaned back, pulling up her com channels but keeping a surreptitious eye for any movement in the rest of the room. Not that she should need to—the room was studded with surveillance sensors. Jacquel claimed their purpose was to let the tech staff link in and discuss their findings with base central at any time, but she thought he was just naturally suspicious and liked to keep an eye on everything around him.

But then, who was she to judge. She hadn't been here during the occupation, had never had to live under the Terrans' boot heel or been forced to hide under the guise of a peasant.

Hathe had been such a wonderful world before the invasion. Advanced in the energy sciences and communications technology, and socially well beyond Earth.

But not in warfare. Why would they waste money on a full-scale military machine? Hathe had a basic military, enough to provide guard duty, and protect against smugglers and other criminals, but interplanetary trade disputes were settled by discussions of the Alliance Council, not territory wars.

Then one day, a fully armed and trained fleet from Earth suddenly appeared in Hathian space. She remembered that day. No Hathian would forget it. She'd been in her last year of college, already a cadet with the DIA and absorbed in her advanced honors project. Just home from a study tour of the Alliance trading worlds, filled with pride and visions of herself as a true citizen of the cosmos. Yet not once in that tour had she heard a whisper of trouble on Earth. Not one Alliance planet had carried rumors of the shortages there, of Earth's desperate need for urgonium—the energy-rich mineral found only on Hathe, and still the principal power source used by Earth and most of the other worlds. But none as wastefully as Earth, none as dependent as Earth.

She remembered the talk in the DIA when the Terrans had demanded more of the mineral. How they had laughed at these Terrans trying to take Hathians for fools, when they already took more than any other planet. Hathe wasn't about to let Earth undercut their hold on the urgonium market by stockpiling it, then on selling to the other worlds.

No one laughed when the Terran ships arrived to threaten them. The look on her mother's face that day. The sheer terror of it; that, Rheia would never forget. Nor the month following, the insane panic to evacuate, to come up with a defense strategy. The faces of the pilots sent out to hold off the Terran fleet while the planet marshalled a defense plan.

So young. Too young to die.

And the long days and nights in the university, the endless sessions, arguments, desperate plottings, as the policy departments worked to come up with their mad, crazy plan. If Hathe couldn't beat the Terrans with weapons and ships, it would have to be by guile and trickery. Fighting would only lead to defeat and the deaths of far too many Hathians.

She wasn't there the day the Terrans landed. Wasn't one of the valiant dirtsiders left behind to endure when the Terrans landed in full conquering mode. Wasn't one of those who had to make the Terrans believe all that was left on Hathe was a downtrodden peasant society dumbly accepting the replacement of their old masters with the new. Not one of those who must tell the Terrans of their old rulers, the mythical Haut Liege, who had fled with the science and knowledge needed to mine the precious urgonium.

An outrageous charade that had only worked because so few Terrans had any knowledge of Hathe before the invasion, and only one had been there.

She'd heard of him—who hadn't? Hamon Radcliff, Hamon an Radcliff he was now. Husband to Marthe an Castre, a onetime Resistance heroine and now exiled traitor—and childhood friend of Colonel Jacquel des Trurains.

Like so many other Mathians, she had avidly followed the exploits of the Resistance heroes, wishing she could be one of them instead of hiding safely up on Mathe along with the political and skilled elite and anyone else best-qualified to work off-planet. "You will be leaving in the next transporter," she'd been told. "Pack what you need, now."

No time to say a proper goodbye. The briefest of hugs, warnings and her mother's tears as she was pushed onto the transporter, then gone. The last time she had ever seen her family.

No, don't think of that. She'd survived till now by shoving those memories to the far back corner of her mind. Her story wasn't unique. So many tragedies from the occupation, so many hurt beyond healing. Survival; that was the priority of Hathians now. Survival, and making a world strong enough that no one, *no one*, would ever hurt them again.

Yet what kind of world had they recovered? Too many Mathians returning with a sense of entitlement, wanting to take back all they had lost, too many striving to turn Hathe into a safe, advanced, *controlled* society such as they'd known on Mathe.

Against them, the dirtsiders. Hathians who'd spent so long as servile, self-effacing nobodies that many had lost the ability to shove themselves forward and stop the grasping self-seeking rife among the returnees. The brave warriors who had kept Hathe safe, now reduced to victims of the restoration.

Not by all Mathians, not by her. All she wanted was the work she knew, and to be left in peace. To lose herself in oblivion.

But that was not possible.

What had made Gilda an Rathman think she and Jacquel des Trurains could make any difference? That they could even work together?

Even if his kiss woke dreams she'd thought lost forever.

She thrust her reader back, jumped up and marched to the lunch counter.

"What can I do?" she asked the cook. "Give me some work, please," and was relieved when the man gave her a supply chart and pointed to a pile near the storage cupboard.

"This stuff needs logged in and checked over," he said gruffly, thrusting the tag to the pantry at her, before turning back to his cookers. She grasped hold of it, grabbing onto the sliver as if to a lifeline, and tried desperately hard for the rest of the afternoon to ignore the questions churning over and over in her head. How could an elite hero of the Resistance and a very ordinary diplomat make a miracle for Hathe, when they couldn't make one for each other?

It turned out she wasn't going to find the answer quickly. Jacquel had been called back to central command in the city, his troop said, and no idea when he'd return.

No idea, or refused to say. Whichever it was, she couldn't talk to the man any time soon, and she had to get on with these dirtsiders in the meantime.

One of them arranged for you to be left behind.

She made it through that night by keeping quiet, finishing her dinner and her share of the evening tasks, then disappearing into her workspace to "finish some reports." So normal, no one questioned it. Sometimes, being an outsider was a definite advantage. Then next morning it was back to the site again, with two troopers counting all staff on and off the transporters. A caution put in place by the Cap, they were told, to stop any more *accidents*. The glares made it quite plain who the dirtsiders blamed for her being left behind.

Once at the site, Rheia made no pretense of doing her job. Not today. Instead, she climbed to a hilltop to where she could get an overview of the site. From up here, the changes in the hollow were all too obvious, the damage to the plants she knew twisting something deep in her heart. What had been done here, done to this fragile and beautiful land she called home, was so *wrong*.

In time, it would heal. That's all the comfort she could find. From the techs' talk, she'd learned there were so many of these dump sites that Central had been forced to rule they would do what was necessary now, and the rest would be left to nature to heal.

How long before her home was hers again?

No, not a path to venture down. She switched her gaze to the tech staff working to save this place. Varda was working with Maria today. Or to be specific, Varda was working in the same zone of the dump site as Maria.

Rheia studied the pair. Varda was easy to figure, the rigid back and blatant rudeness a classic move to put an inferior in her place. Except that Maria looked to have sorted how to handle that, ignoring the chemical engineer and quietly getting on with her own work. Rheia smiled. It was the best thing the ecologist could do. After a time, the strategy seemed to pierce the chemical engineer's thick skull.

Rheia was no scientist, but even she could tell that Varda was duplicating Maria's work. Both were working on line scans and, to Rheia, they looked to be exactly the same; both taking scanner readings at the same point, then Varda would march over to Maria and insist on checking Maria's readings.

Rheia pulled out her own DIA scanner and linked into their equipment. They wouldn't know about it, not with the encryptions she had layered into her little darling, and she had to smile when she saw the readings Varda insisted on reviewing. Measurements of plant dieback, chlorophyll output, degree of parasitical loss on plant leaves. All ecological measures, and how the chemical engineer thought she could make a pronouncement on the results was beyond Rheia. But Maria said nothing, merely passing over her results for comparison and in turn only sought the readings from Varda that did appear to be necessary for an ecologist.

Not an efficient work pattern, not when Maria's body language showed how carefully she must word those requests. A slow burn of anger kindled in Rheia. She liked the little ecologist. More, she respected the woman's work, and a troll like Varda had no right treating her like this. But she grit her teeth and told herself to stay out of it. She had a job to do here, which didn't include picking fights with bad-mannered scientists. Not in this environment. Not when someone had already tried to hurt her.

She was safe today. The troopers kept watch at all times, with one clearly pegging her position and she made sure to stay in full sight. They watched her, and she watched the team below, making notes in her com as she worked out the dynamics of the group. What went on inside a man or woman's head was never completely known, nor the reasons for what they did, and Rheia had learned the hard way never to trust in absolute loyalty.

So she watched Jacquel des Trurains's troops as well.

His squad were good, that she had to concede, watching as they smoothly moved to cover each other so that not one of their charges was ever out of sight, yet always alert for outside hazards. The way they walked over the rough ground told her they were very familiar with the plateau country. And those slight body movements, those twitches of arm or head, movements of hands and clothes, had to be the secret language of the Hathian Resistance she'd heard so much about. Like all Mathians, she had tried to learn the basics, enthralled by this secret patter of talk the brave heroes of the Resistance had continuously carried out right under the Terrans' noses. Their com patches formed a part of it, but not all, and none of what she'd learned on Mathe seemed to work here. She'd tried to tap into it on her first day, to get only a garbled spatter of words, quickly shut down and followed by the scowl of the nearest trooper. The Resistance hadn't told those up on Mathe everything, and the Security Department was the most paranoid of all the Resistance groups.

She'd also learned that the devices used by ex-Resistance forces outplayed all her clever toys from her diplomatic days.

"Lunch is ready, Madame asn Postrova," said the formal tones of Ras den Koprorth, breaking seamlessly into her top security rated, supposedly unhackable diplomatic com stream. She looked across to where he stood beside the transporter, a quick grin on his face when she rose and nodded she'd heard.

They're keeping you safe. She hoped.

By the end of the day she was exhausted, her brain snarled in a tangle of conflicting questions. Who was her enemy, what was she doing here, what made these dirtsiders so different from the people she'd lived with for the past five years?

How could she ever understand them when the only danger she'd faced had been mental. She'd lived in hotels and embassies, while they scratched in the ground and daily risked death or injury.

It was with relief that she saw the chemical engineer packing up her gear. As usual, Maria had yet to finish, nervous glances flicking to the end of her sampling line. Rheia sighed, as she looked over to the flyer. The rest of the team were there already, chatting together as they compared results and packed up for the day. Mind you, she'd seen what happened when Maria tried to join the rest if Varda was in the group. Putting down the best expert on the team to make yourself more secure seemed a stupid tactic, but because of it, Maria tended to arrive last at the transporter.

"Time to go, Madame asn Postrova," came a curt crackle in her ear. She looked up at the sky, and she realized why the troopers were hurrying. Those clouds didn't look good; tonight would be no time to be caught out on the plateau. She quickly stood up, brushing the dust off her seat and hurried down to help Maria, a habit she seemed to be acquiring. Yet again, she made the girl go on while she finished. Another curt reminder from Ras den Koprorth, and she hurried to the transporter.

A thoroughly irritated trooper stood in the doorway. "You're the last, asn Postrova." He touched his comtab and added her to the on-board count, then let the pilot know they were ready for take-off.

Slowly the ramp began to rise, while Rheia searched for a seat. There was one only, right by the door, and the trooper waved her impatiently to it as he stalked off to the troopers' seats down the back. She thrust her bag into the locker above as the hatch began to close. Then turned toward her seat.

A hard shove in her side, a clawing at the comtab on her wrist, and next she knew she was tumbling out the rapidly disappearing gap of the closing hatch and rolling down the hillside. Above her, the unmistakable clunk of the hatch closing and the transporter's engines engaging. Lifting up, leaving her behind. All she could do was roll hastily away to escape the backwash. After that, she had to watch as the transporter disappeared over the ridgeline and back toward base.

Leaving her stranded on the plateau without backpack or com unit.

The only consolation: she knew exactly where she was. Her father's grave sat just over the far side of the hill above her. She looked up at the hillside, searching for the telltale hump, then looked higher, over the ridgeline, at the threatening sky above. A furious cauldron of black cloud and patchy sky tossed by a vindictive stream of furious winds barreling right toward her. The plateau was about to welcome her home in all its outrageous fury. And all she had against it were her wits, her brains, and the capsules and kit secreted in the pockets of her tunic.

"I think I'm in trouble, Da."

CHAPTER FIVE

Priorities. That's what she must decide.

First: shelter. The cave from last time was too far, but there was a small one close by. Not as deep, not as warm, but it would keep her dry.

Food: she had the energy bars she carried in her pockets whenever she was out on the plateau, thanks to her childhood training, and she could worry about finding more in the morning.

Water: unlikely to be a problem given what threatened. The only trick would be to find something to collect it in, unless she wanted to stand outside in the full force of the weather and open her mouth to collect the raindrops.

Not too bad a list. She could manage it. She'd have to. No pilot would agree to bring a vehicle back to rescue her in the kind of weather threatening to hit this region. Time to get a move on if she was to have any chance of surviving the night.

The cave was on the far side of the nearby hill. She scrambled up the bank, grabbing onto the tough grass to haul herself up quicker, then up and over the ridgeline. Today, she had no time to do more than place a small stone by her father's grave, whisper a hurried plea for help then plunge on down the hill. Tumble, fall, barreling down in a mad scurry.

Halfway down, it happened. A sudden twist as her foot caught on a rock, an unmistakable *snap*, and a searing pain shooting up her leg.

No, no, no! Not now.

She refused to look down, refused to see what she'd hurt. Not yet. Half-fainting, she kept up her mad race for the cave entrance, crawling more than running in a flurried race for cover.

The rain just beat her, driving icy spears of water through her clothes and drenching her to the skin before she could tumble through the entrance and out of harm's way. She could no longer walk, just drag her stupid, frozen body inside and away from nature's fury.

The cave wasn't deep, and the wind hurtled straight into the opening. A slight bend in the wall and a long-fallen boulder offered her some protection. Hands scrabbling in the dirt and grabbing at the walls, she maneuvered herself around the barrier, then collapsed. But her hideaway couldn't protect her from the pending hypothermia from her sodden state. Already her fingers fumbled as she tugged out the precious capsules from her pocket. The gray one; that's what she needed first.

Her father had long ago taught her the knack of opening them, but that was on a clear, sunny day when her world still glowed with childhood's warmth. Today, it took long precious moments before her fingers found the notch and dug in, just so, to break the pressure seal.

An explosion of soft, billowing cloth, floating up and draping over her shoulders. Next instant, a delicious warmth enveloped her. A thermal blanket with an inbuilt heating unit.

Heat that right now was saving her life. She sat, tugging the cloth tightly around her and luxuriating in it. Slow. Still. Ignore the savage attack of the storm, the lonely isolation and the agony in her ankle. Wait for the blanket's warmth to stop the feverish shivering.

A beloved voice rang in her head. A voice that had taught her the tricks of this land.

"Don't ever think you know them all, my girl. That's when Old Man Plateau will get you."

"It's got me good today, Da. But I'm alive and that's a win." Another of her father's favorite sayings. She was alive, and she was going to stay that way.

And when she got back, she was going to find out just who had given her that shove in the back and pushed her out of the transporter. It was no accident, nor was it a disgruntled prank. Given what the mission dirtsiders knew of her background, that shove was intended to kill.

Was it personal? Maybe, maybe not. Her guess: she'd stumbled onto something a whole lot bigger than a rogue dirtsider who resented moonies.

It still felt personal. Suddenly, it all became too much, overwhelming her in misery, and she sank into a gray gloom. Reality receded, and she welcomed the misty fuzziness of oblivion.

Time passed uncounted.

Walls, brown dirt, a flurry of wet grit hurtling around the boulder and slamming into her face, bringing her back to harsh reality.

Enough. No more wallowing, no more self-pitying indulgence. That only brought death out here. Why she was here could come later. Right now, she needed something to strap her foot. The pain of it was becoming a serious problem and the slightest of movements set off a searing shiver of agony, slicing right up from her foot to her head until the ache of it spawned a cannonade of drumming in her head. All ranger children learned survival-level first aid, which meant she could make a splint out of anything to hand, and sticks and branches abounded outside, strewn on the ground about the base of each kryptark bush. But the storm meant they might as well have been up on Mathe.

She forced herself to look down and examine her ankle. It was hard to see in the dim light, but enough filtered through the cave entrance for her to see the shape of it, to confirm what she had known from the moment of that awful snap of sound.

A deep breath, then she forced herself to coolly assess her situation. Panic did nothing for you, not out here.

The angle was wrong, but not as bad as she'd feared. So not a complete break, though given the position there would be more than one bone involved and a hellish recovery period. *When* she got back to base.

When, not if; not a word she would consider. *When* she got back to base, when she was evac'd out to a proper hospital, with proper pain control and clean bedding and soft, warm, gentle cleansing units to luxuriate in.

Dreams, dangerous dreams.

She studied the ankle, blocking out the pain, or trying to. What to use to fix it, to let her concentrate on the other things she needed to do. She had two capsules left: one, the light weight tent, and the other, sachets of electrolyte gel for an emergency boost. Plus her knife, compass and energy bars.

She wouldn't need the tent tonight. It wasn't storm proof, not against the kind of weather hitting outside. The cave kept her dry and the blanket would keep out the occasional flurries slithering in the entrance. So the tent could be sacrificed.

She opened the capsule and watched the tent fill the remaining space in the cave. Her father had given it to her so long ago and she'd kept it for when she could return here. The tent was to be her small home as she made friends again with the plateau on a dreamed of summer holiday.

Friends—hah! Some friend her old homeland turned out to be. She stabbed down with the knife before she could change her mind, rending the tough fabric into slashed remnants that lay sadly on the cave floor.

Don't be a sentimental idiot.

She picked up the first piece, rolling it in a practiced twist against her thigh to turn the long strips into tough tubes of solid fabric. They weren't completely rigid but would do the trick. Next, the bit she dreaded. She looked long at the ankle, noted the angle, thought, guessed, then grabbed down and wrenched.

Blackness, pain, gasping breaths and too slowly reality returned. Her head dropped back against the wet dirt, and she lay still, dizzy and sick. Recovery came far too slowly. Time for the last capsule and her fingers scrabbled desperately for the trick of it. A pop, and the first of the three gel sachets tumbled through her fingers. Too hard to reach for it, nausea choking her as the pain leapt to life again. Later, she'd find it later. A second plopped into her lap, and her hand closed gratefully around the tube, lifting it and squeezing the beads into her mouth. One, two, yes take another. Three—and a good shot of adrenalin and sugars flooded into her mouth, momentarily pushing back the shock that hovered, waiting to claim her.

She would survive.

Then bend, slowly, slowly, letting her head settle as she reached carefully for the stack of rolled fabric tubing. The angle; still wrong but better.

Soon she had a protective cylinder of tubes, laid lengthwise around the break. More strips, unflinchingly wrapped round and round the stacks of tubing.

It wasn't the medic's splints that should have encased the ankle in a properly aligning stasis field, but the pleasure of tying that last knot and feeling the ease the supporting tubes gave her rapidly swelling leg, was immeasurable. She could do no more now. Spent and sick with agony, she curled up against the wall and gave into the threatening weakness.

Let me sleep, she prayed. Just for a while.

It was dark, the next time she came to awareness. The true dark of the wilds, with only the weakest of fitful light from the occasional peek of the moons finding its way into her haven. Then true blackness again, broken only by the sudden rending of the night with a flash of lightning.

She didn't care. There was nothing she could do that needed light. She lay back against the dirt, trying vainly to find a soft cushion for her head. Then wavered in and out of consciousness again, time a boundless and changing thing, one face hovering just out of view with that touch of laughter lifting his mouth.

He came for her once.

Don't be stupid, Rheia. Heroes belong to the vids, not real life.

The vids—and the war.

A sneaking shaft of yellow daylight slithered over the cave floor. She opened her eyes blearily, trying to remember where she was.

A stretch of achy limbs, suddenly and too viciously stopped by the streak of pain, and it all came back.

Her ankle, she'd broken something there. And she lay back gasping till the pain receded and memory fully returned. She was stranded on the plateau, with no com unit, no water and only an energy bar and two more sachets of electrolyte gel left.

No, she'd dropped one. Suddenly, finding that sachet seemed the most important goal of all. She wriggled sideways, careful of her ankle, and her hands desperately swept the ground around her. She'd dropped it to one side. It should be close to where she'd been lying.

Nothing, nothing, and the tears she'd fought against stung her eyes.

But no, she would not give up. Stop and think. Keep still, turn and look.

There, a small packet half buried by the dirt she'd thrown up. She grabbed at it, feeling the squelch of cool slush under her clenching fingers.

Two packets of energy gel, a knife, a thermal blanket, one more energy bar in her pocket and her old-fashioned compass, and a clear day outside from the feel of the air coming in the cave. Cold, yes, but the heavy charge of the storm had passed and there was no scent of rain.

It was enough. She would make it out of here and back to base.

First, find water.

There was a creek at the base of the slope. She could crawl there if she had to.

A place to relieve herself. A bush to hide behind. Then remembered. *There's no one out here to see you.* Maybe, but she'd learned to value her privacy after so many years as a diplomat on constant public display. She slowly levered herself up using the wall behind her for support, resting the broken ankle gently on the ground, then collapsed the blanket into its capsule and stuffed everything into her work pockets.

Already the ankle ached badly, and she discovered the hard way that it would bear no weight. There was a shrub a short distance from the cave entrance, with branches that could be broken. She studied it, measuring the distance and the ground surface between.

Hopping? Not over those ruts. Sit then, and carefully, patiently, bottom it along the ground as the damp seeped through her clothes.

Too many lingering twinges. Only halfway there, she had to stop and lash tight her makeshift splints. They really were makeshift, little more than a thick bandage, and couldn't stop all movement.

If only she had some painkillers on her. She gulped, brushed ineffectually at the dirt clinging to her legs, then set off again. A truly makeshift bandage, that had her gasping in pain by the time she reached the shrubs.

The pungent odor of oil-laced native leaf extensions filled her nose as she gingerly crouched behind it. A pompous horticultural major had once castigated her for referring to them as leaves. "That's what Earth plants have. Hathe's so-called leaves are quite different in structure."

Rheia thought it stupid. Leaves, she'd always called the blue-gray twig extensions on the kryptark, and leaves they were, just as on all Hathe's unique trees and shrubs. Hathians would choose what to call their own, not some pedantic off-world textbook.

"This is my home," she said defiantly to the skies. Enough of her family lay beneath its soil. This was her home and she was not yet ready to be laid under its soil as well. Not so soon after the end of her long exile. One day, when it was safe, she would return to the site of her old home. Best of all, show it to her children and tell them of the happy days she had spent there.

Children? Hah! You think? On Hathe, children were highly valued and meant to be raised in a secure, stable family unit. Who would take on someone with her history?

An image of a finely cut face filled with intelligence and humor touched her mind, and the next moment had her doubled over with laughter. Talk about aiming high. Jacquel des Trurains wasn't for some nobody moonie with a family name no amount of wishing could make respectable again.

She must be light-headed and hallucinating.

A quick burst of the energy gel and she pulled out her knife. Two hacks, and she had a couple of serviceable enough splints to add to the tubing. She tugged and twisted, then leaned back, gasping as she finished tying them into the makeshift supports. Then she saw it. That branch, the tallest, thick one near the middle of the shrub. That would do nicely.

A quarter of an hour later, she was still sawing at the base of the branch, trying to dislodge it.

Give up? No, never.

But even Rheia's stubborn determination was badly frayed by the time she finally freed the branch. A few more hacks, a smoothing of the top, and she had an almost perfect walking stick. Yes, it was maybe a hands breadth short, but she was now mobile.

Using her new stick, she levered herself off the ground and slowly hopped down to the creek. One goal attained and now the splashing of water in the creek reminded her how long it was since she'd last drunk anything.

Kneel and bend over, to greedily slurp up handfuls of the crisp high-altitude water. No burr of ozone, no residue of urban treatments, just the delicious tang of plant and long-dead leaf flavoring the clear water. Like a precious cordial or long-forgotten prized wine. She slaked her thirst in a furious spasm of slurp and swallow, then slowed, savoring each mouthful.

Now she knew she was home.

The trip to Central had been a waste of time, as far as Jacquel was concerned, with no need for him to appear in person. The whole thing had a hint of one of Anhuilla's interventions, intended to bring him home. But surely she could have found a more believable excuse to have him ordered back. A minor budget conflict elevated to a major storm, thanks to some office flunkey demanding to know why Jacquel's returns consistently failed to match his budgeted expectations, and a red herring report on a case of moonie wealth grabbing.

The last had been true enough but was backed up by an impenetrable web of legal blatherings that made it irreversible. All he could do was make sure the disenfranchised dirtsiders were reimbursed and made financially stable. It wouldn't ease their bitter anger but did keep them from the humiliation of the welfare queue. Those queues were as dangerous as anything on Hathe at the moment.

And the reason his budgets were so unpredictable. He was trying to prevent civil disaster with little more than the proverbial patch in a leaking shuttle.

For once, he was glad of an excuse to get away from it all, even if the plateau was the last place he needed to be. And to top everything off, his long-time assistant had just announced it was time for her to retire, to live quietly with the husband she'd been parted from for most of the occupation. Graia wanted peace, she said, not the risks that came with working for a target of the most dangerously disaffected on Hathe.

Too much of him understood her too well.

He docked his flyer and climbed out feeling as if poleaxed by a week's forced military training. The clear plateau air filled his lungs and finally something felt right again. The plateau may have been scarred by the Terrans, but it had survived. For the first time, he was glad of this assignment.

"Hey Cap. How was the City?"

Jacquel scowled at his second. "About as expected." The smothered grin on Ras's face said he'd already read Jacquel's mood and knew it exactly. "Graia's retired on me."

"Oh, er, a shame."

That was all Ras could say? He'd worked with Graia as long as Jacquel. "She told you she was planning this?"

Ras gave a non-committal shrug. "Guessed she was thinking of it."

There was something more in his second's face though, a too casual glance before turning away and walking beside Jacquel to the barrack. Almost as if avoiding his gaze.

"So, what's the thing you don't want to tell me?" said Jacquel.

Ras missed a step, and Jacquel's momentary lift in mood plummeted. "Out with it," he said, and Ras grimaced.

"It's the moonie."

"Oh? Who's upset her now?"

Then felt a twinge of fear, and something else he couldn't quite put a finger on. "What's happened?"

"She missed last night's transporter."

"Again? So where is she now? I swear I'm going to tear a strip off that girl if she keeps pulling this kind of trick."

"Well, that's it. There was a bit of a storm last night."

"And…?"

"She's not back yet."

"She was out all night, on the plateau?" A plummeting, a moment of dark horror, then his heart began to beat again. "The pilot and trooper in charge of the field crew, my office, two minutes."

Jacquel swung his bag over his shoulder and marched into the building, angrier than he remembered being for a long time. He flung his bag into his room and stalked to his office. Thankfully both the pilot and trooper were waiting for him there as ordered, or he didn't know what he'd have done. Ras stubbornly positioned himself by the door. Watching out for whom: the nervous pilot, the trooper, or Jacquel? He suspected it was him, but merely nodded in grim acknowledgement.

He locked his stare on the trooper first. "You left one of your team behind last night."

"She was late. We waited, and I counted her on board. She was sitting down as the door was shutting. I'd gone to take my own seat. She wasn't on board when we got back to base."

"She just vanished from a locked transporter? Where does her com say she is?"

Shuffling feet and silence. Suddenly that clench in Jacquel's gut grew ten times worse. "Her com unit?"

"Umm, well…"

"Ras?"

His most trusted and senior trooper slowly pulled something from his inside pocket. Then laid a small sliver of shimmering iridescence on the table. Jacquel immediately activated his own wrist com, held it over the sliver, and his heart seized. "This com. It's hers."

"Ah, yes," said Ras, in a voice devoid of any tone at all. "Her gear pack was found stowed on board, along with her com unit. Seems she'd placed it in her pack as she stowed it."

Jacquel had to walk, had to move. "No one leaves their com behind. Not deliberately. You went back as soon as she was found missing? Any signs?"

The pilot was feet-shuffling again and going red in the face. "Pilot?"

"Not in that storm. Nothing was lifting anywhere in weather like that."

He glared again at Ras, deliberately ignoring the trooper.

"A plateau storm. The pilot's right. Nothing was going to lift in that—you'd have ordered the same, Cap."

He would have. It didn't make him feel any better. "When did the search party leave this morning?"

"About to. You were so close, they decided to wait till you landed."

He couldn't decide whether he was relieved or furious. Rheia, his moonie, out on the plateau in a storm, and they hadn't left yet to find her—or the body. It was a probability he couldn't ignore. The hammering in his head accelerated. "Give me ten minutes to change. Full emergency medical and survival gear on board."

Someone was going to pay for how he felt right now. He remembered the storms of this region, remembered trying to fight his way through one years ago and having to give up. The plateau was a hard foe to beat, and no one in their right mind would stay out in a storm. But a pampered moonie diplomat? *She survived the last time. She knows more than she lets on.* It was all he had to hold on to, all he had to keep his temper and his nerves under control during the loading up and flight to her last known position.

They came to a hover over the pickup point and the pilot began her scan. Kaya deln Trannis had served in this sector during the war and knew the plateau's tricks as well as any of them. But it was no help today. The read outs showed nothing useful, the cold waves of the grasslands refusing to give up their secrets.

Plenty of body heat signals registering. Small gnur, hastily digging in to the softer earth as the flyer hovered over them; large and swooping aerions circling in predatory glee, looking to clean up the detritus of last night's booty. But no signal matching a human female.

"Try the next valley over." Then he had a thought. "Last time she took shelter in a cave. Anything like that around here?"

The pilot nodded. "Ground strata scan in operation now."

The flyer traced over the rising line of hills, tracking up the slope, along the ridgeline and down the other side.

"Wait. What's that?" said Jacquel.

The pilot came to a hover, checking the scan readout. "A cave, sir, of sorts. Not big."

Jacquel looked at the shadow on the com, searching for any sign of life.

Nothing. No hand signal, no gear lying about the cave mouth. The ground was roughed up, the dirt churned, but that was only to be expected after the weather of the night before. Everywhere spoke of the toll visited on the area by the storm's fury. Grasses twisted this way and that, twigs and gravel hurled in chaotic patterns, like so many dancers suddenly dropped at the end of a mad party romp.

"Put us down," he ordered.

Something in his gut said this was the place. It had to be. There was nowhere else, not that would give her cover before that storm hit.

As soon as the struts hit ground, he punched the release on his strapping, thumbed the hatch open and jumped out even before the ramp was fully down. Then sanity hit him and he stopped dead. Rushing in might obliterate any trace of her.

"Scanner," he snapped at the trooper coming down behind him, "Full track and obs' mode. An Thanis, the cave." The ranger-born man was their best tracker.

An Thanis stepped lightly over the ground, his eyes peeled. Jacquel watched intently. The man stopped suddenly, body tensing.

"Drag marks, sir."

"Size?"

"A match. Human, lighter built. Not a man, but not small."

"It's her." Rheia came near to his own height. Not small, but definitely a woman. And there was something about that lean, strong body that called to him.

The lure of the unknown, that's all, scoffed his rational side. Maybe, but the signs of her presence eased the ominous burden squeezing down on his shoulders.

"Record, mark and enter," he ordered the trooper and followed as the man tracked the marks into the cave. She had come here, he knew it.

More drag marks inside, the ground disturbed enough for even Jacquel to see clearly.

"How many? Any other tracks?" he said to the man crouched down in the small space, hands examining the rest of the cave floor before pulling out his com unit.

"One only. She rested here for some time. Got wet coming in—see the clumps of mud there—but here's smoother, as if she'd wrapped herself in something." He peered closer. "Light."

Jacquel switched the scanner beam to bathe the area in light.

The tracker's hand reached down to pick up something. A rag that shimmered in the beam of light, and then Jacquel heard a sudden gasp of breath.

"This is ranger issue. Part of an emergency kit tent. Haven't seen one like it in years." An Thanis looked up. "Who is this asn Postrova—that's no ranger name." His tone said the demand was only saved from being an accusation by their long years of working together.

"Her records said nothing of being on the plateau before."

"Maybe, but where did she get a ranger issue tent? We don't hand them out, ever."

Jacquel knew enough of the closed ranger caste not to say what he thought: that if their gear was so superior, shouldn't they have given it to every single Resistance group needing it during the war. But if Joshan an Thanis said that strip of fabric was ranger-made, then it was, and he had one more question to add to a rapidly growing list for asn Postrova.

When he found her.

"So where'd she go from here, and why all this dragging and scraping? Why not walk on two feet?"

He got the answer all too soon. The tracker quickly checked the rest of the cave, then followed the marks outside again. "She left after the storm but while it was still wet. First thing this morning, I'd say." He began to walk downhill, toward a patch of shrubbery. Jacquel had a fair idea why she'd be heading that way and was about to tell the tracker to look instead for where she'd left the bushes.

"She's hopping, one-footed."

"Injured?"

"I'd bet on it."

That twisting clench of his guts was back. "There was no blood back there."

The tracker shrugged. "Leg's broke, twisted, whatever. She stopped here and cut some branches, including one for a walking stick. See the points of it digging into the dirt?" A sniff, deep, then stopping. "And over here's where she—"

"Yes, I know what she was doing there," put in Jacquel hastily. "After?"

The tracker pointed downhill again. "The girl's got brains. Gets mobile, relieved, next stop is water. She's headed for the creek."

Now Jacquel pulled out his scanner again, swept it around in an arc, setting it to full scan. The tracker ignored him and loped off downhill, making for the splashing of water over sharp mountain rocks. Jacquel finished his sweep. Nothing, still nothing. Where had she gone?

Down by the creek, the crushed grasses and dislodged rocks showed where she'd stopped to drink. A few damp patches of dirt, a smooth skid mark on the gravel at the edge where a body must have slid towards the water to drink, but that was all. No actual body, no man-made residues, nothing *concrete*.

"Can you read anything, see what she's done next?"

An Thanis cast back and forth, stepping from stone to stone to cross over the creek and check both banks upstream, then down. The creek gurgled on, as if laughing at their futile efforts. It was a typical high-country stream, fast-running, cold and crystal clear. The kind that would leave you chilled to the bone after the briefest of dunkings. She can't have tried to use that. He watched his tracker in frustration. Was the girl *trying* to avoid being found?

Finally, finally, an Thanis stopped some distance downstream, leaned over and checked an innocuous clump of the native grasses, their brown-gray stems trailing in the water's edge.

"She got out here, dragging herself again. Not sure she meant to come down here. There's a bit of blood on a rock, not much, more like she's been roughed up a bit by the creek."

"Fresh."

The man nodded. "It's this morning's."

On foot, injured, and using a stick. Which meant she can't have gone far. So why was his scanner not picking her up? He touched his com unit, ordered the other troopers to follow their trail, "…and bring a full med kit."

Don't think, just do your job.

"Lead on, and hurry."

An Thanis nodded, the grim look on his face a match for Jacquel's fears. Nothing about this looked good.

Too much time later, and still following the tracks, he felt like swearing. "You sure she's injured?" he growled at an Thanis. They were both running now.

"Yeah, but she knows this country. A moonie maybe, but this girl knows what she's doing and where she's going. She's only stopped a couple of times, and there's no backtracking."

At last, Jacquel's scanner woke and gave a blip. A location reading. About time. "There, up that hill and by the rock face at the top."

An Thanis hadn't waited, still following the signs marking the ground and running hard. Jacquel raced after, roaring into his com unit as he went. "Follow my signal. Kaya, I want that flyer set down as close as possible to her."

He was breathing heavily now, silently cursing the easy lope of his tracker. Jacquel had imagined he was fit, but too many months stuck in an office and arguing with command had taken its toll and his trooper pulled easily ahead of him. Jacquel stopped, gasping for breath as the man reached the rocks, rounded the biggest one, then swung back, urgently waving him up.

"She's here, sir."

But she hadn't come out with him. Breathlessness forgotten, he surged on, digging in and powering up the slope. Around the rocks, to see a familiar shape huddled in abandoned misery. He put out a hand, felt her damp clothes and touched her forehead.

"Too cold. Kaya, hurry up with that flyer."

The ranger pulled out a flask, put it to her mouth and tried to get her to swallow. A cough, a weak wave of her hand, then shivering, dangerously vicious shivering. Jacquel had rarely felt as helpless. He swung about, searching the skies. At last, the gray shape of the flyer, swinging onto the flats at the base of the hill. Jacquel went to lift her up, arms wrapping protectively around her, then saw the sadly padded leg and the puny sticks serving as makeshift supports.

"A splint. She needs one better than this. Now."

An Thanis hunted, then wordlessly passed him a pair of thick sticks, and Jacquel used the strips holding her makeshift support in place to bind the new splints around her. She made no sound, no response at all when he knew he must be hurting her. He bent his head to her chest, had to hear if her heart still beat, her breath still whispered in, then out. Quick, urgent, but he *needed* to know. Then he lifted her again and began the march down the hill, clutching her tight.

"You want a hand with her, sir?"

He shook his head at an Thanis. "Check out the area and bring anything she's dropped."

The flyer had landed by the time he made it to the bottom, the hatch sliding open. He carried her up the ramp and laid her on a nearby seat. She was half-conscious only, muttering in distress as if searching for something or someone.

"Possible hypothermia" he said to the hovering troop adjutant. "Get a blanket, warm fluids and alert the medical team at the Citadel. She needs a proper requilibration unit."

A bustle as his team swept into action. The tracker arrived and passed him a small, half-open capsule. One the tracker recognized, by the look on his face. "Ranger made?"

The tracker nodded. "Reckon she's got some questions to answer."

Jacquel pursed his mouth. Definitely yes, but not till she looked a lot more distant from death's door. He jerked his head, the tracker thumbed the hatch, and they buckled down, Jacquel taking the seat next to their reticent stray, one hand on her shoulder, needing to touch her, to feel that slight rise and fall of a breathing, living woman.

"Take her up," he ordered the pilot.

CHAPTER SIX

Coming back to the Citadel never got any easier. Too many memories of the war soaked its walls. Jacquel hadn't been here since he came to take away Marthe's cursed Terran husband, just after the end of the occupation. Many dirtsiders felt the same, but not all. For some, the Citadel had come to be home, to be a known place, safer than the streets and valleys of the new, post-war Hathe.

It was also too useful to be discarded. Once the Terran headquarters for all of Hathe, the fortress now served as the regional administration center and hospital. There was also a first-class spaceport in one of the surrounding suburbs. The one-time port for undercover trips between Hathe and the secret base on Mathe, it still served as a hub for intrasystem space flights.

It didn't change anything for Jacquel. He hated the place. But this was the closest medic unit, and Rheia couldn't wait for help. He hovered watchfully as her foot was straightened, a real splint in place, and they began to ready her for the requilibration unit.

"You a relative?" a stern-faced nurse demanded.

"Her mission leader."

"Then you'll be waiting outside," she said with that look all nurses seemed to acquire, and Jacquel could only bow meekly, whatever he felt inside. He was only allowed back in for the shortest of visits once Rheia was in the requib unit's tank, fully immersed in the healing fluids behind its opaque sides and safe from offending eyes.

He gestured at the control panel of the tank. "How long?"

"Come back at meridian plus four and she should be out and able to talk. We've added a probe to the unit to mesh the bones of that leg in place, but she won't be able to use it fully for a week at least."

With which, Jacquel properly assumed, he was dismissed. He took a long look at her blurred outline in the tank, relaxed, floating, comfortable, then listened to the steady pulse of the readouts confirming she was breathing and her heart beating. All normal, all good.

It made leaving her no easier. He'd lost too many who mattered to him, and for some reason this DIA-planted moonie woman had been added to that list.

You like the woman. She knows what she's doing and expects nothing of you.

She ought to, an aggrieved niggle inside him whispered. Should have expected him to keep her safe. But no, she held back, put up that drekking wall and refused to join the stream of people who did need him to fix something for them. A whole planet full of people, all needing him to find a way to haul the rapidly diverging strands of Hathe back to a united whole.

The nurse waited, one foot impatiently tapping on the floor, and he couldn't think of a single excuse to stay. He must walk out that door. One look back, one brief glance at those reassuring monitors. She lived.

But what to do while he waited?

"Is there a spare office I can use?" he asked the guards on her door. Local sentry staff, from their uniforms, but Security by their reply to Jacquel's discreet hand signal. Gof deln Crantz was keeping an eye on him, he guessed sourly. One of them waved him down the hallway and showed him to an empty room in a cluster of offices. A woman sat at a desk in the foyer outside.

"Jannie here acts as general admin for this block," the guard said. "Just ask, and she can deliver most things."

"Thanks. Privacy is all I need at the moment."

No quick smile of understanding from the woman. She solemnly promised to make sure he wasn't disturbed by anyone, then pointed to a door. He headed that way, then had to turn back. Graia would have known what he meant.

"Unless it's from any of my superiors or my family," he added, sighing inside. "I'm setting my com to silent. Or if someone really needs my help and can't wait."

She nodded, but he had little real hope she'd understood what he meant, and he locked the door of the office with little expectation of the room offering any kind of refuge. But it did have a direct com link to Central's system so he could access the personnel records on file in head office, and that's what he most needed.

Who was Rheia asn Postrova and what was her link to the rangers? Too many of the plateau natives had been lost in the occupation, and many of those left had withdrawn into a protective isolation that few in Hathe's new administration cared to pierce. The rangers had earned it the hard way. But

Hathe needed their knowledge of these wild places if there was to be any chance of reversing the damage the Terrans had done.

Because we need those wild places. They remind us of how we fit here, of how we must make a new Hathe that's right for this planet, this living world. You cannot sanitize a wild place, no matter how hard those who'd lived on the artificial, controlled base on Mathe wished they could.

Then he wondered again about Rheia asn Postrova. On which side of the line did she sit?

"Time to wake up, young lady." An unknown voice barked in her ear and a less than gentle hand shook her shoulder.

"Go 'way," she grumbled, burrowing down again. Then realized she was floating, not tucked in her familiar cot. She flailed about in a panic, stuck in what had to be a nightmare, and felt herself sinking under the waterline.

Those gruff hands hauled her back, forced her up, and she discovered she was sitting in a large bath not floundering in an unknown sea. No, she was sitting *naked* in a bath with an unknown person grabbing at her. She cracked open her eyes.

Thank the Pillars, yes. Her unknown assailant wore a nurse's uniform. Not altogether kindly, but brusque and efficient. The woman passed a scanner over her, checked a control bank, then ordered her to stand and climb out of the tank. "You're about back to normal, or near enough as to be no point keeping you in there longer. Next time, treat the plateau with a bit more respect."

So a local, she guessed. Either that, or a dirtsider who knew where Rheia had spent the war. But competent enough to give her confidence she was truly safe to climb out of the unit. A requilibration tank for hypothermia treatment, that's what held her; standard equipment in all plateau medical units. Cold was the biggest killer on the plateau, and Rheia had come horribly close to being the latest statistic.

The creek had been her downfall. Balancing awkwardly on one leg as she maneuvered herself into a sitting position, she'd had to lean right over the water to take a drink. To the point where, thirst slaked, she must scramble backwards to pull herself up to standing again. That was when it happened. A trip over her injured ankle, pain again, too much pain, and she had half fainted, recovering too late to stop herself tumbling into the freezing waters, too late to use her hands to stop before the spiteful creek pitched her end over end, bashing her against the sharp-edged rocks sticking up from the turbulent bed. All she could do was hold tight to her precious stick and wait till the momentum of the current released her enough to grab hold of a trailing tussock to stop her headlong plunge.

She didn't feel cold then, too full of adrenalin and fear. Only later did the shivers hit, when she had dragged herself as far as she could across the unrelenting country. Till finally she had sought shelter, taking to a hidden pocket like a gnur retreating from a seeking aerion. Only it was the land itself that hunted her, the persistently searching, needle-pointed winds and the trap-strewn earth pitted with roughs and ridges, playing with her soaking body and turning the drenched rags of her clothing to clinging icicles of pain. She'd collapsed into the beckoning hollow, curling up in a protective huddle, and that was the last she remembered.

The warmth of the cleanser's drying currents drove back the last memories of cold, and she stood basking in their promise for as long as possible, till with a grunt, her nurse firmly cycled them down and told her to get dressed, shoving some new clothes at her and planting a splint field on her ankle. A proper, modern support field instead of her makeshift field job.

"Come on, we don't want to undo all the good that unit's done you—and the captain's been waiting long enough already."

"The captain…you mean Colonel des Trurains?" She couldn't stop the furious heat cascading through her cheeks. "He saw me…in there?"

"What kind of department do you think we run here? Of course not."

She was too relieved to be angry at Jacquel des Trurains. Although that didn't seem to be the case for him when he marched through the door minutes after the nurse had installed her in a nearby chair with orders to stay there and get some rest, then left her.

"Your back records are locked. Who the hell are you, and what exactly did you do during the occupation?" A finger jabbed at her. "And how did you end up outside that transporter? Did you jump?

She shook her head, appalled. "Pushed. Someone pushed me."

"Why would anyone do that. You know a reason because I sure as hell don't. Why in Mathe were you planted in my team?"

"I…"

"Don't deny it. You knew those records were locked, and why. Are you a risk to my team?"

She could answer that one. "No, not by my intent anyway."

"Apart from being a moonie, yes, I know that." He chopped a hand to one side. "Do you know my security clearance?"

"I can guess."

He took a turn around the room, as if she hadn't spoken. "I'm about as high as you can get. Deln Crantz and the Council outrank me, but that's it. Yet I can't even find out where you were born. Who the hell are you?"

"It's not because of me," she said.

He stopped pacing, glaring at her as if at a coded snare lock. "Your family? You're protecting them?"

She tried a shrug then shook her head. "Dead," was all she managed. The stunned look on his face should have given her satisfaction, but she was past that.

"In the occupation?"

Again, she could only nod.

"My sympathies, and my apologies for my team's boorishness. If we'd known…" He shoved a hand through his hair, drummed a staccato on his thigh with his fingers as he studied her.

"Because of you?"

She shook her head and jumped up, unable to face that too probing scrutiny. He wouldn't allow that, putting out a hand to stop her going anywhere, one finger tilting her chin up, and she let him. Felt the calluses on the fingers that belied the public image, looked into eyes gone dark as a spring squall.

"I'm sorry, Madame asn Postrova, sorry for your loss and sorry to inflict this on you. But I have a team to protect. They don't need a stranger coming in and putting them at risk again. Why is that file locked and who does it protect?"

She shook her head again, forcing herself to meet his eyes as she refused him.

He had such beautiful eyes, such a beautiful face. Alive with that trace of a smile that never quite left the corners of his mouth and so much sorrow buried in those clear blue eyes. This was one secret he must not find out, not if she was ever to see a smile of welcome on his face again—not when he found out who her father was and what he had done.

And that, she would not apologize for. Plenty of others had laid enough scorn on her Da's head; his daughter would *never* join that chorus.

Jacquel's mouth tilted, but there was nothing humorous about it now. "I will learn your secret, Madame asn Postrova— and your real name."

Then he was gone as abruptly as he'd arrived, leaving her to the mercy of the medical staff, and she found herself breathing as hard as if she'd finished a race.

But what had she been running from?

Jacquel had a pile of work waiting for him. He should be on his way back to the mission base, and marched down to the flyer station with every intention of heading there promptly. He laid a flight plan in to the field station and lifted straight into the air, ignoring the harassed calls from flight control.

"Priority one," he said curtly, refusing to feel guilty for abusing his security clearance. He levelled out, went to make the turn north towards the field station.

His hands had other ideas. "Change of course entered," he said to the irate controller screaming in his ear. And his flyer turned and headed west and down country, back down to the City.

Next stop: Gof deln Crantz's office. Someone better give him some answers.

Short and blessed with an acute case of eagerness, Gof deln Crantz looked no less incongruous behind the desk of the Security chief than during the days of the occupation when he masqueraded as the general handyman, Old Raphe of the Citadel. These days, he was Jacquel's boss. Not that Jacquel was about to defer to him or watch his words. Deln Crantz had never encouraged it, and Jacquel had no inclination to pander to anyone's sensitivities today. He could do it if he had to, could do it very well, which had always been one of his strengths as an undercover operative, but not today.

"Who in hell is Rheia asn Postrova and why have you inserted her into my team?"

Deln Crantz studied Jacquel over tented hands. But Jacquel had seen him use that tactic too many times to be cowed by it.

"She has a locked file, carries ranger gear and knows the plateau like a native. She's no green moonie."

"Fortunately for her, as it turns out," said Gof too smoothly, with that smile of his guaranteed to set your back up. "How is Madame after her adventure on the plateau?

"I'm not in the mood," Jacquel said. "Who is she?"

"What exactly are you complaining about, young des Trurains: that she is good at her job, that she knows more about the plateau than you, or that she doesn't buckle under your charms and tell you everything you want, including information to which you have no right?"

"Is she a danger to my team?"

"Not in herself, no."

"But if they find out what's in that locked file."

"That wouldn't be good for her, but it won't hurt your team."

Now that, he didn't expect. "The file is locked to protect her?"

Gof pursed his lips. "If I say yes, you will turn historian and researcher again, dredging up any snippet to find the answer.

Leave her file alone, and that's a direct order, Colonel des Trurains."

Jacquel stared. "You're serious?"

The sudden change, the sudden revelation of the deadly intellect under that round, cheery face, told Jacquel just how serious he was. What in hell was in that file?

Jacquel had never been one to take orders easily but had grown up as the peacemaker between two volatile and trouble-attracting twins. Bendin and Marthe asn Castre had taught him when it was best to be silent, and when to prevaricate. Sometimes the quickest route to what he wanted was the roundabout one.

"Understood, sir," he said now, as if hating the order but compelled to obey.

"Nor do I want to hear of any trouble anywhere near that file location."

Jacquel set his face to wear a look of chagrin. "Understood, again, sir. Will Madame asn Postrova be returning to the team once she is recovered?" he said stiffly.

Gof studied him for a minute, and Jacquel had the uncomfortable feeling the man wasn't fooled in the slightest. Then he gave a brusque nod. "She's good at her job, and we need someone like her. I leave her safety in your capable hands."

So now he was duly warned as well as chastened. He grit his teeth, finding it all too easy to give an impression of being thoroughly annoyed. A brisk nod of acceptance was about all he could manage. Fortunately, Gof chose not to push it further and dismissed him. Or let him escape, depending on your viewpoint.

If the man imagined Jacquel was going to leave this alone…

Next stop, the central library. What could be more natural than his paying a visit to his beloved stepmother, and if he happened to ask about an unusual surname, Gof could find nothing to complain about in that.

The building was as beautiful as ever, and Anhuilla as adorably ruffled, the soft fluff of her hair pulled into a haphazard coil at the back of her neck as she bent over to carefully dust what he recognized as a very antique, late-empire period Terran novel. Utterly priceless.

He reached down and made to swipe it out of her hand, causing her to grab the precious relic close to her chest and swing around with an angry gasp. But then came the smile she reserved for him alone.

"Jaca, that joke was old the first time you pulled it on me."

She never could stay angry. He let her put the book carefully back into its climate-controlled repository then gave her a huge hug. A tiny woman, he could pick her up effortlessly, but her size was as misleading as that of her niece. She and Marthe were the only ones in their family to inherit the small stature of a distant matriarch, and both had been born with the same zest for life. The occupation, and what came after, had altered it irrevocably in Marthe, but it remained in her aunt.

"What are you up to today, young Jaca?"

"Can't I just be visiting my favorite step-mama?"

Soft of heart she may be, but never stupid, and waited now for him to answer properly. He let her wait, until the tapping of her foot on the floor said his time was up, and he threw his hands in the air.

"I need a favor." She smiled in triumph and kept waiting. "It's the family archives," he explained. "I've got a new team member with a name I've never heard before."

"And you want to know who he is, and if he's a risk to your team."

"Who said it was a *he*?"

Anhuilla sighed. "She's pretty then."

"Pretty? Not the right…," he began then stopped, frowning. "Not in the accepted way."

Strangely, Anhuilla said nothing to that, waving him on to the genealogy banks instead. A silence that was not at all her usual response, and one he totally mistrusted.

"She's a team member."

"Yes dear. Whatever you say." She logged into the banks and unlocked the search records. "Now, what did you say the name was?"

He scowled. "I didn't. It's asn Postrova. And not a word to Father about this."

"You know I can't promise that—you are his son; I will not keep secrets about you from him."

He did but had forgotten after so many years away. The love between this extraordinary woman and his restrained father was the unbreakable core that held his family together, and something neither he nor his young half-sisters had ever doubted. "Just don't make it something it's not. I like the woman, admire her in a way, but her position in the team is awkward—she's a moonie," he added by way of explanation.

A gurgle of laughter greeted that. "As am I, and all your family. You are becoming as one-eyed as you claim we are."

"Not you, Mama. Never you."

She gave him a quick hug, then turned to the search. It took rather longer than expected, her brows creasing at the repeated failures. Finally, she spread the search and went back a few generations, and then at last a result.

"One person. That's all, and she can't be your team member. There was a Marisa ka Postrova two generations ago, and the reason you don't recognize the name is because it isn't Hathian."

He stared. "Not…"

She chuckled again. "We have had some immigrants here over the course of history. Not many; outsiders seem to find us too hard to live with for some unknown reason. This Marisa came from Samarkan, the daughter of a family trade vessel that called in here."

She kept reading, pulling up files, diagnostics and images. "Oh, what a lovely story. So romantic."

She set it to display, linking to his com, and a holo-image formed in front of them. Small, wiry and with a striking face, filled with strength and a sparkle of adventure. He recognized those eyes. "She could almost be Rheia."

"More like her great-grandmother."

He read on. A headstrong young girl on her first trip into space. The excitement of her first shore leave. Then a meeting with a young ranger from the plateau country, one with hair he also recognized. "They ran away together. That has to be Rheia's great-grandfather."

Anhuilla sighed blissfully, further into the story than him. "Ran away, to a long and happy life together, with three fine sons and a parcel of grandchildren. Oh, that is a good ending."

So, what was their family name? Jacquel brought up the ranger's face again, along with his public genealogical records.

"An Pientos. Rangers in the northern parts of the plateau, though few rangers remain there now." He scrolled down through the listed descendants. Nothing to explain that locked file, nothing here that spoke of danger to Rheia. But there were other files, more complete ones.

"I don't suppose you can access the official genealogical records?" he said, with a half-laugh at the shocked look on his stepmother's face. "Sorry. Wishful thinking."

"Those records are the true treasure of this institution, and only the comptroller and his deputy have full access. The privacy guarantees are there for a reason—as you well know, young man."

He did. The records were full, accurate and absolutely trustworthy only because the people of Hathe knew they were also absolutely confidential. Family ties were both a blessing and a burden; Hathians respected those ties openly expressed and asked no questions if a family chose otherwise. It was their right, and that must not be put at risk.

Those records would have answered his questions, but his stepmother's love and respect was one of the few bastions left to him. So he'd have to find the information he needed some other way. He would find out who his moonie was, find out what threatened her. It was his duty as mission leader.

Or so he told himself.

He stayed in the City another three days, tracking down his own leads and waiting for Rheia's release from the Citadel medical unit. Two days in which he managed to pick yet another fight with his father, ending in a night that made even his stepmother look askance at him when he walked in the door the next morning.

He had a place of his own in the city, a state-provided apartment, and guessed sourly it was past time to move there. The restoration of his family home was sufficient to leave it in his stepmother's hands to finish off. Not that his father noticed what Jacquel had done before they'd returned. Not from the pained look he'd given the place when he first strode back through the grand front entrance.

Not a day too soon, Jacquel got word that Rheia was to be released. But before he could leave to collect her, deln Crantz ordered him into his office to discuss his plateau mission. He finished with a warning. "You're always on about reunifying the dirtsiders and moonies. This is your chance. You and Rheia asn Postrova come from the same mold. Use her to find a way to make this work; and keep her safe. She's earned it."

"Maybe I should order armed protection for her, *sir*."

An uncharacteristically grim look passed over his boss's face. "Good idea. Have it in place before she returns—and Colonel, I better not hear of any unauthorized attempts on the genealogical data banks," he added, eyeing him dubiously.

Twice warned now, and Jacquel wasn't stupid. "Her identity is her business."

As long as it didn't put his dirtsiders at risk. A familiar feeling sat hard in his gut, one he recognized from his undercover days. There was something here he *needed* to know. And he'd learned the hard way to never ignore that feeling.

He took off from the City with a wave of profound relief to be heading back inland. Of heading where he was meant to be. That lift in his step lasted through the landing at the Citadel and as he made his way to Rheia's room. Then he saw her face. Drawn and pale with the pain she tried to hide from him.

"What imbecile signed your release?"

Her head shot up. "My doctor." Her eyes lit with a defiant sparkle. "I'm ready to get back to work."

She meant it too, and Pillars take it, he doubted he could do anything to stop her. Nor did he make the mistake of offering to help as she pushed off the bed. Instead, he quietly appropriated her bag and kept as close as he could without crowding her as she walked out. The limp was still there, the leg able to take weight but not yet healed properly. He'd had injuries enough of his own, and she was still days away from full strength. The stubborn set of her shoulders told him not to even mention offering to help.

They exited to the parking area and he palmed the hatch on his skimmer. She stopped dead.

"That's a reserved space. You can't park there."

He'd taken the closest one to the exit, reserved, as she'd said, for emergency and official vehicles only.

"No one's about to complain. Get in." He gestured to the passenger seat, wondering if she'd be able to manage the last steps.

She looked dubious, eyebrows lifting. "Your funeral."

He had to grin at the tone. Not a shred of defeat in her voice, quite the opposite. For the first time in as far back as he could remember, he opened his com to display his ID certificate.

CHAPTER SEVEN

An executive security tag, the highest level of clearance. Deln Crantz had one, as did the councilors and her boss, but that was all. He'd told her his clearance was high, but she hadn't fully believed him. This man seriously outranked her. Not only a hero, but a hero with the political weight to discover all her secrets. How could she have missed that in his file?

Because it wasn't in the levels she could access, of course. Worse still, one glimpse of the twinkle in his eyes and she turned into a prize fool. Jacquel des Trurains was a prime scalp for the vidcasts, as was anyone seen too often with him. "I can get a shuttle back to the site," she said hastily. "You must have more important things to do."

A too knowing smile touched his gorgeous mouth. "At this point in time, no, and that's official. I have orders to see you safely back to work."

No point arguing then. She'd learned enough of him to recognize the steel beneath the easy charm. She climbed into the flyer and buckled in without another word, answering in monosyllables all his carefully beguiling lines.

"How's the ankle?" he started innocuously enough. Then moved on to, "A fine job on that field splint. I couldn't have done better during the war, and Pillars know I had plenty of practice."

A short grunt to that one.

"Looks like you had plenty of practice too. When you were a youngster?"

"Yes."

"Was that on trips to the plateau, or somewhere else? It sounds like you must have driven your parents as crazy as we did," said with the kind of chuckle that included you, that made you feel like you had been welcomed into a select group of old friends.

She just shrugged and refused to look at him, but it didn't stop that captivating voice or that clever mind. He kept trying all through the trip, and it wasn't till they were nearly back at camp that he finally relaxed into rollicking waves of laughter.

"You're good. You sure you weren't with the Resistance?"

She had to smile; that grin on his face and the deep-throated belly laugh were irresistible, far more so than his practiced charm. "No, just another moonie cowering off-planet from the big bad Terrans."

He stopped laughing, peered quizzically over at her.

"Hey, watch where you're going. That's a hill up ahead."

All that did was send his grin into the stratosphere. There should be a warning pasted to it. He glanced lazily at the controls, pointing to the auto-track panel as the skimmer lifted safely over the hump and back on course again.

"You can't always rely on those things," she protested.

"On my craft? Yes, you can, and don't prickle up on me." He leaned over, tilting up her chin and pressing a quick kiss to her startled lips, chuckling shamelessly at the cross look she sent him, even as the touch of his lips did things to her she fought hard to ignore.

Worlds apart, Rheia. How often did she have to repeat it before her stupid senses gave up hope? She gave him a polite smile and stared pointedly out the window.

"We're nearly at camp."

His eyes followed hers. "Yes—unfortunately."

She absolutely refused to answer that one.

They were on final approach before he spoke again, and this time the Security Department colonel spoke. "I want your promise you'll tell me if there are any more incidents. No keeping silent to keep the peace. Two attacks on you, so similar and so close together, cannot be taken lightly. I have orders from the top to keep you safe. Hathe can't afford any public attacks on moonies by dirtsiders, or vice versa."

She scowled. "I can manage."

"Maybe, but I'll still have your promise."

She shrugged gracelessly. "All right."

"And, Madame asn Postrova, a friendly warning: I will find out who you are and why your file is locked against me."

He'd turned to speak into his com to his team second before she could argue, even as the struts settled into the dirt of the plateau. Then they were unbuckling, collecting bags, offloading all the ordered packets from the City. They had landed just after the dinner hour, when the whole field team was gathered together in the barracks for the evening. The general hubbub of their arrival gave no chance for more talk, leaving him with the last word. A warning, ringing in her ears.

He would discover her true name, and then what would he do? The worry of it stayed with her as she trailed after him into the common room, only to be brought to a sudden halt by the dead silence of the room. The laughing companion of her trip had stopped square in the center of the room to address the team—in full colonel mode.

"Do we understand? Madame asn Postrova is here to do a job. There will be no more *incidents*. An Vathin or der Phebasin will accompany her at all times."

Did he see the looks on the tech staff's faces? But yes, of course he did. This was a man used to command, one who knew exactly how his words would be taken. All his troopers stood at attention, carefully blank-faced and with eyes fixed on the rest of the room. And every single one of them had the hard edge of an experienced Resistance agent, a match for any tech.

Or so she hoped, as the only moonie here. The tech staff had all survived the Terran occupation, doing who knew what. She'd never liked to ask, fearful of crossing unwritten lines of painful memory. Now she discreetly studied her peers.

Not one looked intimidated by the troopers, not one was afraid of them.

The only one in that whole room who stank of fear was herself.

But she'd survived the war too. In comparative safety, maybe, but stripped of all she held dear. The sole plateau plant she'd managed to take into exile had held pride of place in her room on Mathe: a small and deceptively delicate astelia. Though she'd rarely seen it during the occupation, travelling endlessly from one Alliance planet to another. A sliver with a holo-image went with her instead, a precious link to home and the nearest thing she had to family in those lonely years. The rangers had been hit so hard by the war, her home village scattered and gone. Even if there were survivors from Hyrvettin, she was barred from seeking them out. No welcome waited her, not after what her father did.

But she had survived, and learned to live without expectation of support or friendship. She would get through this night, and all the days left on the plateau. Her head came up, and her eyes stared straight back at all those hostile faces, with a face wiped clear of challenge and the nerves churning up her guts as she listened to Jacquel des Trurains set out the new security arrangements in force.

As he told the rest of the team they were now under watch, as he told them exactly how uncomfortable she was going to make their lives.

His voice snapped to a close, and he dismissed all ranks. She went to follow the rest, desperate for the safe haven of her room.

"Not that way, asn Postrova. You've been moved. You're in the squad area."

So much for quietly slipping back into her role. The colonel had just painted a target in glowing iridescence on her back. Worse, trooper an Vathin peeled off and followed immediately behind her.

"I will be on guard outside your door tonight, Madame asn Postrova. Trooper der Phebasin will take over in the morning."

"I'm sure that's not necessary."

The trooper ignored her, her voice flat as a pan slate. She could have been an automated guard panel. "The colonel has ordered it."

Which meant it was going to happen, whatever she thought of it.

At least her new room had a lock on it. She shut the door firmly on her guard and took a slow turn about. Nothing fancy.

This was a soldier's space, and she took refuge in that. Protected and safe, with nothing here to remind her of what had been. And no one to hear or see her. For the first time in too many years she let slip, for the briefest of moments, the heavy shield of her defenses.

Jacquel watched Rheia leave, her assigned guard close behind her. The trooper wasn't happy about having to babysit a moonie, but she would do her job; an Vathin had been with him long enough to have confidence in that. As had all his troop. He lifted a brow at Ras, nodded briefly at the far corner and the bare little room he'd commandeered for his office.

He sat at his beaten-up excuse for a desk and beckoned for Ras to shut the door and take the other rickety chair. Jacquel was tall, but Ras had a few centimeters and at least ten kilos on him, all of them hard muscle.

"The troops?" he said as Ras lowered his frame dubiously onto the chair and propped those long legs out in front of him. "Will they hold?"

Ras raised an eyebrow. "Have they ever failed you?"

Heat touched his cheeks, but Jacquel refused to apologize. "Someone tried to hurt Madame asn Postrova, and Central isn't about to let that happen. The question had to be asked."

"Just don't ask it of the troops. They don't deserve that from you."

Fair point, but Ras hadn't seen the bruises on Rheia or watched as she hobbled out of that hospital bed, determined to get back to work. "She's here to do a job, and so are we. Hathe needs her to do that job."

He looked down, studying his hands. If he couldn't trust Ras, who was there left to trust. A deep breath. "You've seen the records of the tech staff. Any of them likely to have done it out of spite? Or is one of them working for a group we need to know about?"

"For the first, yeah, could be all of them. They're dirtsiders like us. We've all had to face that lot on Mathe coming back and stealing all the jobs we fought so hard for."

No hint of apology in Ras's voice. They'd both seen plenty of examples. "For the second…" He shrugged helplessly. "There's too much stuff building. Does Central understand that?"

He'd asked the same himself, many times. Deln Crantz did, but how many others?

"You need to talk to Joshan an Thanis too," added Ras. "He hasn't said much, but there's something about that girl he's not happy about."

"Ah, yes. The thing is…she may be ranger stock."

Ras sat up. "May be? You need better than that, Cap. Know how few of them are left?"

"Yes. Not nearly enough. I said *may*."

Ras had a good eye for trouble, and his face said it was staring them hard in the face. "Find out, Cap. We can't afford a blow-up out here."

"You think I haven't tried? Would she talk to you?"

A dry quirk of his lips. "Try where your charms failed? You've been swindling secrets out of poor innocents since you left the nursery."

"Not this time. That woman has a defensive wall a river wide inside her. Whatever she's hiding, it's big."

"As I said, Cap: find out, before it explodes in our faces. We do not need a moonie martyr to rusticated dirtsider prejudices."

Jacquel recognized the quote. The tabloid was still underground, but its subscriber numbers were growing fast among disgruntled moonies, eager to restore Hathe to what it should be, as they termed it.

Strip it bare and keep all the profits for themselves, from the viewpoint of too many dirtsiders. He stood up. "Keep her safe, Ras. And leave the rest to me."

With a brisk nod, his second stood. "That girl won't breathe heavily without one of us knowing about it. I'll organize a second rotation of covert surveillance for her. But Cap, make sure you know what you're doing. Is the threat real, or has she become another of your strays?"

Jacquel glared at him, then had to chuckle at the wry grin on his friend's face before he quickly strode out the door. He had a point; that was the annoying part of it. Was it only pity he felt for their moonie?

She didn't need it, and wouldn't thank him. Strong, brave—and more than capable as it turned out. Rheia asn Postrova knew the plateau country far better than she let on. Her quick thinking and determination had kept her from serious harm twice now.

Serious harm? No, too miserable a phrase. Not nearly sufficient for the pain in her face and the pummeling of her body. She'd come close to dying out there, and he still had no idea how to deal with the terror lodged inside him since he'd found her curled up in that hollow.

Yes, he wanted the woman, but it was more than that. The fact was, he plain liked their gorgeous moonie. There was something true at the core of her. She may be hiding a secret, but she made no attempt to hide what she was. A capable diplomat and trained observer, fully aware of the animosity around her, Rheia asn Postrova showed no signs of trying to profit from the postwar period. Her clothes were reserved and elegant, rather than ostentatious and flashy. Not cheap but not wastefully expensive either. The kind of clothing suited to work.

But not personal, not for partying or fun.

He would like to show her how to party.

The night took forever for Rheia. Bad dreams played tag with hours of restless shifting to avoid the aches plaguing every part of her. Until she began to do all she could to stop sleeping. To avoid images of collapsing caves, of being lost to the power of cold, trammeling waters, of walking on and on in a haze of pain, never finding her goal.

Bleary eyed and with a sponge-filled head, she peered into her viewscreen the next morning. Ugh. Her face. Not good. Today, she was going to need all the help she could get. She switched the controls to groom mode, something she hadn't needed to do since her last diplomatic posting.

"Set to rested, lightly tanned and five years younger."

She lay down and stuck her face in the screen's field, re-emerging ten minutes later. A whole ten minutes it took the viewer to repair the damage. She peered into the screen again. Better, but she had a sinking feeling the camouflage would fool few, and not at all her mission leader.

It didn't.

"Good morning, Madame asn Postrova," *Colonel* des Trurains said to her greeting. That's who he must be. Not the Cap, and definitely not Jacquel.

He gave her one searching glance but said little else, pulling out a chair for her at the commons table and directing trooper an Vathin to the food counter with a brisk tilt of his head.

Fresh fruit, soaked grains and a good-sized dollop of Katcherin cuikh arrived in front of her. Real vat-grown cuikh. Vitamins, minerals, carbohydrates and protein, all readily digestible and high in nutritional value. But no tiny wafer of Huithian collop, her favorite morning treat for keeping away the dismals. Of course not. Mostly fat and sugar, and one hundred percent a delicious bite-sized morsel of delight. At least the hot drink was her usual, a strong blend of bitter, hot stimulation. But it would have tasted better with a collop.

A slight upwards twist from the untrustworthy lips of the colonel. "Doctor's orders, designed to ensure you heal quickly."

She managed to suppress a sigh as she dug her spoon into the healthy bowl of mush and had to concede it wasn't too bad. But she still mourned the collop. Or did till the drink finally hit her brain cells enough to notice the rest of the room. In particular, the wide exclusion zone around their end of the table. All the other staff members, including the troopers, were clustered down the far end of the room. No one appeared to so much as glance at their end of the room, yet she had the uncomfortable feeling they missed not a single thing at her table.

"Your doing?" she said with a crook of her fingers towards the bare zone between them and the rest.

He didn't have to look, just shook his head slightly with the barest of grimaces, his head turned away from all those fascinated non-watchers.

"Oh." She bent her head to her cup as she summoned up every germ of courage she possessed. "We need to talk."

"That would be a start." He did turn toward the other end of the room then, with one long, challenging stare that would have had her squirming if he'd turned it on her. Every trooper jerked upright in their seats and nodded stiffly in reply, then bent their heads to their food without a word.

But not the technical staff. So, one of them? One of the people she worked with had given her that shove, had tried to kill her.

She swallowed.

"Der Phebasin, I'll meet with Madame asn Postrova at first quarter break. She is not to leave your sight until then."

No, he didn't mean…Never out of sight! Even in the field bathroom? But the grim cast of his mouth and the barely glimpsed grimace from der Phebasin confirmed it.

She swallowed again.

She felt no better when she entered the colonel's office, not after a morning navigating the frigid currents washing through the team whenever she tried to open conversation with one of them. Even Maria was being cautious around her

He gestured to her to take the seat opposite, vacated by his second-in-command who now leaned up against the wall, taking up all the remaining oxygen in the tiny space.

Was that why breathing was so hard? Why her lungs felt as if they refused to function? Keep it brief, low-key, *formal*.

"You wanted to see me, Colonel?"

"I need to know what's in that locked file of yours, and I need to know it now," said Jacquel des Trurains, and all her fears exploded.

A knock on the door, and another trooper entered. Joshan an Thanis, the squad's tracker. That name, it had a familiar ring.

With nowhere else to sit in the room, she eased her chair along to make room for him. He took no notice, stepping just far enough in to shut the door and leaning against the wall beside Ras den Koprorth, all while looking stonily ahead.

"Trooper, repeat what you said to me when we found Madame asn Postrova." Jacquel leaned forward, catching her eye and refusing to let her escape the snare of his gaze.

"She had ranger capsules, sir."

What little air remained in her lungs escaped in one last whoosh. How could he know? Then thought again, forced the memories to come flooding back. That last name. It was a ranger name.

"These?" said the colonel now, pulling out two non-descript and battered capsules, one still filled with traces of shredded tent, and planting them on the desk in front of her. "Are you sure they're ranger made?"

Of course they were, and of course the colonel would have someone in his troop who would recognize them. They had saved her life out on the plateau; now it looked like they would condemn her.

The trooper made a show of examining them again, before nodding perfunctorily. Rheia had spent too much of her recent life observing others to miss the anger in his rigid stance and scowl.

"Who are you, Rheia asn Postrova? What is your real name?" said Jacquel des Trurains.

Not a question Rheia was going to answer with the truth. Not now, not ever. "Rheia asn Postrova."

The colonel thrust a capsule across the table, holding it in a clenched fist. "And this? You happened to find it one day?" It was as if he was challenging her to try this lie too. She shook her head and glanced at the tracker lounging against the wall. His eyes never left her.

"Growing up…my family had a distant ranger connection. They gave me this as a present at the time of the invasion."

"Their names?"

Again, a shake of her head. "They're gone now, all of them."

A slap of a hand on the wall and the ranger abruptly moved, shoving into the too small space. "Rangers don't give away gear."

"Not often," she agreed.

The man picked up the empty capsule with the shredded tent. "Never," he said. "Where did you get this?"

He turned the capsule over and over in his hands. She had to grip hers closed in a fist to stop the protest. That was *her* capsule, her memories. She glared at the tracker, refusing to give way. Then caught the flare of interest in the colonel's eyes.

The man was an expert in subterfuge. His failure to hide what he felt had to be deliberate.

"You will talk, asn Postrova. One day, you will tell me all I need to know."

"Not today."

He studied her with that cool stare of his for long, long moments.

"Not today," he finally agreed, but it left Rheia feeling no more secure. She'd been let off the hook for now, but that was all.

"That's it?" The tracker looked set to explode.

"That's it for today. You have a problem with that, trooper?"

Most definitely he did, but the tracker pinched his lips closed at the tone in his commander's voice.

"Dismissed, trooper."

The trooper stalked out, followed by Ras den Koproth, leaving Rheia facing Jacquel des Trurains who still held her capsule, turning it over and over as he studied the scratches and battered surface, before looking up at her.

"Remind me again why you were sent here"

"Councilor an Rathman thought it was a good idea."

"To help in healing the breach growing between moon-based and dirtsider Hathians. An interesting idea. So far, you seem to have done your best to split it wide open."

She shrugged.

Jacquel studied her, studied the careless pose that said she didn't care or saw no reason to do anything about it. That told him to leave her alone.

Except he had too many images stuck in his head to do that. His oldest friend Bendin, cold and white on a slab instead of towering over him with a mad grin on his face. The desolation on Marthe's face as she spoke of her journey to say goodbye to the home world she loved before leaving for exile. Too many others: defeated, hurt, or stone-cold dead.

"You have closed files. The reasons for that are good?"

Her mouth set in a firm line and she nodded.

"How many have access?"

"The Council, deln Crantz and the head of the diplomatic division."

"The reasons for that going to harm my team—or any dirtsider?"

This time she shook her head. "It's in the past. Everyone who could be hurt is dead."

"Except you," he said. Her slight flinch was as full an answer as her barely muttered "Yes."

Just who, by the Pillars, are you, Rheia asn Postrova?

The wind tugged at his hair. How many nights had he spent out on the plateau, shivering and—yeah, admit it—cold-hard scared witless. Those times, he'd had reason to be out. Tonight, he needed to walk, to try to figure out the "what next."

Asn Postrova. Rheia asn Postrova. It suited her. Strong, fluid, but what, by the Pillars, lay behind the name?

He could back her, or throw her to his tracker. Except what would that achieve other than making his tracker happy? He'd watched her with Maria asn Rostrum and noted how well she picked up on the undercurrents of power-broking in the team. Maria was the key technical expert on this region, and everyone knew it except Maria. No one else had her gut-deep understanding of the plateau. Like most dirtsiders from this region, the rest of the team had spent time here during the occupation and come to respect the harsh environment. But to have it in your bones, you needed to grow up with it, and Maria and his tracker alone had that.

And Rheia asn Postrova? Could she be another?

As soon as he got back to camp, he called in Joshan an Thanis. The tracker came to a formal halt in front of his desk and snapped out a salute. First time any of his team had done that. Jacquel leaned backwards, eyeing the man.

"You can relax, trooper, and that is an order."

Thankfully, his men knew exactly how far to push their commander and when to not even try it. The tracker shoved his hand down, pulled across the other chair and threw himself into it.

"You going to do something about that moonie—sir?"

"Yeah, I'm going to watch her. And you are going to leave her alone."

That had the man shoving forward. "She's hiding something."

Jacquel shrugged. "And she has backing right from the top to keep hiding it. *I* can't break her file."

"If she's ranger bred…"

"Highly probable."

The tracker gave a frustrated growl. "Do you know how many of us are left, *sir*?"

And Jacquel had to nod again, sighing inwardly. The ranger families had been hardest hit by the occupation. One whole village in this region no longer existed, only the silent homes remaining as witness to owners long dead.

"Regardless, her file is closed, and orders are it stays that way."

"Rather unusual, sir."

"Cut it, an Thanis. One more *sir*, and you're on the next transporter out of here."

"You need me here, s…"

"You'll still be on that transporter."

The tracker grunted defeat, a brief eyebrow lift in acknowledgement. "So you know a good reason for that file to be closed?"

Jacquel had his own thoughts but he kept them to himself. "All Rheia would say is that all involved are dead."

The tracker scowled. "Except her, conveniently safe in her cozy spot off planet? Nobody can say otherwise because of a closed file, and she refuses to talk. So you still think she's innocent?"

"For now, till evidence proves otherwise," said Jacquel firmly.

The tracker glared at him, then threw up his hands. "All right. Maybe it's just survivor guilt talking—or not, in her case. Or guilt over the easy run she had during the occupation."

"You remember getting any choice about staying or going at the time of the invasion?" Jacquel snapped.

The man reluctantly shook his head.

"The open part of her file," Jacquel went on, "does show what she did. The Diplomatic Corps, and good at it," he added, to the tracker's whistle. "I don't reckon she had too many choices at the time of the invasion either."

The tracker didn't argue further, just shook his head in frustration and Jacquel left it at that. But he couldn't forget the man's words.

Survivor guilt, or some kind of post war trauma disorder. Most of them had a degree of it; they had all lost so much. Too many lived with the missing and hidden grief. Was that enough to suspect her of being an enemy to dirtsiders? Whatever the cause, the mystery remained of how she had managed to leave the ship unnoticed. His trooper swore she was on board when they lifted, but Rheia asn Postrova was very definitely *not* there when they landed. He could think of only two possible explanations. The first: she'd slipped out herself as soon as the trooper's backs were turned, but if that was the case why leave her com behind? Those injuries of hers were real enough. She could have died out there.

She was too agile for it to be an accident, which left the only other possibility. Someone had pushed her.

CHAPTER EIGHT

Rheia tossed yet again, fruitlessly trying to find any kind of comfort in the primitive barracks bed. The hard thrust between her shoulders on the flyer matched too closely the unforgiving base of the bed beneath her. An instant in memory she couldn't shake. That shove was no accident. Given the weather and the terrain, someone had tried to kill her. Someone seated on that transporter with her, someone she'd eaten with, talked to, met eye to eye.

For the umpteenth time, she scrolled through the list of team members. None of the names struck a chord, none known to her before this mission. Or was she only a sacrificial nobody in some larger plan, targeted solely as a moonie?

The tracker, Joshan an Thanis? If that shove was personal, he was the most likely suspect. She'd seen the look on his face in the office when he looked at her ranger capsules. *You're not entitled to these*, that look said.

Even though he must have known she'd acquired them before the war, given she'd been off-planet most of the occupation. Not during it, and certainly not after. With so few ranger families left, none of the survivors would part with a single piece of precious ranger gear. Not when so many memories lay attached to them.

He was a possibility, said the facts. But she couldn't bring herself to believe it. Anger, pain, yes; but deceit?

Yet Jacquel des Trurains's troopers were all trained ex-Resistance agents, skilled in using guile and subterfuge.

But a killer? It just didn't ring true, no matter what her head might claim to the opposite. Not the tracker, or any of the squad members, said her gut and heart.

Which left the tech team.

Too many of the tech team, unfortunately. So many possible suspects.

Make a list. The obvious first: Phillipos athns Kronkist and Varda an Tarkst. Both plain hated her, and both had good reason to dislike a moonie from the DIA sticking her nose into their business. Her gut instinct said "dirty" for both of them, and Rheia had learned never to ignore its warnings.

What about Maria? The sweet, naive ecologist who knew and loved these plains as much as Rheia. Her heart said no—but her head said *could be*. Again, Rheia preferred to go with her heart. Put Maria down as the innocent she appeared to be.

The other technical crew?

Another toss in the sheets. Someone wanted her dead, and Rheia wasn't about to give them the pleasure.

She woke the next morning with the same feeling she remembered from the start of negotiations with one of the less predictable planets of the Alliance, where all the odds were against her. A feeling she'd thought to leave behind once the peace was won.

But peace wasn't turning out to be that simple.

She walked out of her room wearing the professional air that had carried her through her years as a diplomat. The pleasant smile and bland look of hidden secrets, giving nothing away and betraying no anger. A brief frown from the colonel said he recognized the false game she played, but she had a job to do and if the man didn't like it, that was his problem. She bent to pack her gear for the day's mission, doing her best to ignore the twitch of complaining muscles and throbbing of her ankle, despite the hospital's meds.

"What do you think you're doing?" he said.

"Stand back. How can I pack this kit with you breathing down my neck?"

A hand reached around her and snatched the offending bag out of her hand. "You're not going anywhere today. And that's an order."

She shot up, swinging around and only slowing as she accidentally caught that drekking ankle. So much for it not being a problem. "The docs cleared me, and I have a job to do. One which is supposed to be important, according to the council. Nor am I under your command, whatever your boss may have told you. The council sent me here, not deln Crantz, and that's who I answer to."

From the look on Jacquel des Trurains's face, it was a long time since anyone disobeyed his direct order. Tough. She grabbed back her bag and stomped out the door. Nor, to her surprise, did he follow her. She did glance back as she clambered into the transporter, and the cast of his face was about as dark as expected.

Tough, she thought again, as she banged up the ramp and settled into her seat. Then gave an extra thump on her harness catch as the ever-present guard settled into the seat beside her.

Silence was the only possible answer to that constant shadow hovering over her, thanks to Jacquel des Trurains and his drekking orders, and she turned her shoulder away from the woman to stare out the window the entire trip out to the site. Unfortunately, she couldn't push Jacquel—the Colonel—des Trurains, out of her mind as easily. She'd won this fight, but it didn't feel like much of a victory.

Rheia arrived on site feeling more an outsider than ever, and it got no better over the morning. They had come back to the hollow near her father's grave, the meds barely held off her body's aches and her footsteps were dogged by her personal guards—all her attempts to break through to the dirtsiders were thwarted by their hulking presence, or her own watchfulness.

Was this the person who'd shoved her out the door to face the full blast of a plateau storm? Which one of these highly trained scientists, these people who were meant to act only on evidence and reason, hated moonies enough to kill her? Which had suffered badly enough under the Terrans?

Every single one of them. The only good part of the day came when she heard that the final logging of this site was complete, and they were moving on to formulating a plan to deal with it.

Then she began to listen to their talk.

"So we're all agreed," one said. "We blow the site and use some of the surrounding hills to bury it."

The techs were huddled together, studying meaningless screeds of data that she had to assume meant something to them. The waste management expert, Varda, the hydrogeologist, even Maria was nodding her head.

Braken das Shondreth, the hydrogeologist, drew some lines in the dirt and the others followed the movement of her hand, nodding in understanding. "The substrata are on our side here at least. With the pan on the southern side and the changes in formation here," his finger stabbed down, "any leachates will be confined to this basin. Those hills are mostly clay and shale. The right charge will pulverize them finely enough to form a surface seal over the buried wastes."

Charge, hills, pulverize. Horror engulfed Rheia. She stood, rooted to the spot and staring up at one particular hill, one small ridge in the many curving around the site. "You can't!"

All she got were disgusted looks. Did they think she knew nothing about what had happened here? "If you destroy even more of the plateau, you're no better than the Terrans."

A growl of rage, and the tracker stepped forward, fists clenched. "You know nothing of the Terrans."

"Yeah, where was it you spent the war? In high-class hotels and safe on Mathe." Phillipos, the geotech. "Show her the holos."

The hydrogeologist flipped out her scanner, stabbed at the controls and stood back as the holo-field shimmered into place, hovering over the dying plants littering the soil. Her finger stabbed down into the field, down and down again. "Those red patches? They're dump sites, just like this one."

There were literally hundreds. Then the woman played with the controls again, overlaid a splattering of purple spots, smaller but in the same sites. "That was the extent of leakage from these sites two months ago. The red is now. They're spreading and the only way we can quickly stop that is by explosives and removal. You think we *like* having to destroy any more of Hathe?" The woman glared, then closed her fist on the holo-unit and swung around, marching off. "Come on, we're wasting time with this moonie. I've got proper work to do if we're going to have everything in place to finish this tomorrow."

Rheia later realized the woman's action alone saved her. The circle of dirtsiders ringing her echoed with menace, with lowered eyebrows, tight shoulders and thrust forward chins. One more word, one more protest, and the tensed-up guard at her side would have brought her weapon into play.

"Not another word, madame." The guard's finger hovered menacingly over the control pad of her weapon as the muttering techs followed the hydrogeologist. All Rheia could do was clamp down on the tears and the threatening scream inside her.

"I need to talk to the colonel."

Her guard shook her head, no sympathy in those cold eyes. "He's busy. To be disturbed only in an emergency. Is there one?

None she could tell this man, or their precious colonel. "Then patch me through to Central, to Councilor an Rathman. I need a secure line."

"Only the colonel has that, and only for genuine emergencies."

That word again.

"What about her assistant?" She paced back toward the transporter and activated her DIA com link to raise the assistant, to be met with a cool voice telling her. "The Councilor is in a meeting. Can I help?"

Frustratingly, no. "It's a priority clearance issue," Rheia said.

The woman showed little interest, merely saying, "Please hold while I check your status. Your name and priority code?"

Rheia gave it and silence followed. Then the woman was back online. "Thank you for your patience. Unfortunately, that code is not on the list to allow interruptions to this meeting. I'll let the councilor know you called. Your priority rank is 3.56."

Over two, meaning sometime in the next three to four days. The hill would be history by then. "Thanks for nothing," she muttered as the woman signed off and a wall of silence confronted her. There were three more possible contacts on her list, and she frantically linked into each one of them, then into her boss's personal line, usually reliable.

The outcome was the same as all the rest. Nothing. Blocked by assistants, deputies, in-between minions. All her links too busy to deal with personal matters from a non-ranked underling, they implied.

So much for the promises she'd been given so many years ago.

Someone had to listen to her. That hill must not come down.

A cold wind brushed her cheek, dragging her hair into her eyes and clogging her mouth. She impatiently brushed it back, ignoring the shiver as she sought for one more link, one more potential contact.

"Time to go, madame."

"No, not yet. There's ages to go."

"Respectfully, no," said her guard in a voice that was anything but. "The sun is nearly at the horizon and the rest of the team are loaded. You will not be spending another night out on your own. Colonel's orders."

"What?" Rheia glanced up, seeing for the first time the darkening sky and low strike of the last rays of the sun. "It can't be." She had to keep trying, and out here. Not back at camp where any outgoing com calls must register on the troopers' screening monitors.

But the woman gave her no choice, plucking her comtab from her hand and stowing it out of reach in the security tote all of des Trurains's people carried on their hips. Her years as a diplomat had made her intimately familiar with the paraphernalia worn by security staff, and Jacquel des Trurains's people wore the latest, most discreet available. Top of the line and impossible to access.

She was trapped, blocked from getting help by des Trurains and his overzealous troopers, and tomorrow the team was going to demolish the hill where her father rested in peace.

"No, no."

A faint flicker of unease, even possibly of sympathy in her guard's eyes at Rheia's unguarded murmur, but it quickly vanished and the woman again wore the stoical mask of all the troopers. "This way, Madame asn Postrova."

She did try to make a break for it, with some crazy notion of climbing the hill and staying put. Plant herself up there and refuse to budge for anyone.

The guards foiled her before it began, clutching her arms and pulling her into the transporter before she could do or say anything. Two stood over her as she strapped in, then took the seats either side of her, all the while refusing to make eye contact. Orders from their esteemed colonel, she would guess, orders neither were happy about. Not when faced with a *looney moonie*.

By the time they arrived back at camp, she was so frantic with panic that the label fit her all too well.

"Get your paws off me," she snapped at the guards holding her.

"It's for your own protection, madame. Maybe you would prefer to go to your room and rest before dinner."

The carefully soothing tone only wound her up tighter. "Can I have access to a secure, *unmonitored* link there?" No, she didn't think so.

Even worse, the first person she saw after stepping from the transporter was Jacquel des Trurains, returned from some no doubt essential affair to monitor the unloading of the day's samples.

"Madame," he said, nodding briefly.

"Don't *madame* me, you hypocritical, self-appointed dictator." She slammed a hand into one of the guards trying to hold onto her, dug her heels in, then surprised them by suddenly thrusting forward to break their hold. Free at last, she stalked inside and headed for her quarters. Slapped a palm on the door, thrust it open, then slammed her hand against the inner control pad. "Lock, my code only. No one is allowed entry."

At least that she could control.

Jacquel watched her march off in stunned amazement. "What was that all about?"

Trooper an Vathin watched too, shaking her head. "She's been acting weird all day."

"She has?" It didn't sound like Rheia asn Postrova. He'd swear the woman was born shielded, so tough to penetrate was the reserve around her. "Did something happen out there? Something out of the ordinary?"

The two troopers looked at each other. First one, then the other slowly shook their head.

"Just another day on site," said an Vathin. "The techs, they took samples and did their work."

Except it can't have been. "Asn Postrova—what did she do?" he said.

"Same as every other day. Made her way around the different groups, talked, listened to what they were saying. Then she went crazy."

"And the techs," said Jacquel. "What were they talking about?"

"Site recovery. Blowing up the surrounding hills to pull them down on the site and seal it."

Jacquel had seen her briefing notes; he'd written some of them himself. "She's known all along we have to destroy parts of the plateau to protect the rest."

The scrunch marks on Dreya an Vathin's forehead dug deeper, eyes squinting tight in concentration. "It was the hills, that's what set her off. The destruction of the hills, not the burying of the land in the hollow," she said finally.

Jacquel had had more than enough of secrets. He swung around, rapping out orders and strode through the commons room and into the tech lab. "Get the geotech, Phillipos athns Kronkist, in here now. No, I'm not interested in what he's doing. I said *now*."

The full ten minutes it took the man to obey wound Jacquel up twice as tight. Only the years of training kept his hand from shoving the man into a chair and strapping his fingers to the control board of his equipment.

"Send up your probes and scan those hills. Deepest level, and for all bio, chemical and physical anomalies. If there's a pebble out of place, I want to know about it."

The man began to rise, looked about to protest. Jacquel's hand clamped down hard on his shoulder.

The man could go free once he had done his job.

Figures tracked down and down, waves of energy particles scoring through the substrata, tracing patterns across the screen. Layered over it, colorations and shades of data that no doubt meant something to athns Kronkist. On his left, the scans showed up as columns and patterns of numbers; on his right and too slowly building, a holo-field representation of the physical reality.

Suddenly, a pause in the stream of data, a jerking of the muscles under the grip of his hand.

"What? What is it?"

"There." The geotech zoomed down on the holo-field, arrowing down through the north-eastern ridgeline. Soared over and down, like an aerion plummeting to its prey. "By that rock. They're bones. Human bones."

The zooming stopped, the holo-field glowing in one patch as the geotech brought in the highlight function. A rectangular box shape, filled with an unmistakable pattern of shapes, laid out in formal repose.

Jacquel took a step forward, lifted his hand, and stabbed a finger at the dark shape. "That's a grave."

But whose? Late into the night, with only Ras left in the room, he was no closer to finding an answer. All he knew was that it was important to Rheia. "That gravesite; it has to be someone connected to her."

"Maybe." Ras looked slowly at the huge gaps in the stream of data on screen. Gaps that refused to be filled with anything more concrete on the grave's contents. "Someone's gone to a lot of trouble to conceal it."

But why? Jacquel cursed again those hidden files. "There's nothing for it. We'll have to ask deln Crantz."

Easier said than done. "He's in conference," said the annoying voice of his assistant. He switched to visual, and the smug, determined look on the man's face was no help at all.

"This is important."

"Of course it is, Colonel. The commander has many important matters under consideration. I will log your request and ask him to come back to you as soon as he has a spare moment." A blank silence, and the furious knowledge that he'd been fobbed off and patronized.

"Ras, find me something to hit. I swear…"

No way in hell was he letting some upstart assistant beat him. He had a woman depending on him to fix this mess, whether she asked him to or not. He tried calling her com, but nothing, not even when he used his personal line, setting the display codes to show it was a tight beam from him only and unmonitored. No luck. He glared at the return message; the standard one for fobbing off unwelcome calls. "Get me a way into that room of hers—even if it means hammering down that door and dragging her out of there."

The field station had never been designed for security. Simple, pre-built shells dropped down here after the war for just this kind of expedition. They were warm, dry, had all the basic amenities—and door locks easily overridden in an emergency, it turned out when they checked out the building's files.

"The master code of the team leader will open anything," Ras told him in short time.

A spike of glee shot through Jacquel. "Team leader? That would be me."

A cough from Ras. "Aah, and what are you going to say to her when you get in?"

Jacquel halted mid-stride. Right now, he had no idea at all. "We need to talk to deln Crantz," he growled in frustration.

"You reckon he knows what this is about?"

"That old crook? 'Course he does." But there was one other who could help. "Gilda an Rathman—she sent Rheia here. She'll know."

No sooner said than Jacquel was at his com unit again. This time, he shamelessly exploited his family connections. The councilor always kept her personal com line open for family and friends, and Jacquel just happened to have that link.

"Young des Trurains. A pleasure to see you," said the quietly elegant woman in his com-field, a wry smile on her face. "And so soon after my assistant tells me there had been another call from the very same field station. Please tell me you aren't asking me to arbitrate. Sorting out squabbling children is something I left behind years ago."

There might be a smile on her face, but he knew her well enough to hear the warning. "Rheia tried to talk to you already?"

"Yes." That frown demanded a good explanation, or else…

So Jacquel told her the full story, and the private face of the woman behind the senior councilor vanished.

"You will leave that gravesite alone, Colonel. And yes, that is an official order. Further, you will wipe all trace of your findings and of this conversation from the records."

Jacquel had never been good at taking orders. "You have a good reason, I assume. Just who is in that grave?"

A trace of annoyance washed over the councilor's face, a brief glance of the steel Gilda kept well-hidden. "Yes, I have a good reason, young man. I gave my word that grave would never be disturbed, and I keep my word."

"Whose is it?" Jacquel persisted.

This time, she glared back at him, but he refused to drop his gaze. Finally, a sigh of surrender. "He's one of the Unsung."

"Ah." Jacquel sat back. It was final, then. The Unsung: that legion of Hathians who had suffered, sometimes died, under the Terrans' arbitrary rule. No public acclaim, no records, just ordinary men, women and children who had tried their best to beat the Terrans. Sealing the chemical dump would be difficult without disturbing those hills, but it would be done.

"I'll send out the order immediately." He turned to signal Ras. "Give us a moment, will you?"

Once they were alone and the door secured against listeners, Jacquel turned again to Gilda an Rathman. "His name—can you tell me?"

"No." Simple, short and final.

After a long moment when the councilor gave nothing back, Jacquel nodded his acceptance. "Honor be given. He will be left in peace."

"Thank you."

"And Rheia?"

"Is not to be questioned," she said in a tone of finality. With which, she signed off, her holo-image zapping into nothingness.

Unfortunately, Jacquel really was not good with orders. He would obey them if they seemed reasonable, but this time…He slapped his com into life.

"Ras, time to wake Madame asn Postrova."

CHAPTER NINE

To be fair, he did try banging on her door first. Loudly enough for the whole building to hear, so she must have too. When that didn't work, Jacquel fit his palm to the lock and entered his master code. The door slid open—and all glee in him vanished.

She lay flat on the bed, one arm flung over her eyes, but he had no doubt she'd been crying. He didn't need the crumpled and sodden wad in her hand to know that. He'd made no sound, not since entering, but she shot up to sit ruler straight on the bed, one hand tugging at her hair and her face smashed into the composed mask he'd begun to hate. It couldn't hide the raw smudge of her eyes or the grief lodged within.

"You wanted something?" she said coldly.

"Answers," he said. "Who lies in that grave?"

Nothing, not a blink, not a nod or head shake. Nothing. She stared back, silent and steadfast. She was not going to break; not tonight, not ever. Who in Mathe was that man in the grave? Why was he so important to her?

Stalemate, long moments of her staring back and him trying not to sink into those dark, glistening eyes.

It got him nowhere.

A curt nod of acceptance. "Ras, Madame asn Postrova and I will be leaving at dawn for the worksite. Please be ready, Madame."

That shook her. "Ready?"

"I am going to check out that grave, and you're coming with me. Just the two of us; no surveillance, no guards. I *will know* whose grave that is."

Something passed over her face—shock, nerves—fleeting and hard to read, and behind him, Ras told him not to be stupid. It was too risky. He knew that, but it made no difference. Nor did the closed-off and chilly look on her face the next morning. The Resistance years had taught him to never ignore that clenched feeling in his gut, warning that something was important, and he was getting it in spades right now. Whoever lay in that grave mattered, to the woman in front of him, to this project and maybe even to the future peace of Hathe.

"Ready?" He swept her bag out of her hand and lifted it into his personal flyer before she could argue.

Her eyes scanned the area. "We're really alone? Just you and me? I thought you weren't allowed out without your watch guards?"

"Sometimes, if I order it and the reason is sufficient. My squad ran a check on the site this morning, but now, it's just you and me." He held out a hand, challenging her to accept, and couldn't hide his relief when she took it and stepped up into the flyer, then took the seat beside his. He punched the controls for the hatch to close before she could change her mind, but left her to settle into the seat and fasten the webbing down. No need to rub his win in, though his hands twitched with the need to check the straps and make sure she was safely fastened in.

The sky was unusually clear, but the weather could be treacherous on the plateau.

"Set?" he asked.

"Yes."

Would she ever again talk to him in more than these abrupt replies? Her face said no. Controlled, taut, and definitely hiding something. Pain and suffering, said the blanched fingers clenched on the strapping.

Suffering he must honor, just as he would honor the Unsung man buried in that lonely grave. Though why there, why so far from home? The scans showed he'd been buried with care, a formal internment with honor and, it appeared, with love. He'd had the geotech do a second scan, looking for traces of decayed soft materials. His clothes, any ornaments, keepsakes, special treasures buried with him. And yes, he had been buried with full ceremonial wear, in an expensive ranger dress outfit, with three more of the unique ranger capsules laid beside him. Inside them, a long-range locator, an ornately carved knife and a woman's dress scarf. Wife, daughter, who knew who it belonged to, but it had been precious to this man. Of that Jacquel was certain.

Who was the man to the woman beside him? And was that why Jacquel was so hell-bent on finding out his name? That warning clench was so tight, so clear, but suddenly he knew doubt. Of what was he really afraid?

He bent to the controls and forced himself to concentrate on the route.

It didn't help. Her silence still screamed at him, and no matter how he tried, she was too close, too impossible to ignore, too damn beautiful—and too unhappy. It tore at his gut. It was almost with relief that he recognized the line of hills surrounding the worksite and set his course to land on the base of the slope where the gravesite lay.

Suddenly, a hand touched his arm, and she spoke in a voice cracked with strain. "Not there. Please. Back a bit."

He stopped, hovering over the flat herb field that had seemed the safest set down point. "Why?"

He didn't think she would answer, and she ducked her head to hide her face. But a mumbled offering came out. "The astelia, you'll crush them."

They would recover, retreat to a tangled root ball and rebound within a year. Astelia may look delicate but they were as tough as this land, and he strongly suspected the woman beside him knew that. Yet he lifted higher, scanning for a bare patch of land with no vegetation to be harmed. The terrain around here was too unwelcoming. Nothing for it but to go over the slope and down onto the dump site.

He lifted, hovered and drifted down the hillside to the plain below where the bare earth would allow a landing. They clambered out and he looked up to the hilltop.

"It's a bit of a walk."

She shrugged, held out her hand for her pack, and set off as if all the furies were behind her and she hadn't already broken one ankle.

"Fine then," muttered Jacquel. They reached the base of the hills and began the slog upwards. She walked on, ignoring him and clambering over rocks and hillocks as if they didn't exist. Then a stumble, a brush of her knee on the hard ground and a flinch as the barely healed bone protested at the knock.

"Slow down before you hurt yourself again." He reached out a hand, but she shoved it back and powered on as if trying to escape him. Then another stumble and this time he grabbed hold of her arm. "For the Pillars' sake, wait up."

She shook her head, tried to toss him off and strained forward when that didn't work.

"Just stop!" He grabbed her free hand and tugged her around. That was when he saw her face clearly, saw the etched grief and terror carved into every line of it. "Oh, Pillars. I mean you no harm. You have my word. I just need the truth."

Yet still she refused him, still she clamped her mouth shut and set off in a mad scrabble up the hill.

"Have it your way. But you have my promise of safety."

Then they were at the site, and she finally came to a halt. A small astelia flourished at her feet but she made no effort to touch it, though she carefully stepped around it. Then simply stood, staring at the ground. He walked up beside her and deliberately crowded her. He'd told the truth: he would not harm her. But he had to find out whose grave it was. Gather all the facts. It was the only way he knew how to protect her. Too often, some small, overlooked detail had come back to bite him, and that grave was no small detail.

"You know the man who lies here. No one's that tense for no reason."

A deep breath, a long look at the land below and the sky above. Then she stepped back, shoulders straightening as if drawn painfully into line by the strength of will he was learning was her most enduring quality.

"You have no right to this knowledge," she said.

"Yes, I do."

A head shake, and that intense gaze.

"This man means something to you."

"If you'd asked her, Councilor an Rathman would have refused permission for you to come here. This grave was never to be disturbed. She promised me that."

"Gilda is not here, and I'm the one who gets to make on-site decisions."

A flare of eyes. "She ordered you away from here?"

"The gravesite will not be disturbed. That has been decided. Councilor an Rathman marked him as one of the Unsung, and that's enough for us." Dirtsiders had lost too many like him, but he didn't say that. Not to a moonie.

Then suddenly that grief became clear. She shared their pain. She'd also lost someone special.

"Who is this man?" His voice was too harsh, but he couldn't help it. "A family member, a friend, a *lover*?"

She looked so horrified at the last accusation he could have sung with relief, and suddenly realized why he was in such big trouble.

But the man who lay here was precious to her. Geotech scans left so much out. Bare shapes only, enough to show the bones belonged to a man, and fabric remnants that said he came from the plateau. That a ranger lay here.

Nothing that tied him to this woman. Yet that intense protectiveness of hers said this man was important to her. He had to be family or friend.

"Who? Brother, schoolmate, uncle? Father?"

And knew he had it then—but she had to say the words.

"Who?" he demanded again.

A *zit*, and Rheia dropped to the ground, clutching her arm.

"Hey." He grabbed her, saw blood and tore open her sleeve, checking frantically for the source of the bleeding.

A flesh wound. A pinpoint straight furrow directly across the top of her arm. A furrow that could only be caused by one weapon. A C70 long-range sniper weapon. Security and Resistance issue.

"Shh, shh, sweetheart." He swung around, standing above her and scanning. So many places around them to hide attackers, but nothing but grasses close to them, and the sniper already had them targeted. He had to trust it was ex-Resistance fighters they were up against, and a Resistance sniper issued with a C70 would be a good enough shot to have killed either of them easily if they had wanted to. Their attacker and anyone else with him did not want her dead, not yet.

He refused to feel betrayed. Since Rheia's first stranding, he'd known her attacker must be an ex-Resistance dirtsider. There was so much anger boiling up among too many of them.

A sharp pain in his thigh, and he crumpled to the ground. They'd shot his leg out from under him—and that intense pain and tingling came from no legal setting.

"Drop your weapons, Colonel. Then throw them well away from you."

That far rock, uphill on the ridgeline. The voice came from there, and he'd heard it before.

"The next one will kill the girl."

After that shot, he believed him.

"Don't. It's me they're after." A whisper from beside him. He'd landed in front of her, protecting her from the shot, but there was too much drekking cover out there. They could be surrounded and not know it.

"Have to," he gritted out. Then called out to their unknown assailants. "Hold your fire." Slowly his hand reached for his shoulder pouch. "I am not going to lose one more person," he told Rheia. "Not one more. We're both getting out of this alive."

Her mouth dropped open in a silent protest, and her eyes flared wide and dark at his stubborn stare back. He pulled out the last of his scannable weapons, a small hand knife concealed in his boot, and threw it wide. It landed in the dirt just in front of the sniper's rock, blade buried in the hard ground, and whipped back and forth with the fury of his throw.

A chuckle from the rock. "That's it?"

A shout from the left, from behind a cluster of bushes. "Nothing on scan."

Slowly, slowly, bodies stepped out. The man behind the bush, two from the outcrop on the left, a heavy step at their rear, and the sniper from behind his rock.

He'd guessed the voice, but it was still a shock. "Phillipos. Doing a bit of work on the side?"

"Sorry, Cap, but something had to be done. It's time for us to fight back."

The man didn't even have the grace to avoid his eyes, staring him straight in the face and keeping that deadly weapon locked on him and Rheia. The man wasn't Security now, but he'd been an active Resistance member, almost as well-trained as his own troopers, and that weapon had some very nasty Resistance add-ons. If Jacquel made so much as one move to expose her…

"That's enough."

The voice came from directly behind Rheia. She struggled to a stand, reached down a hand and Jacquel shamelessly accepted her help to pull himself up and face this new threat.

The voice was deeper, older than the rest. The leader of this jolly band of traitors, he'd guess. He staggered to a stand, hands clutching Rheia's good arm and hating the grimace of pain on her face. She wasn't used to violence, not like dirtsiders. But she lifted her head and stared straight ahead, with a face showing a calm mask of assurance.

He looked past her, towards their enemy.

The man was older, in his forties, and Jacquel recognized him with a shock. As he'd expected, all of them were ex-Resistance from the ease with which they moved in and out of cover. Something he'd deal with later. But this man wasn't a front-line soldier. No, he'd worked behind the scenes in the Resistance's underground control center. He knew his face only from his rare trips between Hathe and the secret base on Mathe. The man who organized tickets, arranged his flights; useful but just a face at the end of the day.

Now that man pointed a weapon directly at Rheia. For that alone, Jacquel would make him pay one day.

"Colonel des Trurains, I apologize for the injury but if you would stand aside…"

"Your name? I never heard it." A man known by no one, unlike Jacquel des Trurains, and Jacquel made sure his stare said it. Nor did he stand aside. Instead he tugged Rheia tight into his body, wrapping her in his arms and angling them both sideways to the two weapons pointing at them. She started to struggle, trying to step out of his protection. Trying to save him, by all the Pillars.

"Don't make me beg, madame," he murmured. "I'm not about to meet these thugs lying down, and I need help to stand." Not quite true, but it had her instantly standing still. Athns Kronkist and this administrative nobody would have to risk shooting Jacquel to kill Rheia.

"You kill me, and you lose the dirtsiders," he said to the ringleader.

A quirk of annoyance twisted the man's face. "Not if they know you were helping a moonie."

"You think they'll believe you over me—or whoever is behind you?" Too many owed their lives and survival to Jacquel for that to happen.

Unexpectedly, help came from the sniper behind. "He's right."

Phillipos athns Kronkist, coming down from the rock with that drekking C70 still trained on them. Jacquel moved to keep himself between it and Rheia, until she put out a hand and stepped around him.

"Let the colonel go. It's me you want. A dead moonie, to trigger the authorities into clamping down on the dirtsiders and foment your rebellion."

Jacquel moved to shield her again. "Thanks, sweetheart, but I don't trade anyone's skin for mine. Never done it before—no intention of starting now."

"You have to."

"No point, moonie." His erstwhile team member. "Cap's right, and he's stubborn."

"That's Colonel des Trurains to you," said Jacquel.

The man's face stiffened, but what did he expect?

"You'll have to bring him along," athns Kronkist said to the ringleader. Then glared at Jacquel. "You've seen what the moonies are doing to us, *colonel sir.* That's not what we fought for."

"No, but nor is this," said Jacquel coldly. "What *I* fought for was to have my planet back, whole and complete, and no greedy moonie or misguided dirtsider is going to take that away from me."

For long moments, it looked in the balance. Then the nobody behind them, moving faster than expected, stepped up and held his weapon to Rheia's head before Jacquel could stop him.

"Cuff them both, and, Colonel, I will shoot her if you make so much as one wrong move."

Jacquel looked hard at the man. He could have disarmed him easily in a fair fight, but that weapon sat hard against Rheia's temple, and in her eyes Jacquel saw the dark shadow of terror.

She would be dead before he moved a muscle.

He held out his hands.

Rheia watched Jacquel closely as a flyer landed in the nearest patch of flat land, crushing her astelia plant. One more thing they would pay for. Their captors had thrown a support field around his injured leg so he could walk, but as soon as they were both properly secured inside the closed in cabin of the flyer, the guards switched it off and his face flashed stark white. They took off, not gently, and with each bump, each swerve of the flight, that flash returned.

"Put that field back on," she demanded of their captors.

The one in charge gave a grunt of laughter. "No, madame— not a man with his reputation. It keeps him quiet."

What kind of animals are they?

The kind who will kill you.

She nudged as close to Jacquel as she dared, silently setting her leg against his to provide what little support she could. "How bad?" she asked quietly.

"Not...not just blaster. Nerve disruptor."

She gasped. The weapon function was as illegal as they came, and incredibly painful. The only plus: the effects would wear off in time—hopefully.

A soft groan, touched with a breathlessness that betrayed the level of self-control he must be using. "Not permanent," he said. "But…can't use it, not yet. The support field…Thanks for trying."

She'd tried, but not succeeded, and slumped defeated against the seat. He leaned back beside her. "Trying matters, but don't do it again. It puts you at risk—and I don't intend waiting on them for a chance to escape."

A slight chuckle in that light voice, the one she'd seen him use to rally spirits and spur the troopers to mingle with the technical staff. That light, easy voice worked its magic on her too. For some reason, she believed him: they were going to make it out of this.

A belief she held onto, though their chances looked more and more bleak. Their flyer landed, and she was bundled out with a thick cloth over her face and hustled into an unknown building, one that had certainly not been built by rangers. No windows and the place had that dank smell of the underground too long without ventilation. It was on again now, the faint hum of it vibrating through the walls. They were still on the plateau, but she knew that only from the length of the flight and that unmistakable feel of the air outside. Crisp, light, and drenched with the scents of childhood. What their captors intended or exactly where she was remained a mystery, though she had a nasty suspicion. Most importantly, she had no idea where they'd taken Jacquel. All she had was his faint call to stay strong as they were separated.

They pulled off the hood and locked her in a room. Dark, cold and with only the barest of amenities. After rifling through the contents of her pack, they left her alone with only a warm overwrap for comfort, and she huddled miserably into its welcome heat, reviewing every clue she could of the parts of the building she'd seen. A picture was forming, one that matched a file she'd been sent long ago. It did nothing to comfort her, and she needed comfort badly. They had banged her ankle and the ache of it worsened as the cold seeped into the newly healed bone. Nor could she banish the memory of her last sight of Jacquel. A grin on his face and the tautly held muscles of a man in pain. What next?

Finally, a noise in the distance. Then a stomp of booted feet and the door rattled open.

"Up with you."

A new man. He grabbed at her arm, hitting right on the spot where the tracer fire had gouged a furrow; she'd managed to ignore it so far, but the heavy clutch of his hand had her stumbling as a jab of agony shot threw her, a partner to the throb of her ankle. He just grabbed harder, and she had to grit her teeth to concentrate on putting one foot in front of another as he manhandled her down a corridor. When she was thrust into yet another dark hole of a room, all she felt was sheer relief as the man released his hold.

Until she saw who else was in that room. The leader of their kidnappers stood at the far end of the small table and cuffed to a chair in front of him sat Jacquel des Trurains. He looked worse than when she'd last seen him, the ridgelines of pain gouged into deep trenches and his body held awkwardly, arms dragged back and tied behind the chair. That he'd been badly manhandled was all too obvious and a fury arose in her.

"Hello again, sweetheart," he said in that deceptively light voice of his. The one that said he was in charge. *Just hang on a bit longer*, said that voice to her now.

"Put her down opposite him. I want her to see his face."

"Thank you. Always a pleasure to look at a beautiful woman," Jacquel said with one of those courtly nods of his, the kind only those raised in the upper levels of Hathian society could pull off with ease.

The man behind him scowled, then snapped at the guard in the doorway. "Bring me those results, now. And the technician who carried out the test."

She had a bad feeling.

A woman entered, with a glitter in her eyes that had Rheia sitting up even straighter. The boss man held out his hand for the compad she carried.

"I have been looking forward to this, Colonel," she said.

Jacquel leaned back in his chair, as much as he was able within the bounds of his restraints, and raised an eyebrow.

"Oh, yes, Colonel. You see, we did a bit of snooping on this moonie woman you brought out here, the one you're so fixed on protecting."

The leader moved around to the side of the table then set the com down and activated the screen's field. Graphs and patterns shimmered into formation; horrifyingly familiar patterns.

Jacquel leaned forward, mouth set and eyes cold. "DNA screening. Illegal without full consent, and that law has not been rescinded. Not even by the emergency measures during the occupation." He looked across at her. "Yours, I take it, madame. Did you give consent for any samples to be taken?"

"No." She held herself rigidly upright, refusing to react to the images. She was who she was, and she would never apologize for that to *anyone*.

"But they are hers, Colonel," drawled the obnoxious man in charge of this mob. "Hers. Rheia asn Postrova. Or should I say, Rheia asn Forvrad, daughter and only remaining offspring of Garin an Forvrad. The only one safe from his treason because she was far away, up in her comfortable niche on Mathe."

She would not let them do this to her. Her nails dug into her palms, but she held them well out of sight of her tormentors. No, she sat straight in her chair and stared into the deep well of darkness behind Jacquel.

Not at his face. Not at the shock she must see on it or the final loss of that flare of desire in his eyes.

"You have that wrong," she said. "I spent most of the occupation off-world in hotels offering a far superior level of amenities. Mathe was not nearly comfortable enough and diplomats learned eons ago how to secure the best for themselves."

But Jacquel wouldn't let her play alone, it turned out. "Interesting antecedents you have, madame. Asn Postrova—a family name?"

She nodded, forced to look directly at him. To see a cool, detached look on his face and that trace of amusement in the slight tilt of his mouth. But she'd been fighting her own battles long enough, by the Pillars. She didn't need his help here; not when she was trying her best to keep him safe and out of it.

"My great-grandmother's," she said. "She was an offworlder. I used her name when I first attended the central Hathian university." A careless shrug. "Rangers' offspring don't attend top-ranked universities and I didn't like the questions some asked." This time she rocked back on the chair, crossed her ankles and dared Jacquel des Trurains to call her on her ancestry. But instead their obnoxious captor moved around and grabbed her by the chin, forcing it up. She refused to back down, refused to do other than meet that sneering look head-on, eyes wide open and with every particle of self-possession she could dredge up on display. His hand tightened as a shadow of temper crossed his face, and he let her chin go with a snap.

"Offworlder spawn, as well as a moonie and daughter of a traitor. No loss to anyone, but the authorities will have to pretend to care what happens to you."

She lifted her shoulders, shrugging carelessly as if dismissing the man's words. But the man did have the right of it. Gilda an Rathman may have promised to keep her secret safe, but Rheia had never assumed that meant she cared about Rheia herself. She'd always known it was guilt talking: the failure of the Resistance and Hathian regime to protect her father, her family and all those other Hathians who had paid the highest of prices during the occupation.

She knew how Gilda felt. She lived with the same guilt. It was worse in the early days, when the Terrans stomped all over Hathe and inflicted their power in the most basic of ways as she and the other moon-based Hathians watched in horror. So powerless, so completely barred from doing anything to help as the reports seeped in.

And then had come the news about her family.

CHAPTER TEN

Garin an Forvrad. Jacquel had to fight to keep the shock from showing on his face, just as he fought to stay seated until the moment was right, instead of struggling madly to break free and destroy the man who'd hurt Rheia so badly. She'd been hurt enough.

Of course he'd heard of Garin an Forvrad. Every Resistance agent knew the name of the man who had betrayed his family and home village to destruction, all so the Terrans could get easy access to water. *Good thing they killed him, but a pity it was so quick,* was the commonly heard opinion, particularly among dirtsiders.

Except Jacquel had seen the secured file on the incident, and the sick horror of it rose in him again. Everyone had heard the story, but only a handful knew the truth behind it. Jacquel had been the one to debrief the agent involved in the failed attempt to rescue the an Forvrad family—mother, daughter and son. No trace of their bodies was ever found.

Rheia's family.

Now he knew why the daughter was missing, but that didn't change the truth about the mother and son. He'd asked the agent about it once and could never forget the guilt and the grief scoured into the man's face.

"All dead; they're all dead."

It was back in the early days of the occupation, before Marthe's husband had taken over the security services. The sad story in that restricted file came from the time when the Terrans were building their stronghold on the plateau. The buildings that became known as the Citadel.

A fortress town that needed a reliable source of water. The Terrans captured a former ranger posing as a local herder, guessing rightly the man would know the secrets of where the locals got their water. The small plateau streams couldn't supply the volumes needed for a place like the citadel settlement and the water in them was frequently contaminated by flooding. Yet the local village appeared to have no such problem. Hyrvettin had been a ranger town hastily turned into a primitive-appearing village housing local herdsmen and hunters in the month before the Terrans landed.

Jacquel had seen the Terran prison reports on the man, the reports containing the facts never made known to the public. Dirtsiders under the occupation lived in enough fear as it was without hearing of this family's treatment. The ranger had been tortured past any man's limit but still he wouldn't crack. Not till the Terrans tracked down his wife and son, and brought them into the Citadel to torture in front of him.

Even then he'd tried to hold out, begging for their release. But only when they were being dragged away to their deaths did he relent, agreeing to reveal the source of the locals' drinking water in exchange for his family's lives.

He should have known not to trust the Terrans. His wife was dead even as he finished speaking, his son carved up in front of him. That hidden spring was the only safe supply available to the nearby settlement of rangers. They had to destroy their own Hathian built water plant before it could be found and watch as the Terrans took over their spring. Then the invaders had forced the villagers to build a new water plant to supply the Citadel. Worked them long and hard, without the safe water or food they needed.

So many had died—from overwork and disease, or from despair, none could now say. The last he'd heard, the ranger's body had been found on the high plateau, tumbled into an open grave. The few in High Command who knew his story had buried him properly with full military honors, but his grave lay unmarked to this day. Unmarked, alone and stripped from the records, until he'd come across it.

To the rest of Hathe, Garin an Forvrad was the most hated traitor of the occupation.

Rheia must have seen that file too. This brave, defiant woman sitting opposite him must have read the same words as him, felt that sick horror, and been totally powerless to do anything about it. No one could, not at that stage of the occupation. Everything was too confused, too fragile, the Resistance scrabbling to do the best it could with scarcely any resources.

Jacquel had checked out her file, along with all the other team members', in his pre-mission briefings. It barely mentioned her family, and they hadn't seemed important. An ordinary company worker and a teacher from a remote township, the file had said of her parents. At the time, he hadn't thought anything of it. Nor did his searches with his stepmother show up anything, but then he'd been concentrating on possible ranger connections, not her immediate family, and never dreamed those spare details in her file to be totally false.

But he did know what she'd done during the occupation. Yes, she'd lived in relative comfort, based in planetary capitals all over the Alliance as well as the secure and modern facilities of the Mathian university. But he'd grown up in the world she inhabited. His father was one of Hathe's foremost academic experts on the dynamics of political civics and interplanetary relationships; his best friends' father was Sylvan an Castre, a member of the Hathian supreme council all through their teenage years. Jacquel had been attending top-level political and diplomatic functions since he was old enough to be trusted to behave acceptably. He knew the uncharted, predator-strewn seas of human undercurrents Rheia had been navigating for all those long years of exile.

For five years, the dirtsiders had fooled the Terrans, playing the part of a peasant subclass, barely literate and abandoned to the perils of the occupation by a technologically superior class of Hathians, all of whom had escaped. Five years of hell they had endured, working undercover to prepare for the day when they could take back their home.

One of the least painful overthrows in the history of humankind. All the pre-war predictions had showed significant loss of life if Hathe tried to fight back against the invaders, so they had chosen not to. Their only chance was to wait for the Zenith of the Pillars of Mathe. That special astrological moment when the planet's two moons would align in a configuration unique to the Hathian system, one that rendered useless most Alliance technology.

The only injuries received that day were by the few Terrans with sufficient wit to fight back, Hamon Radcliff among them.

An injury Jacquel could still not regret despite his grudging respect for the man.

But it was only thanks to the efforts of the diplomatic corps, including Rheia asn Forvrad, that Hathe had been able to keep the secret of its grand hoax for the five long years of waiting. Rheia had endured years of wheedling, negotiating, downright begging and bribery, to keep that secret. The woman had guts, strength, and was owed a debt her planet could never repay. She was as much a hero of the war as Jacquel, and he would not see miserable nobodies like these use her family's tragic history against her.

He sent her a bold smile of defiance. "Manners are certainly lacking here. Had enough yet, sweetheart?"

"More than enough, thank you," she said with a glint in her eye.

He shoved suddenly forward, leaning towards the table and thrusting with his feet on the floor. A sudden rise and hard shove against the table's edge sent it careering away from him. Rheia followed his lead, jumping sideways, letting the table catch the guard behind her right in the gut and taking him out completely. Grinning in satisfaction, Jacquel rocked his chair sideways, knocking down the nobody, as the other guard hurtled toward them.

"His sidearm," called Jacquel, flicking on the small wrist com concealed in his sleeve cuff. A quick flick of fingers and a sudden slash of energy raked across the room, right toward the light controls.

Darkness, complete and filled with menace.

"Yow."

A crash, a screech of agony from the guard. A smothered scream from the lab tech. A scrabble of feet. Jacquel cursed, clenching and unclenching his fists.

"Rheia, here," he said softly.

No sound, nothing. He'd seen her dive sideways before he shoved at that table, so where was she now? He strained to hear, all the time wriggling his cuffed wrists.

A slither of blood on the tight wrist cuff, and one hand was free. He reached around, tugging at the other. "Shh." The softest of sounds and a small hand slithered over his leg. Something sawed at his ankle ties. A brief moment of panic as the silence returned. Then the ankle cuffs gave way. He was free.

A whisper of sound in his ear. "The door is directly in front of you."

"You have a knife?"

"Never leave home without one," she said.

So quiet, so contained, together they slithered across the floor and out the door. Jacquel used the wall to lever himself up, and palmed the door shut. Beside him, a flash hit the control panel, burning it closed.

Jacquel couldn't stop his grin. "You got a blaster."

"I figured we needed it more than they did."

He had no idea how many were pitted against them and knew it would be sheer luck if they got out of the place without meeting any more. Nor was he in a fit state for much more fighting. His leg was barely holding up and the bruises gifted by his captors were starting to make themselves known, when that small hand touched his shoulder.

"Two more, on our left."

She had a trick of pitching her voice just loud enough for him to hear. The hand on his shoulder pushed gently and she merged with him into the shadows. Then a brief tug on his arm and he sensed rather than saw her move in the opposite direction.

The light dimmed as they drew farther away, intermittent flashes coming from the men hunting them and the occasional spasmodic light glows still working. This place had been empty for some time. Too much dust, too many stray pieces of debris littering the floor and impeding their progress. Over it all, that steady hum of machinery.

But the key of it was wrong. Not Hathian, was his gut feeling.

And beside him, despite all she'd been through, despite the trace of a limp still, Rheia never once stumbled. He'd swear she had the sight of a night-hunting aerion and she could move like a whispered breeze. He wasn't as able, not with that drekking blast to the leg stopping his usual stride. But then she did miss a step, the slightest of trips. A brief pause, before setting off again. Purposefully, intent. As if she knew exactly where she was going.

Yet every file he'd read said Rheia asn Postrova had never set foot on Hathe during the occupation. Now, it was as if she'd forgotten he was with her.

"Hold up," he called softly.

For a space, it was as if she hadn't heard him. Then a halt, a shake of her head and, at last, she stopped and turned, all with that same eerie silence. He caught her up and touched her arm, and she jumped as if shot. Her whole body rang with tension.

Then it came to him. "You know this place."

She was going to deny it. He saw it in her backward step. "I've seen your father's file. The true story," he said, and hated the tears that sprang to her eyes.

"You can't have."

"I told you before. My security clearance is top-level, and I had to debrief the agent sent in to investigate."

She still looked wary.

"He had to be pulled from active duty. Not something we could afford back then, but he was too drekking angry." He reached out to cup her cheek. "Gilda warned me your father was one of the Unsung. She was right. Everyone knows the public version, but I've read his file," he said. "The one that tells the real story of why your father betrayed his village. Your father deserves every protection possible from the Council, and so do you. It's little enough to show him honor."

She didn't move. Not for a long time, nor did she speak, staring back at him. Finally, she seemed to accept what he said, nodding slowly. She bent her head to stare at her twined hands, then slowly raised it up.

"Yes, I know of this place. It's the water plant building. The one they built over the site of our spring." A swallow and a deep breath. "This is what they tortured him for. What they promised him the life of my mother and brother for."

"When he was near to death from their treatment."

Another quick nod of that head and a glance down at those tightly twisting hands. "They killed her anyway. When he saw them…My brother…"

One more wrong word and she would shatter. "I've read the file," he said again. "You have my word I will do nothing to put you at risk."

She shook her head this time. "Too late. Thanks to them." A jerk of her shoulder back the way they'd come. "If we make it away from here, it's still too late. They won't keep that secret."

"Not from other dirtsiders," he agreed, "but the Council can deal with them once we're free. They won't talk to moonies. No dirtsider would, not even these misguided idiots. And they've made a mistake. How well do you know this land?"

A slight lessening of the clutch of those hands. "I grew up here."

"The child of a ranger family." He risked another touch, a soft squeeze of her shoulder. The lightest touch that said *I'm here, and not going anywhere.* She glanced down, swallowed hard, and gave the smallest of shakes, as if throwing off the ghosts haunting her.

"Yes, by the Pillars," she said. "Yes, I'm ranger born. I know this area like the back of my hand." The smallest of smiles touched her mouth. "Follow me, city boy. I'll get you home again." And there it was. That wicked glitter of challenge in her eyes, and Jacquel felt his own lips lift in response.

"Lead on. Just not too fast," he added, glancing ruefully at his damaged leg.

She followed the glance. "Was it just the nerves zapped? Can you use it yet?"

A shake of his head. "Muscles took a pounding, but it'll do. I can put weight on it, but it's not going to hold up to much hiking. Guess I'll be leaning on you this time."

At which she grinned, really grinned, and the fight came back into her face. The pain lingered in her eyes—would never be fully banished, he suspected. But that enormous strength he'd sensed in her the first time they'd met was back.

Some time later, her cockiness appeared to have returned also.

"You sure you know where you're going?" he said.

She stopped "Better than you," she said with a definite challenge in her voice. "Heard any pursuit following us?"

"No," he had to admit. Not for some time. There had been shouts, echoes of trampling boots at first, but they no longer saw even flashes of light from the area used by their kidnappers, and were working as much by feel as by the dim outside light filtering in through dust-covered tunnels and skylights. The place was a veritable warren. "They'll have the exits covered though."

"Not all of them; not if the initial plans of this place were followed."

"You pulled them from the Terran files?"

"No, the investigating officer—your friend—pulled them for me. I didn't ask him to, but he said he hoped it would help to know what my family had…What they …"

"Did it?"

"Not much. A bit, maybe."

"And it would have helped ease his guilt," guessed Jacquel.

She stopped. "You think?" Then began walking. "I hope so."

"So how do these plans help us now? That lot back there will have the same plans."

"Yes, but they don't know this country."

He could swear that was an actual skip in her step. "Remember, I'm not as fit as I'd like." More than once, he'd had to use her shoulder for support, feeling bad every time he felt that slight limp telling of her own just healed foot, and he was drekking near hobbling now. His leg throbbed horribly from the blaster bolt and he had a nasty suspicion he was going to be confined to a hospital ward for some time when they made it out of here. He hated hospitals.

A clatter of rocks at one side, and he froze. Rheia had heard it too, melting into the shadows behind him. Dead silence, then another clatter. He held his breath, feeling every strand of injured leg muscle. They can't have come so far, only to be stymied now.

Then a small slithery shape scuttled over his feet and he breathed again.

"Cursed dynat," chuckled Rheia.

Second cousin to the verminous nystats of Hathian cities, the small animals infested any underground complex out here, having long ago decided that men made tunnels far superior to their own wet, dirty burrows. They also had a marked partiality for human foodstuffs, particularly of the sweet variety, and Jacquel knew from childhood trips to only use ranger-designed storage containers. The Terrans had tried shooting all dynats, then resorted to locking up their supplies in triple-graded security canisters when that failed.

The dynats still got in, much to the Resistance's delight, and they became a symbol of hope. To see a dynat meant your mission would succeed.

He grinned. "Hey little buddy. Go safe."

Rheia groaned. "You wouldn't say that if you'd spent a childhood having to chase those pests out."

"Don't even think that, not in front of a dirtsider."

"Wha…Never mind." She shook her head as if to say it was a gulf too wide to bridge, and maybe she was right. But she was also the moonie who was helping to get him out of here, and a Resistance agent never forgot a debt.

Though he wasn't so sure some time later when they finally emerged from the maze of passageways. The woman had an uncanny knack for directions, but this?

"You sure you've got the right exit?" He stared at the solid wall of water cascading down in front of him.

"Yep, this is the one. The access chute to the plant's spillway. Even if they know of it, that lot behind wouldn't expect us to come this way. The only way out is under that waterfall and over the side of the spillway."

"Which is also full of water."

"Yes." She grinned.

"So we'll get soaking wet and both probably die of hypothermia."

A very pleased-with-herself grin this time. "It's what that lot will think, anyway."

"There's a way through this without getting wet?"

"No, but nor will we get hypothermia."

He only hoped she knew what she was doing. A few minutes later, he was even less convinced. A ledge led off to one side of the powering torrent, but it was filled with a thick cloud of water, and that was where she headed. They pushed through it, the spray soak righting through everything he wore, leaving him drenched and shivering madly as they emerged on the outside of the plant. To be greeted by a narrow shelf of rock teetering under an overhanging bluff and standing just above a pouring torrent of water careering down the spillway. One wrong move and they were lost. At least they were hidden from sight by the thick misty spray from the falls, but Jacquel was left shivering and barely able to hold his position.

"Come on," called his partner. "You will get hypothermia if you hang around here."

In her excitement at beating their enemies and making it out, she seemed to have forgotten about his leg, and Jacquel was too proud to remind her of it. One hand on the glistening wall beside him, he gingerly crept along that bare shelf separating safety from oblivion. He risked one glance down. A very long drop down onto wicked rocks at the bottom of the gulley.

Then he cleared the bluff and Rheia disappeared into the screen of kryptark thorns pointed straight at him. Sheer cliff face above, lethal drop below. Only one way forward. He shoved on through the vicious barrier.

Not just one bush; a whole mad tangle of them. Had he done something to this woman in a previous life? Head down to protect his face, he could only hope he'd still have some clothing on as he emerged. Then a thought: he wouldn't be at all upset if Madame Rheia—walking-trouble—asn Postrova was minus her gear. A chuckle and grin on his face as he pushed past the last bush.

Only to find that she'd passed through the wicked patch with little more than a scratch. No deliciously torn scrap barely concealing enticing breasts, no scraped and pricked battle wounds needing his care and attention. His own sleeve was barely hanging on, his soaking wet tunic plastered to him and he had scratches up and down both arms. She ran her eyes slowly up his torso, too obvious to be accidental.

He couldn't remember ever having the tables turned on him so neatly. "About that hypothermia…"

A widening grin and that shimmer of laughter in her eyes. "You'll need an antiseptic phaser too, by the looks of you."

He had to glare at that, feeling every one of his scratches. His tormentor at least had the grace to say nothing further. Added to which he could feel his shivers worsening.

She noticed, and it finally wiped that grin from her face. Though the laughter still lingered in those gorgeous eyes, he was glad to see. He'd known little laughter in the last few years, and he suspected the same was true for Rheia asn Postrova/Forvrad.

"This way." She waved a hand toward the nearby gully bank. They were still well below the ridgeline, with behind them the roar of water plummeting down, down into a twisted, boulder-strewn mountain creek below. One slip on that treacherous slope and they would end up impaled on the fractured boulders and scree-filled creek-bed. He grabbed at the nearest tussock, holding on tight as he watched Rheia. She was heading out along the slope, not up as he'd hoped.

Another imperious wave, then she disappeared behind a tussock clump.

"Hey."

Her head popped back into sight. A finger to her mouth in a shushing motion, and that commanding wave of her hand before vanishing again.

Nothing for it, apparently. He placed a foot on the narrow indentation in the land, stepping hand over hand from one tussock clump to another till he reached the one she'd disappeared behind.

A last tug, and he swung around behind it, to find a gaping, man-sized hole in the bank covered by the shimmer of a security screen. She grabbed him by his tunic, pulled him through the screen, and he tumbled through a doorway as she slammed a hand against a control panel. Behind them, the bank slid back into place, a soft light came on, and he just stared.

It was a common room, filled with tables, shelving, and with walls decorated in a unique spiraling of color and shape. A style he recognized from texts but had never seen before.

"Ranger art," he said in awe. He stepped closely, finger tracing the whorls but never touching. "How old?"

"Old," was all she said.

"And this place?"

His voice was hushed, and for the life of him he couldn't imagine raising it. This place did that to him.

"It's an old trail lodge." She shrugged, a rare defensiveness in her face. "We had them near most water courses for anyone getting caught out in bad weather."

He slowly swiveled, taking it all in. Tables, chairs, lounge cushions dominated the main area. Lockers on one side, an open corridor leading off it on the other.

"Bathrooms, sleeping alcoves," she said, her hand to the doors opening off the corridor. "There's spare clothing in the supply store and the cleansing units should still be stocked with personal supplies."

"How? This…always here?" Then the significance of it struck Jacquel. "How many places like this? The Resistance had no idea."

She thrust out her chin. "Some they knew about. Where it was needed. Others…most of my village died or were scattered in that first year. My father took some secrets to his grave, and I never saw a reason for this one to be revealed. It's all that remains of my home."

Jacquel felt the anger rising in him, too many bad memories surging to life. So many times the Resistance could have used hides like this one. Then a shiver racked him, bringing him back to the reality at hand. No time for anger, not if they wanted to survive. Get dry, get warm. That came first, for both of them.

Or neither would be feeling angry, defensive or anything at all.

CHAPTER ELEVEN

Rheia took a calming breath as Jacquel des Trurains emerged from the communal cleansing unit, wearing the clothes she'd left out for him. Dried and dressed in proper ranger gear again, she felt more herself than at any time in far too many years. She was also warm again, and had to trust her guest was the same. She'd seen enough of hypothermia to recognize the early signs of a man in a too dangerous state.

Without that cleansing unit and change of clothing, Jacquel des Trurains would be well on his way to a slow and stupid death.

"Feel better?" she said with forced brightness.

He nodded, brief and devoid of emotion. Just a glint of something he quickly shuttered. Something not friendly.

Was he blaming her, blaming her father? No one had a right to do that, not even this son of the City elite eyeing her ranger gear dubiously.

"You can't deny who you are when we get back, not wearing those clothes," he said.

"You're wearing ranger gear too."

"Yes, but I doubt I look born to it."

She wasn't so sure of that. Jacquel des Trurains had a knack for merging into and looking good in whatever he wore. How he'd pulled off appearing servile for five years, she had no idea. Right now, he could have been one of her cousins.

No, not cousin. But one of the ranger wardens most definitely.

Whatever he looked like, he was still studying her with a look on his face she'd seen too many times before. The one on the faces of jumped-up sprigs of the upper echelons at university, and later in the diplomatic service when they heard her plateau voice. She hadn't tolerated it then and wasn't about to now, though she did change to Hathian standard after her family's death. She'd earned her place in Hathe on merit. As had the man before her, she had to admit, but that still gave him no right to look at her like something he'd walked in on his boots.

"There's food on the table," she said coolly. "We can rest up here then move off in the morning."

She set down the plates with a clatter and filled a bowl with the steaming hot broth she'd unearthed in the cold storage locker. From the taste, it had been frozen for some time, but she didn't care. The read-out said the nutrient factor was still in the allowed range and she'd heated it to piping hot. Dry, warm and fed were her goals right now.

She shoved a second bowl of the broth across the table and, after some hesitation, he limped over to sit down, and bent to his own meal. Dead silence reigned, and not the friendly silence of shared suffering.

Finished, she raised an eyebrow and he passed his bowl over for more with a muttered thanks. She filled it, passed it back, and pushed over the plate of stored crackers and rehydrated fruits for him to choose from, all without a word.

The only sound to break the silence was the grinding of teeth and the thump of mugs. By the end of the meal, she was ready to strangle someone. Preferably the man on the other side of the table. She shoved back her chair, enjoying the raw scrape of the legs on the sticrete floor, and stomped with her dishes over to the sanitizer. The mug should have broken when she shoved it in—would have if it was Terran made. But no, it had to be Hathian tough. The kind that survived anything.

She swung around. "That's enough. Out with it. What dirtsider rule have I violated now?" What right did he have to be mad at her, or any ranger. He was *alive*.

An equal shove back of his chair on his side of the table, and he marched over to the sanitizer, daring to stand over her. His eyes stared her down, flat, stormy and cold with anger. She glared back.

"Comfortable, are you?" he said. "Safe in this hide of yours, this safe, well-stocked, *concealed* refuge right under the Terran noses." He shoved closer, leaning right over her. "Know how many nights I've spent out on the plateau country, needing a place just like this one? Me and too many *nobody* dirtsiders with me."

"It's ranger territory. Not for outsiders."

A thump of his hand on the table. "It was war."

"We noticed. Too many of us *noticed*." A wave of her hand. "The council knew of these places, and you shouldn't be here. Wouldn't be, if I'd known any other way of keeping you alive."

"Thank you, madame. Too kind of you."

She dare not open her mouth to speak, had no words for the inferno inside her. How dare he. All she could do was stalk off, giving an imperious wave for him to follow. What she was about to do was absolutely forbidden. She was just so far past incensed, she had to do *something* to wipe that arrogant, self-righteous glower from his face.

"Follow me," she said with clenched jaw.

A slam of her hand on a concealed panel at the rear of the main corridor. A grating of doors long shut, though they shouldn't have been. Not if any were left to care for this place as it should be.

Darkness lay beyond, a darkness filled with a silent sadness. She marched into the shadows, head high and leaving him to follow in her wake. A light shimmered to life in the nearest ceiling panels as he stalked into place beside her. A wave of her hand, and one by one, bank after bank, the lights penetrated the gloom.

She felt more than saw his sudden halt. Heard the swift intake of breath, then the eerie silence as he held it, then slowly released it, very slowly as if fearful of disturbing the sleep of the bodies lying on every side.

But these bodies were beyond disturbing. Row upon row, in alcoves banked up to the ceiling of a cavern cut from the living earth, and held in plain, clay-colored sarcophagi, the dead lay here in the sleep that never ended.

"What is this place?"

His voice was low, barely audible and heavy with somber reverence.

"Our ancestors, the last place of rest for my village. This is where my father, my mother and brother, and all the others of our village should lie."

Another deep breath, and he pulled himself straight. "And the council knew of this."

"Some of them. The ones we trusted."

"My apologies," he said.

She nodded acceptance, brief, the barest acknowledgement. She *should not* have let him in here. "The council agreed to keep the secret of our refuges. We had agreed to let them be used if there was extreme need, but…"

He shivered. "Few of our people would have wanted to use them. Being on the run, it can make you wary. This place…"

"…feels haunted. Or a place of ill omen to those who risked their lives daily." She heard the dryness in her voice, but couldn't help it. She was coming down from her rage, leaving a sick feeling in its place. This was wrong. She turned and began to walk back out.

But the man stayed where he was, kept staring at all those rows where the dead rested. She turned back to see why, and he surprised her once more, kneeling and laying a hand on the dirt of the floor. He dropped his head.

"We will bring them back, all of them. You have my word."

He wasn't speaking to her. Barely audible, it was to the dead he made that promise, and whether she heard the words or not made no difference.

A long pause, as the silence grew calmer, more welcoming. Then he rose swiftly, gazed around in one long, considering sweep then turned and marched out the door, waiting at the entrance until she joined him, and with a quick nod back at the dead, closed the door gently on their long good night.

For some reason, she believed in that quiet promise of his. She'd been let down so often, met so many trials, but this man would keep his word.

"So, what now?" she said.

"You mentioned something about beds and sleep."

"They'll be hunting us hard out."

"And know nothing of this place, you tell me."

She shook her head. "Only rangers and the Council—and now you."

"So an Thanis?" Jacquel des Trurains's tracker, a ranger-born like her.

"No, wrong village. This is not his home area. Nor would he intrude here even if he did know of it. We do not disturb the caves of other guilds."

He looked puzzled. "*Guilds*?"

"The rangers of a given area. A brotherhood."

"Yes, I know the meaning of *guild*. But why not tribe, or clan?"

"Because we're not." It was all so simple to her. "Related, or born to only one guild. Well, not originally, and ranger folk still occasionally move between guilds. We all know the plateau—but your local area, that's your heart, your guardianship area."

"And you? This area is your heart?"

Too close, far too close. "It was." Outsiders never learned of these places for very good reasons. How many times had her grandmother told her that, long ago when she was but a child running freely over these lands.

At least that was one body she knew where to find. Far back, safe within the cavern next to the friends and family who had made her life a joy. A smile as wide as the sky, that's how she remembered her grandmother, with a chuckle that she could almost hear still. And a voice that could cut the sky when crossed. She would be horrified at Jacquel's intrusion into the cavern, as would all of her village. One more betrayal from the an Forvrad family.

But Jacquel des Trurains was not just anyone. A hero, yes, a vidcast star admired and desired by most of the young women on Hathe, thanks to an image from the victory parade of him marching down the avenue in full dress uniform with medals proudly blazing on his chest. But Rheia had come to know the man behind the image, had begun to learn the reality of the cost of those medals. *I think I'm falling in love with him, Grandma.* Falling for a man to whom she could never belong, thanks to her history and his background. And Marthe an Castre.

So why did she show him the cavern, except out of pique and a stupid flare of temper? Guilt slashed her. She twisted back, gestured at a doorway, unable to stop her suddenly harsh tone. "That's your room. I'll see you in the morning."

He looked stunned at her abrupt change of mood, then his face closed over, eyes flat and cool. "My apology, for whatever you think I've done now, madame."

He stepped back, and she felt like she'd been slapped in the face. A curt bow, and a far too polite goodnight that ratcheted up her shame-driven temper.

She swung around, fled into her own room and slammed the door on him. It did nothing to remove him from her thoughts. No matter how she paced around the room, settling in for the night, adjusting the room temperature, the bedding, anything she could find to stop listening for the man in the next room.

He'd sworn as she'd marched off, short, pithy and furious, followed by a heavy clunk of boots on the hard floor as he'd stalked off to his room. She'd shown him a sleep room at the end of the row, as far away as possible from her; but, true to type, he'd ignored her, and the door slamming shut behind him was to the room right next door.

It was going to be a long night.

She lay on the bed, tossing, listening to the sounds from next door. Then cursed as she remembered the clunking of those footsteps. The thump-drag of an injured man refusing to give in. A man who had put himself in the way of a blaster to save her, but whom she'd left to suffer, thanks to a fit of temper. She slammed open her door, then palmed the door pad on his. The telltale thump-drag again, and the door slid open.

He glared at her.

"That door was shut. What do you want?"

She gestured. "Your leg. There's a med unit down the hall and you're not up to travelling yet. Not without treatment. We need to leave tomorrow."

A long stare then a brisk nod. "Show me the med unit, then go back to your own bed."

It was a sort of win, she guessed. They couldn't linger here, or too many would use their unexplained absence to create mischief. Spreading tales, stirring up trouble on one side or the other.

She led him down the hall, opened the door to the med clinic and set the codes to let him access the healing unit.

He nodded, then pointed a hand at the door. "I can take it from here."

A dismissal, unmistakable and final, but a nagging sense of responsibility kept her standing there, needing to see he really was fit and able to use the controls. "I've used units like this more times than I care to remember," he growled at her, beginning to tug at his tunic and undershirt. Yet still she lingered, until he cursed and pulled them off, revealing the scratches and bruises of his trip through the kryptark and the treatment by their captors, mottled over the telltale scars of old hurts and a sleek musculature she couldn't ignore.

She tried hard to look away, but that body, those marks of a difficult past, and those muscles. She coughed, then looked up at his face. "I, uh, need to apologize. For before…."

She felt more than saw him fall still.

"My history." Another clear of her throat. "It's been a secret kept so long. My father…The stories told about him sound so bad."

He studied her face, his eyes intent on her and she felt like squirming. Then he gave a slight shrug and his mouth twisted. "Hathe needed scapegoats to blame."

She didn't understand the raw pain in his voice. Then remembered. "Marthe an Castre. She was your friend."

"*Is.*"

"And…"

He sighed. "All the stories, they're as wrong as the ones about your father. Marthe is a double-starred hero, and can never be safe on Hathe again. My oldest friend left alive, never to return home. I don't even know where she is now. It's kept secret from all but her family and a select few to protect them from those who hate them—both Hathian and Terrans."

So much grief, so much affection in his voice. The sudden stab of jealousy surprised her, and she thrust it back down, locking it deep inside.

"My apologies," she said again, but made no attempt to move. Held there still by duty, by shared pain, by…

A long silence, a moment in stasis. Then he nodded acceptance of her apology and waited. When she did nothing, he slowly lifted his hands to his waist.

"I'll leave you to it," she said. But she made the mistake of looking up, to be caught by the bright shine in his eyes. Not sparkling now, not laughing. Something far deeper, far more dangerous.

"You," he murmured, "should go now."

Except that her foot stepped forward, not back, and her hand lifted to touch a faint scratch on his face and trace slowly down that enticing line of body, of muscles, tendon and scars. "This one," she said, her finger drawn to a faint line of ragged white, running from shoulder, down and across his chest, then down again. His hand finally stopped hers.

"Long ago. The first year. It's done with now."

But that line remained, that white pucker that told of healing coming too late. "You need to use the med unit. There's a phaser function as well—for the new scratches."

"Yes." His voice softer now, huskier, and neither of them moved. Her hand began to trace the line again and his followed, covering hers. "You sure about this?" he murmured.

Her eyes followed her hand moving down, watched as he released the final closures on his pants. "No, but…Yes."

That was when he bent down, when his lips caught hers, and the anger and fear of the past day lost all power to hold her. His body bent to hers, gathering her in, and the couch of the med unit beckoned. He backed towards it.

Or did, till his leg hit the side of it, and he broke off, cursing. What had she been thinking. She pulled back, careful not to hurt him any more.

"I'm sorry. I shouldn't have…You're in no condition."

He cursed again, his face white and one hand clenched tight on the side of the couch. "No, I'm not," he admitted. "But, madame, I very much wish I was," he added softly. "And I would very much appreciate your help—with the med unit. If you care to stay?"

She had put out an arm, offered her shoulder to help him into the unit, but it was her kiss and what came after that healed Jacquel more. This was not the right place, too full of ghosts and memories, and neither of them was in any state. But he had wanted her so badly for so long. At first, she was intent only on healing him, and he didn't argue as her fingers played in the control field, too enthralled by the gorgeous body bending over him and the soft blush touching that delectable skin when the unit finally released him and freed him to climb out, pulling her laughing into his arms and batting at his body.

Then a yawn caught him. "I'm getting old," he muttered, disgruntled.

"No, just beaten up, battered and not yet healed. A med unit can't do miracles."

And he had to agree. His leg took his weight better now, but the twinges hadn't left, the warnings of his weakness lingering still.

"My bed is not far," she whispered. "If you think you can sleep…"

Unlikely, but his battered body wasn't going to let him sleep anyway. He propped an arm over her shoulders and let her lead him to her room.

He woke early in the morning, to find her nestled beside him, trustingly coiled into his body in a way he found far too easy to like. He smiled, remembering the night. All those things he'd planned to do with her, and then accepted he couldn't yet. Not when he badly needed rest and the smallest movement left him grimacing in pain and frustration. Then a grin as he remembered she'd overcome that too, both inventive and generous in finding ways to share her body with him, until he had forgotten his pains. He'd made love to Rheia asn Postrova that night with passion, with tenderness and with all that had been building in his heart. Though not, admittedly, with all the skills he prided himself on. So not as he'd planned—but yet so much more than expected. Next time…

But then other thoughts intruded. Darker and with no comfort. Their kidnapping. The betrayal by one of his own. By *dirtsiders* no less. As soon as he returned to the City, Phillipos athns Kronkist would learn what betraying his own kind meant.

But Phillipos and the rest of the gang, maybe even their arrogant leader, were no more than cogs in a bigger wheel. That was Jacquel's real target. His, and the woman who'd been kidnapped and threatened along with him. Whose life their captors had directly threatened.

He felt the rage of it in his blood still, the panic and the fear, and the cold certainty that he would not tolerate a risk to Rheia asn Postrova. A certainty that frightened him even more than the kidnapping and told him he must leave this room, this warm bed and the haven of her body.

With all the stealth of his training, he lifted the covers, shifting carefully from the bed so as not to disturb her. He moved slowly to gather his clothes and slipped out the door, causing only a soft murmur and a shift of her body, a hand tracing the sheet as if searching for something lost. It caught him mid-flight, halfway through the door. But then the hand stopped, a soft huff of breath and she settled again.

Safely in his own room again, he climbed into his cold bed. Nor could he sleep for a very long time after, and this time it was not their captors, not the hidden forces behind them, that held his thoughts.

No, he couldn't get Rheia's words from his head—the bitter cynicism of her voice echoing over and over as she'd called him on his prejudice. He'd judged her as a moonie, condemned her on that alone. She had good reason for her anger, standing up and reminding him that most moonies had as little choice in where they went at the time of the invasion as had dirtsiders.

Yet she'd still made sure he got the treatment he needed. For all her stubborn independence, his moonie was a woman who would not shirk a duty to those under her care. Last night, that had included him. And later…?

He woke again much later, rested in body and mind. The unit had healed his scratches and the worst of the battering, though the leg muscles were weaker than he'd like, thanks to that curse-ridden nerve disruptor. But he didn't fool himself he was fully fit yet.

As for his mind…for that, he had to thank ranger medicine. But how she felt…

He mulled it over as he cleansed, luxuriating in the facilities opening off his room. The place can't have been used since the locals had been summarily turfed out of their homes and carted off to the labor details that so drastically few had survived.

Children had once played here.

He slammed a hand against the wall, abruptly switching the cycle to dry, and forced his thoughts elsewhere. He should have learned by now.

Those first brutal months of the occupation.

Don't think. It did no good, not to him, not to those lost.

And not when he needed his wits about him. He doubted he'd ever lose the anger that boiled inside him, but today was not a day he dared indulge that loss.

Rheia had allocated another ranger's outfit for him, showing him how to access the supply slot in his room, and he pulled out each garment and considered it carefully. The rangers knew their world. Tough, thick and warm, their gear was well-suited to surviving out here. He pulled them on, and discovered they were also soft, flexible and more comfortable than he'd expected. A good stomp of his new boots, and he was ready for action. He emerged from his room, hoping to beat Rheia to the food area and have a chance to settle his thoughts about this place.

Too late. The woman sat finishing off her plate, and with a warm cup steaming beside her. She saw him, smiled and fetched another mug.

"Food selection's over there. You might like to try the priuets. They're our local breakfast special."

Matter of fact, no hint of last night. As if it had never happened. It appeared she was no readier than he to figure out what it meant. He considered helping her to decide, unsure whether he was insulted or relieved and aware of a knot of regret buried deep inside him. Could he strip off her veneer, expose what she really felt about last night? Should he? Then thought better of it.

Last night was a memory he would keep for a very long time. But to let it mean something…to let it grow, to plot how to finish it when they were still caught in the middle of so many unanswered questions…

Maybe not. But he couldn't resist leaning down to kiss her, teasing those warm lips to open to him, then breaking off with a soft "Good morning, madame." He walked over to the food station filled with delight at the soft blush on her cheeks.

He coded priuets into the food dispenser, waited and soon a delicious smell filled the room. Priuets turned out to be a kind of pancake, stuffed full of grains, fruit, and protein clumps, with a fresh, tangy sauce lifted by a touch of spice.

"This is good," he said as the last mouthful disappeared in far too short a time.

He got a half smile out of her for that, and she wordlessly ordered up a second helping for him.

"Someone should put this on the City menu," he said as the last spoonful of his second plate also vanished. "Capital bureaucrats would pay a fortune to the designer."

Then suddenly remembered, and abruptly shoved the plate away, "I'm sorry. That was thoughtless."

She shook her head. "It was my grandmother's recipe and she passed to her final rest a full year before the occupation. And I've had years to get used to what happened here."

A diplomatic sop to put him at ease. How often had she done the same for others—and had any others questioned the truth of it. He watched as she took their plates and loaded them into the sanitizer. Her hands were steady but he couldn't see her face from here, not till she returned to the table wearing a polished smile.

"So what's our next move?" she said brightly.

Talking to this woman was like walking through the booby-trapped approaches to a Terran outpost. To think he'd always assumed moonies had it easy.

For the first time, he wondered what his family had thought of his Resistance work during the war. His father never mentioned it; his stepmother was the opposite, forever wanting him to talk it through. Both walked on eggshells whenever an old memory threatened to overwhelm him. The day Marthe had left Hathe forever, his stepmother put on his favorite dinner and his father retreated to his university office for the rest of the week. Neither reaction had helped, but for their sake he'd tried to pretend to be dealing with his latest loss.

Although maybe his rampage through the streets of the City that night hadn't been all that stable.

This woman took refuge in business, and right now her face gave nothing away. Any illusion he had that he was starting to learn to read her was banished by the forced cheerfulness of her question.

One day, Rheia asn Forvrad would learn to trust him.

"Back to base, then head into the City to report this," he said in answer. "Though part of me is tempted to send you back while I get recaptured, to find out who's really behind this."

"No."

It was short, loud and—from her sudden gasp—had surprised her as much as it did him.

"You think that bunch of amateurs organized this on their own?"

"No, but you need help. Proper help for those injuries."

It was too pat. What had really caused that sudden shriek?

"Then we go together," he said, watching her. "I rely on you to get us back unseen."

No problem at all, said her cool nod. Not to a ranger born. But it was only when they set out and began trekking across her home territory that he fully appreciated what that meant. He had traipsed across these lands so often during the occupation, believing himself to be a master of them. He was a fool. This was her home and she slipped into the hidden byways of it with an ease and skill unsurpassed by any in the Resistance not from the plateau.

Which only told him how good she must be as a diplomat. The Resistance wouldn't have agreed to lose someone this talented unless she could do something even better. His father had hinted at an off-planet role for him too many times for him to remember, but the senior Resistance figures had ignored it.

"You're wanted down here, des Trurains. This is where you will serve." Which had suited him fine, but if he'd argued harder would they have also pulled him off?

Or was this woman even better at negotiating the pitfalls and convoluted pathways of interplanetary wrangling than him—and he'd grown up in the world of government intrigues. Just how good was she? He knocked his leg against a stone, sending a sudden spasm of pain arcing through it. She looked back, waited for him to recover then offered a hand as he gingerly tested it.

He shook his head. After last night, better to risk a stumble than brave her touch; the woman was dangerously appealing.

By the end of the first day, he'd changed his mind—or was beyond thought. His leg had ballooned, abused muscles protesting violently at the tough hike on top of the still healing injury and more than once he had to call a halt.

He felt like the rawest of recruits, blowing out after a bit of a stroll, while the remains of Rheia's own limp appeared to barely trouble her.

"We stop here for the night," she said finally.

The sun wasn't even on the horizon. "I can keep going."

A wave of her hand, encompassing the dip in the slope. "This hollow has the best shelter around here. Nowhere else close is as safe from the elements and anyone hunting us."

Nowhere close enough for a cripple like me, thought Jacquel bitterly. Worse, she was right. He needed to stop. He slumped to the ground, watching her set the camp, weaving a rough shelter out of a tall clump of tussock grasses and heat up their rations, all with the ease of familiar routine. He did once struggle up to help but she waved him back, telling him curtly she could do it quicker on her own. A line carved into her forehead as she looked pointedly at his injured leg.

She was right in that too.

He humphed back against the slope, eyes half-closed and watching her *efficient* movements. He was supposed to be the one in control, and he wondered which of his officiously interfering family members had decided a dose of Rheia asn Postrova/Forvrad would do him good. He already blamed Gilda, but excused her from any personal goal. Her close friend, his beloved stepmother, however…

They talked little that evening, and at first neither sought a repeat of the closeness of the previous night. Despite her facade of well-being, he suspected she was nearly as tired as he was, and as torn about what came next.

"We should make base camp by tomorrow afternoon," she said as they ate. "It's only a few hours more by the direct route, but that way will be watched. Safer to swing east and use the broken country as cover. If you're up to it," she added belatedly.

This space between them was too big. He reached out an arm and she moved closer, letting him tug her into his side. "I will be," he promised.

By the middle of the next day, he wasn't so sure. They stopped at the top of a bluff, the wind blowing and the only cover a sprinkle of grasses. It had been a long push up a broken slope, and both of them fell exhausted to the ground at the end. "We stop for a good hour. Get some sleep."

She shot up at that. "Why, what's wrong?"

"Nothing, but when was the last time you spent two days hiking around the plateau? And we spent a day before that in that hellhole. I know what they did to me. What…"

Suddenly, he couldn't finish it. Had the bastards done something she wasn't telling him?

"Nothing. No one touched me. Just left me in a dark room with no food."

That better be true.

"We still stop for an hour." He sat up, keeping just below the grass line and scanning the lands below. Nothing to be seen, but a lone aerion patrolling high up. "We're safe. Take a break."

She must have been in a worse state than he thought as she stopped arguing and flopped down beside him. Yet still alert, still casting her eyes all around. Still watching over him even when she had nothing left to give.

Enough. He leaned forward to prop his elbows on his knees, deliberately ignoring her and kept watching the lands below. Motionless, conserving energy, but on first guard. *I will keep you safe. Rest easy.*

She refused for too long, but finally, finally, she gave in. Lay back and showed she trusted him enough to let her breathing slow and sleep take her.

From here, he could see all the world below, facing straight toward their base camp and back across the plains from where any pursuit would come. Behind them lay only wilderness and trackless wastes. The plateau protected its own.

He had no intention of sleeping on watch. Not when Rheia had given him her trust.

"Up, you."

A boot thudded into his side and he instantly woke, rolling over to face his assailant and protect Rheia.

Another boot while he still lay on the ground, barely grazing him but having the luck to catch him on the leg injury. Blackness took him under for precious seconds.

Rheia. Struggle back to consciousness, with a quick roll away from possible attack, learned the hard way.

Use the rocky ground to lever upright; hide his weakness.

Rheia. What had they done to her?

He went to sit up again, to find that a whole squad of troopers surrounded him, in a uniform he recognized too well. The same as the one he wore on the rare occasions he needed to look official.

Why in hell were a full squad of Hathian Security troopers attacking him?

Rheia!

Two jumped on him. He twisted away, leaping up and using every trick he knew. They fought back but lacked his training. Moonies masquerading as seasoned soldiers. Any one of his people could lick them in an instant.

Four onto him this time. Another twist, two grappling him on each side. A kick from his sound leg then a quick shift of sides, moving his weight off the injured leg before it gave way.

Rheia. He broke free, spinning sideways and searching frantically for her.

Over there. Free, but cornered. Three of them backing her into a large rock.

"Leave her alone." He made for her, just as a blaster shot from behind stunned him with full force and he crumpled forward.

The squad leader bowed ostentatiously to Rheia. "Madame asn Postrova. You are safe now."

Jacquel grit his teeth, scrabbling toward her. Another blast wave, backed up by a neuro-sim forcefield immobilizing him as the rest of the troop jumped on him, hauling his arms behind his back and snapping full grade security cuffs on his wrist and ankles. Unbreakable, even by him.

"You are charged with the kidnapping and assault of Specialist Madame Rheia asn Postrova."

"Wha…"

Another boot to his ribs. Another blast, a full body stun this time and a scream from a woman. "Leave him alone!"

Then nothing.

CHAPTER TWELVE

Rheia stared in horror at the idiots surrounding her. "Let him go."

A wasted cry. The soldiers dragged Jacquel's limp body across the ground, ignoring her tugs at their hands, clothes, anything to get them to release him.

"Do you have any idea who he is?"

They kept dragging him, down the far side of the hill to a waiting flyer hidden in the long scrub below a rocky outcrop. She should have heard it coming, but tiredness had beaten her.

She thrust herself in front of the lead soldier. "He's Colonel Jacquel des Trurains. A decorated hero. You'll be in serious trouble if anything happens to him."

They tossed Jacquel carelessly into the flyer. "We know exactly who he is, madame. But even heroes have to obey the law."

What was he talking about? The man bowed, gesturing her into the flyer, as if they were the ones rescuing her.

From Jacquel?

"No, you've got it wrong. The colonel was kidnapped too. He's the one who rescued me."

A sound, and she suddenly realized Jacquel was awake. He stared up at the squad leader. A brief glance at her from those bright eyes, then back to the leader.

"Don't bother, sweetheart," he said. "The senator is unlikely to listen."

A look of shock on the man's face, then a cruel grin of confirmation of who sent them.

"But the Council. They overrule the Senate," she cried, and refused to think of it as naive. Hathe traditionally had a two-tier system of governance. The ruling Council, with members appointed by the wider family groupings, based on a complex system of affiliations known to every Hathian, and the Senate, representing the various regions of the planet. Fully elected in peacetime by all the local citizens, the Senate was meant to balance out any deficiencies in the Council. But then had come the Terran invasion, and the aftermath. The post-war Senate was a quite different body.

"Not in this climate," said Jacquel to her protest. "Not with Hathe on a knife-edge. That's what he's counting on." Jacquel painfully hitched himself up, propping his back against the ship wall for support. "But there will be a trial."

"Maybe, but the facts speak for themselves," said the squad leader.

Rheia glared at him. "What facts? You assaulted this man while he was helping me. You think I will say nothing?"

"Yes, Madame asn Postrova. Or should I say, asn Forvrad?"

He can't know that. But the leer on his face said otherwise. Only the Council should know her name. That's what they promised.

And their dirtsider kidnappers, who claimed to be fighting against moonies…

"Enough." The ring of command in Jacquel's voice, even when cuffed and beaten, still had the power to silence the man. "Madame asn Postrova, please take a seat in the flyer," he said now, as if he were the one in control. "This will be sorted."

He may be able to project his authority still, but she had spent too much time with him and saw the effort it took. What could she do but climb in and take the seat nearest to where they'd flung him, while the squad took the rest and she wondered how this insanity could be true. Gilda had promised. She kept her eyes fixed on Jacquel, watching as he braced his legs against the wall. He should have been buckled in too. Instead, he was forced to use every one of his abused muscles to keep from being thrown around as they lifted off and took flight.

This was all so wrong!

Even more so when she realized they weren't going back to their base camp. No, they turned to the coast, across the vast stretch of the plateau and toward the City. By the time they landed on the main City pad, Rheia had inveigled the squad into telling her the full names and rank of every single member, and worked out exactly what charge she intended to bring against each of them. What punishment she fully intended they be made to suffer.

And all the long way back, over the dividing ranges and through turbulent skies, Jacquel des Trurains sat on the floor, bracing himself stoically against the sudden lurches of the flyer.

The pilot could have flown a smoother path. She suspected it was deliberate, and she hated to think of the state of Jacquel's leg and bruised body. But he made no sound, no comment, his face closed tightly and his thoughts hidden.

They landed, and the squad leader held out a hand to help her up, even as his troopers released Jacquel's ankle cuffs and manhandled him to a stand, still holding him tight. From the looks of him, he'd drop to the ground without it, let alone walk unaided. She shook off the leader's hand and stepped forward, head high and ready to give someone, anyone, a piece of her mind.

"Not a word," said Jacquel.

Surely not. Then she heard the slap of a hand as she swung around. Jacquel ignored the blow, catching her eyes and looking intently at her. "Not a word, no comment, nothing. Wait till it's time."

Another crash, and the squad leader yanked her away. She twisted out of his grasp, erupting through the doorway of the flyer. Only to see the crowd waiting.

"Not a word." A cool voice from behind her, a hint of breathlessness only showing the effect of the latest beating. She nodded and had to believe he had a reason, must honor his call when it had cost him so much.

But then she stepped out into madness. Vidcasters with dronecams, reporters thrusting into her space, crowds jeering, calling out for the man behind her with venom in their voices, calling to her, asking her how she was, did he hurt her. Keep silent, keep her nerve and courage. Say nothing, Jacquel des Trurains had said, and say nothing she did. It was safest when the world had gone mad.

"Madame asn Postrova, over here."

"Did you have any idea this was going to happen?"

"Will you be filing charges?"

An imperious lift of her hand waved the plague of faces away but couldn't banish the flitting of the spybots or the vidcasters' dronecams. All of it recorded, all broadcast in full holovision to a world hungry for distractions—or for a spark to ignite an inferno engulfing all of Hathe and leaving the instigators of this farce as the survivors and victors. An icy chill swept over her as Jacquel's words suddenly made all too much sense. She thrust her back straight, refused to look at anyone or answer any questions and marched in funereal dignity through the melee. A rising tide of sound to her left signaled Jacquel's emergence. She risked one slow turn of her head, her face a careful mask, one slow gaze to make sure he saw her, that she needed to see he was still whole. It was only a short distance to the terminal offices and the security wing, but never had it felt so long.

And every step marked with the sight of Jacquel walking rigidly contained, held too tightly by his guards for his limp to be obvious, and his face stripped bare of any response to the thronging tumult surrounding him as the troopers marched him through the densest part of the crowd and all the way across the square to the waiting justice van. If he could do it, so could she.

Then she was inside the flyer pad control center, the security doors snapped shut on the noise and clamor, and Gilda an Rathman stood with arms stretched wide waiting for her.

"They've got it all wrong. You have to help him."

Gilda hugged her tight. "Don't worry, we'll get him out. I failed Marthe. I will not be failing Jacquel."

"Why are they doing this? He's a *hero*."

"Yes, he is. The most well-known one we have left."

Another hard hug, then Gilda set her back. "Did he say anything to you when they took him?"

"Only to keep silent."

"And do you know why?"

"No," but too many scenarios ran through her head, and none of them reassuring. "The Senate is out for his skin; that's all I gathered. But the Council has power over the Senate." If she said it often enough, it might come true. "At least get him medical help. He's been blasted with a nerve disruptor, beaten up by our kidnappers, had to slog across the plateau when he should have still been in a med unit, and been thoroughly manhandled by that bunch of thugs masquerading as Security troopers." She told Gilda the names, and made sure she noted them on her com. "Every single one of those so-called troopers needs to be hauled up on charges. They went far beyond arresting him, and he was already in a bad state. He's been surviving on his will for the last two days."

A harsh grunt of laughter from Gilda. "And the Pillars know that will of his can beat most problems. Pig-headed, bloody-minded *hero*."

It was the sheer weight of grief in Gilda's voice that finally calmed Rheia. This woman would not abandon Jacquel.

"Come on," said Gilda. "Rest, a cleansing and food, then I need you to talk to some people."

She shook her head. Comfort could wait. "We talk to them now. Jacquel won't be offered any of those. Find out where he is and get the medics in there before they make it worse or hide the evidence."

A nod and a promise from Gilda as she began hurrying them down the corridors with her security detail clearing away any bystander. But Gilda an Rathman had made promises to her before. "One more thing," said Rheia. "The men who captured us, the Security troop. Their leader knows my name. My true one. Either someone leaked it or that Security squad is in league with the dirtsider rabble who first captured us."

That stopped Gilda short. "They can't be. Our systems…"

"…are compromised. The squad leader called me asn Forvrad. Too quietly for his troopers to hear, but he said it."

"Aaah. That is a problem." Gilda switched direction, took a lift tube through to another story and entered a trans-urban gateway. A secured cab carried them swiftly down into a deserted tunnel she had to assume was for top-level politicians only, and minutes later disgorged them both into a plain-walled foyer. The Councilor stopped, arms out to let the security devices probe her thoroughly and a slight tingle told Rheia she was being subjected to the same.

Then she recognized the disembodied voice of the security protocol. It was the same one she'd heard the first time she met Jacquel des Trurains—in the main Central Security building.

She rounded on Gilda. "What are we doing here? I told you, it was Security troopers who seized us the second time. They're the ones holding Jacquel now."

"Yes, and they will be dealt with. The Senate may have succeeded in planting some tame troopers into the Security Department, but Gof deln Crantz is nobody's fool—and especially not of a Senator who spent the entire occupation safely on Mathe."

"As did you, and I was either there or in high-class hotels on friendly planets."

"Yet Jacquel seems to trust you," pointed out Gilda.

Maybe, and despite herself she had come to trust the Resistance hero from the heart of the City elite. It didn't mean she felt very safe right now. Gilda leaned over and patted her hand.

"Don't worry. We're going to free that young man, whatever he thinks we should be doing."

Maybe, but Gilda was renowned for having the most trustworthy face on Council, a bland niceness that the woman wasn't above using when it suited her purposes. "This way," she said briskly. Too soon, Rheia found herself catapulted into another office, facing yet another political heavyweight.

Gof deln Crantz had captured the imagination of the public, but Rheia had never met the man in person. She'd heard enough of him. Notoriously varying between cheerful, shrewd, and blunt, said the pundits, but all agreed the man had a razor-sharp intelligence. He was also known as a man who played his own games, regardless of what others might want him to do.

The physical reality of him was another matter. None of the holo-vids had revealed how very short he was, as if the man had been squashed from the bottom up, a slim rectangle squished into a lumpy square. Nor did they catch the life of the man. The sudden lift of his brow and the vivid intentness of his gaze that belied his physical appearance. A man who sat behind his desk with a glare that had Rheia quaking in her shoes. "What's that young man up to now?" he said.

Gilda appeared immune to it. She calmly seated herself in the only other chair in an office surely too small for a man of his importance, leaving Rheia to stand, squeezed in against the wall. Deliberately, she was sure.

"You've seen the reports?" said Gilda.

"Seen them? Can't avoid them. Not with every vidstream blaring them out to all and sundry." He scowled, humphed, and squidged back further into his chair. "I thought the boy wanted to heal the rifts on Hathe, not tear it to pieces.

That was unfair. "He did nothing. He's barely fit to walk, let alone kidnap anyone."

"We know that, young madame." Gof scowled blackly. "To think, I thought him the sensible one of that unholy trio."

"He means Jacquel and the asn Castre twins," said Gilda. "They grew up together."

Rheia had known that, had shamefully spent an evening while stuck in hospital after Jacquel had rescued her, searching out every vidcast available of him with the asn Castres before the invasion. So many showed him with an arm flung around Marthe asn Castre, laughing merrily into her eyes. The very beautiful Marthe asn Castre.

Rheia knew she was pretty enough. A fine figure of a girl, one silly uncle had once pronounced her. But Marthe asn Castre was stunning, and the look in Jacquel des Trurains's eyes those days when he looked at her…

But Marthe wasn't here, only Rheia, and Jacquel des Trurains badly needed a friend. No time for childish self-indulgence or foolish dreams. "How do we get him released?"

"*We* don't. Or more particularly, *you* don't," said Gilda.

Gof leaned forward. "What did Jacquel tell you to do?"

"Keep silent." An order she had no intention of obeying, whatever his reasons.

But a smile of delight creased deln Crantz's face and she could almost see him mentally rubbing his hands in glee. "The boy always had very good instincts."

"No." Rheia thrust away from the wall. "No. He needs help now. If I tell the truth, say it was no such thing, they have to release him."

"And your name and history are dragged into the open, to be broadcast to dirtsiders and moonies alike. You want to handle that media firefight?"

No, but she couldn't stand by.

Except Gilda nodded agreement with Gof. "Our medic is on her way to him. Every bruise, bang and twitch will be indelibly recorded. You're also going to a medical facility as soon as we're finished here, and we need you to set down a record of everything that happened, starting from the first kidnapping."

It wasn't a request, but Rheia had no thought of refusing. Anything to help his defense.

"Jacquel will be released to the civilian judicial system and under dirtsider guard as soon as we can organize it," added Gilda.

"His guard is also being replaced with our own troopers," said Gof.

"It was Security force troops who arrested him," she protested.

Another scowl on Gof's face. "The Senate flexing its muscle, and not for the first time."

Rheia knew what brought that look of distaste to the man's face. Even off-planet, she had picked up disturbing signs. In the turmoil and bluster of restoring peacetime to Hathe, most ordinary citizens were too busy getting their lives back to bother with seemingly irrelevant political games. Leaving the Senate to become the puppet of the powerful heads of returning moonie families hell-bent on securing their place in the new Hathe.

Were they who Jacquel suspected? She wasn't going to find out today, it turned out.

"Don't worry. We have it in hand," said Gof deln Crantz firmly. "You may go now, Madame asn Postrova. Thank you for all your help."

She wasn't stupid enough to try arguing. But Gof deln Crantz wasn't her boss, nor did he know her. Always have a backup strategy, was the unspoken rule for DIA officers, and if no one's offering an alternative, then make one.

Gilda rose but the look she gave Rheia was far more considering. "Do you have a place to stay in the City?"

Rheia nodded. "An apartment." The one organized by her ministry. She assumed her gear was still there. She'd barely had time to do more than check that the few pieces she'd picked up on her travels were safely stowed, before she'd been ordered out to the plateau.

"I'll drop you off after we've finished everything up here," said Gilda. Rheia looked at her suspiciously.

"Just to make sure you're safe," the woman promised.

After that, she discovered what Gilda meant by *everything*. A very apt word for it. In a short space of time, she was thoroughly examined by a team of medics, interrogated by a cold-eyed team of truly scary professionals from Gof's department and left feeling as if no private corner of her body or life had been left untouched.

This time, when she exited the building with Gilda, the security was so low-key as to appear nonexistent. A councilor would have security at all times, at maximum and the best available, but to warrant this level of discretion impressed Rheia anew with the importance of the seemingly nondescript woman beside her. Yet Gilda was largely silent on the way to her apartment, quietly taking note of the streets they passed through. They travelled above the hubbub of ground level, keeping to the priority traffic level where all they could see were upper level apartments and walkways. Not too busy, with people moving in orderly fashion. Plenty of gardenscapes covered the buildings, but nothing too glamorous, nothing worthy of a designer's vidcast. This was a zone for government workers like Rheia, where the extraordinary was frowned on and neutrality actively hunted. They pulled into her parking slot and Rheia turned to say thank you and goodbye. But Gilda was already climbing out.

"I'll see you safely inside," she said, beginning to walk toward the bank of skyshafts. "Your room number?"

"6C4," said Rheia automatically.

They exited the shaft and walked the short distance to her door. Rheia dutifully opened it, blushing at the bare walls and scarcely concealed blank spaces.

"When did you return to Hathe?"

Rheia told her.

"And bare days later you were marched out to the plateau. This is a ministry service apartment. Good enough security for most situations, but not this one. You're coming home with me."

"No. Not necessary. You've done enough already," said Rheia hastily.

"Yes. It's for the best." Gilda an Rathman ignored the rest of Rheia's splutterings, lifting her wrist to speak into her com unit. "Gerardo, send a removal squad, full security mode. Our team only. Madame asn Postrova will be returning home with me."

Rheia could only stand by, mouth agape, as Gilda signed off.

"Now, don't you worry, young madame. This is best—for you and Jacquel. You will be safe from those viper aerions out there, and I am a good friend of Anhuilla deln Vestros, Jacquel's stepmother. Which means you will be seen to be in the fold and on his side."

"No, please, I'm safe enough here."

Suddenly Gilda's face changed, and Rheia was dealing with a senior councilor in the full force of her power. "Jacquel des Trurains is a hero to the dirtsiders for very good reasons, which is why he is a key target for the moonie clique causing this current trouble. The boy is too angry, too sick at heart to stay rational if they push him too hard, and I will not have you being the trigger point for him. One wrong move right now will blow Hathe wide open."

Rheia suddenly felt like a soldier under orders. "You will come home with me," said Gilda. "You will be seen as a concerned friend to his family. You will *not* be seen as a moonie victim, but one comfortable, happy, well-cared-for citizen confident in her position in the new Hathe."

"I am?"

A wave of Gilda's hand. "Of course you're not. Few of us are. But you've been a successful diplomat for five years, and all diplomats are actors. This is just as important as any diplomatic stratagem or social bluff."

A deep breath. This was not how Rheia had thought to return to Hathe, but Gilda an Rathman spoke a language Rheia understood.

"Is that why Jacquel asked for my silence?"

"Partly, although mostly I suspect to keep you out of the direct eye of the media. You appear to be his latest wounded Unsung. He will protect you first, last, and before seeking any help for himself." An angry glint of pain in those usually placid eyes. "He's lost too much already. You may think speaking out would help, but quite the opposite. The greedy always want more, and tabloid vidcasters are the greediest we have."

How could Rheia argue with that?

Gilda waved to her security head, and Rheia was engulfed again in the efficient force surrounding the councilor. Back down the shafts to another secured van set down by the rear service entrance, then transported to a modern mansion in the heart of the political establishment where she was politely shuffled off into a guest suite the equal of any luxury hotel from her travels. She suspected the level of surveillance was also equal and made sure no expression on her face gave any hint of the fear and turmoil within her.

A man was in jail, was charged with a crime against her, and only she could prove his innocence. But the very heart of the establishment she expected to shelter him was keeping her a virtual prisoner here and well away from doing anything about it.

That made her feel guilty. Of course it did, but didn't explain the turmoil, the stewed-up cauldron inside her that demanded she break out of here and *do something*. That clamored for Jacquel's release, immediately. She barely knew the man!

After spending days with him on the plateau? After showing him the deepest secret of her home village? After that night together?

She paced the room, opened her luggage, picked out some essential clothes to pack into the capacious storage units. All of her clothes, all her special, most treasured possessions: all here. Gilda an Rathman's staff were thorough. They had packed up and carefully stowed each and every one of the random objects that measured the timeline of her life. Each small, unique thing that gave her life meaning, tucked away in orderly fashion and pored over by a stranger tearing out her secrets.

Rheia felt sick.

She unpacked, then repacked everything, checking each item. The crystalline globe from Arcturus, her first off-planet post; a transcab schedule from Pontrains, a planet renowned for its efficient public transit system; the ticket from her first interstellar voyage, tucked inside the anti-nausea bag. The spare one; she'd used up the original. A training simflight had turned out to be little use in coping with the real thing. Right at the bottom, a small white pebble traced with amber marbling. The kind of pebble found only on the high Hathian plateau. Gilda an Rathman had sent it to her, taken from the spot her father had stood before tumbling into that lonely grave. She gripped hold of it now, clung tight to its familiar smoothness and couldn't stop thinking of another man beset by the unfairness of the times.

She had to see him, had to let Jacquel des Trurains know he was not alone. He would not be abandoned like her father. Not while she could stop it.

Jacquel paced, back and forth, measuring the confines of the miserable hole he'd been thrust into. Ten paces one way, six the other. Plain white walls, with only one small window high up to give an illusion of sunlight filtering in but his inbuilt sense of place had been honed to a fine edge over the occupation. He was underground, buried in the depths of the prison building and held here by the drekking force shield covering the fourth side of his cell, a shield he knew too well was impregnable. He'd been on the team supervising their installation. Not that there was anything to see through it, even in the glare of the harsh prison light. Just the equally blank corridor wall opposite. All he could so was pace and pace again, stomp, drag, stomp drag, anything to keep his leg supple and functional.

Doing all he could to deny his captors, by refusing to give in to the battering of his body and by fighting off what this cell did to him. He would be out of here soon. He knew that, had faith in his troop and the ability of Gof deln Crantz. It made no difference to how he felt now. Too closed in, too lacking control, too damn *vulnerable*.

Too much like he'd been made to feel for five years. And echoing inside him always, the terror of that first year—before the Resistance was properly organized and a change in the Terran leadership stopped the more vicious brutalizing of the native Hathians. Before he became numb to the sight of a dead body or lost the shock at the blows raining on his body.

He punched his hand against the far wall, a bloody fist mashing to a pulp the skin over his knuckles and grounding him in a reality far too familiar. Pain, sharp and throbbing. A physical hurt he could deal with.

A few months ago, he'd been feted by all of Hathe, paraded in honor and granted the highest of military honors by a grateful populace. He jeered now at his innocent pride on that day, before the saccharine icing of independence had been blasted away.

"Hey, hero. You've got a visitor."

All his guards were moonies, this the latest in a jeering chorus of motley no-hopers apparently drafted into a new branch of *his* Security forces. He swung around. About time. Then saw the face of the man walking slowly down the corridor to his cell.

His father, and the professor had heard that jackass comment.

He stopped just outside the cell. "Don't worry, son. We'll have you out of there and this little mess sorted in no time."

Jacquel stared. Not what he'd expected to hear. He stopped his pacing. "Hello Father."

"Harrumph." No smile of welcome, but nor was this the time. "Yes, well then. At least the young woman has no connections of note to worry about. The lawyers are already preparing a settlement package and confidentiality documents."

Jacquel stepped back. "You do know I didn't kidnap her? That we were escaping together from a group who *had* kidnapped both of us."

A flush and his father had that look on his face again. The same one he'd worn on Jacquel's furloughs back to Mathe during the occupation, the one he'd worn when Jacquel was delivered home on the night after Bendin had been killed, and again when Marthe had flown off to exile. The one that said that his son should try harder, his son had failed him again. Jacquel stepped back further, out of the light from the corridor and into the protection of the cell's gloom.

"Thank you, Father, but my own lawyers have the matter under control. There will be no settlement package needed."

A sigh of relief. "You've already got her to agree to keep silent. Thank the Pillars for small mercies."

"There's nothing to keep silent about."

"Yes, well…" A noise at the far end of the corridor, a door sliding open and a murmur of voices. Military passwords and a woman issuing orders, the sounds falling like leaden shards into the hollow space.

"If you'll excuse me, Father, that's my people coming now," he said in cold dismissal. It had been a long few day, or he would never have let his father's words and lack of belief get to him. It was the only reason to account for his next piece of stupidity. He stepped right up to the cell barrier, right into the full glare of the corridor's light where he could face his father, then compounded the blunder by putting too much weight on his shot leg and crumpling momentarily against the sidewall.

A harsh intake of breath. His father, staring now at his face and for once abandoning his air of disinterest. "What happened to you?"

Another voice, a woman in the uniform of the City Hospital he'd too often dreaded seeing but right now couldn't thank enough. "His captors trying to break him, would be my guess. Prize idiots that they are."

"Doctor an Mathson. A pleasure as always," said Jacquel.

A scoffing laugh. "I can see that, young man. Now stand back and let this oaf here," a glare at the guard hovering by her shoulder, "open the door and let me in. Gof tells me he wants a full workup, so I would thank all of you to leave. Including you," she curtly told his father.

It was a night for surprises. "I don't think so, Dr. That's my son in there."

"Hmmmph. Well, keep out of my way. And you, you big lummox," she turned on the guard, "open up that door, turn the lights on in here, then go guard something useful, preferably a long ways elsewhere." The man obeyed the first two but stood obdurately by the far wall. Then the doctor switched that stare of hers onto him. "As for you, young man. Lie right back down on that sorry excuse for a bed before you fall down."

Jacquel knew better than to argue but wished he was fit enough to have reason to. Anything to keep his father from seeing this. The doctor nodded at him, a curt lift of her hand and he dutifully pulled off his jerkin.

"And the rest."

He glanced toward his father, cursing silently, then reluctantly obeyed her. Lying back, he tried to pretend he was anywhere but here.

Silence, too much silence. The doctor had seen him before, so he expected no less—she always worked in silence, calmly noting down and treating each bang and scrape. But his father was a moonie and had never seen the scars of the occupation. Jacquel made sure to keep them covered on his visits home. Partly from a knowledge of what they would do to his kind-hearted stepmother, but mostly from a kind of thwarted pride. After so many years living under a yoke, he had no desire to be the subject of any kind of pity. He'd survived; he had beaten their enemies. *That* was what mattered.

The silence thickened, the quiet of shock and tautly held breaths, then a gasp and a harsh intake of air. "Pillars almighty."

Jacquel refused to turn and look, refused to acknowledge the pain in that softly whispered cry.

"Jaca. You never told us. Doctor, how bad?"

"This one? Looks worse than it is. He'll recover quick enough once we get him treatment. Seen worse on him."

Another harsh breath. "Worse. How much worse?"

The doctor was leaning over him now, scanning his torso. He knew he must be a mess of black and blue, but the pain from the boot and fist that had slammed into him was already easing, thanks to the shot she'd infused. He saw her shrug as she kept working, not bothering to stop as she answered. "This is just a beating. He'll be sore for some days yet, but the only real damage is to that leg. And someone had the sense to give it the proper treatment in time."

"Rheia asn Postrova," Jacquel said to her raised eyebrow. "She knew of an old Hathian way station with a med unit." The doctor wouldn't ask more. She'd worked with Resistance troops too long.

Footsteps pacing. Followed by a concerned face thrust into his field of vision. He couldn't turn away. Not from his father. "It's nothing," he told him.

"*This* is nothing?" That loved, yet stern face turned back to the doctor. "During the war…How much worse?"

"He ain't dying today. He's been near enough to that plenty of times before," she added, "but not this time."

A curse, the kind of foul words he'd often used himself when caught in a tight fix, but never heard from his academy-bound father. "You never told us. Not once. Why? Why go through this? Have you no idea what those years of silence did to your mother and your sisters?"

To me, Jacquel heard under the words for the first time he could remember. "Because I'm good at it."

"At fighting? You're a trained historian, not a brawler."

"Specializing in ancient Earth political stratagems. It uniquely qualified me to lead troops in the battle against them." He shut his eyes, too tired, too sore and too stunned to argue.

Still, his father refused to leave. "That scar. How?"

He had to open his eyes to see where his father was pointing. A jagged line running from his back to over his hip. An old mark he rarely noticed now.

"A disagreement with a Terran trooper."

A grunt from his doctor. "It wasn't the lashing from the trooper that left that scar. A simple enough injury if you'd got help quicker."

He tried glaring at her but Doctor an Mathson wasn't easily intimidated. "It was the septicemia that set in when he stayed in the field. The boy was near dead by the time Marthe forced him in to see me. Not that she was in much better shape, and she should have known better."

"We came in as soon as we were free to."

Jacquel wasn't about to let his father find out what had delayed them. A group of villagers forced into a work party then abandoned to their own devices when a storm threatened that area. The Terrans had hightailed it home leaving the Hathians to walk to safety. It was earlier in the war, soon after Marthe had been pulled from medical duty in the mines.

Forced to abandon her patients, as she saw it, before the grief of what she couldn't do for them killed her.

"Marthe asn Castre. I should have known." His father almost spat the name. "Those asn Castre twins. Always leading you into trouble."

"Not this time."

"At least the Council finally shipped her off to exile."

"Father!"

"Professor, you are leaving now." Doctor an Mathson called out to the door and gestured the guard in. "The professor has finished here."

"Not yet," his father said belligerently.

An Mathson glared back. "Yes, you have. And a word of warning, Professor. Do not malign Marthe an Castre. Not to us."

Us, as in dirtsiders. As in everything his father was not.

"Do you know who I am?" growled his father.

Doctor an Mathson rose to her full height. "Of course I do. And I also know exactly what Marthe an Castre did to save the hides of you and the rest of that miserable bunch thinking they run this place now."

His father opened his mouth, and Jacquel sat up sharply, silencing the pair of them. "Thank you for coming, Father. I will come to visit you and Mama when I am able."

The professor gave one solid glare back at the furious doctor before deliberately shrugging and assuming the air of aloof superiority Jacquel was more used to. He stepped back, his eyes scanning Jacquel's body as if noting and remembering each scar.

"Please do so. Your family is always there for you. Your own family. Not a foreign invader. We will be there when you remember we are as much Hathian as those who stayed here."

You do not belong with them. His father's words on too many occasions.

"I will," said Jacquel, "when those who fled also remember that we who stayed are Hathians, and to be respected. And a word of warning, Father. Do not abuse a dirtsider, not to us. We protect our own."

With that, all the old barriers clanged down again, and Jacquel no longer cared that it was he who had done it. Not today.

A spasm rippled across his father's face. He turned to leave, then stopped. "You are so like her, you know. Your mother."

"Who…?"

"Your real mother, that is," said his father.

He had never talked of her before, and Jacquel had no memory of her. To him, she was just a face in old holo-vids. But today was truly a day for surprises.

"I was angry at her for so long, for leaving me alone without her," said his father.

"But, I was told…it was an accident."

His father nodded. "Yes, an accident that happened because she insisted on helping out an old school friend. A small concert, she said. It was our anniversary. She would be home in time to celebrate." He tightened his lips, and Jacquel was fascinated to see a hint of a pained frown spasm across his brow. "There was a power surge. Her keynola took the full hit. Her friend's group had formed on a nothing budget. They couldn't afford proper surge shields, and your mother didn't know."

A deep breath, a long sigh as if releasing so much bottled inside. "She should have asked. You were so little…and you look so like her."

Then, it was as if the dam was plugged. "When you are finished playing soldier, you know where we are," he said. "Our family lawyers are on call if you need help in sorting out this mess, and the family funds can support whatever compensation the young woman cares to demand."

With which, his father walked out. Just like that, leaving him stewing in a bare cell. Capping it off with that last offer, the kind of offer only made to a man his father believed guilty.

Leaving him to cope with a landslide of emotion churning up his guts.

"Shut your mouth, young man, and lie back down on that bed. I haven't finished my examination." The doctor pushed him back, the lightest of pats that had him toppling backwards and falling onto the bed, sprawled at the mercy of her scanners and probing fingers.

It didn't matter. He felt none of it.

CHAPTER THIRTEEN

Rheia had pictured her return home to Hathe so many times. Walking freely in a park. Taking a cup of tas in the central boulevard. Sitting at a table and watching her people pass by, free and happy.

Laughter, children playing, seeing the breeze rifle through the branchlets of proper Hathian trees. Leaf bracts of sage and silver, aligning properly to the sun in joyful tribute, rather than the randomly moving, garish plants of foreign worlds or the sterile, controlled ventilation of the air currents in artificial habitats.

"Rest, recover," Gilda had said, consigning her to her room.

"We have it under control," promised Gof deln Crantz in a voice she mistrusted.

Don't worry, keep out of it, this is not your concern. The clear message underlying every soothing note.

Jacquel des Trurains was in jail because of her. Rheia had never backed away from a responsibility, and wasn't about to start now, while Gilda and Gof were both quite capable of letting Jacquel rot in jail if it suited their purposes. She'd had too much to do with senior statesmen to think otherwise. She paced the confines of her room. There was a guard on the building and she had no doubt sensors would activate as soon as she tried to leave. If only they were back in her own plateau country where she knew the rules better than any of them.

Not something she'd ever thought to wish for. Not when her home region was haunted by too many ghosts.

Where were you when we needed you?

Safe on Krassus Minor.

There because her talent had marked her out. Creating alliances with unfamiliar worlds, formulating plans, subtle and complete in their complexity. Which meant she should have no trouble finding her way out of this building, despite it being designed to thwart the most sophisticated technology available on Hathe. A wicked sense of mischief pricked at the darkness threatening to smother her. Diplomacy was built on more than technical know-how.

She paced back and forth. This room had to be monitored. With Gof deln Crantz in charge, you could count on it. And a mere storm of tears wouldn't be enough against a man who'd survived the Terrans. She frowned, pacing harder. Heavy clumping footsteps echoing through the room. Then threw herself into a chair, and stared at the door, before flinging her head back and throwing an arm over her eyes.

Again and again she pushed out of the chair, paced heavily, frantically from one side of the room to the other. Paced till her legs felt like solid rock and the room shrank and shrank.

An hour, two. They must be watching her. Circle madly, desperately, flinging cushions, objects, annoying encumbrances out of her way. Including one charming statuette of an aerion in full flight. A vicious hurl from one side of the room to the other, against a cushion already tossed in a lopsided huddle against the far wall. One wing clipped the wall, the snap audible in the silence of held breath and sudden stillness. Two fists clenched on either side of her face, she stared at the broken body of the ornament lying drunkenly on the floor.

"Sorry, sorry. Aerions are…" Another lurching gasp, heaving breaths dragged right from the core of the pain lodged deep inside her.

Stare at the shattered ornament, silence, then hurry into movement. She flung open every cupboard and cabinet in the room. Where had they hidden the kitchen unit?

There, in a cupboard behind a panel. Bare of utensils except the obligatory spoons for drinks. She flung them away, watching them land in a jangle of fury.

Around the room again, picking up a chair, testing the legs but they were too tough to break. Set it down, and back to the broken aerion. A wing in one hand, the jagged fracture of the body in the other. Sharp and vicious. She studied the fragments then held one wrist out, underside upwards, and lifted the shard of the wing in the other, held it high and aimed it. Down to the pulsing beat of the blue vein lining her wrist.

A crash. A trio of guards burst in. Just in time to stop the slash of dark red blood seeping from her wrist.

"Get a medic in here."

They had cut it fine, but Rheia was relieved to find she'd judged it well. A guard clamped a vice of a fist on the mess she'd made of her wrist, dragged a cloth off the table and wrapped it round and round, tightening till the sodden mess stopped leaking.

"Put her on the table."

She added a moan for effect. Strong arms picked her up and lay her on the cold surface. A muttering of unintelligible phrases into a com unit near her head. Unconnected words, abbreviations, nothing she could understand. The secret, coded shorthand used by the Resistance during the war, she guessed, exposing her guards as ex-Resistance dirtsiders.

So, on Jacquel des Trurains side, but probably no friend to her. Not by the hard thump onto the table, the tight fist on her throbbing wrist, or the next words of those charged with protecting her as they abandoned their coded language, maybe thinking her comatose.

"Just the wrist. An amateur job."

"Moonie desk junk."

"Lucky for her. Our people would have made a proper job of it."

Another commotion at the door. The whoosh of a medic's gurney and the tramping of feet from new bodies. The emergency services had arrived.

"Victim's name?"

"Rheia asn Postrova. Guest of the department." The silence of code, or hand gestures she guessed, then the voice answering someone. "Nah. Mathian ID chip. Diplomatic office."

Their scanners must have told them she wasn't fully unconscious. She just didn't matter. Not to these dirtsiders.

They lifted her onto the gurney, and she had to concentrate on staying limp and unresponsive. As Gilda had said, acting was second nature to her, thanks to all those years of diplomacy. These medics were easy bait.

The hospital lay a few blocks from Gilda's home. Down the skyshaft, across the lobby, then out a side entrance from the dank smell of a back-service alley. From there, she concentrated on listening for traffic signs to follow her route. Engines roaring, a sudden blare of noise at an intersection, the tooting and susurration of vehicles changing levels. The louder shooshing of a public unit, whistling through the multi-transport level.

Slowing, gently settling to ground level. They must be approaching the entrance to the hospital service tunnel.

How many would walk beside her during the transfer? That was the critical point.

Sliding to a halt. The carrier door opening. Her gurney lifting out and a wash of chemical odors telling of a parking bay, with the nearby sliding of doors that must be the hospital entrance.

Her ears strained for footsteps.

Two medics, one on her right, one at the foot. Watching to keep her safe. They would hand over to hospital staff at any moment.

Her gurney halted, voices speaking, the one from the foot moving around to stand with her partner on the side. Other voices, hospital staff, transferring details between com units. She carefully opened her eyes a crack.

Four heads, all turned away from her. Silently, swiftly, she rolled over and slipped to the ground. Sliding away as if passing through the tussock country of home.

Another crowd of people, a bank of gurneys passing through the doors. A traffic snarl-up disgorging victims. Rheia slipped into the crowd, through the doors then down another hallway. Walking swiftly and purposefully down the corridor, through a doorway, following the signs to the public waiting room.

A faint shout behind her. She was missed. She kept walking, fighting down the urge to run, to flee.

She'd been in this hospital before. Student friends had more than once ended up here. One more corridor, through the crowded waiting room, then a doorway opening in front of her. Daylight beyond, beckoning, and then she was outside, sliding into a crowd of passers-by. Across the street, down an alleyway and into a park filled with bushes and trees offering welcoming smudges of light and dark for cover.

Now to find the prison—and find a way to get in without setting off a full Security Services call-out. She glanced up at the sun. Late afternoon, by the angle. Close to the chaos of homeward-bound traffic.

Not much more than a year after the restoration, and the City had already reverted to form. Right now, those crowded streets suited her nicely. A wicked grin lit her face. There was only one department that could match the Security Services for power and guile—her own. And the Department of Interplanetary Affairs had been at logger heads with the Security Services as long as Hathe had had a government.

The main office stood a block away, but the DIA had a pathological dislike of displaying its full colors. Two further complexes opened onto this side of the park, their connection to the main building hidden from public view. Nothing marked them out as different to the rest of the commercial office buildings lining the street and they were less likely to be watched by the Security forces. And as with all the other offices lining this street, this time of day brought the change of shift with crowds going in and out. All she had to do was blend in with the staff going in, an anonymous figure lost in a crowd.

A night drone would be her safest cover, one of the horde of administrative staff keeping the night surveillance programs ticking over. Low-grade technos interested only in doing their job and heading home. She looked down at her clothes and frowned. No one bothered with what you wore at night.

Comfort first, no point dressing like a model in the basement levels. But the splodges of blood were a different matter.

The sun still warmed the park, enticing later strollers and early seekers of romantic havens. She stole through the bushes, checking each group. Finally, a too warm overcloak flung over a shrub by a couple oblivious to their surroundings. Thank the Pillars for young love. Had she ever been so enthralled—felt safe enough to ignore the world around her, all for the joys of a lover?

A memory flashed into her mind. Night, a lean body, and a face marked by clear, all-seeing eyes and a mouth curved in laughter. A memory she thrust firmly out. Why dream of the impossible. Jacquel des Trurains was not for her. But she did owe him, and he would not be hurt by her.

It was easier than she'd expected to get into the building. A bump into one of the night shift data drones mobbing the staff entrance doors in the side alley and a smothered curse.

"Forgot my stupid pass again," she muttered. "I'll lose my job this time."

"Don't phase it," said the young man. "Keep close. My pass will cover both of us."

She nodded anxiously, as if nervous of losing her place. "Stay with me," the young man reassured her again.

"You're too good," she whispered breathily.

Yes, far too good. Head down, cloak clutched around her, and tucked safely into the side of the kind young man, she made her way into the building right in the middle of the hustling crowd. There was a jam at the doorway as too many people tried shoving in together, as if by starting quickly they could somehow make the night go faster. Pushing, cursing, com chips flashed in all directions at the same time, along with the young man's. Once, then the quickest of flashes twice.

Quick enough to fool the scanners. He'd done this before, she guessed.

Then she was inside. A quick lift of one eyebrow in thanks to the young man, and she peeled off to the lower levels. She let herself be held back by the crowds, losing any who would remember her coming in with them and drifting along with the masses as they made for the staff chutes at the end of the back corridors. Not for these workers the grandiose front foyers built to impress councilors, ambassadors and off-world officials. No, drone space was allocated on the bare necessities for completion of their job. Plain corridors, narrow work spaces and utilitarian service areas. In her present guise, she fit right in. So many worked down here that few expected to see a familiar face until they reached their own department.

Nearing the chutes, she sidled across to the margins of the crowd. Then slipped down the alley leading to the staff toilets. It also led to a narrow access way for the service technicians to get to the power and ventilation feeds. Part of her early training had been to memorize the full plans of the departmental buildings as part of the security protocols. All diplomatic staff were considered potential sabotage targets and were required to know how to keep safe. She dredged up the memory of those plans now, tracing the ventilation shafts, the service chutes and the alarm sensors.

Tricky, but doable, even if the fit was a bit tight. She wriggled through the tubes, moving as smoothly as possible in case someone below should hear her. The one problem: if her clearance level had been changed and her com unit set off the alarms. She breathed deeply as she passed into the screening zones, heaving a hearty sigh when she'd slipped safely through.

The cleaning bots had been over every square of this building at the end of the war before the department moved back in again, but whoever programmed them seemed to have forgotten more than a few corners. By the time she reached her target area, she was filthy. An even more disgusting spectacle than when she started. The slow seepage from her bandaged wrist only added to it. All she could hope was that her boss kept to his usual routine of working late. Anyone else would take one look at her and throw her out before she could say anything. He should be alone in his office. The change of shift was a rare space free of interruptions and her boss liked to make full use of it. One more corner, drag herself along the last straight, and she was on top of the grid at the end.

A scrape of a chair and a tall, thin man appeared below her, streaks of gray at his temples and a resigned scowl on his face as he looked up at her. The sensors had warned him she was coming. He reached up, unclipped the covers and helped her down, cool gray eyes tracking her slowly from head to toe.

"You could have tried the front door."

She risked the barest of shrugs. "I've just come from Security accommodations, courtesy of Councilor an Rathman."

"And you think we let Security decide who comes in and out of here? Not on my watch, young lady. You ought to know that."

At the tone of his voice, something inside her relaxed. Myron ven Raden had sponsored her since her first entry into the department. He had been a few steps down then, before taking the reins of the department soon after the invasion. He'd apparently seen something in a gawky, raw recruit from the wilds of the plateau and fresh from university, and she owed much of her career progression to his judicious watch.

"So, what can we do for you, apart from the medical care that Security appears to have felt fit to ignore."

"I did this to myself," Security didn't need the blame for it, "so I could escape from the hospital waiting area."

A slight lift of his lips at that, in something approaching a grin. "Good to see your defense training had some use."

She had to return the smile. He'd caught her moans on that subject more than once. As to her reason for being here… She took a breath.

"I need to get in to see Jacquel des Trurains."

A sudden tightening of those lips. "Haven't you been watching the vid screens?"

"No. Why?"

"You're going nowhere close to that prison. Not today."

He punched orders into his com unit and a panel shimmered into life on the far wall. Rheia looked across and gasped. "What in all Mathe!"

Crowds mobbed the street, raucous calls of angry protests ripping through the evening air.

"Listen to the names." He switched off the background filter. Angry shouts filled the safe office.

"Free dirtsiders!"

"Down with moonies!"

"Postrova, go home!"

The last repeated, over and over. Interspersed with "moonies go, moonies go," and the sheer hate slicing through the streets shafted straight home to her heart.

"This *is* home." How could they not know that? "How long?"

"Since the first reports hit the stars-cursed vid channels. They get louder each time one of our esteemed Senators goes on a vidcast to repeat the litany of charges against des Trurains."

"Litany?'

The director switched views and brought up a Senate document. Her eyes traced the list, heart beating and breath lodged somewhere in her gullet.

"They think he did all that? To me?"

A bright flush of shame rushed across her cheeks and the director thrust forward a chair. She plumped down on it, hard.

"I take it none of this is true?"

"Of course not." Why would he think that? "You know me; you know Jacquel."

"I had to ask," said the director. "Now you want entry into the prison?"

She nodded. "He needs to know I'll do whatever is takes to clear up this mess. That one moonie will not desert him," she added defiantly.

"An empty gesture," suggested the director.

It was true. They both knew it. "I still have to try," she said, unable to explain even to herself why it was so important.

A shrug. "Your call." He stabbed at his com unit, to call in his assistant. Then folded his hands calmly in front of him as he faced her again. "I'll call Gof. You'll need a way in that keeps you out of sight."

She didn't know she'd been holding her breath until she let it out in a long, long sigh. "Thank you." She glanced down at her wrist. "Ah, and yes, I guess I need something done about this."

After that, her department fulfilled all her expectations, and matters went as smoothly as she could have hoped. The necessary fussing over by a medic, a change of clothes including a full shrouding cloak, then a DIA squad lead her on foot by a route that took her through the quiet streets and dark byways of the city. Only once did they approach the screaming crowds swelling the streets around the prison. A mutter from her guards, a harsh order to keep her head down and keep moving, and they scurried through the shadows past the angry faces. Then into the complex of tunnels open only to the Security and diplomatic agencies. Myron ven Raden had given her a pass, but the official stamp on her transmission made no impression on the Security Department guards at the prison end.

"Authenticate verification," the squad leader snapped into her com unit. The resulting beep and green light brought a scowl to the woman's face. "You're cleared for entry, Madame asn Postrova. You only. No one else."

Her guard thrust forward. "She's under our protection."

"Not here. This is Security territory."

Gof deln Crantz did say he was putting his own people around Jacquel, and she guessed this proved it. One moonie might enter, if the Security's hand was forced, but not a whole squad.

She turned to her squad leader. "Thank you for bringing me. The Security forces can take me the rest of the way."

"It was the Security forces that put Colonel des Trurains in here."

"Not *our* Security," growled his opposite.

For an instant, Rheia feared an armed scuffle, and didn't know whether to laugh at two soldiers crowing over this dung heap of a place, or weep tears that Hathe should come to this.

"Enough. Squad Leader, wait here. I won't be long. Security agent, please lead on."

Her guards had no choice but to obey. They released her with an exaggerated salute and made it clear they would not budge a micron, not till she returned.

The Security team shuffled her into the middle of their squad, before hustling her into the building and up and down a seeming maze of corridors. All deserted, all uniformly bare of anything showing their use. Cold white walls and harsh lighting. Nothing to tell her the way out again.

"Are you sure this is the quickest route?" she said after a while.

A curt shake of the squad leader's head. "Safest—for you."

Rheia was left to wonder who they were keeping her safe from: the angry mob outside, the dirtsiders inside, or the despised new moonie Security troops. Nor did the blank astonishment and the furious "What are you doing here?" from Jacquel help, when they finally reached his cell.

"Making sure you're all right," she said calmly, fists clenched together and nails biting into her palms so he couldn't see what the sight of him did to her.

A medic had treated him. The bangs and scrapes on his face no longer blazed an angry red and a support field braced his injured leg, taking the weight as the healing unit wrapping over the blast zone did its work. They had brought him his own clothes, and someone had provided a decent sleep pad for his cot.

But he still stood in a bare prison cell, stripped of all but the necessities and held inside by a full-strength confining field shimmering in the air between them.

"I'm fine," he said impatiently. "You should not be here."

"Well, I am." She lifted an eyebrow at the squad leader and waited. One of the troopers hastily brought forward a chair and she settled her cloak around her as she sank into it to avoid giving way to the quakes in her legs It couldn't stop the mushed-up mess of nerves tearing at her insides. "How long before Gof deln Crantz gets you out?"

"Soon." A warning snap in his voice.

But the squad leader was studying Rheia. "The Senate is blocking the colonel's release, due to the seriousness of the charges."

She turned to consider the woman. The trooper held herself rigid. As if waiting for a blow to fall, Rheia suddenly realized. All the squad were dirtsiders. All had been brutalized during the war, and all, it seemed, now expected nothing from an outsider.

Even from a fellow Hathian?

"No one has asked for my statement yet, and nor will anyone take it," she said to them. "Not till I have recovered, they tell me."

A slight slump of the woman's shoulders, as if confirming the worst. Another self-serving moonie failing them. A slump mirrored in the whole troop. Oh no, not happening.

"That is not the end of it, Squad Leader. I will contact my own lawyer as soon as I return, ordering her to place a statement on file with the Senior Court exonerating Colonel des Trurains. They will have to release him then."

"Thank you," the woman said stiffly.

"You do know they won't believe you," Jacquel said to Rheia.

"But it will force them to let you go, sir," said the squad leader.

Rheia stood, catching the look Jacquel gave the squad surrounding her. One that excluded her, one between a Resistance leader and his troops. Slowly they forced their shoulders back up, faces contained and standing as if braced to meet a battle. And suddenly she understood.

"This? This is what you are fighting?" Not the moonies, not the jeering crowds outside. This, in front of her, was the greatest threat to the dirtsiders. How to make them feel valued again, know they could win against the smugly confident and privileged moonies now ruling too much of their world.

A slow nod, the light of recognition in his face but still he stood at attention, still he held her out.

"But you're a Pillars marked hero, all of your dirtsiders are. You gave us back our home world. There was a *parade*." How could anyone forget the cheering of the crowds that day when they celebrated the restoration of their world?

"I will be released soon," he said. "Gof and the Council have it in hand. Your testimony is not needed."

"Without it…No one will believe you're innocent."

A shrug. "It's all right, Madame. You don't need to trouble yourself further."

She shot up. Madame? Was he serious? "I *will* testify."

He glared at her. "You will *not*. It's too risky."

She glared back. "That crowd out there are ready to skewer me if I don't."

"And whoever put me in here is counting on your loyalty as a moonie to keep you silent. Counting on *your name* to make you."

"They don't know me."

A trace of a grin touched his lips. "Were you born this stubborn?"

He shoved a hand through his hair and he waved her to sit down again. Then pulled over the stool in his cell and straddled it, elbows propped on his knees as he leaned toward her.

"Madame…Rheia, please." That famous disarming grin, familiar from so many news vids, but not as sure, not as in control as usual. "I'm sorry, but…you shouldn't have come." Another pause, then a soft whisper. "It's good to see you."

A wash of sudden warmth in those bright blue eyes, gone as soon as glimpsed. And now he put on the kind of smile she'd seen before, though never in person. The one familiar from the more strident news vids, when he'd been trying to fob off their worst platitudes by disarming the reporter.

"Rheia…," he started again, and never before had her name sounded so beguiling, or so suspect. "Gof has it in hand. I—we—Hathe needs you to keep silent."

A cold hand clutched at her belly. "Hathe. Not you?"

He nodded, sitting straighter. As if withdrawing from her. "This divide in our people. It has to be closed." His hand took in his cell. "This was a mistake."

"You think so? That riot outside sounds very real. Come tomorrow, a lot of dirtsiders will be stagnating in jail, feeding their anger and reinforcing moonie beliefs in their superiority. *Dirtsiders can no longer be trusted to behave in a civilized manner. They can't give up the war.*"

"There's enough truth in that to be dangerous. Look at Phillipos athns Kronkist and his cronies. So angry at what's happened they became a prime target for the unscrupulous trying to stir up trouble for their own ends."

"So where's the mistake?"

"Targeting me, using you." Another of those slight smiles, but this one looked forced. "They didn't do their homework properly." Then the smile disappeared, and a chill entered her heart. "Hathe needs your help, Rheia asn Postrova."

That fist about her heart clenched tighter and she clutched at her arms for support.

He was too good at reading others and his face closed over, as if forcing all feeling back behind the solid barricade of his will. "I'm so sorry," he whispered. Then continued, speaking as if reading from a prepared script he must follow. "Hathe needs a favor from you. You have given so much; can you give more?"

What could she do but nod senselessly.

A twitch of his eyebrow, that beautiful mouth set straight and hard. "We need you to keep silent so that the moonie faction behind all this will come to trust you. They must think they have a hold on you because of your background."

Another drag of his hand, a bitter clench of his mouth. "It's the only way we can prove who is causing this mess."

"You don't know?"

"Some. We know who is at the root of this incident, at least, and suspect who is pulling the strings above them. But we don't have enough evidence to prove it. That's what we must find if we're going to bring all Hathians on side. Moonies and dirtsiders together; those who want a united Hathe back again, as much as you and me."

Her breath whooshed out. "You want me to go undercover."

The squad leader stepped forward. "Cap, that's insane. She's not trained."

"Yes, she is," said Jacquel des Trurains. "Ranger raised, and held her own against the diplomatic predators of the Alliance for five years. She's as well-trained as any of us."

Another whoosh of lost breath. "Thank you, I think."

He said nothing.

"Was this your idea?" she demanded, suddenly needing to know.

A grimace of an apology.

"The commander," said the squad leader. "It's got deln Crantz's touch all over it."

Rheia gripped her arms tighter. Gof deln Crantz, yes, but the thing also had Jacquel des Trurains's touch. She'd read his files, knew his talent for command in the field and for subterfuge. Of course he would think of using her like this, and the worst of it was, he was right. It still hurt that he should think to make her no more than a tool in their wider game, denying whatever it had been between them. His eyes darkened as he watched her face, saw the pain she couldn't hide, and she hurried on before he made it worse.

"While I'm waltzing through the stews of treacherous moonies, what happens to you?"

"I go free." A wry smile, but no twinkle in those eyes. "Without your testimony, they have no evidence."

"But every moonie will think me a victim, and every dirtsider think you a wronged innocent. That puts us both at risk."

"We need that proof—and you will be kept safe. Gilda has promised that."

She suddenly stood up, unable to go on.

"All right," she promised, hugging her arms tight to her body.

He stood as well. "Thank you. Please, sit down again and I'll tell you the full plan…"

"No, no. I can get it from Gilda and Gof." She stepped back. "Squad leader. Let's go." She couldn't stay a moment longer, but his voice stopped her as she gained the door.

"I'm sorry. I just…I cannot fight another war for Hathe."

She turned and saw the stark white of his face. He took another breath, took a step back.

"And Rheia. Once the proof is revealed…" A hand reached out, then dropped. "Once it goes public, we won't be able to keep your father's name out of it. Not when everything is revealed."

She swung around at that, marched away from him and up the long, long hall to the door at the end. Her troop of dirtsider guards hurried after her as she reached the obstacle of a shut door at the end, slammed a hand on the control panel, and escaped through it, the pain curling its talons tighter and tighter.

Did he think she hadn't realized that?

CHAPTER FOURTEEN

Jacquel watched her leave, silently mouthing every curse he knew. A slap of flesh against the wall at the end of the row, and the outer door whooshed open to her command. A farewell salute from the squad leader, disappointment clear on her face. The beat of retreating footsteps, another slap echoing in bitter mockery against the hard prison walls, and the outer door banged shut in a resounding finale.

She was gone.

A squat figure emerged from the shadows at the other end of the long hallway. Numerous cells opened off it, but Jacquel's was the only one occupied. A dubious sign of his importance.

"Well done, young man," said Gof deln Crantz.

"You think so?"

Gof humphed back, his mouth a mixture of smug grin and scowl. "She didn't look happy."

She deserved to be.

"This better be worth it," he said.

That unreliable smile on his commander's face again. "Once the vids get a glimpse of her face and realize she's being smuggled out of here by council troops? Followed by your exit, looking your most charming self? Oh, yes, that will bring out our scum."

Deln Crantz was right. His ramshackle plan was their best option, and the only way Jacquel knew to make his world one again—and safe for Rheia. Someone was behind the group of dirtsiders who had captured them both. It was too well organized for that group of ragtag leftovers. Someone, and he bet it was a senate moonie, was deliberately stirring up the disaffected among the dirtsiders. Trouble they didn't need. The Senate and the radical elements of the media needed little encouragement to start demanding action be taken against anyone threatening the new order on Hathe.

"So when do I get out of here?"

"Right now." Gof signaled, and Jacquel's faithful squad marched through the far door, in full protective ceremonial gear. "And by the front door this time. With all the leaks we've dropped, that crowd of vid reporters out there should be at riot pitch by now."

Jacquel would have groaned out loud except for the satisfaction it would afford Gof. He managed to survive the formalities of prison release, but emerging through the doorway to a screaming crowd of reporters all hungry for their bite of publicity nearly had him scurrying back inside. Only the sardonic cast of Gof's face and the memory of Rheia's hand slapping the door kept his back straight and his course forwards.

He shoved a smile on his face, paused for effect at the top of the steps and hoped by all the Pillars he would someday be rewarded for this charade. "You owe me," he muttered to Gof, before stepping forward to greet the predators waiting below.

Rheia saw it all on the vids that night, punishing herself with the full, multi-senses mode from the live drone feeds closest to Jacquel. The noise and claustrophobia of the packed street, the screams of abuse and support, the scuffles and the smell of bloodletting in the crowd, quickly swamped by the Security forces. Jacquel carried himself through it all. The familiar tricks were there. The warm smiles of welcome, the elegantly high carriage of his head, denying the limp that still dogged him, the cool air of authority he'd worn when he'd marched down this same avenue in the victory parade.

But Rheia had seen him hurt, brought low and injured. She recognized the small signs that said only pride and training carried him through this. The sudden, barely seen tensing as the crowd shoved in on his protective circle of guards, the flinch as a flying clod of dirt caught him on the cheek. A sudden stare at the thrower and flick of his head brought the security forces down on the agitator before the crowd got even more out of control.

And always those eyes of his scanned the crowds. She would have to learn the Resistance codes, though she suspected the ones he used today were unique to his troop. His own people surrounded him, Ras at the fore. She didn't see any commands but had studied this man with his troop since she'd joined their mission and it was Jacquel des Trurains in charge out there.

She paced the length of her new rooms. Not her old apartment. Too dangerous still, said Myron ven Raden, and her gut agreed. Not Gilda an Rathman's elegant home that had been like a prison either. This place belonged to her own department. She was back in moonie territory; safer with the open hostility to her from many dirtsiders and a statement of loyalty to her side of the divide.

No.

The denial was automatic. Moonie, dirtsider. Names she refused.

She was Hathian.

A ping on her door. "Identify," she ordered the security system. A holo formed by the door, with the public record filing beneath.

Gof deln Crantz. Of course. The smiling web-weaver at the center of all these strands of intrigue. She scowled and slapped the door open.

"What do you want?"

He stepped into the apartment, despite having no invitation, locked the door after him and glanced at her viewer. "You've seen the coverage. Good."

"Jacquel? Is he safe?"

That unreliable smile deepened worryingly. "Of course, madame. Security has him under full protection."

"It was Security who *arrested* him."

At last, a break in the smiling exterior. "A matter that has been attended to." A betrayal she doubted Gof or the rest of Jacquel's troop would ever forgive.

"And the dirtsiders who first captured us? You do know they must have been in league with the moonie Security troops."

"Knowingly or otherwise. Yes, we are fully aware of it, and it is also being attended to."

Which meant what, exactly? That they'd been shipped away from the City, somewhere they couldn't cause trouble but were being looked after? Dirtsiders were famously prone to close ranks.

"His own troop are in control," snapped Gof, "and I personally ran their security checks again. No vermin will get near him—of either side."

"So pleased to hear it," she said caustically.

"He is safe and back working with Security."

"As if nothing happened?" The gall of the man was truly astounding. "You think the vid channels will wear that?"

"They will, when the next minor scandal hits."

Unfortunately, that was too true for most scandals. But not all.

"Hathe Central, The Enquirer, Rastus pen Cuthmin?"

"Of course not," said Gof, "but even they cannot spread a story when there's nothing to support it."

"The Senate will, if what you suspect is true."

"I'm counting on it." Rheia could almost see the man metaphorically rubbing his hands in glee.

"And Jacquel?" Rheia couldn't contain her fear any longer. "How badly hurt is he?"

"Given what those amateur dirtsider thugs and the so-called Security troopers did to him? Always knew there was a stiff-backed stubbornness in the boy. It was the only thing that got him across that plaza today."

"How bad?" Her voice cracked, a whisper of sound that must tell deln Crantz too much.

"He's in the military hospital under the care of ex-Resistance staff and hating every minute of it." A pleased chuckle. "The interested vid channels have been granted full access to his records and he's agreed to talk to a select few."

She choked. "He can manage that?"

"For brief spells." A scowl. "His doctors are in charge."

Thank the Pillars. "So which channels asked for access?" she finally thought to ask.

"Hathe Central, The Enquirer, Pen Cuthmin Today."

Now she knew he was rubbing those mental hands in glee. She sighed, stepped back and waved a hand at the seating area. "I guess you better sit down and give me the whole plan."

It was breathtaking, though she wasn't sure whether it was breathtakingly brilliant or crazy.

"This whole thing relies on their believing that I can be blackmailed? My father's name is out there now, thanks to our first kidnappers. What can they offer me against that?"

"Protection. You already know some streets are not safe for you. But while your name is out among the dirtsiders, it's not yet out among the moonie population. A rare benefit of the split in Hathe—dirtsiders don't talk to moonies about the war, not any more. Any moonie who knows who you are must be in league with the people manipulating that band of naive idiots who first kidnapped you. Moonies who will promise you safety by keeping the secret of your name—in return for you supporting them when they demand it, with no questions asked." Deln Crantz had the grace to lift his hands in apology. "They are people who value power, which means they only feel safe if they have control. They need their people to be dependent on them."

"I will side with them, just to protect my own hide? They believe I fear and hate dirtsiders that much?"

"That's what they'll be telling their supporters, and we're not about to do anything to show them they're wrong. Not till we have them where we want them."

She shot up. "I need a drink."

"Thank you, that would be pleasant."

His voice followed her as her hands made busy with drinks and snacks, flatly giving her the details.

"So I disappear into the moonie side as a disgruntled and wronged innocent."

"It's the only way to lure these muckrakers in. Once you break all connections to Jacquel…"

An unexpected shock jolted her. "No contact?"

"No, no reason for it. And every reason against."

"I had thought…had assumed…Won't he be my contact?"

Gof shook his head. "Too risky. You need to be seen to be at odds with him." He leaned back, crossing his feet. "It's nothing to what we endured for those five years."

There it was. The divide that would always separate them. Dirtsiders could never forget those years, and moonies would never fully understand what it had cost them to stay on-planet and be treated as less than nothing. The Terrans had much to answer for—but so did Hathe's rulers.

The Great Plan, they had called it, but look how it turned out. A way to win what looked like a hopeless battle and save as many Hathian lives as possible. Rheia thought that too, in those heady days when her university was part of the planning. Then the Terrans landed and reality crashed down on those left on Hathe.

She needed this over.

"In brief, then, I retreat to my old place in the department and shun all contact with dirtsider communities. They know who I am." That hurt. Who she was meant so much to her. No one insulted her father. Not to her face.

Gof nodded. "It's why you avoid us."

She smiled bitterly. "I hide out at work until this moonie group contacts me." That bit, she really didn't like.

"You're a wounded victim," said Gof firmly. "Fake it. You were a diplomat. This is no different."

Didn't mean she had to like it. "How long do you think it will take?"

Gof eyed the snacks she put out, one hand hovering first over the plate of granda fruits, then the chorodin tarts before settling on the slices of roasted fremen, munching each one down with every sign of relish. "Hard to say. Months, no more than a year." His head bent back to the delights of the table.

"Year?"

His hand plunged down, seized on the plate of fremen. He picked up another slice, opened his mouth and munched it down with a long moan. "Exquisite."

"A year," she prompted, taking the seat furthest from him.

"Oh yes, I should think so."

"You want me to go undercover for months? To have no deliberate contact with any dirtsider?"

Gof's hand reached out again, hovering between two dishes then swooped down on the Pathean pastries. "You set a fine table, madame. I can see how you were such a success in the diplomatic service." He crunched down, odd flakes of pastry escaping his lips as his eyes closed momentarily. "No dirtsider contact? Of course not. It's not possible. Out and about, daily business under DIA protection, yes. But socializing, whose company you seek out and enjoy…" Another munch. "Moonies. Definitely moonies."

She stared at the rapidly disappearing plates of food and felt absolutely no inclination to join him. "I continue as I did for the last five years."

Gof stopped eating, sat back and looked at her with pity in his eyes, Pillars blast him. "I am sorry, madame. You are too good at your work, an acute observer of those whom you must influence. Your reports from the short time you managed to spend on the plateau will be very useful. It's a talent we cannot waste."

There wasn't much to be said after that. Gof seized one more pastry, rose and bowed his acknowledgement. "Myron ven Raden will liaise with you." Then he paused before opening the door. "Your com, if you please."

She saw no reason to refuse, reached out and touched her wrist unit directly to his. A red line spasmed between them. The highest security transfer. "If you need us…" *Or don't trust your department,* said a flick of his eyes at the com units.

An emergency link. A necessary backup—if she trusted Gof's Security forces. They still included the troop that had arrested Jacquel des Trurains. If their enemies could penetrate the tight bonds of the Security forces, rich with ex-Resistance fighters, what sector was safe from their influence?

She palmed the door control as it closed behind Gof, switching the entry codes and locking it securely against him. Then checked her com unit, angling the visual display panel to avoid any watching sensors. The emergency code was one word only.

Bupha.

Her dead little brother's nickname.

Jacquel glared at his commander, unable to believe the message that had been waiting in his desk queue when he escaped from hospital. That nightmare parade across the plaza had been bad enough. The dirtsider half wanted to carry him shoulder high; the other half wanted to rip his head off.

"No contact, nothing? Leave her alone in that nest of vermin?"

Gof set his hands on his office desk, waiting with that infernal patience of his until Jacquel gave up and threw himself into the opposite chair.

"She's returned to her duties with her own department, to carry on the work she has so admirably managed for the last few years."

"Laid out as bait for a pile of bloodsucking traitors."

Gof shrugged, not denying it. "Ven Raden has her under full surveillance at all times, as do my Security forces."

"Trusted ones?"

"I've run the files of every member of the team. You're free to do the same," said Gof.

Jacquel stretched out his arm. "Pass me your com and transmit the links."

Gof reached across to touch coms and sent across the files. "I've also given Madame asn Postrova an emergency code, set to my coms only. You want me to keep you posted if she uses it?"

"Yes." And no order would stop him if she asked for help.

"Remember, one contact and you blow her cover sky-high."

"I'll do whatever keeps her safe," promised Jacquel. He desperately needed to be able to watch over her but would not put her at risk. "You *will* keep her safe."

"On my oath."

Gof put out a hand, and Jacquel reached across and grasped his arm. "I'll hold you to that."

A rare smile lit Gof's face, one that was genuine. "Madame asn Postrova seems to have become important to you."

A shake of his head. "She's in danger because of me." That should be answer enough, and it was true. If not the whole truth. And when he knew what that was, he might admit it—but not to Gof deln Crantz.

"What now?" he said instead. "More rubbish duties for me?"

A wide grin lit his commander's face. "No, that pleasure has been given to another hero. You go out and celebrate, young man. Party, enjoy your freedom, join in with the crowds in the capital. Go and have fun after your dreadful prison ordeal." He folded his hands across his stomach, that unreliable twinkle back in his eyes. "That's an order."

Jacquel could only groan.

"Enough, Cap. Time to go home."

Jacquel cracked open an eye. His gut jerked him back to life, a spasm of filth that left him gasping and loosing a string of curses.

"Past enough, Cap," was Ras's dry comment. His face loomed close, peered into his eyes, then retreated. "Mairfin. Definitely past enough. Didn't think to see you stoop to taking that poison."

"Keeps me inebriated but conscious." His head hurt, every joint in his body creaked and he wanted nothing more than to fall into a bed—alone—and collapse into a coma until this whole nightmare was over. "Can't…"

"…talk? I know. Mairfin. First choice of spies, diplomats and their victims. Looks like you're the last one tonight."

He cracked the other eye open. Or tried to but gave up when the swollen lids stuck together.

"And what caused that shiner?"

Jacquel touched a finger to the eye and flinched. "Someone said something."

"Aahhh."

Then silence, the kind he hated.

"There was a vid on."

Another long silence.

"They booed her," he said, the fury of it still clutching him.

"And you won't have a thing to do with her. Your idea?"

"Don't be stupid." Jacquel was past niceties. "Deln Crantz is pulling the strings."

"And you're dancing to 'em. Not like you."

Jacquel leaned back in his chair. It creaked alarmingly as he cracked open his sound eye again.

Ras took the chair beside him, waiting for an answer. Not that Jacquel had one for him. The room swung around and he levered himself up, trying to sort out the pieces of the puzzle that were the unfamiliar place. A layer of grime coated every surface and dull light filtered through the cracks in the wall.

Night? He squinted, started to shake his head then stopped, cursing again.

"It's near dawn," Ras supplied helpfully.

"Aah." He scanned the room. "Weren't there more people here?"

"Gone." Ras shoved an arm under his shoulder, elbowing him upward. "Time you were too, Cap."

Jacquel lurched forward. Noooo. His entire stomach contents rose up to meet the floor this time. He fell back into the chair, embarrassment pummeling him. Ras ignored it, tucking his shoulder tight under Jacquel's and helping him up again. Between them, they managed a slow crash toward the exit, one ugly step after another.

"How long you planning to keep this up, Cap?"

He considered that one. There was a reason behind all this; he did remember that. "Can't talk about it."

It was the only clear thought in his head. Don't speak. Don't talk about why he was there, what lay behind it. Don't talk, ever, about Rheia asn Postrova.

Don't talk, or she was in danger.

Yet tonight he'd broken that. A vid had been playing overhead. Talking voices, holos of news figures. His release from prison, and the crowd around him had cheered uproariously.

Dirtsiders all. His people. Heroes of the Resistance, now second class in their own home. Even those like him, sons and daughters of the top political ranks, weren't immune.

That's who he partied with. The once leading lights of their generation. Many decorated for their war efforts, others among the Unsung. All heroes.

All missing out in this new world. Without his military rank and position in the Security forces, he'd be the same.

Then a vid came on. A delegate of officials ironing out a new deal with the committee of allies now running Earth. Those helping get that cursed planet the help it needed so never again would it try to take it by force. *She* was one of them. A back-room, quietly-dressed, anonymous suit, exactly what she wasn't. But then the vidbots zoomed into the silent face at the back of the crowd.

"The former diplomat, and rumored ex-ranger, was implicated in the recent incident involving Colonel des Trurains, son of Professor Gauvan de Trurains."

The sensors had zoned closer on her, the holo showing each strained line, each hollowed out edge to that lovely face. The crowd erupted. Vicious boos echoed off the walls, and that's when he'd exploded.

She didn't deserve that.

"When do you think she last laughed?"

Ras stumbled. "Who?"

"Rheia. Madame asn Postrova." Who else would he mean? "She was so quiet. They've shut her up in a box."

A crack of laughter from Ras. "And you want to let her out? Yeah, I can see why. She is a stunner."

His fist was swinging before he realized it. Fortunately, the rest of him wasn't working as well. Ras easily blocked it with a hard chop that left his hand numb, all while staring at him in shock.

Jacquel felt the same. He'd just tried to punch the man he trusted most of all those left on Hathe. "Um. Guess 'sorry' doesn't cut it."

Ras slowly dropped his fist and waited for Jacquel to rub the life back into his hand with a stunned look on his face. Then the corners of his mouth suddenly lifted.

"Looks like it's me owing that 'sorry.' Didn't know it was like that."

Jacquel blustered, gone the glib tongue that usually sprung to his aid.

"She's a colleague," he managed to mutter.

"Yeah. If you say so."

Ras swung his arm around Jacquel again and help him onward, lurching with him toward a skimmer parked discreetly around the corner. Then home, up the shafts and into Jacquel's City apartment, where he helped Jacquel shed his dress outers and gave a quick push that had him keeling over onto the bed.

"I've coded in the security system to get help if you vomit or show medical warning signs."

A wave of his hand was all that Jacquel could manage.

Ras turned to go but halted in the doorway. "Reckon you've done enough drowning your sorrows. Time to move on to the next stage of the commander's plans. Much more, and it'll start looking real even to those of us who know you better."

Jacquel peered up at him. Ras looked like he was going to say more. But then he lifted his hand, half in farewell and half as if batting something away, swung around and left. The front door whooshed closed and the beeping patter told of the security code engaging.

He slumped back and stared at the empty ceiling. He'd had it colorized with the skies over the plateau on a rare clear day, the artist brilliantly capturing that endless expanse of crystalline blue found only there. But nothing lived on his ceiling, nothing spoke of the drama, the terror and exhilaration of the living sky of the plateau that was Rheia's home country.

Why did Ras apologize? Rheia was…what?

A question for which the inanimate ceiling gave no answer.

CHAPTER FIFTEEN

"Anhuilla wants to see you."

His father's voice smashed through his drug-hazed sleep. Though sleep wasn't the right word. He'd shut his eyes and surrendered to the darkness, but true sleep evaded him.

Jacquel groaned and elbowed his way up from the depths of his bed.

"Make yourself presentable. I've told her you'll be there this afternoon."

"Can't," he mumbled.

His father had *that look* on his face. "You can, and you will. You haven't visited home since you got out of…that place. I checked with deln Crantz. You have no business scheduled."

Haven't had for some time, lay unspoken between them. But his commander wouldn't tell his father the reason why. That Jacquel had never stopped working was known only to a select few, and his establishment father was certainly not in the loop. Meaning that he had no credible excuses now.

"Is she at home or work today?"

His father's mouth tightened. "It's her day off." Which Jacquel should have known if he hadn't been avoiding the family home for weeks "She's expecting you for afternoon tiffin."

A small reprieve then. There would be others there: his half-sisters and a smattering of colleagues, friends, and her latest social discard.

His stepmother was one of the good ones. Those who recognized that the new Hathe was vastly different from the old. For a while, it had been covered over by the jubilation after victory; the glorious parades and medal ceremonies. Jacquel had shoved his own medals into the deepest corner of a storage locker, to be dragged out only when forced to wear them by his commander to impress some useful bigwig. Then came Marthe's trial and exile. The tide of feeling against her Terran husband and the shock at her marriage created a temporary veneer of unity.

But through it all, the knocks of the dispossessed still landed on his front door. His father finally put a stop to them. "It's upsetting your stepmother," he said, and by mutual agreement Jacquel moved back to his City apartment.

But that hadn't stopped his step-mama's efforts. A constant stream of "old friends," as she called them, made their appearance at her ceremonial tiffins, along with various company and government officials who Anhuilla had strong-armed into helping her friends to recover their lives.

It was old-fashioned, low-key, and his charming and quite without scruples step-mama was extraordinarily effective. She had grown as beloved among the dirtsiders for her social work as she was by the moonies for her fierce protection of the central library.

Jacquel palmed the front door, wondering whom she'd wrangled to appear today. He strode down the hall to her parlor with a sudden lift in spirits. A knock on her door in their established family pattern, followed by the an equally old call to "Come on in, Jaca. Since when have you asked permission?"

He walked in, smiled at his stepmother in her favorite chair and glanced around the room, ready to bow and make himself known to the others.

There was no one.

He straightened, the smile wiped from his face.

"I thought it was time we talked," she said.

The last time his stepmother had looked at him like that was the day she'd told him of Bendin asn Castre's death. He'd already heard about it of course, but that look of fear and desperate pity on Anhuilla's beloved face was the same as now.

He sat carefully on the least comfortable chair, the one opposite her, needing the hard support of the rigid frame, and waited. His stepmother operated on her own time frame.

She clutched her fingers, then leaned forward, grabbing at the pot handle. "Tiffeas?"

He hated the stuff, but her knuckles were nearly white on the handle. "Yes, please."

She took care in pouring, giving all her attention to the timeless ritual. Thin brown liquid, filling the cup to precisely halfway, a careful dribble of scalding water to top it up—she remembered what he thought of the drink then. Even watered down it was barely tolerable. Then finished with a sliver of parma leaf for its pungent spice and a mere dusting of sweet cafka powder. For looks as much as taste. He disliked anything oversweet.

A quick check, the cafka spoon set down on one side of the tray, and she passed the cup over to him. The smallest tinkle of the metal spoon against the tray betrayed her but the tremor in her hand was otherwise barely noticeable.

"Thank you."

So polite, so meaningless.

He took a requisite sip, then placed the cup carefully on the table by his seat.

"Have you eaten?" Anhuilla waved a hand at the collection of dishes on the side table. All his favorites.

"Not now, thank you."

"Oh."

She leaned very slightly forward and carefully poured her own tiffeas, before fussing over her selection from the plates, placing one item, then glanced at him and placed a second on the fragile best-occasion tiffeas dish.

Jacquel shoved himself upright in his chair, began to stand, till the flinch on her face cut through him and he sat back down again.

"What is it?" he said, gentler than the churning fear inside him urged.

His beloved stepmother, who had been listening to all his confidences since he was a small boy, set her plate carefully aside, ducked her head, then lifted it again with such sorrow in her eyes. "You are well?"

"Well enough. Deln Crantz is keeping me busy."

"That's not what we heard." Her hand shot up to cover her mouth.

"Why? What have you heard?"

She closed her eyes, then opened them, took a breath and the passing wave of her hand encompassed him from head to toe.

"Was it Marthe's trial, the changes at the end of the war? That nothing is as you imagined it would be?" She swallowed. "Your father?"

He stared at her.

"Something's wrong. Don't tell me it isn't. There are programs, you know."

He opened his mouth.

She looked the same, looked like his calm, wonderful, *sensible* step-mama. "Programs?"

"Yes, for, you know…"

"Those of us who can't cope? Unreliable, no longer fit for this world? Dirtsiders?"

She shook her head. "No, it's not like that. It isn't." He wanted to stop her words but didn't know how. She ploughed on. "There's nothing for you to be ashamed of. What you went through. You're a *hero*."

Who was she trying to convince?

"Are you using?" she finally said, and the shock of it roared through him.

"Is that what you think?"

A tear escaped her eye and he hated himself more.

"Using what, Mama?"

That's who she was to him, always. The only mother he'd ever known. But this time, she said nothing to take away the hurt. "Are you?" she said.

Her eyes traced his face, stared closely into his eyes and he had no doubt she saw the same as he did every day in his mirror. The suspicious blankness of pupil, the hollow shell of his cheeks and the sallow washed-out skin that spoke of too many hours away from sunshine haunting the dark halls of the night.

At least she was spared the bruising that mottled his torso courtesy of various brash moonies.

Yes, she was right to ask her questions but the suspicion that lay behind them?

"You can still trust me."

"Can I?"

"You can." That was all he could say. He was under orders. She should understand that.

The tears shimmering in her eyes said otherwise.

He ploughed on. "My sisters? They are well?"

She nodded, hands clutching her cup. "Yes, yes."

He glanced at the door, having expected them both to come barreling through it by now.

"They're away," Anhuilla said hastily. "Staying at Aunt Clothilde's for the day."

"Oh. I'll have to catch up another day."

"Yes, yes." Her hand waved vaguely. "Although they are both very busy these days. It's their age. Friends, you see…"

Yes, he suddenly saw exactly. Ashes in his mouth, he pushed the cup away from him. "I have to go," he said. "Thank you for this." He nodded at the cup and plates. "For now, I am needed elsewhere," he added, in the nearest to deliberate cruelty he had ever inflicted on her.

Hating himself and not trusting himself to say more, he rose, muttered something, he couldn't say what, and escaped.

The lasting image: a teardrop glistening on each of his stepmother's cheeks. An image that stayed with him through the raucous goings-on, the vapid nothings of the mind-numbing weeks and months that followed. And once every few days he would slip in the concealed side door entrance to make his way to Gof's office to give his report.

"I'm getting nowhere." Gof barely changed position. Had he heard Jacquel? He shot out of his chair, paced in front of his commander's desk, fingers jabbing at him with each footstep. "There was a riot in the Quarter last weekend. No real reason."

Gof raised an eyebrow.

"Nothing out of the ordinary." Jacquel's finger stabbed the air, thrusting toward his commander. "Just a group of highly capable, well-trained Resistance heroes celebrating that one of them had managed to find a job." A wall blocked his pacing. He swung around again. "As *janitor* in an office block."

A wall blocked him again. He swung about.

"The man is a fully qualified service mechanic. He kept all the ventilation systems going in the Citadel bases on a shoestring—in the time wedged between the laboring jobs the Terrans forced onto him. He's a drekking genius when it comes to servicing machinery. Yet he's now emptying garbage bots in a building he tells me he could get running at twice the efficiency for half the cost."

A wall, always a wall in his way. He smacked a hand against it and swung around to face his commander.

"Only they already have a service engineer. Qualified barely a month before the end of the war, but a moonie cousin of the man in charge of the maintenance company. Both Mathian moonies."

Gof pleated his hands together. "Your friend won't starve and he has paid work."

"Oh yes, he has that."

"And the celebration?"

Jacquel slammed a hand against the other wall—they were getting closer together now, or his strides were increasing in speed. "A few drinks and a laugh. Happy dirtsiders. Imagine that." He glared at his commander, though the man had done nothing. "How dare they."

"Someone objected?"

Jacquel came to a halt. "Objected? Beat them to a pulp. A feat the scum only managed by attacking them from behind as the cowards they are, then getting the local security patrol to charge the dirtsiders with *causing a public nuisance*—who then threw them into jail to cool off."

Gof palmed his com but was waved off by Jacquel. "Ras has already set the legal team onto it. They're in Medical now."

Gof changed the call pattern. "Mathis, there is a party in need of your attention. Contact Ras den Koprorth for the details." He signed off and looked up at Jacquel.

Jacquel nodded at the com. "Mathis an Begum?" The head of the prosecutions department at the local judiciary and younger brother of an old friend.

"Your moonie friends will be in custody very soon. The Council is taking these issues seriously, you know."

Jacquel grunted.

Gof's mouth twisted. "They are, but the news is having trouble filtering down to street level patrollers. We're working on that, and I trust you have some information to help us."

But Jacquel didn't. Oh, he knew the obvious suspects, the open abusers and supporters of moonie domination.

But who was pulling the strings in the background? That was hidden behind murky layers of blind alleys and dead ends, and increasingly he doubted he could penetrate them. For that, they needed Rheia.

No. Too dangerous. He had to find the truth before she put herself at more risk.

He'd lost too many already.

More days, more useless nights passed in a blur. His only success: being there as witness as the violence escalated. Moonies beating up dirtsiders, fed-up dirtsiders like Phillipos athns Kronkist refusing to wait longer for justice and the world they had been promised, and starting their own mini riots. Chaos increasing while he did nothing more than party.

He increased the mairfin dosage so he could prove he was taking something. To look as despairing as all the other dirtsiders partying with him.

Another club and a familiar face. But this one was wrong. "Jochin, aren't you supposed to be at work?"

A shrug and that look of studied indifference he was coming to hate. "They found someone else."

He didn't ask who. He'd heard those words too often. "So what now?"

But the man raised a hand. "Don't. I won't be one of your charity cases. Not yet," he added bitterly. "Ask me again when I'm starving and at death's door."

Jacquel stepped back. "I wasn't—."

"You were." The man crashed his drink on the table. "Take a seat and have a drink—one I'm paying for, not you."

Because one day, you'll be the one sitting here with no options left. Except he wouldn't be. Not given his privileged birth.

"I'm working; you're not. This is on my credit."

The man nodded. "Working for now. Until they get rid of Gof and his cohorts on Council."

"Not going to happen."

The man slugged his drink down, deep and long, and slammed the mug on the table. "Yeah?"

Jacquel's inner gut sense sparked into life. "You've heard something."

"Sit and let me buy you a drink first." The man's eyebrows squeezed tight and he glared in challenge. Jacquel met it, frowning directly back, then shrugged.

"As you ask so politely. "He thumped into the opposite seat, taking care to look put upon, and gave his order to the control panel, scowling as Jochin input his credit code

"Thanks," Jacquel said grudgingly as the tray arrived, lifting the mug in a toast and slugging it down as deeply as Jochin. "So, this office block you worked in…."

The other man gave the darkest of smiles, leaned closer, and started to talk.

The names were familiar, too familiar. The senator whose son he'd pilloried. He'd expected that one, but the others, the quiet ones. The ones with connections known to only a few.

"You could take the names before Council."

The man shrugged. "Yeah, I could—for what it's worth."

Jacquel's inner alarms roared up to screaming level. "Not every moonies has forgotten this planet belongs to all of us," he said carefully.

"Yeah, well some of us shed actual blood. False tears of sorrow aren't the same."

The man moved off soon after, looking like he thought he'd said way too much. And he had. Jacquel put in an urgent call to deln Crantz. This went higher than they'd guessed. Though he wasn't surprised. The political loyalties of the Council were balanced on a knife-edge.

He looked at the door where the man had disappeared, swallowed up by the streams of street traffic. *Don't give up, not yet.* But who Jacquel addressed, he daren't consider. A determined swallow, a nod at the bartender, and a barely perceptible flurry of hand signals between old Resistance colleagues. *Keep an eye on Jochin.* Then an answering *Yes.*

Hathe Central knew the official Resistance com codes and body signals, but in five years the field staff had changed the ones used on the ground. Only a former agent could have read all the quick messages passing through the crowd, the secret language of the Resistance second nature to all these men and women who had used it as often as speech during the war. After his silent order to the bartender, Jacquel retreated to a corner, leaned back against the wall, and simply watched the room.

Sullen, a bit drunk maybe, drugged certainly. That's how he'd appear to any who bumped into him, but after a while few noticed him, letting him merge into the background, observing the quick change of finger, shoulder, the set of a tunic, the silent signals that told of a growing anger. Or more dangerously, the sloth of despair.

They were good at covering their feelings, these ex-Resistance folks. Years of pretense had made the carefully blank face of a peasant second nature to all of them.

But here and there, he saw the baffled fury on the face of a teenager who had grown up on a promise of paradise after the fall of the Terrans, or bleak sorrow as a woman turned to talk to someone who wasn't there, and never would be again.

But none of that cut to the bone as much as the children in the streets the next day. He was in full military dress for an official meeting, belying the stinging pain of his reddened eyeballs and pounding head. No sooner had he set out from his home block than a crowd of ragged children surrounded him.

"Carry your bags, sir?"

"Two credits to guide you?"

"Oz, get out yor. I was here first. This one's mine." That from a big boy at the back. Sharp elbowed and jostling forward.

All said in Terran.

"Speak Hathian," said Jacquel, too harshly as the faces of the boys caved inwards and they huddled back. The elder tugged his forelock and hustled the young ones behind him.

"Oh, Pillars." Jacquel spread his hands out wide, displaying his lack of visible weapons. "I'm not going to hurt you. You don't have to…" Beg any more, was what he was going to say. But his voice was lost in the knife thrust of agony lodging in his chest. "Go home to your parents. You are free now," he ended wearily, knowing it for a lie as much as the children. The leader gave him a hand gesture a child of that age should never have seen, they all whooped with laughter then swept off. Discarding useless prey and flocking to their next target.

Jacquel had to watch, a strong streak of protectionism demanding he march the young delinquents home where they belonged. The pack of them poured around a smartly-dressed woman on the pedway.

"Carry your bag, lady?"

She clutched it tight. "Shoo, get away." She flapped her hands and they obediently hung back, a picture of injured innocence.

"Aww lady, just two credits. We only want to help."

A pitiful wail from the youngest, most angelic of the brats. "I'm starving." The child looked well-fed to Jacquel. He knew what real hunger looked like, as did these children.

The woman scrabbled in her bag, pulled out a cheap flash-drive com, the kind carried for casual, untraceable purchases. "One credit to that child only." She touched the pad to the crying boy's arm com, then snatched it back, thrusting it into the capacious depths of her expensive bag, and hurried on as if chased by demons.

"Horrid little vermin," she muttered as she passed him. "Somebody ought to *do* something about these dirtsiders."

Jacquel thrust his hands behind him, fists clenched tight together and grateful for the shading pitch of his regulation hat. Anything that stopped him telling this woman exactly what he thought of her.

As for the wayward boys…his superiors could drekking well wait. A set of very explicit instructions travelled over the Resistance com network that all dirtsiders kept logged into.

These boys clearly among them. They stopped dead, swung around and stared at him with mouths stuck open.

Home, now, he signaled to them.

Maybe they would have argued, but all around them others had also heard Jacquel's message. A man fixing a street bot, a shopkeeper wandering out of his doorway, a pedestrian strolling down the street who was ex-patrol by the looks of the eye he cast over the bunch of wayward youths.

We've got this, said the coded message in Jacquel's ear. *Thank you for your help, sir.*

Jacquel lifted his hand in acknowledgement and moved on. Heartsick didn't begin to describe how he felt.

They were children; the future of Hathe.

No moonie put them in the gutter.

Jacquel wandered for hours after that, not knowing where he was going. Not surprised with where he wound up. The City cemetery, fourth row down. The section for the fallen heroes, in the plot reserved for the pilots who had held the Terrans off-planet while Hathe desperately organized their outrageous defense. A suicide flight that had been. Puny little ships flown by pilots who had never fired a phaser in anger, pitted against a Terran armada of heavy-duty interplanetary warships.

The name on the tombstone said Pilot Officer B asn Castre, gold class.

"Hey Bendin."

He knelt, touched the carefully tended plants surrounding the sarcophagus and wished anew that his friend still lay in the hastily dug rawness of his wartime grave. Basic, but so much more honest than these pompous, ordered rows of tombs surrounded by tasteful and precisely tended gardens. Each had a plaque on the front inscribed with a citation detailing the fallen hero's actions. Jacquel's fingers traced the now familiar words. He could almost hear his friend's crack of laughter at the weighty tones.

"Have some dignity, mano. You are a decorated hero."

...selflessly faced the enemy in a valiant act of great sacrifice...

Nothing in the words captured the terror, the shock and the sheer insanity of those days. He remembered Bendin's face as he stepped aboard his craft that day. His friend had known exactly what he faced.

"Keep her safe," Bendin had made him promise. "Keep my sister safe."

One more promise Jacquel had failed to keep. And now he had sent another woman into battle. Another woman he loved.

Strangely, the words didn't shock him. Rheia asn Forvrad answered the question lurking inside him; the one that left him feeling rudderless and bereft of meaning or place. The one not even Marthe could answer

Love. The word felt good, not terrifying. He was in love with Rheia asn Postrova/Forvrad, and the jittering cogs inside him settled into place in a way they hadn't for a very long time.

Except what had he done to her? To himself? Loved her, then betrayed her with this scheme of Gof's.

He stood up. No more. The Council and Hathe owed him, and it was time they paid up.

CHAPTER SIXTEEN

Rheia woke to another empty morning. As empty as all the other mornings since walking out of that cell block and finding out she was no more than a tool in Jacquel des Trurains's campaign to restore Hathe.

It should have made her angry, except that he was right. Hathe must be reunited. Too many had sacrificed too much to let a fit of self-pity by her put that at risk—and Jacquel des Trurains had never been for her. She'd been a fool to imagine he could be. Even if she matched him in background and wealth, she couldn't compete with a planet—or his past. He was already pledged, and not to her.

All she could do was make sure he succeeded.

At least this crazy scheme came with a good room. She could almost be back in the days of the Terran occupation, waking in yet another off-planet hotel to face a day of dissembling diplomacy. A marked step up from the Security barracks she'd been shoved into for the weeks of training deln Crantz had decreed she needed before starting this crazy masquerade. Now, the real task began. As a cover, her departmental boss had set her up with a high-powered job in the DIA trade and export section.

"It suits Security's purposes, and your connections from your previous missions are very helpful to us there. A bonus, you might say."

The wide grin on his face had been suspiciously angelic. Which told her two things: he knew everything about the mission from deln Crantz, and relished to the full twisting the Security boss's schemes to the DIA's advantage.

She got the distinct impression this was a game Myron ven Raden and Gof deln Crantz had played for many years. Harmless enough, unless you happened to be the latest toy caught in the middle. It changed nothing. She would play their game; had to, if her work was to have any meaning. She thrust off the covers, dialed the couch back to wake mode, and rolled slowly out of bed.

"Dress: business casual. One meeting. Three meet-and-greets."

Her high spec wardrobe program's suggested range of outfits materialized in holo form beside the bed. The first three, she waved away, then paused on the fourth.

"Change the color. Dark, harsh tones." She was in a mood to challenge her hosts today. A twist of her hand, and the holovision scrolled slowly around.

"Lift the hemline." She pointed a finger to chop it back to her preferred length.

A cleansing, then she stepped out of the bathroom unit to see her selected outfit emerging from the state-of-the-art wardrobe, a big step up from the basic storage unit in her last apartment. Now it presented her with a full tunic and underdress in the latest cut. Pristine and shiny new, ready for her to be poured into and emerge properly coifed and uniformed. She peered at her image in the holo-mirror, setting it to revolve slowly. A precisely marshaled bureaucrat stared back.

Professional, unflappable, powerful and determined. The required image for her current position, with no hint of a ranger background or, Pillars forbid, any stain of dirtsider sympathies.

Who are you?

A strand of hair had come loose. She shoved it back into place, the mask of perfection complete. Then tugged it free again. Not so perfect now.

She smiled.

The morning's meeting with her senior team ran to a familiar routine. Gripes, ruffled ambassadorial piques and the rocky state of the latest trade project. Much the same as all her meetings over the last five years, except that today the clear light of Hathe's sun streamed down on welcoming bushes in the gardens below, and jaunty Hathian zitters buzzed at the window demanding entrance. No doubt sensing the odors of food wafting from the side table.

Nothing here for you today, little ones. Fly free and find a dirtsider in the path below.

"Senator an Kroth has heard of your work and suggested you sit in on the next meeting of the Senate trade committee."

Rheia jerked awake, hastily smoothed her tunic and plastered on a thrilled expression as she turned toward her boss.

"That would be very useful," she said, adopting the neutral voice of a cautiously pleased official.

"They have created a list of potential trade opportunities, and the regions best suited to fill them. It synchronizes well with the contacts you have developed for urgonium sales during the occupation, so they would value your input."

She bet they would, glancing through the table he sent to her com. The very first entry should have been barred from consideration by the normal standards of government. The proposing Senator's company would do very well out of it. Or to be precise, the one nominally owned by his son.

But she gave no sign of her thoughts.

"Excellent," she said. "I look forward to it."

The lies dripped so easily off her tongue but her boss nodded, with that touch of a smile lifting the corners of his mouth that signaled recognition of the layers under her words.

A few days later, she walked into the Senate committee room with all her emotional armor in place. An Kroth rose slightly to welcome her, and she offered the obligatory hand touch.

"A pleasure to see you, Senator."

The man was much as she remembered from when she'd last seen him on Mathe during the exile. A bit plumper, his clothing as immaculate but now even finer. A man taking full advantage of the restoration to normality on Hathe, she decided. None of the team on the plateau, the Security forces, nor the ever-elegant Jacquel des Trurains wore anything so ostentatiously expensive.

The man took her hand, clasping it with his upper hand in the manner of one of higher ranking, and she made herself allow it, setting a cool smile on her face as he released her hand and gave her a less than avuncular pat on her shoulder before sitting down again.

"And you, madame. I see you have recovered from your awful ordeal. That des Trurains scamp should be shot."

"You are mistaken. Nothing of note occurred," she said blandly, hating the glint of triumph on the man's face. She couldn't stop the blush burning her cheeks, and only prayed he put it down to embarrassment and not the anger scalding her veins.

Jacquel des Trurains had defended her from her enemies out on the plateau, and one day, this slug would pay for making the world think otherwise. But not today, not if they were to save Hathe, and she set herself to placate, beguile and downright flatter the obnoxious piece of humanity in front of her. As ven Raden had said, she was well versed in all the nuances of this game.

But none of her targets in the past had been one of her own. None had been Hathians.

By the end of it, she felt she could claim the meeting as a success. The man was either stupid—unlikely—or too greedy and vain to recognize her twisted falsehoods. When she rose to leave, he gave her a horizontal hand clasp and a warmer smile.

"To a prosperous future together," he said. A firm grip, and he released her hand. "When you have that reprobate out of your system."

And her smile slipped.

That night she gave up resisting temptation. Setting a multilayered protection into her com, breakable only by the Security forces, she pulled up all the vidcasts of Jacquel des Trurains.

It wasn't difficult. The man had been hitting the nightspots hard, flagrantly drowning in the sybaritic excesses on offer in the newly liberated capital.

Some of the voice-overs were indulgent. *Our sexy hero enjoying his rewards,* was the one she liked best. That inbuilt elegance of his combined with the effects of dissipation did nothing to dampen his appeal. Injured, broken but not defeated, he had set fire to something in her she was desperate to deny. But that wicked grin of his as he played up to the cheering crowd, that brash wave to a jeering onlooker as he threw bits against ever increasing odds in the latest hellhole?

She was lost.

Then there were the other tag lines. *"Fallen Hero"*, *"Bright Hope Lost"*.

"Hollow Hero" was the one she hated most. Jacquel des Trurains had done every single thing in his awards citation while the snarky vidcaster had sat safely on Mathe, reporting on the latest petty squabble among its too closed-in society. The vids were no better. Jacquel slumped against a wall, Jacquel wasted on a surfeit of uppers and drink, stumbling out of yet another seedy club. The vidcams zoned in on him, showing in minute detail every sagging, drawn line of that beautiful face. And he knew it, his eyes staring directly at the vidcams as if daring them to show him at his worst.

She gasped. Those eyes.

"He's using."

Mairfin. A filthy drug, only too familiar to everyone on the diplomatic squad, and now she realized, the Resistance. Mairfin had one big advantage: its user could drink or get doped up, all while staying conscious and in control, however inebriated he might choose to appear. A ploy to get the opposition to relax and spill much-needed secrets. Its use was closely controlled by her department and the Security forces, the only agencies authorized to use it. Too much, and it could kill.

The drug had not made it to the black market, of that she was sure. Notoriously hard to manufacture and with few pleasurable effects, it held little attraction for the underworld, and the two agencies clamped down hard on any whisper of misuse. Not the kind of attention any criminal outfit wanted.

So, if Jacquel had it, the Security forces had supplied it. Rheia knew well the telltale signs. She'd used mairfin herself on rare occasions. A night here, a few hours there; that's all their bosses usually allowed.

Those constricted pupils, the lines etched around his mouth as if in constant pain, and the slight abrasions on his hands and face from an accidental stumble. Jacquel des Trurains had been on mairfin for some time and was dangerously close to the edge.

Her heart wept.

Next day, she set out for her scheduled meeting with a hard glitter in her eyes and rock-solid determination in her heart.

"We start with the province of Kashtarn," said Senator an Kroth, calling the meeting to a start.

Across from her, his team sat to attention, screens lit up and Rheia quickly scrolled to the first item on the agenda. Kashtarn was a lush and fertile region, well-protected during the occupation by illusion screens to keep the Terrans out and preserve the food bowl of Hathe.

"Your home province, is it not, Senator? I hope your family have all settled comfortably back into their homes again." She gave the man a cordial smile but that was all.

"They have, thank you. And your own?"

"I have none. They were lost in the occupation." The glitter in his eyes confirmed he'd known that, knew exactly *who* her family had been and would use it when it suited him. "I have no family connections left, not to whom I owe any duty," she added with a cool stare.

The smile slipped on the man's face and Rheia felt a warm glow of satisfaction. *If you dance with the best, an Kroth, expect to be forced to complete all the coils of the dance.* Game on, as her little brother used to say when she'd dared him to do something outrageous.

Game on, little man.

She looked at her com screen. "For such a prosperous region, there are few alternatives listed."

The Senator harrumphed. "This is a final list. The regional staff screened all the available business cases to come up with the best possibilities."

Rheia set herself to scrolling through the list again. "They do offer interesting options, but more are needed. These are too limited in scope. Our trading partners do not like being herded down one track only. Far better to create a number of attractive pathways and let them feel they have a choice."

"So you allow other planets to set the parameters for Hathe?"

She smiled, a touch of her lips and the barest lifting of the corner of her mouth. "They like to think that. It's called diplomacy, Senator. All partners must feel they have gained something."

Stop being so obviously greedy, little man. The public won't stand for it.

A tic of his cheek and his eyes narrowed. She shrugged mentally. He and his cronies were threatening to blackmail her, and logic said they shouldn't expect her to like it.

After that, things settled down and they got to work. A long, tedious discussion, with Rheia insisting on bringing up the original list for the Kashtarn region, bartering and haggling over each deleted entry till they came up with a new list for her. Still too short, still bearing the blatant mark of a family bent on fattening itself, but enough leeway remained to offer a chance for other parties. By the end of it, she suspected that an Kroth regarded her much as he did Jacquel des Trurains.

He stabbed at the final list. "That's it. No more."

She made a play of studying the list. The Council and her department could live with it, unlike the man's first brash attempts.

"Yes, this will work," she said.

The man slapped his com unit, shutting down the meeting files. "It will."

He marched out before she could take away any more of his toys. His team followed him out. One of them was an ex-trader and lawyer specializing in interplanetary trade and the rest came from backgrounds in business or upper level regional administrations. The Senator had good advisors; all as hell-bent on making the most of the new Hathe at the expense of those who won it back for them, but intelligent and experienced enough to recognize the wisdom of the deal on offer. She had no doubt they would make him accept it.

Ven Raden said much the same when she reported to him, scanning down the list. "He'll whinge and moan, but his people will bring him around. Good work." He looked at the list again, then cast her a wry look. "We trained you well. Maybe too well. You quite sure you know what you're getting into?"

She started to shrug it off, but that shrewd scrutiny couldn't be denied. "It's necessary."

He nodded. "Too much has been paid by too many?"

"Something like that."

A grim frown marred ven Raden's face. But he knew as well as she there was no other answer and sat back as he moved on to the rest of her report. "You bluffed him today, but you can't keep doing that. I'll talk to deln Crantz about getting Council backing to apply pressure on him."

"They know about this?"

"A few only," he conceded. "Those who recognize the problem."

Gilda an Rathman and Sylvan an Castre's clique, she assumed he meant. They could bring in a third of the Council, with a group in the middle who would at least refrain from meddling, she hoped. But then there was the bunch at the other end. Not bad people, but these councilors had never had to face the cost of the grand plan to beat the Terrans. None had family members who had served in the Resistance or had lost those dear to them. A small group only, but like Senator an Kroth, many had used their position to keep their loved ones safely up on Mathe.

So few others had been offered a choice. She had been ordered on board a ship, her family told to prepare to downsize their lives and accept Terran rule. No choice mentioned to any of them. And now she alone remained; she alone lived to uphold her family's honor. "Then I better get the evidence needed to convince the rest of the council to take action."

"You'll be on your own in the Senator's camp." Her boss looked grimmer than ever. "I can assign you an assistant, one with security training."

She shook her head. "You can't disguise a bodyguard." All those muscles and their trained alertness. Any experienced diplomat or trader learned quickly to pick out who was the brains and who the shield, and ven Raden knew that. Not that he looked happy about it.

"Be careful then. This is not like a short off-planet job."

No, it was going to be a very long game. But not five years, not as long as Jacquel and the dirtsiders had endured.

That night, she gazed around her apartment. One in a DIA complex designed for career officials on short-term returns to Hathe between assignments. High-end luxury it may be, but it still looked utilitarian and temporary. Not a home. She'd been in many such places, and usually did whatever she could to make it feel like a place she belonged. Time she did the same here to make it look like the home of the moonie woman attending those Senate meetings. She sat down, opened up a com screen and began to plot.

In the past, one rule had always guided her. Keep as close to the truth as possible. Diplomats, whatever their planetary origin, shared one very salient characteristic: they were all, by training and inclination, very good at reading other people, so lying to them was rarely successful. Prevaricating—now that was quite another matter.

Now she faced a new target group. Not as subtle, not as well-trained. But, by treating the dirtsiders like the peasants they had been forced to impersonate, and preying on their engrained patterns of survival, these greedy moonies had succeeded where the Terrans had failed. They had beaten down the brave and long-suffering heroes of the Resistance into a second string and powerless new reality.

Which meant they were not a group she could discount. The so-called leaders—the ones like Senator an Kroth who fronted for them—yes, those she could hoodwink. Puffed up with visions of fortune and greed, they were an easy target to hate. But the more she came to know of the senator, the less she believed he was the real power. Somewhere behind him, powerful men and women pulled the strings for their own profit, and she meant to find out who.

She turned slowly around, studying the apartment again. She'd been deposited here by ven Raden with a warning that she was staying here whether she liked it or not.

"Your true name is out among the dirtsiders. Soon, it will spread. To keep safe, you stay here, or go back off-world."

With no hope of helping Jacquel or clearing her father's name. She could only growl and give in, but up till now had refused to add anything of herself to a place that felt like a glorified way station.

Enough of that. She had a job to do, and the best way to start was to restore a front of normality. Whatever spy an Kroth and his cohorts set on her must see what they expected. More, she must look like she enjoyed her life and work, must make them believe that was her only interest. Not rescuing her home world or protecting a certain enticing hero of the Resistance.

By the next night the room had sprung to life. On the shelves, the favorite pieces collected in her travels. On the walls, an ever-changing array of images: waves of plateau tussocks, the teeming seas of Migrath Minor, her great-grandmother's ancestral home on Samarkan—a place she doubted her adventurous and space-loving ancestor had stayed long in but the dramatic lines of the clan homestead, set on a vast sweep of broken hilltops, called to something in Rheia—and her favorite, a cheeky mountain stream bubbling merrily over rocks and overhanging grasses. A kaleidoscope of color to welcome a visitor, while the far room had become a cozy nook of sleeper, deep-seated chair with her reader set on the table on one side and a bowl holding a living astelia plant. A reminder of home and a beacon of hope in this lonely path she followed. She walked through the rooms, pacing, studying. Yes, any who penetrated here would see exactly what her history said to expect. Someone who liked fine things, cherished mementos and adored her home region. The fact that home was the plateau had been something to hide up to now, but always her apartment had included some reminder; this time, she'd made it more obvious.

An Kroth and his cronies thought to hold her past over her. By blatantly showing her roots, she sent a message. *Your threats are empty.*

She doubted they would read it but felt better for the sending. And the higher-up ones, those who pulled the strings—they would see it in the reports. Their response to that would betray them and bring their downfall.

She grinned, striding over to the shielded window and staring out at the streets below. The man loitering by the far door, the girl wandering down the walkway, stopping at the odd shop window, the elderly woman picking her way over the broken path at the base of her building; which of them watched her, which belonged to her enemies? Ven Raden had assured her that the Security's best surveillance systems protected the apartment. Sensors monitored her continuously and screened the rooms for any intruding scans. She still watched what she did here, unable to trust fully anything originating in the Security Department. Not after their rogue agents arrested Jacquel. Only in the open air, where she was free from surveillance, and only with her DIA secured com link did she dare speak truth, and even then, she used a DIA top-level access code. Ever changing, known to none but off-planet officials, the mathematical probability of it being broken even by another official should keep her safe. She hoped. She needed one trusted route, needed to know it was there even if she used it only when she must. Her courage depended on it.

Who was her enemy? She peered closer, studying the shadows in the streets and lanes below. No one lurked, but eyes watched. The prickle on the back of her neck never lied. So do what they expect. She crossed the room, kicked off her boots and curled up on the seat, pulling up reports on her com. A workaholic who avoided unforced social occasions. That had been her routine for the past few years, living in a world where she didn't belong, and forced to hide her background from colleagues and opponents alike.

Yet attendance at gatherings of the well-connected was a necessary part of her work, and on a good night she enjoyed the company, relishing the challenge of the chatter with its underlying currents. With her name exposed, she must now be fearful of all but those carefully vetted by her assigned protection service, and tonight none of the gatherings of the City glitterati had passed their screening. Instead, she read reports and tomorrow would hand out her advice again, wanted or otherwise by her enemy.

Hopefully an Kroth's backing team lived up to her expectations and had the sense to recognize the worth of what she'd told them. That was her surest route in. Get his team to tell their boss to bring her on board and make him want her so badly he begged for her help. Turn the tables so he had to earn her trust, rather than she pleading for his. A woman of her ability had plenty of other work needing her attention. Whatever he offered had to be good enough to make her drop everything else.

And that was when she would find out who was behind him.

CHAPTER SEVENTEEN

Jacquel had never been so angry. Those children were the final humiliation. He dusted off his trousers and looked down once more at the grave of his friend. "You paid, we paid, we keep paying. It stops now."

Luckily, he was in full dress regalia. Slicked up to impress some insignificant bigwig deln Crantz planned to inveigle into one of his schemes.

Just like he'd done to Jacquel and to Rheia.

He marched, faster, boot heels cracking on the paved ground as he headed for his nearest club. Not to drink, not to carouse. Not this time. In the door, straight to the bathrooms.

"Out."

One look at his face and the moonie daring to slum it with dirtsiders slunk out. Jacquel accessed the grooming unit, scrutinizing his holo-image when he finished.

Spotless, official. Damned impressive. Exactly what he needed today. He activated his com.

"Ras here. What's up, Cap?" The man had never learned protocol, one of the reasons Jacquel trusted him completely. That, and the number of times Ras had saved his sorry backside.

"Tell the squad to take the day off. I've got something I need doing that won't work with a troop of soldiers surrounding me."

A short laugh. "We'll scare off your victims?"

"Yeah, something like that."

Silence. Then Ras came back. "Sure, Cap. Go do your worst. Just get back in one piece." A quick flash of an old holo, the one of a much younger Jacquel spewing his guts out on his first off-world trip. Bendin had posted about it afterward and Ras had somehow acquired a copy. Now he used it whenever he wanted to rile his commander. Jacquel sent back a pained grin and signed off, hoping he'd fooled his second but not totally convinced.

He grimaced. He'd done the best he could, and not even Ras would pick what he planned next. He slammed open the bathroom door and marched into the club then out the front door, willfully ignoring the gibes from old friends loitering in the rooms and halls on his way through.

There was a public transit link just down the street, but today he chose to walk. It would take a good few hours; hopefully enough time to cool down and come up with an argument that would work. Right now, he could barely string two effective sentences together.

"Cap, where you off to?" A girl lingering in a doorway, a woman he remembered as an astute undercover agent and as brave as they came. Her tunic looked no better today than when she'd manned a street stall during the occupation.

A laughing cry from an old colleague. "You lookin' mighty fancy, Cap. Your mama know what you planning?"

"Not likely. Not with that get-up."

"A bit upmarket, ain't we, Cap?"

He marched on, ignoring the gathering crowd. They'd tire of it soon enough.

A low murmuring as he switched direction. He refused to look back. They must leave him soon. He had to do this alone. He had enough bodies on his conscience already.

The noise followed, rose in volume. Didn't they know he wasn't safe? Not today.

He veered sideways, plunged into an alleyway, out the other side, then down a rickety set of steps from a long-disused shortcut. One not needed in the modern Hathe, where flitters and walkways carried the new citizens of the City to their destination. It would take much longer, but few knew of it.

Then down an abandoned track. No one followed him, yet the sound of beating footsteps still lingered in the distance. He marched on, half running, veering around one corner then another, finally coming to a stop as reason asserted itself. Much more of this mad flight and he'd arrive looking like the worst dirtsider caricature, hair askew and his carefully smoothed uniform a bedraggled disgrace.

He switched on the holo from his com and restored the facade of his dress formals, then moved back into the main roads, mingling with the crowds on the walkways at a more sedate pace. Through the upmarket shopping boulevard and across the City Gardens filled with happy children and dancing trees—though few of the laughing youngsters had the sunbeaten skin or the sudden panic of dirtsider children, brought up with the constant fear of soldiers bent on destroying their latest refuge.

It's not these children's fault. Leave them in their innocent joy, and know you helped give it to them.

A woman grabbed a child out of his way. He walked faster, hating whatever she had seen in his face.

Then he stopped. A small island of calm in streets filled with business, a paved circle surrounded a statue of the commander of the first ship to colonize Hathe. Beyond it lay the long avenue lined with office blocks, the heart of government on Hathe. Midway down, Security headquarters, and at the far end, surrounded by Avenue Park, the home of the Council. The building dominated the avenue, straddling the entire end of the vista. Hathian tourists once came from all over the planet to stand where he stood now, to see this panorama. The most uploaded holopic in all of Hathe.

He glared at that facade of pristine officialdom, then set off right down the middle of the avenue.

"Going somewhere, Cap?"

A hand snaked around his neck, another blocked his chest, and he moved instinctively to throw off his attacker. Too late. More arms flung around him and a webnet engulfed him in its sticky tangles.

"Let me go," he growled.

"Not happening Cap."

He couldn't believe it. "Release me right now, Ras."

"Why, you got some better place to be, Cap?"

Yes, he sure as hell did. "This is *not* your affair."

"Yeah, about that, Cap," said another voice. One Jacquel knew well.

"Dreya, stand down. Keep out of this."

Who else? He struggled, but they'd locked the net fast to the ground. One by one, as if on parade, every single member of his squad, the men and women who'd fought, laughed and mourned with him, came and stood silently in a line, cutting him off from his goal.

Each one gleamed in full dress parade uniform.

"You don't do this alone, Cap," said Ras softly. He signaled to Anton, and the strands of the net released enough to let him turn, but not leave. "Look behind you, Cap."

He turned, slowly, fearfully. Silently, row by row, the streets filled up. Here, a man he remembered from the second year of the war; there, a group of women, arms steeled by the hard muscles that only came from tough labor; flitting in between them all, the very pack of harum-scarum kids who had precipitated this flight. And squeezing into the front row, the family he'd thought safe in Marthe's house on the plains. The once terrified wee girl standing up defiantly, still scared, but belligerently sticking out her chin.

Dirtsiders all, the valiant, the brave, the rank and file of street-sweepers and foot troops who had won the war by plodding along, enduring day by day the menial lives that had so effectively duped the Terran conquerors. All standing in ranks with him today, and all clearly determined to go nowhere.

"No. Don't make me put you at risk."

A shrug from that valiant wee girl, and a grin from her father, head high as never before. "We've lived with risk forever, Cap. It's time to step forward and demand the reward for it."

Jacquel stared down the ranks. Row upon row, filling up the streets, more and more adding to it every minute. He raised his voice. "Go home. I will not have you pay the price for my actions. Enough have done that already."

"Hard luck, Cap. This is our fight too, and we're coming with you," said a woman at the front of the crowd. It was as if they had all been waiting for this day. Had to have been planning for it, by the size of the crowd mobilizing here.

"You don't know where I'm going."

Ras stepped forward, tilted his head to the end of the avenue. "Up there, and don't deny it. I've known you too long, Cap, and when something gets you mad and sick, you go straight to the source."

Jacquel shook his head, wishing he could deny it. But enough was enough; the Council must listen, must act before more of his people paid for their heroism.

Before Rheia pays the ultimate price, like Bendin and so many before.

He studied all those faces looking to him. Scared, wary, but determined, every one of them. The same gritty courage that had brought them through the hellish years and today brought them to follow where he lead.

Which meant he must succeed. "Right then," he said, nodding at Ras to release him from the net, and swung around as soon as he was free

Up that long avenue and straight through the park. Dirtsiders marching, heads high, refusing to be quelled by the gawking throngs stopping dead in the street and staring in horror at the ranks filling up their pristine avenue. This was a government area, a zone exclusive to those properly authorized to exercise power.

A zone badly in need of reminding who gave them the freedom to exercise that power. Jacquel had never felt so proud, or so terrified.

They came to the steps and stopped. Guards rushed to man the entranceway, speaking into coms. Most were from Security—ex-Resistance from their hand signals and coded messages. He said nothing, just looked and waited until, one by one, they stood down and formed a file on each side of the steps. An honor guard for him to mount the stairs, leaving behind the murmur of the crowd as a warning to those sitting inside. He marched in front of his team with head held high, dress uniform shining, medals gleaming. They wanted a hero, and right now, in this moment, they would have it. It was the least they deserved.

He carried the masquerade through the doors and into the main entrance of the Council House. Behind him, his squad lined up in full parade formation as if escorting him to a state occasion. A security guard stepped forward and saluted with the old Resistance salute.

"Colonel Jacquel des Trurains, to see the Council," said Ras on his flank.

The security officer's face was dead flat, his delivery giving away nothing of the extraordinary nature of his request. "Certainly, sir. The Council is in private session at the moment, but I'm sure they will see you as soon as they are able."

"No, you misunderstood," said Jacquel, politely but firmly. "I will be going in to see them now."

The officer stared at him. Jacquel merely tilted his head, bringing the man's attention to the crowd outside, filling the parkland and all the avenue. He didn't need to. This place had the best security on modern Hathe and every single person inside this building would know exactly what was happening outside.

"The Council have advised that they cannot be interrupted at present."

"Unfortunately, they are mistaken." Jacquel gave the man a cool smile, glanced at the hand that had come to land on his arm till it was again lifted, then began to walk to the nearest lifter bank. The guards could stop him using them by turning off his security clearances, but they'd need the cooperation of the Security Department, and Jacquel trusted in deln Crantz to prevent that.

It was only as he arrived at the door of the council chambers that he suddenly realized he was holding his breath, and slowly released it. Security troops also manned this door. Friend, or moonie? He took a step forward. One went to block him, the other saluted.

"A moment please, Colonel."

"I have urgent business with the Council that cannot wait."

Then the man who had saluted also stepped forward, blocking his passage. "We know that, sir, but if you could please wait a minute. One of the other guards has something for you."

"I will see him after."

"No, sir, now please. It's important." The man had to be a moonie. Then Jacquel looked again. Something about the cast of face or voice triggered a memory. One just out of reach.

"Jonatheos deln Franzen, sir. I served in the northern border."

"Dirtsider?" He stopped trying to shove through them, shocked to his core. "Then you know I have to go in there. It's time."

"Yes sir, it's past time. But wait a minute, please."

The lifter screen smashed open, a sound of running footsteps, and a man came to a panting halt in front of him. The other two stepped back to their assigned position by the council doors.

"Colonel des Trurains. The Cap?"

"That's me."

The man reached behind him, pulled something from a carry bag, and Jacquel tensed. The man put out a hand. "When you go in there, sir, can you take this?"

A flat piece of acronite, plain, tough and rare as hell. A plaque. He reached out as if on autopilot, took the thing, and wondered what in hell he was doing forgetting every security rule he'd ever learned.

Then he lifted it and read what had been written there.

To the Unsung.
In memory of all those who are lost to us,
whose names grace no monument
and whose graves lie unmarked.
They gave us freedom.

Jacquel stood stock-still. "Where… How, who did this…?"

"I had a cousin, a family, friends. They didn't win medals, didn't do anything outstanding. They just died. They kept quiet, and they carried Hathe's secret to their graves in the mines."

"We all have those." Jacquel could barely say the words. "We all lost…"

"They need a memorial. Dirtsiders need this, sir. Please, take it with you into the Council. Set it by a tree, something living and whole, planted in the avenue park to remember for all time those who didn't make it. You can do that for us, sir."

Jacquel's fingers clenched on the cold metal. He could do this, he *would* do this. He nodded, then pointed at the doors. "Open up, soldiers. The council is about to hear the truth."

"Yes, sir." A slap of hands on their weapons as the guards came to full attention and gave him the most formal, most correct of parade ground salutes. Their leader hit the controls. The doors slid back, and the Council chambers opened to him

A wide-open space took up the floor of the auditorium, dominated by a speaker's rostrum and a simple table draped in the Hathian flag and bearing Hathe's most precious relicts handed down from the first settlers. The colonizing ship's log, a small dense cube of startling black, and the faded hat of its legendary captain. Rising up from that, the circling banks of the Councilors' seats filled with startled faces, interrupted mid speech or brought suddenly to attention. Jacquel marched forward into the belly of the room. Faces now glared and silence fell.

"The Pillars be with you, esteemed Councilors."

Sylvan an Castre was the first to recover, but then he'd been dealing with his twins and Jacquel since they were babies.

"Young Jaca, what can we do for you?"

Jacquel gave him a full, formal salute. "Councilor. I have an urgent addition to your agenda."

A crash of a too hasty standing on the left. "Council sets its agenda, not junior officers." Trundain an Delsin, the computer comptroller and guardian of Hathe's precious genealogical records. The man had never forgiven Marthe for her marriage to a Terran.

"Look at your exterior monitor, Councilor," he said to him.

On his right, Gilda an Rathman rose. An ally, he'd have thought, but was no longer so sure. "Something has happened, Colonel?"

"No, Councilor. Nothing has happened—and that is the trouble."

"Aahhh. You speak for those who stayed down here. We've put programs in place for them, as you are aware."

"Yes, Councilor, I am fully aware."

The chamber echoed with a chorus of annoyed snorts and cries of "That old problem," and Jacquel had to fight to stay calm.

"Programs that so far have been singularly ineffective. Programs that have done nothing for those for whom they were intended." Programs that have only enriched the moonies running them, he could have added, but Gilda and Sylvan already knew that, and the others weren't ready to listen.

"Today, I walked down the main street of this fine city of ours and was accosted by children trying to scam me for petty credits." He drew in a breath. "Is that what we fought for? Children begging in the streets?" He lifted his hand, to a collective gasp, then thumped the plaque down on the table. "You know what this is? A simple plaque. I was stopped before I came in here, not to ask for much, not to do anything extraordinary."

He took another breath. "One simple request. Ask the council to have this placed by a living tree, they said. In the Avenue Park. Don't let our friends, our neighbors, our families be forgotten." He placed his palm full on the face of the plaque, set it to spin in a crazy swirl that obliterated the words inscribed there. "Only you have; every one of you sitting here, comfortable in the success of the restoration and busy *getting things back to normal.* The Unsung, we call them, with good reason. A short word, easily said."

He slammed a hand down, brought the plaque to a sudden crashing halt, then lifted it up and held it aloft. "Easy to forget—only we won't let you. We endured five years down here, giving you your comfortable seats, your fine homes and your honored titles, and *we will not let you forget us.*"

A slow clapping from the front of the room. Jacquel had played at Councilor der Greystan's house during his childhood and had endured the carping of his noxious daughter and son when they lost any game. His father thought the man a shrewd politician but had never said he trusted him.

"A fine speech, des Trurains. What next? A comic turn to keep us further enthralled? One of those humorous japes of yours against the Terrans?"

"No, Councilor. A demand that the Council does its job and stops the decimation of the lives, the wealth and the future of those citizens who served on Hathe under the occupation. Stops it *now,* not in some nebulous time in the future."

He signaled to the ex-Resistance guards on the doors. *Bring in my squad,* said his hand sign. To a shocked gasp, the stony-faced soldiers left their posts, entered their security releases and the doors swung all the way back to their widest opening. Outside, at full attention, his squad lined up. He lifted a hand, taking in the shiny uniforms, the medals standing proudly on each chest, the perfect control of each and every member of the squad. Another quick hand signal, a touch on his com, and they marched forward, lining up in precise formation behind him.

"So now you seek to overthrow the Council?" said der Greystan.

"No, Councilor. I seek to remind you of your duty. Let me introduce my squad." He swept his gaze around the room in challenge, almost sorry that no one stood to deny him, though Gilda and Sylvan looked decidedly unimpressed with his stunt. That's what Sylvan would call it later in private, but for now they kept silent as he began to speak, moving from one to the other of the squad.

"Starting with Squad Second Ras den Koprorth, Valiance Star First Class, Medal of Honor and bar, two Service Commendations, Resistance Award, Three Golden Hearts, and the Official Hathian Commendation of Valor."

Ras might hate every minute of it, but he kept his head high. As did every member of his squad as he announced their names and read out the truly stupendous list of their military honors. Every single one acquired under the harshest and most trying of situations. Jacquel could vouch for that; he'd been there for most of them, and luckily no one offered to return the favor by reading out the quite ridiculously long list of his own honors. He finished at last, and could almost hear the sigh of relief from his squad.

"Very commendable, young des Trurains," said Sylvan, "and you all have the Council's eternal gratitude for your outstanding efforts."

"Yes, Councilor, we know," said Jacquel. "But the others, the ones without honors. The ones filling the avenue, the living Unsung. Do they have your gratitude?" He flung an arm, gesturing behind him. "No. They don't. All they know is that Hathe has forgotten them, has taken their sacrifices and trampled over them, leaving them in the gutter."

"No."

Gilda an Rathman, a cry from her heart.

"Yes, Councilor." Gilda had made a promise to Marthe on the day she left Hathe—permanently exiled for the crime of loving a Terran, despite her heroism during the war. Marthe had more medals than even him. Gilda had promised Marthe to protect the dirtsiders, to restore their world to them. Most of all, to restore a future to the children raised on Hathe during the occupation.

Exactly the opposite of what he'd seen today.

He studied the faces of the Councilors again; which ones twitched, which looked bored, which guilty and which sad. Those like Trundain an Delsin and der Greystan would never be persuaded. Too much to gain and little to lose by preying on dirtsiders. Across from them, Sylvan, Gilda, and the others who had worked closely with the Resistance during the occupation. The ones who understood in their hearts what he was talking about.

Then he looked at the last group: those clustered in the middle of the chamber and who hadn't yet chosen which side to support. Some had dealt with the Resistance, others were fundamentally decent people but as yet undecided. And some, tired of it all and torn beyond their limits, just wanted peace. Those were the ones who would take the easy path, and right now that was to keep quiet and let whatever happened come to pass.

These last ones were the most dangerous group of all. What would sway these men and women who had served Hathe long and well, to their limit and beyond?

He looked each one in the eye and challenged them to respond.

Then stopped, shocked. In those eyes, in all of those eyes—fear. Stark and cold, their eyes wide and mouths crimped tight. Fear of him, his squad, the crowds swelling the streets outside.

No, by all the Pillars, no.

He swung around, a terse shift of his hand, and an abrupt order to his squad. "We leave now."

Ras took one look at him, then saluted, and signaled to the squad. A parade ground perfect salute, every single one in time, and they wheeled and marched out. He followed at the rear, protecting them from this, the most cutting of betrayals from the very body they had all fought so hard to reinstate. So many dirtsiders had given their lives to bring this Council back to power on Hathian soil. Now, not only had these Councilors failed to protect dirtsider rights, they knew so little of dirtsiders that they feared the very people who had saved them.

"Wait," cried Gilda.

Some last vestige of pride said he owed her too much to ignore her. He stopped and turned sharply back. "Yes?"

"The Council is acting. But we need you, need your people."

"You've said that before."

And nothing had worked. He'd heard all the ideas. "We are not one of your charity cases. We are Hathians."

"Yes, you are, and dirtsiders have more than earned the right to control what happens to them."

He stood, his squad behind him, wondering why he didn't just turn around and walk out of here. But Gilda tried, had kept trying. He waited to hear what she would say. Yet not even he could have guessed at her words.

"There is a committee forming to deal solely with the recovery of the dirtsiders and their restoration to their rightful place in Hathe. I want you to head it."

"Put *me* at the heart of the establishment." It was either choke with laughter or give in to the grief inside him. That's the best she could offer? One more meaningless committee. "Have you asked my father what he thinks of it?"

Gilda forced a smile, as strained as his cracked attempt at humor. "It wasn't relevant."

They were serious. "This committee. It will have real power? Or—is this just a way to cover over the problem? Bog it down in committee deliberations until real life out there sorts out its own messy solution?"

Sylvan stood now. "It's real. Something has to be done. My daughter and son's sacrifices must mean something. You owe this to Bendin, to Marthe."

A blow Jacquel hadn't expected and couldn't answer.

"They are part of me still, Doctor an Castre, and will always be so." He fought to keep his voice respectful. Sylvan an Castre may stand straight, but those losses had brought lines to his face that could never be erased.

But a committee. Another talkfest?

He looked up to the other rows, searching out those in whose eyes he'd glimpsed that horrifying touch of fear. It was still there. "And you, Councilors, all of you. You would support my part in this? And will you give this committee real power to change Hathe?"

None spoke. But then der Greystan lifted a hand in agreement. "At least it will stop this intrusion and let the Council get back to work."

Take this on, and let me watch you fail, Jacquel suspected he meant.

"And the rest of you?" He let his gaze travel around the room, pausing at the group in the middle. One by one, they nodded, raised a hand, or mumbled agreement. At the end, it was unanimous.

Leaving the ball in his court. If he refused, he walked out of here with nothing to show for it. How could he explain that to the massed crowd outside? They had been waiting so long for someone to champion them.

He drew himself up. "Thank you for your kind offer, Councilors. I will of course accept."

Accept for now.

Yet he couldn't stop the questions in his head. What exactly lay behind this offer, and why had they all agreed? The ones in the middle were pushed by that swelling crowd of dirtsiders outside. Sylvan, Gilda and their adherents meant what they'd said. But the last faction, the der Greystans and the an Delsins? There was a too-pleased-by-half smile lurking in the corner of der Greystan's mouth.

He gave no sign of noticing it, giving a formal bow of acceptance Then he lifted his hand towards Gilda an Rathman. "Will you accompany me, Councilor? There are a number of Hathians outside waiting to hear the outcome of this meeting."

She did it too. Lead every single member of the Council out the door, down the lifters and onto the portico at the front of the council building. The Chair of the Council was up for nomination next Pillars' turn, and he strongly hoped she stood. The only other contender was Philos der Greystan and he was firmly in the camp of those backing more moonie control of Hathe, a disaster for dirtsiders if he won. The makeup of the Council was the one thing moonies hadn't yet claimed for their own. Up till now, no one faction had even managed to take control of the Council due to the complex interweaving of family and social checks underlying any appointment. One thing that, thankfully, the war had not changed. Not yet.

But it had changed so much else.

He forced a smile of triumph on his face to make it look like this was a victory. That leading a committee had been the purpose of this hurly-burly march of his.

A committee! Not a word that had entered the wild furor driving his mad race here. No, he had meant to tell the Council exactly what he thought of them.

CHAPTER EIGHTEEN

At the top of the steps, they stopped to face the crowd. Gilda stepped up to speak and the crowd fell silent. They knew what she'd done for the Resistance during the war, but a glittering core of anger simmered in that silence. They stayed quiet as she began to address them, but he could feel the fraught impatience straining for release. The councilor talked well, said all the right things, but she was no dirtsider and this crowd wanted more than platitudes.

"To ensure that real action is taken, the Council has formed a committee—and Colonel des Trurains has agreed to head it."

The silence turned disastrous. Wrong words, Gilda. Wrong answer to so much. One breath, two, then the first clod fired up the steps. A second, then an entire volley torn up from the carefully planted gardens flanking the Council House steps.

Ras, shield! he signaled.

A shimmering line sprang up, cutting off the crowd from the Council steps, and he stood on the wrong side. A divide he feared would never be breached now.

Out in the avenue, the buzz started, a wave of long-stifled resentment given voice. He knew faces in that crowd, had been on missions with them and trusted them with his life.

A trust no longer returned.

"Talk's cheap," they shouted. "Action, not words."

"Traitor."

That did it. "Ras, release that shield. One person to pass."

"Not on your own, Cap."

He shook his head, stubbornly facing down his second, his friends and fellow soldiers. They stared straight back.

"Troop," said Ras. They all took one step forward.

Jacquel shook his head, mouth pinched. "I got us into this."

"No, those moonie freeloaders did. Now *we* are going to fix it."

The buzz had grown to a roar. No time to argue. No point, from the set looks on his troop's faces. He had no choice but to give in. He sent a silent code and snapped to full parade ground attention. A swift flick of fingers, a salute to Gilda, and he took one step forward and one step down. Then another, with his entire squad falling in behind.

"Jacquel. It's too dangerous," called Gilda.

"Stay here, Councilor. You'll be safe."

The security guards had swept up to surround the Council in a protective circle. Ex-Resistance all, no one should ask them to fight against their own, but they could be trusted to get the Council to safety if this turned dangerous.

Step, step, down his troop marched, and the roar slowly settled into a quiet hum. The shield stayed up, but Ras had the coordinates to allow them to pass through, shutting out all other outsiders.

Silence ruled, the crowd stepping back to leave a clear space in front.

He walked through that shimmering divide and his squad passed through after. As one with him, they swiveled to stand facing up the steps.

"Enough talk, Councilor," called Jacquel, repeating it simultaneously in Resistance field code. "We need action, and we need it now."

"Jaca, don't do this. Bendin and Marthe didn't sacrifice everything for this," said Sylvan.

"They would have been down here with me, Councilor," he replied in a voice that carried to the far back of the crowd, and reinforced it with a Resistance short code for any who couldn't hear.

Sylvan looked like he'd just broken him.

"How can we fix this?" said Gilda.

He wasn't sure she or anyone could. But they had to try. He flicked out a message on the field band and set his com to collate the most repeated claims. This crowd needed to be heard.

Then waited, letting the silence fall as the Council huddled together at the top of the steps. All except for Sylvan and Gilda, still standing clear of their guards, still facing their people and waiting to listen to their demands.

The list was so long. He sent it to the Council's open com line.

"These are the most urgent. And we need Council to enforce them. Give us back our place in this world. Education for our children, our old jobs and our homes back, and the Council to make that happen."

Der Greystan shoved his way to the front of the pack. "Insufferable. Impossible!"

"We force people to give up their jobs to dirtsiders? To turn over their property to you? You're asking for a police state," said Gilda. "Is that what you fought for?"

"What do you think we lived under for five years? You can deny it all you like, but this planet is still in a state of emergency."

Trundain an Delsin plowed forward. "The rule of law cannot be overturned like this. Without laws, we have nothing."

"It depends how you use the laws, Councilor," said a voice beside Jacquel. He looked across. Yurin an Begum, another familiar face who should not be here. An old friend, Marthe's lawyer, and a leading Resistance fighter. "We need law, but we also need justice," Yurin said.

"Justice, phaw," scoffed der Greystan. "We let you get away with this, and Hathe becomes a peasant world."

An angry murmuring greeted that, and Gilda hastily raised a hand. "No, never again, but it will stay a divided world. How many of you have family and friends who spent the occupation on Mathe through no choice of theirs? Who went there because they were told to go there, for one reason and one reason only? Because that's where they could best serve Hathe. I had no choice; most on Mathe had no choice. We didn't live through what you endured, but we spent those years terrified for our loved ones back here. Today, you risk alienating every one of them. Today, by this action, you reject them all."

She stared straight at Jacquel as she said that. His family, Father and Mama, his sisters. Rheia. That's who she meant. His heart clenched and the muttering from behind said many felt the same. How many had endured conversations like that last one with his father; that harrowing tiffen session with Mama? Had felt abandoned by family twice over as a result?

And how many moonies carried the same guilt burden as Rheia asn Postrova/Forvrad? Forced to live their lives pretending their hearts hadn't been cut out and left behind.

"We waited, we tried. Now we take," said Jacquel uncompromisingly. He held the plaque aloft, sighting the Security guard who'd given it to him standing to the side of the councilors. "Com me the plans for the memorial garden, soldier."

The man looked shocked. *How'd you know?* he sent in code.

A plaque this fine has to have a well-planned site to do it justice.

Jereth has it. He's in the crowd, halfway back.

The guard signaled in field code to a brown-haired man waving up at him, and a file landed in Jacquel's public folder. He set his com to project it to all the gathered dirtsiders. *Is this plan acceptable to you?* he signaled.

Above, the Council began to fidget, and even Gilda and Sylvan looked nervous. They had both dealt with Resistance troops long enough to know when dirtsiders were coding each other, and to know they had no way to break into their com channels.

This memorial, we're all agreed?

Assent came back through the coms. Not surprising, given the rightness he'd felt as soon as he saw the plans. A simple tree, a true Hathian native planted on a small rise to stand guard at the entrance to the Avenue gardens. In the quiet left corner, closest to the children's play area and facing both the Council House and Mama's precious library. Rule of law, knowledge, and democracy combined. He could see children rolling down those slopes and falling into giggling piles at the bottom, then running up and one day reading the plaque under the tree at the top.

That was what every dirtsider had fought for.

Thank you. "Ras, call for volunteers to build this, and make sure they understand exactly what they're taking on."

Then he turned to face the Council. "I've just sent you a plan for a memorial. We are currently organizing the construction and will advise you of the details when ready. For the rest, dirtsiders have waited too long. Just remember, you pushed us into this."

He lifted his voice, sending a field message at the same time.

"Soldiers, guard the Council," he said to the troops standing at attention on the council forecourt.

"So now we're prisoners?" Der Greystan glared from the top of the steps.

"Not at all, Councilor," said the troop leader. "Our duty is to protect the Council of Hathe, and we do not forget our duty."

"Then clear that rabble from Council grounds."

"My apologies, but those people are currently standing on public space, and the Council building belongs to the people of Hathe. Nor are they currently threatening violence against any council member."

"It's a protest, not a lynch mob," said Sylvan sharply. "Protest is a healthy part of any properly functioning democracy."

Der Greystan looked less than impressed. "Denying who rules this planet is treason, not protest. Security, arrest them."

"Not possible, Councilor," said the troop leader. "That shield is controlled by the colonel's squad. We can't get to them, even if we had grounds to."

Der Greystan turned nearly purple, glaring down at Jacquel. "Switch it off. That's a direct order, Colonel."

"My apologies, Councilor," said Jacquel, "but I take my orders from the head of Security, and I understand he is currently in conference. Please pass your concerns on to him." Which should prove interesting, though he wasn't sure yet for whom.

At which der Greystan nearly popped an artery and he swung around and marched back inside.

Ras, check on those moonie Security troops. Make sure they're still off in outer Westfallin doing extra training.

A pause then Ras came back. *Don't worry, Cap. Deln Crantz has extended their placement there. They're far away from trouble and out on exercises in a particularly remote part of the region.*

And the dirtsiders who first caught us.

Another pause. *Still stationed on the other side of the planet in Kraystona. Cold enough there to freeze any bright ideas out of them, I reckon,* he finished with the slight waver that told of a chuckle.

"So now what?" called out Sylvan.

Jacquel recognized that look on Sylvan an Castre's face. Whenever he and the asn Castre twins got in trouble over their heads, Sylvan had looked just like that. "What now?" he'd always asked, before leaving them to figure it out.

Not always for the best, and from the look on Sylvan's face he didn't expect today to be different.

Only this time the stakes were a whole lot bigger.

"We'll let you know when we decide, Councilors," Jacquel answered drily, and turned back to the crowd behind them. What now, indeed.

To start with, how about we organize this crowd by the old Resistance divisions? he coded on a tight band to Ras.

Ras scanned the crowds. *Seems best*, he coded back.

On your head be it, suddenly sounded in his ear in stilted code, and he glanced up startled, to catch a triumphant grin from Gilda as she and Sylvan strolled back into the Council House. Having the last word, as too often before.

He signaled deln Crantz. *How does Gilda an Rathman know Resistance field codes?*

She's Council, young man. She worked with the Resistance all through the occupation.

Yes, but none of the Council had ever before bothered to learn the field versions.

She's not working with us now. So why use it?

You expect her to tolerate you talking all around her in field code she can't understand? You should know her better than that. Did you think they would do nothing when you started1 playing these games?

Now you're against us too?

A hitch, a quaver that might have been laughter. *Don't imagine you know what I think, young des Trurains*, signaled his boss. Then signed off, leaving Jacquel with a sinking feeling that his boss was rather pleased with this latest development, for his own very convoluted reasons

Which meant Jacquel better make sure this went well. Or at least wasn't a complete disaster, which right now seemed a very optimistic hope.

He turned to Ras and the rest of his squad.

It took a couple of hours of talk, arguing, confusion and stonewalling to wrangle the crowd into some kind of order, and step them back from the edge of open warfare. The food arriving in pallet loads helped the most. The ex-Resistance Control Center people had slotted seamlessly back into their former roles, arranging for water and food, a play area for the youngsters, mothers and babies sent to a protected area and checking that everyone's com linked into the new Control Center.

He saw a group of toddlers playing a game of catch the skitterby, in shrieks of laughter as the creature kept just out of reach. Oblivious to the occasion, unlike their mothers. Eyes never left the youngsters, and fingers constantly touched ear or wrist coms. Like most ex-Resistance, they still wore the almost invisible Resistance patches that had kept the dirtsiders in constant contact with the Resistance communication network. The kind of fear they'd lived with couldn't be set aside easily. Today's actions wouldn't help either.

"You reckon we know what we're doing?" he muttered to Ras.

"Nope, but what's new? Come on, they're waiting."

"Who?"

A dubious grin from the big man. "Those come for the meeting of course. All good revolutions start with a meeting."

Sure enough, a crowd had gathered at the site of the proposed memorial.

"Come on, Cap. Best face forward," said Ras.

Jacquel had seen the tabloids too. "Sometimes I think Security kept me on after the overthrow for my face alone."

"Nah, Cap, you forget your *beautiful manner.*"

Jacquel threw a punch in his second's direction and Ras barely blocked it, he was laughing so hard.

"You're coming with me," Jacquel said as soon as Ras showed signs of recovering. "If I have to do the playing-to-the-crowd bit, you can play the dutiful second."

That just set Ras laughing again. Yeah, he couldn't remember when Ras had ever acted like that either. But Jacquel had played his public persona enough times now that it was a second skin he slipped on easily. Too damn easily.

A crowd had gathered in a grove of trees near the children's playground. He recognized faces: all leading figures in the various Resistance divisions before the fall. Several mothers in the group kept one eye on their young, despite the number of caregivers obviously standing guard over them, but Jacquel wasn't about to call them on it.

"Right, who's in charge?" he said as all eyes swiveled toward him and Ras.

A woman looked startled. "You, of course."

"No, I just threw a fit of temper and started this thing."

"And we're counting on you to finish it, Cap. We've all been waiting for a spark like this, and you gave it to us."

"Everyone knows you. Dirtsiders trust you."

"You can't have seen the recent vidcasts," he said, thinking of the damning images.

"Enough of us have served under deln Crantz," said another man. "We know when someone's working."

They couldn't be serious. "I'm not the one for this," he tried again.

"You've got the connections, the political and military nous, and we trust you," said another woman. "You're in charge, Cap."

He looked around the crowd, saw the nods, the open eyes, the same determination linking them all. Heart sinking, he accepted defeat. "On your heads be it. So, give me your plans so far." He nodded to the first in the circle.

They were more prepared than he'd expected, the list growing longer with each speaker. "We need to prioritize," he said.

"But…the memorial…"

"Comes first. No question. But after that? Ideas?"

He let them talk, let them feel the power of setting out ideas and having them listened to. From time to time, he'd see one opening their mouth to talk, then stopping as if caught out. Then speaking anyway, and he watched fascinated as their shoulders came back and their voice firmed. Became the voice of the person they'd been before the occupation.

By the end of it, he'd even had to referee a couple of all-out squabbles. Ras winked, and he grinned back.

"The top priorities, then," he said when he judged they'd had enough, and more talk only pandered to individual vanities. "Proper schooling for our children. Make sure they don't get left behind."

Education for the youngest had suffered badly during the occupation. Too young to hide a knowledge of sophisticated technology, they had been allowed to run wild, learning only the basics. Reading, writing and math, science restricted to what they could see and feel, and tradecraft skills to a level unknown to their Mathian fellows. The older children had stopped school altogether, caught up in working for the Resistance and conscripted by the Terrans.

Now, they needed a syllabus to catch up with those in moonie schools. To learn to be the children of an advanced world again.

"That's all very well, but what are those well-trained young rascals to do after that? They need real jobs."

Ras broke in on his private com line. *Cap, Dreya tells me that food we bought in is about gone and we've got plenty of those 'young rascals' here tonight.*

Pillars, exactly what they didn't need. Hyped-up, over-eager young men and women ready to start a fight with anyone they thought threatened their uprising. *Mobilize all militia reservists and set them on perimeter watch. Then seed the rest through the crowd—and find an ex supply clerk to sort out food deliveries. Full bellies should stave off some of them.*

Done, coded Ras a beat later. *But we also need to give that crowd something to do now. A job with hard labor for the hotheads.*

Which was how he found himself on a hastily organized stage, explaining to the many hopeful faces staring up at him what they were going to have to do next to keep the protest camp running.

"Better make that in shifts," said an older woman. He looked at her blankly. "This patrol of yours to keep us safe and all the other work. I was in the Citadel control room, and right now I need to get my kids home to bed. Every single one of us is coming back here tomorrow, and we don't need some Pillars blind senate mob taking over the park while we're home sleeping."

Bedtime? Jacquel looked up, startled to see Hathe's largest moon riding the western sky and the shadows of evening sending long spikes over the parklands. He gestured at Ras.

"Set up a picket. All children and one parent to go home. We need at least half the remainder to stay overnight to hold our position here." He looked at the woman who'd spoken up. A bit older, and that no-nonsense look on her face said she was used to managing organization and logistics, both of her family and anyone else who dared come into her sphere.

"Bedding and shelter for the stayers," she promised him. "We've all done enough nights out on the plateau or slept in those Pillars cursed peasant beds. This will be a picnic."

He nodded thanks. "No freezing our backsides off or trying to sleep on sharpened rocks?"

"Hah. We can do better than field-duty standards. You need everyone fresh tomorrow." With which she bustled off, grabbing three children from the play area as she went, and in quick time hustled a crowd of helpers around her, talking non-stop even as she herded her offspring on their way.

She was true to her word. As the sun went down, he did a tour of the grounds. A perimeter guard of Security troops tracked him on the other side of the shielding that surrounded the entire area, shadowing the dirtsider troops on this side.

Then he realized he'd seen the dirtsider guard he was talking to before. Earlier in the day, the man had been patrolling the outside of the shield perimeter in an official Security uniform. He took note as he continued his tour and had his suspicions confirmed. Dirtsider troops from the Security Department had come up with their own roster, swapping between guarding their fellow dirtsiders from inside the perimeter then discreetly switching over, pulling on an official uniform for their turn among the Security troops on the outside of the shield barrier monitoring the rebel encampment for the Council.

The spice on the top: a dirtsider collective cleaned the troopers' Security uniforms before turning them over to the patrollers at shift changeover.

Not that he said anything about it. If the Council was turning a blind eye, he saw no reason to do otherwise. It worked, and it kept the hotheads on both sides under control— or so he hoped.

Cap, you're needed.

Or maybe not under control.

A crowd of young dirtsiders had gathered opposite one of the side entrances to the park. Opposite, a street lined with the most popular nightclubs in town, and facing them across the shielding, a gang of the sons and daughters of the elite who had spilled from the clubs, high on the night and whatever substance they'd been taking. Moonies all, with an overdeveloped sense of entitlement, swaggering up to the shield and yelling taunts at the dirtsiders.

"Back to your villages, clodmuckers."

"Dirt lovers."

"A bit late for you, ain't it boys and girls," came back from the dirtsider youths.

"Yeah, your mamas are out looking for you."

"Pretty boys."

"Mud scum."

If it had stayed at yelling, Jacquel might have left it to the Security troops monitoring the ruckus from both sides of the shield, but next minute one of the moonies picked up a rock from a garden and hurled it at the shield, which the dirtsiders answered with sticks, rocks, and whatever they could find

Control, how much can the shield barrier take?

He signaled the troopers on both sides, ordering them in a sweep on the troublemakers—moonie and dirtsider both.

A voice came over his com. *Freneth an Dreyans here, Cap. Senior technician. That shield's holding, but I don't like our chances if both sides make a rush at it.*

Acknowledged. Extra power to this section, and let Security on both sides know to step up patrols on the rest of the shield rim.

He sent a signal to the nearest trooper, and heard the orders rippling through the forces on both sides, both on his Resistance links and the secure Security streams. Suddenly, bright lights washed the whole area, stark and highlighting the smallest action. At the same time, the encircling troopers moved in on the young troublemakers.

It didn't take long. They had the moonies quashed and cuffed in minutes; the dirtsiders took a bit longer. All old enough to have worked with the Resistance, dirtsider teens knew more about self-defense than they did their letters. Jacquel waded into action with the troopers, all of them trying their best to avoid harming their marks. By the end, they carried as many bruises as the dirtsider young, but youthful bravado was no match for stunners, advanced training and top-level cuffs. The guards dragged the kids up in front of Jacquel.

"You think we're playing some kind of game here?" He focused on the boy in the middle—bigger, angrier and glaring daggers at his captor. "You got an excuse for this idiocy, young man?"

"They started it, Cap."

"Is that the best you can do? Every one of you kept your mouths shut under the Terrans, and now you can't do it for one night. Are you soft moonie children, or tough dirtsider heroes?"

The boy lifted his head, pride hurt, but Jacquel didn't let that sway him. Too much sat on a knife-edge.

A younger boy elbowed the bigger one. "Heroes, Cap," he said. "Just don't seem anyone else remembers it." Brothers, Jacquel would guess. The eyes staring straight up at him had the same sharp green as the angry one's.

"I remember it," he said firmly to the boys. "Every single dirtsider here remembers it, and our job is to make sure that everyone else on Hathe remembers it."

He swept into a formal at-ease military stance, hands behind his back. "Remembers you as heroes. Not backstreet punks yelling out stupid names and squabbling with rejects from Mathe. You understand me."

For too long, it stood in the balance. Until slowly, one by one, heads dropped, feet scuffed the dirt. The younger boy elbowed the big one in the middle again.

"Understood?" said Jacquel, staring straight at the ringleader.

Another of those sharp jabs.

"Understood," mumbled the bigger boy. "So what you going to do to make them remember?"

Ah, the crucial question.

"It's still being decided," said Jacquel, honesty being the only option here. "We will sort it out, and you will all have a role to play. Just don't let us down in the meantime."

They muttered, grumbled, but one by one they stepped back. On the far side of the shield, the Security troopers led the moonie kids away.

Detox and a warning? he asked them.

The squad leader flicked a hand signal at him to say he had it from here, then ordered them off. *Seems best,* he coded with a head nod. *Stops any vidcasters stirring up trouble.*

He nodded back and coded his thanks. It may be a far cushier solution than the moonie brats deserved, but the trooper had the right of it. Sober them up, give them a good talking to and deliver them home like any other kids who'd partied too hard and roughed the edges of the law.

Nothing to do with civil strife and dangerous uprisings in the center of town. Too many vidcast channels were out there. Watching, waiting. Hungry for a real story.

Hungry for trouble and mayhem.

CHAPTER NINETEEN

"Cap, you can't keep going without sleep."

Jacquel peered blearily up from his com screen, where vidcasters played their games of who had the juiciest scoop on the protest camp, and on the growing tide of support across the planet by dirtsiders banding together in protest. He'd just seen Varda an Tarkst angrily denying having any part in the Avenue Park camp and giving a scathing interview on his management of the plateau mission. Seemed the woman still hadn't found a comfortable enough niche to suit her. Not that any existed.

"Those reports won't get any better, no matter how long you stare at them."

He should know the woman talking to him. Then placed her. The one who'd taken on organizing a place for everyone to sleep last night, magically rustling up the mini tent city now covering the park before taking her kids home to their own beds. "You're back," he said somewhat inanely. "Your children?"

"Safe at home, along with all the others too young to risk in this place."

Panic flashed. "Security know about that?"

"All taken care of. Dirtsiders know how to look after their own, even if some don't act like it."

He obediently switched off the com feed—nothing worth seeing on it anyway—just as a head popped around the corner of his field tent. "Council wants to talk to you, Cap."

"They can wait," said the woman.

He stood up and waved her away. "No, I'm coming."

But she placed herself square in his way, arms crossed and legs astride. "No, you're not. Not till you've had at least six hours sleep, young man."

"That's the Council calling, not the neighborhood gossip."

"And you're in no state to deal with that pack of slippery endogs. Not with a brain that ain't had a sec's respite since early yesterday." She turned to the young trooper at the door. "You go back and tell the Council that the colonel will get back to them as soon as he's available—and yes, that is all they need to know. Nothing like uncertainty to make a body more amenable."

He couldn't help the dry chuckle. The woman was right. Nor did she show any signs of budging, so he conceded and sent the trooper to deliver her message. The woman still didn't move. "Madame…?"

"Your sleep tent's next door and a fine plate of best Hathian fare is waiting on the table. Food, then sleep, Cap."

He tried glaring at her, but she wasn't moving.

"As you command, it seems," he grumbled.

"Always heard you had a good head on your shoulders." She still watched him as he walked—no, stumbled—to the waiting tent next door. A familiar design, one he'd used so often during the occupation he felt a weight leave his shoulders as soon as he stepped inside. It was as if the months after the overthrow never existed, and life had slipped back into normal gear. Ignoring the food, he fell onto the bed, his eyes closed and he slipped into oblivion.

Only to wake far too soon after, sweating and heart pounding. "It was a dream. Only a dream." But no matter how many times he repeated it, the fear refused to let go.

Rheia, surrounded on all sides, trapped and terrified, holding a knife out in front of her, and a sheer drop behind as her enemies moved closer and closer. One step back, another. Inside he screamed but she didn't hear him. A stumble, and he had to watch that bright fearless hair flying free and doomed as she fell, over and over, disappearing in a soundless canticle of horror.

He couldn't com her, not without bringing danger to her door and setting her on that cliff edge, but he needed desperately to know she was safe. Heart in mouth, he punched at his com. *Urgent message for Gof deln Crantz.*

An assistant came on line after far too long a wait. *The commander will respond as soon as able. Please confirm the priority ranking of this request.*

First rank, he coded in deliberately. Security owed him.

"Deln Crantz here. This better be important, Colonel."

"Rheia asn Postrova. What's her status?"

An exasperated snort. "Hold while I put a call through to the DIA."

Silence. He put his things to rights and put out an update call to all the group leaders. But he did not leave the tent, not yet. Finally, deln Crantz came back. "She's safe, under surveillance and successfully making contacts among the moonies."

"No, where exactly is she now?"

"In her apartment, dressing for a meeting. And under full surveillance by Security as well as her own department. We won't let her go anywhere unprotected."

Something inside him eased. A fraction only, but enough to let him keep going. "Keep her under surveillance. This camp. It's not going to help her."

Another snort. "You should have thought of that before you marched into the council chambers like some fired-up superhero. So, what's next in this brilliant campaign of yours?"

If Jacquel had any doubt of his commander's satisfaction at the turn of events, that trace of delight in his voice banished it. "I'll tell you that when you tell me just how long you've been waiting for me to do this."

A roll of laughter. "Always a pleasure talking to you, young man." With which deln Crantz signed off, leaving Jacquel with a nasty feeling he'd missed a whole chunk of somethings here.

But Rheia was safe, and he could keep the driving need for her at bay a bit longer. "What am I going to do next, *sir?*" he muttered. "Change Hathe. That's what."

Someone had cleaned his dress uniform while he slept. He made a last check in the holo-mirror, checking that all the medals and braid were lined up in precise rows. Then he marched out of his tent, to a huge grin from Ras and a sharp call of "Troop, form up."

His squad snapped to attention, all wearing the identical grin.

"What?" he said.

"We about to cause a ruckus, Cap?" said one.

"Oh, yeah," said Ras, and they all lined up beside him. Disreputable, proficient. The best damn soldiers on Hathe.

He called through to the shield controller. *Let a vidcaster through.* No sooner sent than a vidcam swooped into view. He set his com to discover the channel. Plains Ten-Seven; planet wide and popular. Just what he wanted.

He stopped and stared straight into the main sensor nodule. "You want to know what we're doing here? Be at the avenue entrance immediately after noon prime." He swiveled, set his back to the thing, and sent another order through. To block entry to all vidcams until prime.

"You heard him," said Ras. "Scram, or no gossip for you."

A whoosh of air, and the control room sent the thing out of range. Good. He had work to do.

They cut it fine, grabbing at lunch while they talked to the crowd gathered in the center of the camp. He'd sent the call out on the widest dirtsider bands but hadn't been sure any would answer.

"You're all willing to speak up today?" he said to the volunteers at the front, "and no one vulnerable will be hurt by it?" No child must suffer one more hurt on Hathe; his own personal line he refused to cross. "We ready to do this?"

Eager faces looked at him. "Long past ready, Cap. Long past," called one at the back.

He thrust a fist in the air and they joined him with a loud ringing cry of "Hathe, now and forever."

He could be back on the plateau, hiding from the Terrans and dreaming of the day they could say that out loud. But today was real, today they would bring those words home.

"Right. Let's go."

As one, the group marched with him. A murmur rose as they passed, spreading in a wave throughout the camp. He could feel it as much as hear it, a groundswell of support pushing him on to the waiting cluster of drone cams at the avenue entrance. Drones held outside the perimeter by the dirtsiders' shield and demanding he deliver.

His marchers came to a halt ten paces from the end of the avenue, just shy of the outer shielding. "Let the drones through," he ordered the comms group. "Recognized broadcasting agencies only. No Security forces, no interplanetary forces' drones, and definitely no senate or corporate drones."

A dark cloud of whirring bots swooped through the shrubs guarding the entrance and shimmered as they hit the shield and passed through. An angry clatter marked their passage; the drones of the unwanted vidcasters falling in a racket of useless protests.

Jacquel stood at the entrance and held up a hand for silence. The crowd of supporters stood motionless and his squad eased back to lose themselves in the crowd. Fingers and brains on full alert and keeping him within their protective orbit, Ras assured him.

Leaving him alone, to step forward and face the swarm of vidbots.

"Colonel Jacquel des Trurains, former Resistance agent, and dirtsider citizen of Hathe," he said.

Dead quiet. His dirtsiders waited, barely breathing.

"A dirtsider citizen of Hathe," he repeated, letting the power of his voice ring out, to the hovering drone sensors and through them to every vid screen in every bar, every home, every meeting place and hall focused on this place. "Dirtsider. Just a word, some say. But that word has brought every one of us here today and across Hathe, other dirtsiders are beginning to rally to support us. In every city, every region on Hathe, dirtsiders are saying *enough*. Yes, I am a dirtsider, and I'm proud to say that."

A pause. A gathering in, and he heard the crowd behind him breath again as he gave the bots a cool, brief smile.

"We Hathians all fought for our home world and none of us was given a choice where or how we fought. In those far-off days, each Hathian—man, woman and child—went where Hathe needed them. Some to Mathe, some even farther off-world. And some had to stay and face the Terrans. Dirtsiders stayed. We became less than ourselves, did what was needed to lure the Terrans into the trap our world and our system had aimed at them.

All of Hathe fought the Terrans, all of us did what we had to do to beat them." Then he lifted his head, set his jaw and let the challenge in his heart blaze in his eyes.

"But only dirtsiders died for Hathe."

You've got them, Cap, came softly in his ear from the comms team. *Coverage figures hit the eighty-percentile mark. Every major channel is live streaming it.*

He lifted his head a notch higher, putting every particle of sheer bravado he could summon into his pose, legs astride and hands crossed behind his back. Out of sight of the vidcams, he signaled with his fingers. *Viewing success?*

High. Traffic's stopped, work's stopped, and crowds are gathering in every main park on the planet. The Council and Senate have gone into closed session and refuse to talk.

In front of him, holo figures began forming. Well-known reporters from across the planet—here in the City, this continent, the other lands, cities, and regions, sparse and populous alike. Even some he recognized from long past holidays in the idyllic island sectors where planetary politics rarely intruded. But those islands had been forced to smile while they created a paradise escape for the Terrans brutalizing their world.

"Colonel,"

"Over here, Colonel."

A gaggle of cries as each vidcam, each shimmering human facade tried to attract his attention.

"Heartbreaking, Colonel," called out one, "we all agree on that. But what is it exactly you want?"

He lifted a hand and turned toward the holo-image. A woman, of mid years, sharp-boned and with a sneer on her face. One designed to provoke a reply. Didn't she realize she faced people who'd been provoked in ways she couldn't imagine?

"Heartbreaking, you say, madame. Let me show you what heartbreaking means." He turned to the crowd at his back, gave a nod, and a gap parted in the middle "We talk about the Unsung. We raise songs to them. But let me introduce you to the living Unsung, and to those the dead left behind."

One by one, they stepped forward. At first hesitant, some plain terrified, then stronger as they gathered their courage, heads lifting to stare straight into the vidcam sensors and share their stories.

"They took my family in the first wave. My father to the mines. My mother to the fields. My brother, my cousins, all my friends old enough to carry a plank went to the construction gangs. Half came back. My father and mother's bodies are still lost."

"They worked us but didn't see any reason to feed us properly. I fainted one day building the Citadel walls. They threw a bucket of water over me, dragged in a child off the street and ordered me to get back to work or watch the girl die. I worked."

"I was ordered to work in an officer's home. Clean, organize his household, keep him fed, clothed, run the house and act as secretary. Then at night, my duties changed." The woman stopped and Jacquel signaled to Dreya to stand beside her. But she didn't need help. A few seconds only, before her head rose proudly and she kept on speaking. Told her story in all its harrowing truth. Then stepped back, swung around and marched to take her stand in the front line of protesters, linking arms with the dirtsiders either side of her. Steadfastly refusing to be diminished by her role in the war.

Jacquel stepped up again. "The information Phaedra gathered for us in that house saved the lives of three thousand Hathians during the occupation and increased the chances of success at the overthrow by a full percentage point."

His arm swept back, taking in the line of those who had witnessed. Yes, the vid channels had been full of stories of the occupation in the early days of the peace. All of Hathe had heard the reports of returning journalists, seen the graphic reconstructions by academics, so many and in such detail that most viewers had got far past the point of being immune to horror. All so long ago, said the talk in the streets. And yes, the worst excesses had happened in the first year of war, with the next few years being more a time of dogged endurance as the occupation wore on—largely thanks to Hamon an Radcliff, curse him, bringing the Terrans' focus back to the driving need of Earth to get the ore it must have for survival and away from the wild banditry of the initial invasion. Hathian peasants and Terran overlords alike had settled into a more routine pattern.

But Terran soldiers didn't change, and casual brutality remained always a bare whisper away for the dirtsiders, too often without cause or warning.

The stories were old. But never before had they been told like this. By the victims in a cold, clear recitation that made what they said even more horrific. Never before accompanied by the occasional limp, the prematurely grayed and aging faces, the fear in the back of too many eyes that would never be banished.

"Dirtsiders have paid. Now, we demand restitution."

Jacquel pulled up his com and began to read out their demands. "Provide tailored education programs for our children to bring them back to where they would have been without the occupation. Along with trauma evaluation and counselling."

A reporter stepped forward. "That's already happening, Colonel. You're out of touch."

"The *record* says it's happening, but the programs they put in don't work. Our children are losing their place in a future Hathe. Use dirtsiders to make new programs; ones designed by us to suit the real needs of our children."

A few head nods. Helping children could never be denied.

"Restore ownership of all businesses and all properties back to the day of the Terran's arrival in Hathe space."

Open-mouthed gasps at that one.

"Compulsory retraining programs for all dirtsiders. All dirtsiders to be offered restoration of their jobs; the one's they had on the day of the Terrans' entry into Hathian space."

The murmur became shouts. "What about the people doing those jobs now? Doing them well. Far better than someone five years out of the loop."

Anya ven Fritheida of the Comms Central. A moonie, but known as a straight shooter.

"They'll have to wait for a vacancy, and work to earn it, just like they'd have had to if the Terrans had never come," he told her and watched the shock waves spread over the reporters' faces. "We didn't suffer so much for others to steal the future from us." He shoved up a hand at the chorus of shouted questions. "That's the start. We are preparing a full dossier of claims and will present them to Council once ready. Goodbye."

He gave them no time to protest, signaling the coms team to eject the vidcams, and swung around to walk away.

"Hey, this is a public space," he heard one reporter squawk as one by one, reporter avatars around her zapped into nothingness. A recognizable voice and a respected one, but he couldn't afford to pander to that. She may be in the right, but dirtsiders had too much to lose.

"Clear them all out," he repeated to the security team as soon as he'd gained the protection of the control tent.

"And their questions?"

"Will have to wait. Or are all the reports in yet?"

The look on the man's face said it all. Of course not. Near a third of the planet had stayed behind on Hathe, so many dirtsiders now fighting to get back a life. Yes, not all had suffered in this postwar Hathe. He was a prime example of that, thanks to a solid inheritance, an honorable family and his usefulness to the continuing security of Hathe. But the Security Department couldn't employ all the Resistance fighters. The dregs of war; that's what too many dirtsiders had become.

"Bring up the vid channels," he ordered, and watched the multiple screens as one panel of experts after another scavenged over the bones of his words. "Haven't any of them heard of *research* or *checking the facts?*"

A chuckle from the comms tech. "Cap, you been born too long to expect that."

"Doesn't stop me hoping," he growled. "And the other regions? What's happening there?"

Protests, that's what was happening. Camps like their own in most of the big cities, protest marches in big towns and small, strikes bringing to a halt critical services in region after region. And among it all, violence and outbursts from dirtsiders too frustrated and angry to care about consequences or waiting for an alternative. Those like the group who had been duped into his and Rheia's first kidnapping.

He watched channel after channel, then switched to the official Council newscasts. Der Greystan dominated the coverage. "Irresponsible ingrates," seemed to be the man's favorite phrase, his mouth the disapproving scowl of a spoiled brat.

"Add in the response polls," he said.

The lines plunged downwards every time der Greystan appeared, then wobbled every which way during the vids of protests and dirtsider interviews. Undecided, he'd call the populous—except about der Greystan. Their opinion of the senior Councilor was down and diving deeper into a bog hole. "Suddenly I feel a whole lot better," he grinned. "Take that, Councilor."

"Hey, that's Drushka over there," said the comms tech watching a vid of a protest march.

"And Jermiah. Remember him in that farming gang. Look at him shouting out about how tough it was. Lazy fragger spent the whole occupation pottering in the fields."

"You think? Zoom onto his face," said a dry voice on the side. Jacquel looked around to see he'd gathered a crowd, all avidly watching their fellow dirtsiders shout out their grievances. The comms tech zoomed in on the man at the front of the march in Cloughtarch. Zoomed in tighter again, hovering over the man's right cheek and neck line. Pale egg-shaped patches bloomed sickly against the man's healthy bronze skin.

"What are those?" said Jacquel.

"That's what happens when you work all day in the gardens on Islandia without head covering or sun protection. Peasants don't burn or get dehydrated, you see."

He looked at the speaker, a small woman with an angry curl to the corner of her mouth. "I was the team medic for that sector. I had Jermiah in my emergency recovery rooms more times than I care to remember. That man has reason to shout out."

"We all have good reason to shout out. All honor to Jermiah," Jacquel said quietly. She gave him a short nod back, and many others around did the same. There was a look in their eyes he hadn't seen for a long time. A light he hadn't seen since the first Terran ships landed on Hathe and the reality of what they faced hit home.

"He got burned right enough, but mostly because the man's plain bullheaded," said the first voice again with a choked laugh. "The rest of us knew to pick fast, then slow down in the heat and pick the stuff on the low-down bushes. But not Jermiah. He reckoned he wasn't going to bend down for no man, even to keep out of the sun."

Jacquel tensed, but the medic chuckled. "I may have thought the man was brave; didn't mean he was bright."

And a chorus of laughs surrounded them. They'd all had team members like that. Soon, others on the screens drew notice, familiar faces, all with stories attached, and after a while, Jacquel left them to it. Word of the vidcasts had spread, and throughout the camp, knots of dirtsiders stood and cheered with the other dirtsiders from across the planet. So many marches, strikes, and protest camps had broken out that someone was sure to find a familiar face, and join in the laughter and tears. Dirtsiders finding they had a voice, and using it to tell the rest of Hathe what they thought about what had happened to them.

Jacquel eased quietly off to the side, signaling his squad and the main Security officers present to follow him.

They gathered in a grove of trees near the far edge of the camp, in an area of the Avenue Park set aside for native gardens. A precious area that many had grown up loving as children, now left untouched by the tents and services of the ever-growing camp. Jacquel kept one eye on the crowd, his com links open and on full alert, as he drew his small group in.

"They seem happy enough for now."

Jacquel looked at the speaker and checked his ID on his com. "First officer deln Vladoss, isn't it?"

The man nodded.

"And how long do you think they'll stay happy, deln Vladoss?"

"About as long as it takes the Council to drum up some moonie troopers and try to clear us out of here."

Jacquel let out a silent sigh. Somebody had said it, said the awful truth this camp and all those protests made inevitable and Sylvan and Gilda could hold off the other factions on Council only so long.

Hathians were now set against Hathians.

CHAPTER TWENTY

The walls of her apartment closed in on Rheia. The vidcasts screamed at her, trumpeting of sedition, an armed uprising in the center of the capital, bolstered by interviews with bystanders reckless enough to give a reporter a provocative comment. She switched feeds, searching, searching one after another. All the same, all broadcasting their diet of pulp. Rabid dirtsiders causing mayhem and tension by their uncivilized sedition.

Did moonies own all the channels? She smacked a fist against a wall, ignoring the crack of pain in her knuckles. She so badly wanted to be out there with the protesters, raising her voice in their chorus. To demand justice, demand some kind of return for the years of loneliness and strife.

But no, she must stay here, must carry on as if the streets filled with angry protesters and belligerent moonies meant nothing. Must ignore the vids while Jacquel was out there, body and heart cast on the line, an open target for all the vile spleen spewing from the ether.

And her? Some days, she felt no further ahead than when she'd started this insane endeavor.

These drekking walls. She had to get outside, now.

Not far from the central heart of the City lay a famous stretch of parklands. Called simply the City Gardens in the twisted pragmatism of the capital and famed as a refuge for the native plant systems of a myriad of Hathe's unique ecosystems, it had been protected from the Terrans by shielding during the occupation and maintained by a sophisticated network of sensors and garden bots. Now, the park had sprung back to glorious life under the loving ministrations of its returned guardians. A perfect escape from the prison walls of her apartment and her mission.

She walked in the massive gates and immediately felt the horror ease. A man waved, a gentle smile on his face, before bending back to the tiny plant at his feet. She'd watched the vidcast of the official reopening of the gardens from her hotel on Samarkan. A rare day of unfettered happiness it had been, the returning staff mingling with cries of joy as dirtsider and Mathe-based staff celebrated their reunion after long years apart. Yes, there were gaps in the ranks, faces missing, bodies changed by privation on Hathe or incarceration on Mathe, but that was not for today.

No, that day had been for exclaiming at a beloved plant rediscovered, for plans to further develop and expand the gardens and for schemes for a new area to be made into a living memorial to those lost years.

All together; joined in one purpose. The joy of that day had carried her through that last mission as nothing else could have done, worn out after too many years as a lost stranger in foreign worlds. As she wandered down the pathways today, Rheia breathed in the smells and the sounds, and watched the staff treasuring the work of their creation. She batted away tears at the sight of two men carefully planting out a new area, the work too sensitive to be left to bots. One man marked still with the new sunburn marks on pallid skin that spoke of one returned from Mathe, the other with a slight limp and the wary dropped head of a dirtsider peasant.

But today they worked side by side, talked and argued, called on years spent working together before history tore them apart. Joked, teased, laughed and dropped into serious discussion and good-hearted argument.

Working together.

Rheia eased back into the shade of a swatch of grasses, blending in with the changing shades of light and dark, and watched them for a long time. This was what she labored for. For this, she could endure those meetings. How long she wandered after that, she couldn't say, but knew she would come back to the gardens often.

Long hours later, she slipped back into her apartment. Not unnoticed, the too cool salute from the guard at the door said she'd been watched, her freedom illusory. As she entered the door, her com buzzed an alarm to remind her of tonight's reception in the home of a well-connected City identity. If only she could ignore it. Another evening spent uttering vapid nothings and getting no closer to finding out who lurked beneath the poisonous whispers surrounding her.

For a brief while, she'd glimpsed another path. Those days with Jacquel des Trurains, sharing the fear and the struggle of their adventures, finding laughter—and that one night. For one night, she had belonged to someone again.

Forget it. Pretend it didn't happen. So much easier than to remember light and warmth and know how far out of reach they were now.

You are alone.

The alarm pinged again, and her wardrobe program summoned her. A half-hearted slam of flat palm against the wall, and she turned to see what mirage the apartment's top-of-the-line system had created for her tonight.

A formal occasion, obviously. Coolly elegant. She knew the kind of names on the guest list even before she checked the details on her com. Politicians, government officials and those eager to extract something from them. Prime fodder for her explorations, but she'd thought that on too many other nights.

An angry ping again as her wardrobe reminded her it was time to enter the grooming unit.

"I'm coming—and you're only a machine."

Her wardrobe was not impressed. "Madame scheduled this occasion on the tenth Secator," it said in its most prim modulation.

"Yes, yes." She waved a hand, gesturing at the least objectionable of the fabulous creations, and stepped into the grooming unit, to emerge shortly after gowned and bejeweled and fit to astonish.

Or so proclaimed the image staring back at her from the holo-mirror. She set it to revolve, minutely examining each view. "It'll do."

"Yes, madame."

You are a machine, she felt like snapping back, but being reduced to childish whining twice by the thing was too much. "Time to go," she pronounced instead, hoping she sounded like the woman in charge of this apartment rather than a coward fleeing the battle zone.

The evening was as bad as she'd expected, and as useless. Like everything she tried these days.

Increasingly, she took to haunting the gardens, the one place she found solace as the days became weeks and the vidcasts blared their filth while the lines dividing Hathians soured and hardened. And one day, she realized she was not the only one needing its blessing. Wandering a far path, easing in and out of the grasses she was most drawn to, she glimpsed a moving shaft of bright silver hair on a head disappearing from view, a head engraved in her soul. She eased back into the shadows but couldn't resist the urge to follow.

It was him. Jacquel des Trurains, alone and unguarded. She eased deeper into the protective plant cover, slipping into the subtle ways of childhood, but too soon his swift footsteps took him out of range, forcing her to give up her pursuit or risk exposure. The shadows embraced her as she eased back, watching that familiar figure disappear from sight. Back to the dirtsider camp, to the safety of his guards and away from the hate that flooded all those rooms and places she must live her life in.

She saw him again, brief fleeting glimpses on other visits. Always she was careful to avoid a meeting that might put him at risk—and her, she admitted, the attraction of that lean, upright figure no less now that in those days on the plateau. An attraction she could not afford, and could never allow to develop, even without that final rejection in his prison cell. When he had chosen Hathe over whatever it was growing between them.

Another night, and another party, no different from all the others and with the usual grab bag of guests. Leaders of the business class, up-and-coming new stars of the elite, a cluster of minor celebrities clinging to their temporary veil of importance, and low ranked politicians eager for advancement. By far too early in the evening, she was longing for an excuse to leave. She wandered through packed rooms, stopping here and there to plant a snippet of gossip or pick up a useful tidbit. Always forcing down the urge to scream or laugh outrageously.

Another room, another crowd of cawing gossipers. She couldn't face it any longer and veered sideways, seeking a side passage to a quiet study room she'd found in this house on another such occasion. Blessed silence and the welcome shadow of dimmed lighting enveloped her as she left the masses. One more corner, and her doorway beckoned.

"Oof."

Drek it. No escape after all. She checked her toes for injury, brushed down her tunic and hoped to repair the damage once she was safely hidden, then looked up.

"Rhei…Madame asn Postrova."

That voice. "Colonel des Trurains."

A sudden light from a far-off doorway lit his face. Just as gorgeous as ever. And at huge risk if anyone found him here. "I need to…I was just leaving," she mumbled, stepping sideways to move past him. A hand on her arm. His scent, warm, rich and oh so very inviting.

"Wait, Rheia. Are you safe? At least tell me that."

Her mouth dropped open. "Me, safe? What about you? What if you're seen?" Then another thought. "What are you doing here?"

"I had a meeting. The Security Department…Then I saw you, and hoped…" His hand tugged. "Not here." A strangled mutter. "Please, this way."

And fool that she was, she let him tug her down the hall and through the very door she'd been heading for. A quiet room, softly lit and colored in subtle brown and cool grays. A room designed to soothe. But that did not take in the man whose hand touched her back. The man who had rejected her so willfully at their last meeting. It made no difference. Nothing had changed, not for her, not in how he made her feel.

He pulled out a scanner and ran a quick program.

"Now we can talk."

She shook her head. "No, you have to leave now."

"I've got time, and we're covered." He lifted the scanner. "An old Resistance trick. Monitoring of this section is by autobot; we've blocked the alarm vectors. We're also running an alternative vidtape for the backup check on the feed. It's a technique the Resistance perfected during the war, using existing figures to create a projected reality."

"You are? What happens on it?" Anything to distract him.

"We argue. You are shocked and frightened. Then I leave, and you are left in tears."

She lifted her chin. "Not very flattering."

That unreliable grin of his flashed across his face, "Not what you would really do, no. But a wronged moonie with no backbone?"

She shook her head. "They won't buy that. I've been up against them in too many meetings."

"Not the top-level, but the Senator? It fits his world view nicely."

"He's not *that* stupid. Tears, yes. But not frightened."

He gave a half grin. "How about upset and angry."

"Better," she conceded, still hating it. "So, I fool the Senator into believing we are enemies and put the top dog on notice. Thanks for painting a target on my back."

"No. Yes." His hand tightened on her arm. "Move it to my back. As soon as they show their hand, you pull out." That beguiling grin had completely vanished. She wished the light in here was better. She badly needed to know what was in his eyes.

"You are safe?" he said again, that hand tightening, pulling her closer. She doubted he was even aware of it.

With him here? With her life, these past months? "Yes, I'm safe," she said.

"No, you're not," he said flatly, picking up the lie in her voice as no one else could. "Pillars, I want you out of there."

"I'm safe enough, considering," she argued back.

That had him dropping his hand and stepping back, leaving her shut out yet again.

"Considering the daily risks you run, which I only make worse with my antics."

"No." She took a breath, gathering all her courage. "What you're doing in that camp. It needed done. No one was listening. But why are you here now, in this room with me.?"

"Putting you at even more risk." A bitter laugh, and before she could think, she reached out and wrapped both hands around his shoulders He stood rigid, paused as if in shock, then his own arms came around her and squeezed hard. "I shouldn't have stopped you, you're right. I came here for a meeting. A crowd like this…it's a good cover for the people I need to see to gather in one place. But then I saw you, and…Deln Crantz's game, not seeing you…" A harsh breath, gasped in. "What I said in that prison. When I made you no more than a piece in a game."

Her breath matched his, sawing in, then out. Did he mean…? She shook her head, tried to sound normal. "It doesn't matter. And at least you've stopped using," she added. His arms dropped, shock slapping his face, and she pulled back her own hands "The diplomatic service is licensed to use mairfin as well."

"You?"

She squared her shoulders. "On occasion. For a few hours only. But not for weeks on end. Never that."

He tried to step back, his face closed over. "I was playing. Letting off steam. Didn't you see the vidcasts?"

She grabbed at his arms refusing to let him withdraw, not when she had laid herself so open. "Yes, I saw them. I saw a highly skilled undercover agent trying to unearth information, regardless of the cost to himself, to his sanity, to his very life."

A bitter laugh. "Came close enough to that happening" he admitted. "But don't set me on a pedestal, sweetheart. A cover story only works if there's a grain of truth in it. All those vidtales of me partying madly went viral for a reason One time · hero gone bad."

He believed it. That twisted half smile on his face, the tension in the muscles beneath her hands, but this man was a true hero, and she wasn't about to let him walk away from that. He needed to know someone believed in him still. That someone could desire him, regardless of what he'd done. She pulled his head down, pulling his mouth to meet hers. He held back for so long, body tensed to flee, then his hands came up, grasped her head as he opened his mouth and gave himself up to her. Drank greedily of the fire between them.

But only for so long. Warm arms holding her tight, a hard mouth and greedy tongue joining with hers, but then he must have remembered. The room where they stood, what he had done to her.

He lifted his head and she could have wept for the loss of that sanctuary and the bitterness in his voice. "No, it's too risky. I won't hurt you. Not again. And, Pillars forgive me, I can't even demand you stop your mission. Not after the chaos I've caused. What you're doing—it's more important now than ever."

He may be right, but for now, she badly needed to escape. She hauled his head back down, opened her mouth and drew him back into pleasure. Finally, when she felt him surrender, she lifted her head and glared at him. "We will succeed. You will browbeat those stupid councilors and all the blind nystats out there into doing their duty for the dirtsiders, and I will find out who is behind this moonie nonsense."

A breathless chuckle and a twisted grin. "If you say so, sweetheart, but not at this moment, please." A hand stroked down her back, folding her in, and another traced the line of her shoulder, arm, and caught her hand. He lifted it, touching each finger in turn to his lips, then held it tight. "There is a large bench behind me. It looks very comfortable."

This time, she laughed, low and husky. "*Very* comfortable?"

"But quite firm," he murmured back. "And that vidtape? We argue for a very long time on it."

A whistle cut through the haze of contentment that held her in thrall. Unhindered by injury, Jacquel des Trurains had brought the full force of his skills to their lovemaking. She had been half in love with him since those evening walks on the plateau. Now...

Another whistle; high-pitched, just on the edge of audible, setting her nerves on edge.

"What...?" Where was she?

The firm pillow under her head moved. His arm, lifting up, and she came back to reality. A bench in a room, a side shoot of where she should be. "The reception."

"Yes, sweetheart. Time to return." Jacquel des Trurains leaned over and his mouth caught hers again. "That was my alarm. All too soon, we need to be outside that door, verbally tearing each other to pieces before I make my escape."

"Oh." Then a giggle took her. "Only verbally."

He grinned. "Yes, and not that way. Decorum please, Madame asn Postrova."

She made a play of batting her eyes. "Certainly, Colonel." Then she arched her back and smiled. He groaned again.

"That timer can't be changed. I've already pushed my luck," He gave her one small kiss, that turned into a far longer one, then deliberately let her go and reached for his clothes. She sat up, smiling easily this time, and pulled on her own scattered clothes before using the grooming program on her comtab to restore her appearance A few moments later and she was ready.

He looked at her, brows crunched. "No, too good. We've been arguing, and there is a history between us."

"I will not give them the pleasure of smearing your name like that. You would not hurt me, or any woman."

His smile vanished. "You will, if it keeps you safe. I resent the false allegations about me; you hate all dirtsiders. We are both stubborn and strong-willed. Of course it ends badly."

"How badly?" She crossed her arms, already hating this.

He pulled her in. "Very badly. I need a torn sleeve and scratch marks. You need a slight bruise. Only the slightest."

She choked on the threatening sob. "How does that help? I kept silent when I could have quashed those charges. Please, don't make me prove them real now."

His lips touched hers, touched her cheeks, the tip of her nose, her brow. "I'm sorry, sweetheart. So sorry. It's for the surveillance sensors in the hallways. We couldn't switch their feeds as well—too complicated at short notice. Or in case we're seen."

But she had got herself under control. "It's for Hathe," she said, looking him square in the eyes and setting her mouth. "We have no choice."

"And it will bring this charade to an end sooner."

She shook her head. "Not soon enough. Never soon enough."

He didn't say it, perhaps knew she could not go on if he said anything of what lay in his heart or asked for the truth of hers. His face said it for him, or maybe it was only the hope coiled deep inside her. But he must not say the words; not yet, not till they were free.

"Do it then," she said. "Not a punch. You wouldn't do that. But bruising on my wrists, yes."

He nodded, lips straight and eyes the gray-blue of an ocean storm. Then seized her by the wrists, suddenly clamped down tight, hard and unforgiving and her body reacted for her, flinging him off, her fingers scratching along each hand. Just as he'd planned, she suddenly realized, sparing her from having to deliberately hurt him. Sparing her what he'd had to go through.

Then he tugged at his sleeve, dragged it against the sharp edge of a table, until a ragged gash in the wristband matched the scratch marks on his hands.

"That's enough," she said sharply. He nodded, face tight. "Ready."

One deep breath, two. Then she nodded back and marched to the door. A slam on the pad, and it slid open. She marched out, setting a scowl on her face and scrubbing at her cheeks for the benefit of anyone who might walk down the hall and catch them.

"That is the last time you catch me out like that, Colonel. Never again. Crawl back to your ground scum where you belong."

Was that her voice, that screeching shriek of a wronged harpy.

He glared back, cold as ice and back straight, one hand tightly clenched around the blood slowly dripping from the scratch marks on his hand. "My pleasure, Madame. To never see you again is my greatest wish. Farewell."

She could feel his stare as she marched down that corridor, saw with relief his guard pull him into the shadows and disappear from sight before she hurried back to the party.

Then saw who was coming towards her. Caya der Greystan, well-known socialite and daughter of a councilor. She put her head down and tried to avoid noticing her, hoping the woman would let her pass. No, a hand caught at her arm. She gave an artless gasp, which she doubted this woman would believe, and had no choice but to stop. No friend to dirtsiders, the woman was one of those Rheia suspected as being close to the hidden clique driving the moonie power grab.

"I'm sorry. I didn't see you, madame," she said.

"Yes, you looked to be quite elsewhere," said the other woman. "Are you all right, madame?" She peered at Rheia, her sharp gaze tracking over the marks of disorder and making concerned tuttings that reminded Rheia of a desert nystat chittering over its latest kill.

"I'm fine," she said, taking a discreet step back and setting her wrists out of sight.

The der Greystan woman put an arm around Rheia's shoulders, squeezing her as if in comfort and sending a waft of expensive perfume to assail Rheia's nostrils. Sharp, pungent and in questionable taste. "Say no more, madame. These are dangerous days, but you are safe here. I was about to return to the service area for a touch-up. Will you join me?"

Rheia had no choice but to accept. The woman must have seen Jacquel's faked vidscreen footage, although she should have had no right to it. Which meant this woman was squarely in the camp of those deln Crantz was hunting. She plastered a gratified smile on her face and followed Caya, though it was the last thing she wanted to do. She was nowhere near ready yet to face the melee of social mitherings found in the public anteroom and grabbed a private booth. There, she set the controls to minimize the bruises on her wrists and the grooming cycle to massage her face to maximum elegance phase. Their work had been done; Caya had seen them, and Rheia needed some kind of shield before facing the crowds again.

Not that it fooled Caya. The woman took one look at her carefully armored face, lifted an eyebrow, her gaze raking down her body and resting on her hands, before hustling her out of the booth and back to the main area with ill-disguised glee. She soon had them both buried in a cluster of avid sympathizers cackling with wit and veiled allusions to the bright future waiting. A future without the rude reality of dirtsiders, Rheia soon discovered. The women seemed to delight in each new revelation of the vid channels.

"They've done it now. That's the end of the dirtsiders."

"Yes, the Council won't tolerate this."

"What can you expect? They've been through so much, poor souls. We must do something for them," said one treacly voice.

Rheia had never heard such a welter of hollow claptrap. To be left out of the Resistance on Hathe was a mark of honor for these women.

"I could never have endured it. The drudgery…," screeched one woman.

"Only a peasant at heart could have pulled it off."

"Which we most certainly are not. No one of true quality or rank would qualify. Don't you agree, Madame asn Postrova?"

"As one who showed early on that you belonged in a sphere far above your birth." A waspish comment that set Rheia's gut in a tight knot of tension.

"Possibly," she murmured, "I wouldn't presume to make a comment about those who endured the war on Mathe as I spent very little time there. Most of my war time service was spent off-planet in various diplomatic posts."

"Oh yes, of course," said the sharp-voiced one.

"And I understand you are of off-planet descent yourself," put in Caya.

Every nerve in Rheia's body went on full alert. How could she know that unless she knew Rheia's real name? "A long way back," she said. "A very long way back."

"I'm sure your department found it most useful," said Caya too smoothly.

Since the one fact Rheia had never mentioned on Samarkan was her great-grandmother's flight and rejection of that society, Rheia very much doubted it, but only shrugged now and turned the conversation. Pretending the gaggle of women were a pit of diplomats helped. As shallow and treacherous, and the outcome of her charade as critical.

How could they carry on as if nothing was happening outside their precious walls? Did they think the dirtsider protests would just disappear? That night, she looked at her empty sleeper and switched on all the vid channels she could find. Searching, searching for one face among those patrolling the dirtsider shields. Not till she glimpsed him, could she settle down.

He'd made it back safely.

As for their time in that hidden room…that memory, she shoved down ruthlessly. Precious, never to be forgotten, but too dangerous to bring out. Hope was a luxury she could no longer afford.

She lay down on her lonely sleeper and pulled up the covers of detachment. Survival; that was all she could afford.

CHAPTER TWENTY-ONE

Fortunately, she had no meetings with the suspect factions for some days. Right now, she didn't think she could fool anyone. She went about her DIA duties with all the cool detachment her role demanded and hoped no one realized she could only do it because she was working on auto.

And fled often to the gardens that had become her sanctuary. Her guards followed her in the gates, but she could manage them, although she'd had to use Gof's emergency code once when she ventured out a new gate and ran smack into a crowd of dirtsiders and one of them recognized her face. The speed the Security troops came to her rescue was testament to how closely they watched her, as did the tirade from her boss and Gof deln Crantz when she returned home and got told in no uncertain terms that she was not to escape her protection like that again. She nodded dutifully and inwardly grinned in wicked delight at knowing there was one place they couldn't follow her.

Then there were the other trackers. The ones set on her by those she hunted. That man over there, the young woman laughing with her child. Who had they set to follow her?

Through the gates, head down and refusing to make eye contact, with all her senses tuned. Then activate the DIA's blocking program on her com before a sidestep, a quick flurry of leaves, ruffled branches, and soft footfalls through a sighing avenue of trees to the native grassland section.

She had found a special place there where she could be free; no guards, no surveillance. No constant turmoil of conflicting demands.

A careful wander down one path, a sudden switch to another, then slow, slow pacing, the walk of someone meandering without purpose through the beds. Until she came to the bend. The one blind spot where the path split to two. Today she chose the right fork. Around the bend, a quick step sideways and she was engulfed by the rustling stalks. In a rhythm engrained in her blood, she passed through the waving strands making no disturbance, no noise. A backward glance and she slid through the tufts to the familiar, welcoming hollow.

To run feet first into a body already there.

"Oomph."

"Shh." Her hand shot out, covering the man's mouth, but her fingers tingled in recognition. Those too familiar blue eyes, shock turning quickly to sparkling laughter.

"Rheia," he breathed. "A welcome sight, though I don't usually get assaulted in quite that manner by beautiful women. Hello, sweetheart."

"What are you doing here?"

He grinned, putting on a theatrical sigh. "Much as you, I suspect. Escaping reality until I can face it again."

There was a question in his voice and she nodded in answer. "Much the same," she agreed.

But his head came up and the laughter vanished. "What's happened?"

"Nothing. Precisely nothing."

She used to be able to keep him out, but not today. Not in this place of refuge, with her shields already down. "A meeting, that's all," she tried claiming, but suddenly, all the frustrations rolled out of her. At the end of her litany of complaints, she realized his arms held her and she lay curled into his chest. Embarrassed, she began to struggle to sit up.

"Shh, sweetheart. Stay, a bit longer. Please, just stay."

"This isn't safe. I shouldn't have…You don't need to listen to my stupid gripes. Not with all you face."

A hand covered her lips, gentle, scarred and firm. "Never apologize, not for needing someone, for needing…me. I'm here—when I can. For now," he added bitterly.

She was going to protest, then saw the sudden clench of his mouth as he waited for it and realized she couldn't. To do so would be to reject him and the power of what grew between them. She shook her head. "Thank you for listening," she whispered, and his head bent forward to take her lips in the sweetest kiss he had given her.

"Thank you for telling me," he murmured back.

She took to visiting the gardens at the same time of day, and one day he was there again. This time, it was she who listened, heard all the guilt, the strife, the agony of worry churning him up as the dirtsiders rebellion grew and spread, as too impatient factions like the one that had kidnapped them threatened to escape their control and escalate the rebellion in dangerous ways, and the response from moonies hardened.

"I need to see you again," he said at the end, "but it's too dangerous. If I can find you, eventually someone else will."

"Find a ranger born? Not likely," she said, grinning in challenge, and this time it was he who shook his head.

"If I can come, if I can get away…"

"I will be here," she promised. They set a time, and a series of dates after that, and on the third one, he was there again. Bruises mottled his cheeks that day, but the glint in his eye stopped her asking why. A touch of her hand only, then she switched to telling him of her wardrobe program's latest update. The thing had become even more autocratic, if possible, and she really had begun to wonder who ran her apartment. At the end, she was rewarded with a chuckle, and a quick kiss before he melted away into the grasses.

Then it was back to her own battles. Her evening with Caya der Greystan turned out to be not such a failure. The next meeting with Senator an Kroth's team had new faces: Caya's brother, a tall and imposing man. In his own mind too, she guessed from the way he naturally took over the center of the room, and a very much smaller and less prepossessing man he introduced as a cousin. The brother was a land developer, and the cousin an adviser in Councilor der Greystan's office.

A sudden tightness at the back of her neck, and a clenching in her gut. At last.

"Master der Greystan, a pleasure."

The man had his father's mannerisms, but without the wily edge of the Councilor.

"The plateau. You grew up there," said the cousin.

Pay dirt. That tingle and gut signal never failed. This man knew her real name and didn't expect her to deny it. Not when they were on the same side. She had to be; the rioting dirtsiders gave her no choice but to throw her lot in with a group opposed to them.

"Which means you know the good bits," said the councilor's son.

The good bits? What was this man on about? The parts that she adored? The wild sectors that spoke to her heart?

"Yeah, the scenic bits. All that open space and wild weather. People will pay for that."

Pay—who? The plateau was either public reserve, or ranger-controlled village sites ceded to the local guilds under age-old treaties. Even though the local guild was gone, that land belonged to the rangers, not this blustering man in front of her.

The cousin leaned forward, wearing the smile of a seasoned spin peddler. "Master der Greystan is proposing a wonderful employment opportunity for the tragic survivors of the plateau and those brave Resistance folks finding it difficult to settle into life in Hathe again. Such sad stories. Once this current nonsense is settled, they will need jobs. Not the ones they foolishly demand of course; how could anyone give them anything too complicated or serious. But they will need help."

Rheia had an ominous feeling. "What kind of help?"

The nystat cousin rubbed his hands together and let his mouth droop. "Simple jobs. Something that suits the kind of life they're accustomed to."

"The kind that won't stretch their abilities," said Rheia. "The kind that needs few skills or training?"

"Exactly," said der Greystan, pleased with her understanding. "That's why we're building there."

"Building what?"

"A resort of course," said der Greystan. "After all those years cooped up on Mathe, what better than holidaying in a place as wide open as the plateau."

She stared at him. He looked serious. "They wouldn't find it somewhat agoraphobic?" It was a real syndrome among the returning moonies—those who had spent so long relying on walls to keep out the dead vacuum of Mathe's surface that walking in a street was now beyond them.

The councilor's son waved an impatient hand. "Not them. Too soft. No, it's for those of us taking this place back for our own. We're making it an adventure destination. Use dirtsiders to set up a real-life Resistance experience, with the guests taking a part as one of the brave heroes. Get their hearts beating—and credit bands buzzing," he added with a hearty laugh.

"It's in the early planning stages, you understand," said the cousin. "Nothing concrete yet and all confidential. Not a whisper must go beyond these walls. Not till we get control of those dirtsiders again and have Council approval."

"No problem there," said der Greystan. "Money and muscle talk. Throw enough credits at them, strong-arm the leaders, and those rabble in the camps will fold. After that, not even the likes of Councilors an Castre and an Rathman can argue against a project to look after their precious dirtsiders. Jobs and a place they can belong, right back where they should be."

Rheia felt sick. "And exactly what is it you think I can do for you, Master der Greystan?" she forced herself to ask.

"It's the site, you see." He leaned forward as if offering her a huge treat. "You come from a village in the heart of the plateau."

"Yes. No one lives there now." There seemed no point denying it as long as they didn't blatantly say her real name, and it might secure her way in. But had these people no thought of what talking about her past did to her?

The cousin—what was the man's name? Der Greystan had thrown his name at her in a barely audible mumble she had no hope of deciphering. Now, he leaned forward as well, all sympathy and false concern. "A dreadful memory for you, so painful. You must want to put it all behind you."

Never in a million years, but she wasn't going to admit that here. She gave the briefest of nods, teeth gripping her lower lip.

"You are the last of your village left, we understand? So sad."

Der Greystan went to open his mouth, but his cousin put out a hand, touched him on the arm, and he stayed silent. Interesting. She would have sworn the big man was in charge.

"Which would make you the title-holder of your village," the little man said now gently.

"I hadn't considered it."

"No, far too painful. You mustn't ever want to go back there, even if it becomes safe."

That slithery edge to his voice; she hadn't imagined it. This man had just threatened her. She gave a non-committal lift of her shoulders, her face set in stone.

"So how would you like it if we took all that misery away? Took the village off your hands."

Shock held her still. "My village?"

"Yes," said der Greystan. "It's perfect."

The man was nodding earnestly. Looking at her as if actually expecting her to want to take part in destroying all that remained of her childhood home.

And, Pillars help her, she had to make them believe she would do exactly that.

The cousin stepped in again. "We'll pay you a fair price, of course. After that, you may leave it all in our hands," he added, as if explaining something to a small child.

"How? The plateau—you can't buy land on the plateau." Not outright, not an outsider.

"Yes, you can," said the cousin. "Village sites belong to a ranger group, and you are the last survivor of your village. You own the village site under Hathian law."

This time she could only open her mouth and gasp. No words appeared at all.

"Do you know what those sons of nystats want me to do?"

Rheia raged back and forth in her boss's office, recounting for him every last, miserable moment of the moonies' plan. That cousin, he was the one she blamed, not the bluff and greedy der Greystan. A boulder of a man in build and thought processes, he hadn't come up with this scheme. But that sniveling cousin, that genial, grasping, slimy little man sitting beside him. She'd looked up his name as soon as she'd got back to her apartment.

"You need to check the files of Narvin asn Chrostic. That man…," her hand smashed against the chair back, a defenseless lump in place of the man she wanted so badly to smash.

"At least they're not talking about razing the whole site," said ven Raden, which just had her marching harder. He quickly grabbed at a priceless Venutian statuette, seconds before her heedless rampage sent it careering off the table.

"No, far too valuable. They would rather leave our homes, my parents' house, my grandparents', family's, friends', village elders' homes to be restored as quaint relics of old ranger lore. A living mockery of everything rangers hold dear. And…," a collection of artifacts tumbled wildly off the edge of a shelf, falling in a clatter of protest on the hard floor. They were made of marcasine; unbreakable, but it made her feel no better. She knew ven Raden valued them. She stared aghast, muttered an apology and felt no better after her boss waved his hand aside to tell her not to worry. Still she paced, seemingly unable to stop her wild march. A deep breath to try to settle herself into some kind of rationality. It failed.

"And, to make it really, really authentic," she went on, "they want me to recruit ex-Resistance rangers to live there. To act out what it was like during the occupation, so that their *guests* can play at enjoying their own slice of heroism. Do they know how few of us there are left?"

"To which you said?"

"I would think about it and get back to them with some ideas," she said in disgust.

"You didn't break cover. Good."

"Break cover? No, I agreed with every word coming out of their greedy mouths." Though she'd had to stop twice on the way here, scurrying into a filthy side alley to retch up the pitiful contents of her stomach and wait till the shivering left her. Ven Raden's keen gaze had swept over her when she arrived and can't have missed the washed-out pallor of her face, but he had said nothing.

She ground to a halt and flung herself into the chair opposite his desk.

Looking relieved, ven Raden leaned forward, hands tented and cut straight to her most important revelation. "So this group of moonies knows your true name?"

"Did they call me Madame asn Forvrad? Of course not. They did tell me I was the only survivor of Hyrvettin."

"And the most probable source of that was your dirtsider kidnappers. Your name is out in dirtsider channels, but so far they're keeping it to themselves and not spreading it publicly. Or not that they've let us know. But dirtsiders don't generally talk to moonies; not about something like this."

"Yes, and this lot didn't even try to disguise it," she said in disgust, "which means…"

"They were behind those dirtsider kidnappers, and now they've bought your story, loyalties and all. Well done."

"That's supposed to make me feel better?" She glared back. "Is it true? Ranger sites are held by the guild, not an individual."

"By ranger law, and Hathe has accepted that interpretation till now. No one else wanted the land. But the actual wording of the legislation…yes, you can be deemed the owner of that site, though it would take a court case to prove it. Overturning accepted practice is not easy."

She felt sick again. "There's no one else left? Have you looked?"

He nodded. "The DIA ran a search when you were first assigned to this mission, though none but me knew the reason why. We found no one, though it's not to say some may have survived. The most likely would be children, if their parents had found a way to relocate them."

"I need to talk to Jacquel. The Resistance would know."

"Impossible," said ven Raden. "Not now the boy's put himself in the firing line. But I can get deln Crantz on a com line. He was Resistance too, and young des Trurains is still listed as a fully active Security agent. Gof might be able to get the dirtsiders to look for you."

Nor would he change his mind about her talking to anyone. Thank the Pillars she had never told her boss of those secret meetings in the park. Nor was she surprised at ven Raden's response. Rheia had watched enough vid channels, had seen the sheer anger aimed at the handsome figure challenging the heart of modern Hathe. She had no choice but to nod agreement, though she doubted she was up to facing the wily head of Security.

The grin on the small man's face when he shimmered into view confirmed it. Ven Raden asked about the survivors, to a shake of the Security man's head and a promise to check further. Then her boss updated him on everything that had been said in her meetings, and the glee on deln Crantz's face sent the flutters in her stomach into chaotic flight.

"Very good, very good. The boy's got them worried. Well done, madame."

"Nice to know someone trusts me, even if it is a bunch of selfish grabsters."

Deln Crantz humphed. "After the way that young hothead defended you, it's about more than that, madame. You're a weapon, one they would dearly love to aim."

"What do you mean? Is Jacquel in danger?"

"Any more than usual? Oh yes, of a certainty. After his antics these last days, that boy is target number one."

"I've got to warn him."

"You're staying right here, Rheia," said ven Raden.

"And under full protection," said deln Crantz. "I promised young Jaca that."

"You did? Why?"

"The boy's soft on you, and about time too. You're now under his wing, someone he feels honor bound to protect," said deln Crantz gruffly.

"No." How could they think that? "Duty. That's why he protected me. It's what he does."

A questionable smile lifted deln Crantz's ever mobile mouth. "I'm transmitting a copy of his file to you now," deln Crantz said. "His full one—the complete, security coded version. It leaves nothing out. Read it in here. The copy will be destroyed on leaving this level"

She felt the buzz of her com as a highest-level file pinged it. She automatically clamped her hand over her com patch. This was private, something she must read unwatched.

Ven Raden nodded acceptance. "Use my sitting room. No one will bother you there.," he said. "Gof, we'll be in touch if there are any more developments. I take it you have the matter of the Avenue camp under control?"

"Oh, not in the slightest," said that grinning, gnome-like figure. "That's a flock of wild aerion bolting for freedom, led by a principled hellion. It's all very satisfactory," he added and coded out, leaving Rheia feeling sick yet again.

Did Jacquel have any idea he was no more than a pawn in their game?

Ven Raden waved her into the private sitting room off his office, shutting the door behind him and leaving her to read Jacquel's file in peace. In no time, she had her answer. She'd read the public citations and thought she understood what he'd been through. What a fool. She had no idea how bad it had been. This file recorded every mission, every misstep and triumph, all the backbreaking, tedious, terrifying work that went into the celebrated successes, with every time he'd been pulled in for compulsory debriefing and counselling. A proud, highly-educated man forced to live as a defeated drudge for years.

Jacquel des Trurains knew exactly how he was being used. He'd probably counted on it.

"You say they'll have to go to court to get my village site?" she said to ven Raden when she'd finished reading and returned to his office, hugging all that knowledge to herself and nowhere near ready to discuss it. "That chitbut cousin probably has the lawyers lined up already."

Her boss smiled, in a way she'd long ago learned to mistrust. "Which means that all the players in this scheme of theirs will have to front up."

"Not asn Chrostic. He'll hide in the background, pushing the buttons. It's how he works."

She growled, so frustrated she didn't know what to do next. Ven Raden put out a hand. "Gof may find something useful. The Resistance may know more about what happened to your village."

She grimaced. "They still don't tell us everything."

"The dirtsiders? No. Do you blame them?"

"We can never understand what they went through."

No answer was needed, and her boss knew it. The riots in the streets were proof enough. He frowned. "That first year. It went so far beyond what we expected, and the scars of it cannot be removed from Hathe."

"Too many graves." She shot out of her chair, swinging away before her boss saw the tears threatening. Her family lay in those graves. Some of ven Raden's too, for all she knew. She'd never asked, and didn't have the courage to do so now.

"You do know if that court case goes ahead, you'll become enemy number one to the dirtsiders."

She came to a slow halt, hugging her arm and huddling against the wall, hearing the loss of all hope. Jacquel could never be hers. "Like father, like daughter," she whispered. "I'll have betrayed the memory of every dead ranger." The horror of it swamped her, but she'd spent too many years caught in thorny negotiations and facing the untenable. "This is our best chance to expose these predators."

Her boss nodded. "They can't do anything in the current climate, so we have a little time. And we will keep your village safe; that's a promise. We lure those nystat scum into court, get them to expose all the players, and then we pull you out of there so fast your feet won't touch the ground."

"Thank you." For his optimism, if nothing else. The truth was she may have to stomach the desecration of her childhood home if there was no other way of reuniting her planet. Was there no end to it, no end to the price she must pay? She'd fully intended to never visit Hyrvettin again and still doubted whether she would ever be able to endure visiting the actual site of her old home.

But to let it be destroyed and turned into this false parody…?

More meetings, almost exclusively now with the younger der Greystan and the rest of the group trying to steal her home village, with each more gut churning than the last. And always she refused their claim that she was the last survivor of her village. Hyrvettin must still live in some other heart. It drove her to wear a protective slick over her hands, unable to bear the touch of Narvin asn Chrostic. She could claim it was because of the new stomach virus doing the rounds, a consequence of the growing horde of offworlders visiting Hathe bringing new disease challenges to a planetary health system still in recovery.

Marthe an Castre wasn't the only dirtsider medic burnt out by caring for those enduring the harsh rule of the Terrans.

Marthe an Castre. The lost love of Jacquel des Trurains.

Rheia thrust her hands into the gel, right up to the elbows, then shoved them under the setting light. A hard slap of hands to feel the shell keeping her safe, and she marched out of her door.

"And how are you today, Madame asn Postrova?"

"As ever," Rheia told her smirking nemesis. "Shall we get down to business, Master asn Chrostic?" She put out a hand and saw with satisfaction the exact moment the man took it and realized she wore slicker protection. "Last time, you were talking of the latest developments in getting control of the village site."

Rheia settled herself back into her seat, taking time to graciously bend into the chair. All around the table, the rest of der Greystan's team sat at her signal. Asn Chrostic placed a com unit in the middle of the table and waited as a holo-head materialized. The chief of their legal unit.

The man in the holo-image made no effort to look around or give any kind of greeting, his eyes flicking past her as if uncomfortable at having to recognize her.

"My copy of the report on possible claimants is on your coms now."

Rheia's heart seized. "There are others…"

"Alive? No," said the disembodied voice of the spectral head. "Not that we can ascertain."

"You've traced them all?"

"Not all," said the lawyer. "The details are in my report."

She couldn't do it, couldn't read that record immediately. "Thank you. I need to read this before we go any further. She thrust suddenly up from her chair. "I will review the file and discuss it at our next meeting."

Asn Chrostic shot out a hand, caught hers as she palmed her loaded com. "That record does not leave this room."

She pulled her hand back, letting him feel the tips of her fingernails. "Yes, it does. And if you don't trust me to keep it safe, there is no basis for us working together."

She stepped back, eyes holding his in challenge. Then finally he smiled, the kind that left a smear of ugliness on wherever it landed. "Certainly, Madame asn Postrova. We *all* have so much to lose if the truth leaks out before we are fully prepared to act."

Don't threaten me, you little creep. But she kept the cool regard on her face as she swung around and walked out the door. Then escaped into the nearest service unit where she scrubbed and scrubbed her hands under the highest sanitizing level of jet, desperate to rid herself of the feel and odor of that appalling room and asn Chrostic's touch. Not even the slicker field had stopped her feeling the clamminess of his over eager handgrip.

She didn't dare open the file till she was far from possible surveillance. Her personal com unit was secure. The Security forces and her own department had promised her that, and even the current divergent factions in Council couldn't break either department's safe walls. But her apartment—no. Not at all. She fled instead to the gardens, to the one place that felt safe. And hoped today he could make it.

A warm body caught her as she pushed through to the hollow, and the lilt of laughter welcomed her. His lips claimed hers, and told her she was home again, if only briefly. Then he tilted up her head and she saw blue eyes suddenly harden.

"What's happened?"

She held out her com unit. "Asn Chrostic gave me this. Security can't give any sign they know about it."

He touched his com directly to hers. "They won't pick up even a trace of this transmission," he promised. Then he tucked her into his side and stared into space. He'd set his com to personal view only, not even a shimmer of the report visible. After far too long, his eyes lost focus and he leaned forward and turned to look her full in the eyes.

"Have you read this yet?"

She shook her head and his mouth tightened. "I wish you didn't have to see it, ever, but you do," he said. "Just remember, they don't have access to everything."

She gulped, breathing in long and hard, then set the file to view. At the first heading, her hand thrust blindly out and Jacquel seized hold of it.

"I'm here, sweetheart. I'm here."

For now, but it was enough. She began to read again.

Too soon into it, she wished she'd refused. She'd known the bare facts, but not these details. Not this endless litany of misery.

An Prostet family. 1 adult male, 1 adult female, 3 minors. Consigned to Urgonium Mine 3.

Male, deceased 2 months; Female, deceased 6 months; 3 minors returned to village site. No record at 10 months.

That was her brother's best friend's family. No record after ten months. Lost, dead, or vanished?

Deln Vestren family. 2 adult males, 3 adult females, 4 minors of working age. 1 adult male and 1 female assigned to waterworks construction. Family home site requisitioned. No record of minors or mature aged adults after 7 months.

Memories of a sprawling family complex, home to old Grandpa and Grandma Vestren and her elderly sister, along with the eldest deln Vestren son and his rambunctious brood of boys. The terror of the village with their ability to dream up new ways of getting into riotous trouble. But they'd had the kindest of hearts, and the teenage boys had come to the aid of any child needing it. That wonderful, topsy-turvy home gone, *requisitioned.* A euphemism for destroyed and left in a pile of rubble, the family turned out to find what shelter and work they could in the hostile plateau. The hideaways had briefly sheltered some. A few only. The Resistance couldn't risk the investigations by the Terrans if too many tried to evade their work gangs by disappearing into the refuge and put at risk the peace of their dead.

"I can't…" She thrust the com unit away, slamming shut the personal view mode.

Jacquel said nothing. Just opened the file to scroll through it again, one arm tightly around her shoulders. His eyes focused as he entered view mode, but the rigid muscles and the strong band of protection of his arm promised he was still here. Too soon, he came back. She looked up fearfully, but he only shook his head. "No known survivors," he confirmed.

"None? The Resistance must know of some?" That moonie lawyer had to be wrong. She dashed a hand across eyes brimming stupidly full. This man had lived through the horror, had seen too many such stories.

His arms pulled her in close, tucking her head into his chest and allowing her the peace of staring only at his warm tunic, of smelling only the healthy smell of living male, of grass and soil and that special, unique scent that belonged only to him. Clean, alive, fresh and solid.

"I don't know," he said now. "We've asked, but the rangers aren't talking. We will keep asking—that I promise. But the records show…among the young and the oldest, those the Terrans had no need to conscript, a high percentage just disappear from the database."

"So they could have survived?"

"On the plateau, in winter? The village was destroyed. How many ranger hidden lodges are there?"

"Only two in our zone, and they wouldn't have gone there."

"Preserving the tombs of the old at the expense of the lives of the young?"

"How dare you!" She shot up, burst out of his arms. How could he say that? "No outsider before you has seen the inside of our refuges. You think they would expose those tombs to desecration by Terran marauders?"

She shoved at that stupid arm offering fake support. "And the technology in those hideaways would have exposed the truth of Hathe in an instant. How many dirtsiders died rather than let Terrans find out about a Resistance control room?"

Those eyebrows of his twitched up and a dangerous glitter lit up his eyes. "Welcome back, sweetheart."

"What!" she stared at the grin on his face and the challenge in those laughing blue eyes. "You said that just to rile me up."

"Sorry, love. We still have a fight to win."

"And I was giving in to feminine hysterics?"

He lifted his hands in surrender. "Acquit me of crass stupidity. I'm not brave enough to suggest that."

This time, her fist swung out and he manfully offered a wince as she bumped his arm. He'd had far worse in his time. "Sorry," she muttered, "but you deserved that." She pulled in a deep breath. "Do I need to read the rest?"

This time, the kindness in his face was genuine, the regret real. "Yes, you do. You need to have the same facts that asn Chrostic and der Greystan will use in court."

She shuddered. "Must it come to that?"

A twist of his mouth. "Unless we can crack them first or bring it to a head some other way."

She shuddered again and opened the file. When Jacquel opened his arms wide in invitation, she leaned back, needing the touch of his body to ground her. Her eyes scrolled down and down the horrific record of her home's sacrifice.

She'd known the bare facts before this, had known her village was gone, her family dead, and most of the rest dead or missing. But the clinical retelling, the cold, stark list of names and dates…

At long, long last she was done. She could shut the file.

"I would like to kill every Terran who ever set foot on Hathe."

"Join the queue," said Jacquel. "Politics says they can't be touched at the moment—but not a planet in the Alliance trusts Earth now. They will pay. Destiny says they will pay."

She so wished she could believe him.

One other group who must pay: those who used the horrors detailed in this report against her, all to feed their own greed for profit. She felt like her favorite aerion; her prey of choice, the facile bodies who sat opposite her at meetings, unctuously suggesting ever more outrageous ways for her to betray all she had worked so hard to achieve while they sat in safety on Mathe.

"Teach me your field codes," she demanded of Jacquel. "The ones only dirtsiders know."

CHAPTER TWENTY-TWO

"We got company, Cap."

Jacquel eased one eye open. A boy's head poked through the door to his tent, wearing a grin that had Jacquel groaning. "What kind of company?"

"Troopers marching up the avenue, and they ain't any of ours. They look real pretty too."

"Moonies?"

But he didn't need the vigorous head nod of the boy to confirm it. The Council and Senate must have been busy last night.

He glanced at the timer on his com. Yes, he'd got some sleep. Not nearly enough, but it would have to do. He'd returned to camp late last night, thanks to an emergency call when he was on his way back from his meeting with Rheia. Then had fallen into bed, to wake too soon from a dream that began in bliss and ended in terror. One day, he would make those moonie nystats tormenting Rheia pay for every word of that foul report. She may have known the bare facts for long enough, but he'd seen her face when she put names and faces to cold statistics. He'd met Myron ven Raden more than once, and he doubted Rheia's boss would ever have shoved the full horror of her loss down her throat like that. All dirtsiders knew about grief; you dealt with it as best you could, usually by burying it down deep and getting on with life, one day at a time.

The boy's head shoved further into the tent, and Jacquel lifted his hand to show he was coming. "Tell them I'll be out soon—and no one is to fire on anyone till I get there." The last thing they needed was a bunch of overexcited dirtsider teens setting off a bunch of inexperienced and hyped-up moonie troopers.

He made it quick, pulling on clean fatigues. The kind of dark clothing he'd worn on night missions so many times during the war. Today, he was a working soldier. Shiny uniforms and polished medals had nothing like the punch of worn-in gear. In short time, he stood with his squad, the camp leaders, and senior Resistance veterans, at the shield wall facing the Avenue's entrance, watching a band of moonie troopers in full Security uniform marching toward them. All shiny uniforms and not a medal among them.

"They do look pretty," he said turning to the boy, who was almost hopping in excitement. He looked so young. "I have a job for you," said Jacquel. "I need you to go tell the guardians to keep the youngsters under control. Can I trust you to make sure they're kept safe?"

The boy's chest swelled under his fascinated gaze. "Yes sir," he said, and raced off, yelling to anyone who cared to listen. "Give way. Trooper on important duty."

Ras watched him go. "That's one safely out of trouble at least. When do you think he'll realize why you sent him off?"

"Hopefully never." If he had to sweet talk the whole camp into doing what was needed to keep them safe, he'd do it. "Now, about our guests…"

The incoming troopers closed in on the shield wall.

Do they have disruptors? Jacquel signaled to the comms team.

None detectable, Cap. Standard arms only. Shield wall's safe for now.

"So deln Crantz's been forced to send them out but isn't letting the children play with the real toys," said Ras.

Jacquel grinned back in answer and stepped forward to face the green troops lining up against them. He lifted his head high, plastered on his most wicked grin, and turned slowly to his squad, showing his back to the moonie troopers and raising his voice. "Those are some mighty shiny weapons they're carrying. Reckon any know how to use them?"

His squad grinned back, hefting their own, very much not shiny weapons to firing position.

No injuries, he signaled in field code. *Throwing a tantrum is no excuse for hurting babies.*

Yeah? Ever been a parent? his oldest squad member signaled back. The woman had three teenage children.

Make sure these babies can walk away from this. And that's an order, he coded back.

Aaw, not even one potshot?

He swung back to face the moonies across the shield and lifted an arm high in challenge. He would swear some of them near dropped to the ground in terror.

Just don't nick them too badly, he sent back to his squad.

He nodded at Ras, who raised his voice to be heard clearly by the moonies. "State your business."

One very young, very scared-looking trooper in the middle took a half step forward. "In the name of the Senate and the

Council, you are hereby ordered to disband this illegal gathering and return peacefully to your work and homes."

Jacquel stared him down. "Both the Senate and the Council, is it, boy? Transmit your *orders*." He opened a public link, confident any Resistance comms team could scramble a moonie signal and keep safe their internal com channels. A ping as the document came through. He looked to Ras, who made an ostentatious show of displaying it in a shimmering haze of over-decoration in front of them all. Jacquel scanned it down. Then glanced at his squad, laughter in his voice as he read the terms out, emphasizing each of the more outrageous demands, all designed to add to the power of certain senators and leave the dirtsiders with nothing for their years of suffering.

"Signed by the sovereign command of the Senate of Hathe and duly notarized by the Hathian Council in session." He recited out loud the duplicitous names attached to it, broadcasting them to all in this camp, and all the other dirtsider camps across Hathe.

At the end, he looked across to the boy standing defiantly at the head of his brave squad of green cadets, weapons pointed very firmly straight at Jacquel.

"Let me give you a lesson in civics, my young friends. The constitution of Hathe was written many generations ago and has not been rescinded. The Senate has no sovereign power over Hathe. Only the Council in full session has that. The councilor names attached to this," he flicked a hand at the meaningless shimmer, "are insufficient in number to constitute a Council in full session. Further, the Council does not *notarize* anything. The Council decrees, it rules, it decides. It does not rubber stamp the actions of an overweening pack of opportunists masquerading as a Senate. Take this back to your pretender bosses, with our regards and a strong recommendation they hire a better lawyer than their present one."

He lifted his hand, struck it across and out in a clear signal to the seasoned Resistance troopers standing behind him. "You have four seconds to clear this square and stop threatening the peaceful Hathian citizens behind us, before the duly authorized Security personnel with me take appropriate action to end your threat. Troop, arm," he called out.

With a loud slam, and a swift movement, his troops dropped into firing position and Jacquel slipped in beside them, weapons aimed firmly at the quaking moonie troops in front of them.

You reckon they're stupid enough to fire at us? signaled Ras.

Yes, he did, watching the confused scramble of the moonie squad as they scurried to take up defensive positions behind whatever shelter they could find. Trees, a few skimmer bodies, the corner of a building and a patch of shrubs. Had they even checked the kind of weapons his dirtsiders carried?

Shield strength?

No change, Cap, signaled the comms team.

So, no camouflaged disruptors over there either. He supposed he ought to thank deln Crantz for that. After he'd taken the man to task for the games he played with his life and Rheia's.

A flash twisted through the air and a rainfall of shimmer patterns marked the shield in front of them. Yes, the green moonies were that stupid.

Mark full, he ordered his team as he aimed his weapon. *Remember the order.*

Then he dropped his hand, a volley of light sprang out from his troopers' weapons, and half the moonie squad fell out from their inadequate cover clutching at arms, legs, scrapes on their heads. The other half huddled in shock. No one must have told them about shields programed to let weapon fire out, but not back in.

Run, children, run. If only he could say it aloud, could urge them on to sense before this became a whole lot worse. For a few seconds, he thought they might do it, but then one stood up, lifted his voice in a powerful rally of misplaced courage, then the boy—no, man. No one that brave was a mere boy. The appallingly young-looking man at the center of the squad dropped back into an attack position and fired his weapon at the shield again. Fired, and fired, and fired, till a curtain of shimmering fire stood between moonies and dirtsiders.

He's mine, coded Jacquel to his team, sighting his weapon. Whoever recruited this moonie squad hadn't been totally lacking in judgement. That boy had steel in his spine, and Hathe needed defenders like him. He lifted his weapon, locked it on to his target, set the charge for maximum force with minimum bio-disruption and pushed the fire button. All that brave defiance dropped in a heap and Jacquel immediately checked his status. Alive, stunned and no serious injury. Thank the Pillars.

Full stun, disable the rest, he ordered. Time for this game to end. His squad sank into work mode, moving through the shield to target those hiding behind proper cover, and one by one all the brave and foolish young moonie cadets dropped to the ground.

"Status," he said into his com at the end.

"All alive, all sleeping like babes, Cap," said the voice of the comms team in his ear.

"Clean-up crew," he ordered through the Resistance network. "Treat 'em nice and deliver them to their homes."

"Aah, about that, Cap," broke in a new voice. He checked the signal. Joshan an Thanis, former ranger and his only squad member not here today. Jacquel had sent him out on reconnaissance through the City. The man could move through the streets like the whisper of a shadow, with no sign of his passing.

"Joshan, where have you got to with that sneaky carcass of yours?"

"Residential sector three, Cap."

Jacquel knew the area. Middle class, solid, respectable homes, about half and half dirtsider and moonie. Or had been before the occupation. Now, too many dirtsiders had been scammed or forced into trading in their old homes for the money they needed to get through each day. His old friend Yurin an Begum had a full-time job wrestling the courts to win back the lives of dispossessed dirtsiders. But just a few days ago he'd met up with Yurin and noticed a new spring in the man. "We're starting to win," Yurin had said to him. Jacquel had contacted deln Crantz to double the guard around the lawyer immediately.

"Cap, you don't want to send dirtsiders carrying dead-looking moonie kids through here. Not a good idea," sent Joshan.

A clench in his gut. "Transmit," he ordered Joshan, and watched in horror as he was transported into the visual hell that was sector three. Beautiful old homes with boarded up windows and doors, armed groups of young thugs roaming the streets, stupid clashes of half-grown moonies and dirtsiders, a man dragged from his home and tossed into the street.

"Go back where you belong, dirtsucker," he heard a man yell as a woman aimed a vicious kick right into the cringing man's gut.

"I want a squad in there, immediately," he ordered Joshan. "Pull all dirtsiders back into safe houses."

He turned to his second. "Ras, get these kids into the nearest hospital triage lobby, then detail the squads on rim patrol to up the security."

He stood up, making no effort now to look like the vid star. Not when lives were at stake and the City was falling to pieces around them. *Comms, a full meeting of the leadership team in the control tent at fourth prime. And get me Gof deln Crantz—on a tight beam, fully secured link.*

Gof deln Crantz was no less serious when he linked through. "What did you expect to happen when you decided to play glory boy?" he barked.

"Yeah, and you had nothing to do with it."

The man refused to look even slightly shamefaced. "You started this brave revolt, and I expect you to finish it satisfactorily," his commander said.

"Just keep that lot from the Senate off our backs. I assume we still have full Security resources."

Deln Crantz only harrumphed, and Jacquel took that as a *yes.* "Just don't make it too obvious," the commander added. "Ven Raden and I can handle most of the Council, but there is a core there wanting you to fail. Hopefully this latest dust-up will encourage them to take a stand."

"Expose their sweet treacheries, you mean," said Jacquel grimly. "And Rheia?"

"She's safe, under full observation, and becoming best buddies with the worst of the moonie madames."

Deep in the pit of the worst predators on Hathe, but he already knew that. And that he must stop his visits to the gardens, terrified that someone would follow them and expose her cover. "I take it you'd like our revolt to last a bit longer," he said with resignation, "without anyone getting hurt."

Deln Crantz shrugged. "If possible. Liaise with Security Central about your actions,"

Then the man signed off before Jacquel could protest. *If possible.* Which meant deln Crantz had already factored in the political cost of any injuries or deaths to either moonies or dirtsiders. All very well for his commander, but Jacquel had lost too many people already. *Hathe* had lost too many. Not one more, he vowed, and silently hoped it was a promise he could keep. He'd had to break so many.

He broke this one too. Days into the hell that the City had become, he saw it happen but could do nothing to stop it. His life became a nightmare of brawling youths, stubborn dirtsiders manning makeshift barricades, and finding homes for the increasing numbers of displaced dirtsiders as demarcation lines became the heartbreaking norm.

His face was too well known to move around openly during daylight hours, but old Resistance ways still let him slip through the angry streets and into homes and buildings barred to other dirtsiders—those without his wealth and family connections. Not to the gardens, no matter how much he wished for it. Too dangerous for Rheia, but he still met regularly with Gof's people, trying desperately to find a way out of the mess.

Caught in the middle of it all, those dirtsider and moonie Hathians who just wanted to slip back into the quiet, normal life they'd had before. Not too rich, not too poor, their goal to keep their families safe, well fed and with a future to look forward to.

Not much, he thought bitterly one evening as he watched one more family being quietly moved out of their home. A moonie family this, in a neighborhood of stout, easily defended homes. Dirtsiders needed their house, needed this neighborhood for their young and vulnerable, and none of them felt safe anymore in a place with moonies. Nor could the dirtsider leaders promise safety to moonies in dirtsider territory, not with the tensions running barely restrained in the City, and none of it helped by the more extreme factions on both sides. He and Gof repeatedly shut down cells of dirtsider extremists— the moonie faction was Rheia's to solve—but there were too many like Phillipos athns Kronkist. Disaffected and past waiting for someone else to give them the life they had been promised.

"We will keep your goods safe and give you a full payment for the use of your home until these troubles are past," he heard Dreya tell the woman.

His trooper had a face easily trusted. With her kind brown eyes and a calmness built up through being tested again and again during the occupation, too many of these evictions fell to her to lead. Even the most frightened could be brought to have faith in what Dreya told them. The times dictated that Jacquel use the best resources to hand, and that meant using Dreya for these filthy duties, no matter what he suspected it cost her. "Our people will guide you to your new home," she said.

"But this is our home." The woman wept, hands clutching the shoulders of the two small children clustered at her feet. "We've only just come back. We waited so long."

"And soon it will be your home again, madame, but for now…For your children's sake…"

Jacquel held his breath. The woman's eyes clung to Dreya's face, then finally, finally she nodded agreement and began to walk away. Jacquel let out a silent whoosh. Dreya had nearly broken then. He'd seen it in the too rigid line of her back, but not once did she let it show in her face. He signaled to one of the senior camp women to take over. A mother, a housewife, like the evicted woman. He could hear the check sheet of promises she made to the woman, the cleaning schedule, the guards to keep her property safe, the secured storage for all the family's precious belongings they must leave behind.

"The chair. The old one in the study. It was my father's."

"Don't worry, we'll put that in storage too. When you come back, it will be as it was the day your father last sat in it. Now come along, you've had a hard day and these little ones must be getting hungry."

"Oh, yes. Yes."

Jacquel breathed a sigh of relief. She was going to go peacefully.

Suddenly, a figure barreled through the crowd. A glint of light and someone yelled.

"Leave her alone," he heard the figure scream, then saw a glint of metal. A knife, in a hand plunging down towards Dreya.

Jacquel's body moved before his head could think. Too far from Dreya. His weapon was out, he aimed and shot to stun. No time for finesse. The attacker stopped, dropped, then fell face first, that deadly knife slicing at Dreya's arm as she shoved the woman back behind her.

Full defensive formation, he ordered his squad. The woman began screaming, battering at Dreya. The children joined in, with mighty gulps of terrified sobs and screams. *Get them out of here.*

But the woman fought back, clawing at Dreya and Jacquel when he stepped in to help. He had no option, drawing his weapon again and using it to stun her senseless. She crumpled, and he beckoned to Vanna, his oldest squad member, to take the children.

"Come on, sweetlings. Mama is fine. She's asleep and will wake up soon. Let's go find her a nice bed to lie on, shall we?"

Shocked faces stared back at her. Two little ones who can't have seen more than three and five summers "Sleeping? Padra?" The little girl looked down at the man crumpled on the ground.

"Padra, is that his name, sweetling?" said Vanna with commendable calm.

The little boy looked up defiantly. "He's our brother. He's gonna be awful mad at you when he wakes up."

"So we better find a bed for him too, hadn't we?" Vanna put her arm around the shoulders of both small children and urged them on, talking all the time in a low, calm tone about the kind of bed their mama and brother liked. She gave one slight glance back at Jacquel. A grimace, and he nodded, then looked down at the bodies at his feet. The mother, yes, she was sleeping. But the man? Jacquel knelt, and gently rolled him over, seeing that knife stuck so firmly in his chest and the slow pooling of blood on the ground below him. Then recognized the face of the man. No, a boy, no more than mid-teens, but a man in truth he'd called him when this boy stood up to his squad at the shield barrier.

Sleeping. Yes, but not the kind you wake from. Not when Jacquel had so little time to target his shot properly to control how the boy fell once stunned.

"He's a boy," he said. "Just a boy, and armed with only a knife, for Mathe's sake. What's he doing attacking a fully armed squad with a knife?"

And now he was dead. Somehow, one day, maybe he could explain it to the boy's family. All they could do now was honor his sacrifice. Jacquel stood to attention, gave the boy the full ceremonial salute to a fallen hero, joined by every member of his squad. A click of boots and snap of hands, then back to pragmatic reality.

"Dreya, you hurt?" Blood stained the sleeve of her tunic.

"Just a scratch, Cap. You stopped worse."

True, and duty was met. It made him feel no better. "Find them a good house. The best we have available. I'd let them stay here, but it's not safe—and I doubt they'd agree to it. Not now."

His family had an empty apartment in a safe section near the center of town. Top of the line and filled with every luxury, it was one they'd always kept for visitors from out of town. But he didn't offer it; not to the mother of the boy he'd just killed.

Ras looked up from his com. "She has a sister in Kraschtow. We can get her there by the time she wakes up. Her son's body can go with her."

"Their father?"

"He was a backup technician during the occupation and is still serving on Mathe."

One of the army of support staff who had worked to keep the Resistance safe and able to finally beat the Terrans. Now he'd killed the man's son. "Arrange for him to be told and shipped back to Hathe. He will need to be there for the funeral."

A nod from Ras. Jacquel couldn't think of anything to be done. Not immediately. But his squad still needed him. He waited by the bodies, tense and ready to act, until a dirtsider ambulance arrived, lifted the sleeping mother and her son's body into their care and swiftly rose up and away.

The City was divided, but grief still united both sides. One hospital, one emergency service, busier than ever in these turbulent times and what they thought of it all, he didn't like to ask. Had that been condemnation in the paramedics' eyes when they lifted the boy's body? Or was that his conscience speaking.

It didn't matter. None of it truly mattered. He had a job to do and it had just been made a myriad times worse.

"Cap, you can't do any more." Ras's voice, and his second's elbow jogging him as he stared into space. "Time to wrap this and go home. The next shift has arrived."

Except that he hadn't been looking at empty space. Not when everywhere he looked, ghostly faces stared back at him with the blank, shocked surprise of a boy cut down far too young.

By a Resistance *hero*. By one of those pledged to save him.

"Come on, Cap. Time to give it away for tonight."

He nodded, too worn out and wasted. "Stand down the rest."

"Already done."

"Dreya?"

"Frithan's got her." Jacquel nodded. Her husband. He'd know how to manage the aftermath. He'd had to do it many times before. "That boy came close to killing her," Ras reminded him.

Jacquel nodded at that too. Might have, might not have, but the possibility had driven his reaction. They'd never know for sure, not now.

"Go home, Cap," said Ras, sounding as wasted as Jacquel felt. "Your flitter's waiting. I'll drive you."

He shook his head. "I can walk."

"Not tonight, Cap."

So Ras didn't trust him either. Jacquel didn't blame him, not sure he trusted his own actions tonight, not after…

He rode back to his current billet without speaking, lifted a hand to Ras as he set him down, and walked up the steps. To a room in a squat, with barely space for a bed and cleaning unit, but at least it was private. The building was set square in the middle of the poorest part of the City. Too mean to be coveted by the moonie agitators, dirtsiders flooded into the area in droves, squeezing into ever lesser and lesser space.

The only advantage of the district: a stream cut it off from the main part of the City, providing a clear line of defense. The core of the new Resistance had taken up residence here and had gradually moved to control other parts of the City, always connected by a corridor of dirtsider-held streets so that no one was ever cut off from help.

It wasn't the Hathe he'd debased himself for, but better than the Hathe he'd found. Dirtsiders walked here with heads held high; gradually, slowly recovering from the degradation of the occupation.

He slung his weapon into the secure lock-up, wishing he'd never have to see it again, pulled off the service gear he'd been wearing and found something else. Something that looking nothing like a fighter would wear, then collapsed back onto the bed.

To stare blankly at the ceiling and see again a dead boy's face repeating over and over on every wall and surface. All staring at him with that same look in his eyes. *You killed me. You stole my future.*

A mother crying. Two small children needing to be told why their world was turned upside down again. Two children who only remembered the corridors of Mathe and had never been outside the walls of a habitat before the overthrow of the Terrans. Taken from there and told "this is home." A home now torn away from them, just like their apartment on Mathe.

This is the house your father and I bought before the Terrans. This is the house your brother grew up in. Had the boy—no, he had a name—had *Padra* shown them all the places he'd played in as a child? This closet, that cubbyhole. Here's where I played hide-and-seek. Long forgotten days of laughter and fun. You'll love it here, he would have told them.

Before he died.

Jacquel swore, stood up, shut his eyes but to no good. Always, the faces jeered at him. Lucky Dreya and her Frithan. He needed…someone.

No, he needed Rheia. With that spark in her eyes, that cool stare that said she understood. Her body.

He needed.

The shadows were still his friend. Slipping between buildings, logging into her building security and dropping in an alternative surveillance vidcast, shifting down corridors like a man who had every right to enter a high-security, Department of International Affairs apartment block.

It shouldn't be this easy. If he could break in, so could someone else. Yes, he probably owed his success to deln Crantz. He'd counted on his commander keeping Jacquel's full security rating on all his aliases, but still…

Her door. He slapped a hand on the palm reader, waited impatiently, then slapped it again. No answer, no welcoming slide of door. He slapped the reader harder. Stupid security. He slapped again and again, until finally the door slid to.

She stood there, mouth gaped, then grabbed at him and he stumbled through into the welcoming haven of her arms.

"What are you doing here?"

"I needed…you."

Her eyes fixed on his and he drowned in the molten fires hidden there. They opened wide, her body tensing under his.

"Sit down, now." She pulled him over to the couch and he followed her lead as if stunned. Unable to control anything. He put out a hand, lowered himself down as she helped him sit, as if placing something ineffably fragile in position.

"Food. That's what you need. Wait here."

No. I need you. Each detail, each tiny element that made up the essence of her stood out in sharp relief. The catch in her breath, the soft whisper of hair from the trace of air through the door when he arrived. The way her mouth tightened, the tiny crease between her eyes, the precision of her hands as she checked her pantry menu and the click of her nails against the pad as she made her selection.

The smell of real food filled the air. The smell of childhood. His favorite soup; rich, hot and filling. How did she know?

She filled a ruby-red bowl, pulled out a cloth napkin and placed it over his knee, then passed him the bowl and spoon. "Careful, it's still hot."

His body on automatic, he lifted the spoon, blew and drank a mouthful. Felt the glow of heat sink down inside him, thawing out the frozen husk he'd become.

She stayed quiet, watching him drink, and still the details assailed him. The lift of her chest, each rise of those round breasts, her legs as she tucked them under her, curling beside him on the couch and waiting.

Till he woke up, he guessed. Spoon after spoon. Each one filling the empty hollow inside him. But soup could not banish the jagged blade twisting his guts to shreds. Then the bowl was empty, she took it from him and he must look her in the face again. And what he saw there sent a shiver through him. Life returning. She stared back, then moved.

Leaving him alone? He reached out and clutched her arm, holding on to it as to a lifeline.

"I'm not leaving. Just fetching a wrap for you."

He shook his head, opened his mouth then closed it again. He swallowed. "No, not cold. I don't need…You, I need you."

She stopped, came back and let him pull her close. Then leaned up for his kiss. He opened his mouth and fell into the spell of her. Familiar and new, as every time before. Except this time, he was a drowning man, falling into an endless sea.

CHAPTER TWENTY-THREE

Rheia woke slowly, aware of a strange feeling of contentment. Then registered the strong arm and warm body holding her safe. Hard muscles and a heady scent of clean male. Jacquel des Trurains.

Jacquel des Trurains! She shot up.

"You have to get out of here. You shouldn't be here."

"Wha…" That gorgeous head lifted. "Oh good, you're here." He pulled her back into his side.

She wriggled, then nudged him with her elbow. Not enough to hurt, just to remind him. "This is dangerous." She had a meeting first thing and asn Chrostic had said he'd call on her to give her a lift. "You can't be here."

A wicked grin appeared. "I like it here and it's still early. You like me here too."

With that smile and that body, of course she did, but it changed nothing. "You have to go."

A raised brow, then suddenly his face closed over and he drew back. "You're right. Sorry, I shouldn't have bothered you."

"Bothered me?" She stared. Bothered her—that's what you called dealing with something irritating, a minor inconvenience. As if what had happened between them meant nothing. She pulled up the cover.

"Oh, Mathe, no. That came out wrong. You are…" He shoved a hand through his hair. "I shouldn't be here, putting you at risk. It's just…"

Lost for words? Jacquel des Trurains was one of the most articulate people she'd met.

"Is it me? Did I do something wrong?" she said.

A choked off grunt of laughter. "No, not you."

Silence, the kind that made you fear to breathe lest you break it. He dropped his head and met her gaze. Then looked up with his eyes like two shattered pools of despair.

"It's not you. I've done something…so wrong."

"Tell me."

For a second, she didn't think he would. But then, so quiet the words, the telling of it like the breaching of a broken dam. "Last night. A house. We were clearing a house. Evicting the rightful owners and forcing them out of the home they'd only just come back to."

She nodded. The vids cluttered the news streams, stirring up moonie anger, but she understood the reasons for the evictions, the need for dirtsiders to be safe from attack. Just as she felt the anger at stories of Hathians yet again uprooted, bringing back so many memories of that day when she'd been marched into a ship and ordered off-planet, leaving her family behind forever. To see both sides was no gift at any time, but now she had a more personal stake. She'd read his full file, the one opened to her by deln Crantz, then greedy for more she'd tracked down all the essays of his too brief academic career. Jacquel des

Trurains in all his glory, awfulness and tragedy. She'd been in love with him before she read them. Now…

"Tell me," she said again. He opened his mouth but didn't speak. A head shake only. "Show me," she said instead, and touched her hand to his, pressing it to his com. For a long moment, she thought he'd refused. Then she felt the faint movement of his fingers and the pulse as he transferred the vid to her com.

"For privacy," he said. "So you know it's true."

Then he waited with shoulders tensed as she watched the vid.

A streetscape. Normal, mundane, like any family street in the city. Gardens, houses, courtyards and playgrounds for children. But this street had fallen silent and few onlookers graced its walkways. A family. Two small children and a tired mother… Beside them, a woman she recognized as Dreya from Jacquel's squad. Quiet, stoic and patient, a light hand on the mother's shoulder as she mouthed reassuring platitudes. She doubted it helped. The woman had the look on her face that said she knew what was coming.

Then a noise, a scuffle down the street. A young man, barely out of his teens, streaking toward the family.

It was over so quickly. A lunge from the boy, a shudder from Dreya and an answering twist from Jacquel followed by the flash of weapon fire. Then the boy lay still on the ground and blood dripped from Dreya's arm. The screaming of the woman; that's what broke Rheia. She slapped her hand over the com, pausing the scene in all its awful tragedy.

Jacquel's hand clamped down on hers, banishing the vid. "Her son. Seventeen years old and already a member of the newest Security intake."

"And you killed him."

"Yes."

That was it, short and simple with no excuses offered. Except nothing was ever simple. "Dreya's arm. The boy hurt her?"

"He had a knife. He fell on it."

"So could have killed her. And the *knife* killed him, not you."

"It was my shot that made him fall forward. I killed him."

Technically; no court would convict him of it, but that changed nothing.

"Did you know he'd been trained in fighting?"

"Not when I…But that didn't mean… He moved enough like one. I recognized him after though. He was part of a moonie squad that attacked the avenue camp a while back. He was…He had the makings of a fine officer."

So yes, he definitely could have killed Dreya if Jacquel hadn't intervened. But Jacquel des Trurains, hero of the Resistance, had now caused the death of a young moonie trying to protect his family. "Was there time to do anything else?"

He shook his head, dropped it again but she refused to allow that, putting her hand under his chin. "Don't hide from me. Good or bad, please don't hide from me. I'm worth more than that." She hoped. But this moment was not about her. If she had to use his bone deep sense of duty to pull him out of this, she'd use it. Whatever would bring him back to life. "I don't care what the vidcasts or busybodies say. You are a hero, period. This changes nothing."

"It changes everything. That boy didn't deserve this."

"And you didn't deserve to be shoved in the middle of it. Or would you rather Dreya was killed instead?" A violent head shake. "And she wasn't, because of your natural, automatic reaction. That boy had a knife and he was going to use it against her. Against one of your troopers, a woman who has more than earned the right to expect you to save her."

He dropped his head and fell back onto the bed, staring up at the ceiling. "And that boy had the right to grow old." The barest of whispers, spoken into the air as he turned away from her.

Decide now. This man, forever, or walk away. But there was no choice. She lay down beside him, pulled and tugged at those rigid shoulders, till finally he rolled over to face her. Then buried his face in her breasts and the mighty shudders broke.

The storm lasted too short a time for the burden he'd carried so long, but when it was ended he lay in her arms in silence. Long moments later, he lifted his head, brought her lips to his and kissed her. Sweet, gentle, a kiss that sought nothing but peace.

"Thank you," he said.

She made to shrug, then stopped herself. The stark honesty in his eyes and the laying bare of his soul demanded better than that. "You needed it. You deserved it. I'm here, whenever you need me."

A bare lift of his lips. "If only that were true. Oh, not you, love. I shouldn't be here. You are right in that, and I'm leaving now. But last night…"

She touched a finger to his lips. "Shh. I opened the door to you."

"And now you must close it behind me." He checked his com; something to do with how he'd gained entry to one of the most secure buildings on Hathe, she guessed, but had no intention of asking. Not if she had to tell ven Raden about it later.

One more kiss, one whispered word of farewell. "The Resistance field codes. You remember them?"

She touched her head to his. "I remember," she said.

"Good."

Then he was gone.

Silence, emptiness. Loneliness slammed in and dumped on her in all its awful banality. This was her life, her real life.

Get used to it. You have a meeting to worry about.

She looked around her apartment, and saw too many telltale signs betraying them, small but undeniable signs of lovers and happiness. The rumpled cushions, the warm, lived-in smell of a place that had briefly become a home for more than one. She took a deep breath and began to work her way through the room, picking up the discarded reader, the mugs left on the side table, shutting the door to the bedroom.

A room she must not show to asn Chrostic, and she forced her grief back, shoved it down into that place locked deep inside where she hid everything that was too real. A place none could find, except Jacquel des Trurains, and she suspected he'd known of it within days of meeting her. But then, surprising as it still was, Jacquel *saw* her. Not her father's daughter, not the efficient diplomat, but her, Rheia asn Forvrad/Postrova.

Now to make sure no others could see it.

A flurry of activity that almost banished the memories of the night, and the apartment looked as before. All curios in place and correctly aligned, chairs precisely placed, and the room systems restored to a light, synthetic scent, faintly redolent of the plateau on a rare sunlit day, though she doubted her newly arrived visitor would notice that.

"You're ready?" asn Chrostic said without preamble.

She nodded, collected her com and jacket and walked out, discreetly securing the room with the maximum lock-up. She had enough to worry about today without risking a break-in by moonie snoopers.

Walking into the meeting room in the Senate quarters gave her the usual tingle on the back of her neck. A crowd of street-level bullies would have felt more welcoming.

"Morning," she said.

They had sent through an agenda for today's meeting, but she'd learned to be ready to switch to a new proposal at any time. Whether they were deliberately trying to unsettle her or just had no idea how to organize their plans, she couldn't decide, but it meant she entered the room on full guard. And that was no different than usual either.

The younger der Greystan smiled genially in her direction from the middle of his usual entourage on the far side of the table, a man at ease with himself and the world around him. None of the usual bluff hastiness driving him today, and that set all kinds of alarm signals firing off in her head.

"Morning, Madame asn Postrova," he said heartily. "A fine day for business."

"One hopes so." She pulled out her chair just enough to take her seat, then placed herself at the table, lining up her glass and bringing up her personal com screen display in a precise manner. Finished, she looked up to the rest of the table and nodded her readiness to start.

A sound at the door signaled a late arrival. The others began to stand, and she waited. The door slid to and a man entered the room.

Councilor Philos der Greystan. The father himself, walking in the door in a triumph of chair-scraping and gushing welcomes. She reluctantly stood in acknowledgement of his rank but said nothing and watched as he circled the room to take his place at the only vacant chair. Right at the head of the table.

As for the others in the room, the councilor's arrival appeared to surprise none but herself. So…

She sat down again, saying nothing. Waiting.

The councilor leaned forward, hands clasped, and gazed around the room with a slight curl of his lips. "I see we're all here. Good, time to get on with the real business."

"And what would that be?" she asked when no one else did.

He looked down the table at her, as if mildly surprised at her temerity. "Developing that plateau village of yours of course, young lady, and getting rid of the obstacles."

She stared back at him, cool and unruffled. Did the man think she'd never come up against opponents trying to intimidate her?

"Making sure the courts see things our way and clearing away any annoying hindrances," explained his son, while the councilor went back to ignoring her.

"Hindrances?" she had to ask again.

"Those who let sentiment stand in the way of necessary growth," said the son.

"The lawyers trying to block this project, and others like it that are needed if Hathe is to regain its rightful place in the Alliance," explained asn Chrostic.

A few others around the councilor put in their own explanations, all wordily explaining to the naive newcomer— her apparently—their perfectly justifiable reasons for bulldozing through long-standing regulations and any reasonable consideration of what real people had suffered to bring them back home again.

But there was one obvious roadblock no one brought up. "What about the dirtsider rebellion?" she said.

"Don't worry about them, girl," said the councilor. "A small hiccup only. They'll be sorted out very soon."

Smirks broke out all around the table. "The Council has the matter in hand, I take it," she said.

"The Council? Yes, yes," he said, to a chorus of more smirks and outright chortles.

She nodded slowly, as if mentally turning over their arguments. A moment to compose herself. "That's all right then," she said. "To business."

She set her hands placidly in front of her and waited for them to commence. Her schedule had this down as a meeting of equals between a group of interested parties and a representative of the Department of Interplanetary Affairs, and she wasn't about to let a man of der Greystan's conceit get away with acting otherwise. An amused lift of an immaculately groomed eyebrow and he lifted one soft hand in acknowledgement. The man had walked the halls of power for many years. A dangerous man, said her gut. The son might be a man of single thought and few subtleties; not so the father.

"To business, certainly, madame. And the first order of the day is the matter of Hyrvettin. Your home village."

He didn't say her name. He didn't have to. A lift of an eyebrow said he was as aware of it as every other person in this room and would use it to his advantage whenever it suited him.

She had never liked threats. "You have further information on the matter?"

"Oh, we don't need to spend more time on such fribbles. We have enough and will soon have secured all the rights we need."

What could that mean? Her com was automatically recording the meeting, but she wished she dared send the feed through to ven Raden now. Something warned her against it, some look of asn Chrostic as he leaned back a fraction to better watch her.

"The matter of ownership of that land has not been resolved," she said as calmly as she could manage. "Whether or not any other villagers survived is still unknown."

Der Greystan junior and asn Chrostic both huffed their contempt.

"None have come forward. They should have done so by now. And we know you won't, Madame asn Forvrad, not unless forced to," said asn Chrostic.

A gasp of breath. Hers, she suddenly realized. An open threat, clear and unmistakable. She gazed back, refusing to acknowledge it.

Asn Chrostic gave her a chilly sneer. "The legal requirements are clear. If no descendant emerges, the site reverts to public reserve. But if any do come forward and physically take up residence again on the village site, the precedent of case law gives ownership of that village site to the ranger descendant in possession."

"Guardianship. The rangers are guardians of the high plateau country."

"If that's the term you prefer. It changes nothing. Legally, it's clear. Physical possession grants ownership."

The Councilor placed his hands on the table. "And that is why, Madame asn *Forvrad,* we are leaving for the plateau country. You, my son here, our good adviser and a team of support staff. Along with a legal brief from the house of Brennons and Vidsans."

One of the most prominent property law firms on the planet, an office with a history of experience in land development going back to the earliest days of settlement. A firm that had made sure all its senior staff were among those evacuated from Hathe at the time of the invasion.

She didn't waste time denying her name, though the shock of hearing it still echoed through her. "I have no intention of travelling anywhere," she said. "Nor would my superiors agree to it."

The Councilor looked down his nose at her. "The DIA have not been asked. Your only choice, madame; to come with us willingly, or not. You have a name, let me remind you, that you cannot wish to have publicized."

That had her thrusting out of her chair. "The DIA is not your toy, Councilor. Nor are its officers. This meeting is finished."

"It is. We leave now."

"A message has been sent to your apartment program to have what you need packed and forwarded," said asn Chrostic. "A message hand coded by your palm print."

"That's…" Theft, invasion of privacy, a violation of so many laws she didn't know where to start.

"Very clever of us, yes." The younger der Greystan was almost crowing. "The table, you see. It's got a reader in it."

She had suspected it might, but her com should have blocked it. "I'm still not going anywhere with you."

"Ah, but madame, I'm afraid you are." A sudden sound behind her, a whoosh of air, a whistle of gas blowing down on her face and a heavy footstep.

Then blackness.

Jacquel forced his feet down the hallway and away from Rheia. Last night, he had belonged to someone. A feeling that filled the black hole growing inside him ever since Bendin had died and Marthe had left. Family, friends, duty—they could only fill so much. That hole, and the head-battering futility of the lost years under occupation, had threatened him too many times. One day, he would lose himself to it.

But last night, Rheia had granted him refuge and he'd found...home.

Now to convince her. She had lost so much. The abrupt severing of all the ties she'd taken for granted at the time of the invasion had left a scar he sometimes wondered would ever heal. Last night had given him hope that one day he could banish that seed of doubt inside her, that one day she might come to believe in the truth and power of the attraction between them. In their most recent stolen moments in the gardens, he'd felt her putting up her barriers again. The clearer it became that what drew them together them was real, the more she pulled away.

Then last night, she'd dropped all her defenses and he had tasted a promise of what their life could be. He was beginning to know her but had so much more to learn. The most important; how to get her to believe that she made his life better, not less as she seemed to think. How could he let this be taken from them, merely because of the stories of what her father had done and the stupid myths that had grown around his own war service.

But instead of showing her how he felt and what they could be together, he must skulk out of her home, shifting swiftly from shade to shade as he slipped back through the streets to the secure blocks held by dirtsiders. He'd given so much to Hathe; was this his reward?

And side by side with his anger walked fear. Deln Crantz monitored her schedule and passed it on to Jacquel. That nystat asn Chrostic was due this morning to collect her for another meeting. That was why she'd been so frantic for him to leave.

She's a trained diplomat. That's what deln Crantz reminded him every time he nagged his commander over her safety. Sometimes he cursed that vainglorious parade of his up the avenue. No one else was meant to be a party to it. One protest to the council, one bitter dirtsider giving their rulers a piece of his mind and telling them a few pointed facts. That's all he'd intended. Or consciously at least. After years spent manipulating the Terrans and plotting behind the scenes, had he really had no idea what could come of it?

Had he not in some part of his churned-up brain planned to incite this rebellion?

He usually thought his schemes through so much better. The cesspit ensnaring Rheia was his fault; the pathways luring her into danger of his making. And the guilt of that was something he'd been trying to find a way to live with ever since her first meeting with the moonies.

How had he come to this?

"You're back," said Ras. "About time."

The voice was cool, but Jacquel had known his second too long. "I had to be somewhere," he said to the barely traceable lines scoring his friend's face.

"Yeah, again. Deln Crantz told us. Hope it did you some good."

He couldn't decide who Ras was angry at: Rheia or himself. "Is he monitoring the inside of her apartment as well now?"

"If he is, he didn't tell us. Your secret's safe, or confined to only the squad so far."

"I won't apologize. Not for this, ever."

Ras raised an eyebrow. "Didn't say I was wanting one. She's good people. But you put her at risk, and everyone here if you're caught by those swamp dredgers she's courting. We deserve better."

"And me. What do I deserve?"

Ras's mouth thinned. "You want to go a round with me, Cap? Any day, right now if needed. But get your head on straight first. The news of that boy's death has gone through the City."

"I'll step down then. Dirtsiders don't need a child-killer leading them."

This time, Ras's fist shot out. Only Jacquel's well-trained reflexes kept him upright, but he still copped a hard punch on the jaw.

"If you've finished wallowing in self-pity, *sir*...I don't hear anyone asking you to resign, and until they do, *sir*, you can leave your self-pity at the door and *do your job*."

"I didn't ask to be leader."

"Yes, you did. When you marched up that avenue hell-bent on setting things straight, *Colonel, sir*. And right now, the people you owe a duty to are waiting for you in the hall."

He opened his mouth, but Ras swung around and marched out on him. Leaving Jacquel staring at the four bare walls of his room and wondering what in Mathe he was supposed to do next.

Your job, said the insistent voice inside his head.

When all he felt like doing was crawling into bed and sleeping like the dead until someone else fixed this unholy mess he'd made.

No one's going to do that either.

One deep breath, another, the last echo of grief forced out, and he stepped into the cleansing unit, cycling in a shortened grooming program to hide the signs of missed sleep, and every other part of the hellish day just gone and the precious night after. He checked the holo-mirror at the end and, not for the first time, regretted the lost luxuries of his home apartment. He'd have to do.

First, a call through to Gof deln Crantz. "Do you enjoy causing chaos, or it just happens when you're around?" said his commander.

"How bad's the fallout?"

"The local senator is petitioning for an arrest warrant. Murder, he's calling it."

"Not too far wrong."

Deln Crantz actually growled. "Tell that to the squad member whose life you saved. The Council is debating whether to hear his petition. Whatever the outcome, keep a low profile. Or is that beyond you too?"

Another growl, then the commander signed off. He hadn't said anything about delisting Jacquel's rank or cutting off his troopers' finances, so he guessed that was something.

Now for his team.

Another deep breath. *You can do this.* One step out the door, then another. It was the way he'd got through the occupation. One foot in front of another, keep on going and maybe one day the hell would end.

All the senior leaders of the dirtsiders had gathered in the building's central hall. Silence blanketed the room as he walked through the door. He refused to acknowledge it. *You're a born actor*, he'd been told many times. He marched up to the head table, stared out at the crowd standing around the hall and gathered them all in with one sweeping gaze.

"Status report."

"Status normal, Cap," called out one wit.

"So totally mushed up," he shot back, and the room erupted in strained laughter.

Yeah, mushed up and plummeting down faster than an aerion after prey. He shoved back his shoulders and prepared to do something about it.

To bring to nothing the senseless death of an innocent boy.

Don't go there. You have work to do.

"Ras, the security rosters for the next week, to my com, pronto. Who we have, their specialties, how much Security support we can count on. And double the guard on all dirtsider areas. No entry by moonies. No exceptions." One wrong word, one angry fracas and any hope of finding a way out of this mess would be gone. He turned to the man on Ras's left: a former strategist in the Resistance, now an unemployed math teacher. "Karven, map out the affiliations of each dirtsider camp. I want to know who we can call on, and who's caught between us and a family or has a loyalty conflict."

Most dirtsiders could fit that description. He doubted there were many who didn't have moonie family, friends, relations.

But the man merely nodded, looking as calm as he'd been throughout the occupation, planning missions with split-second timing and risk factors sky-high.

"Madame da Festran," he said to the amazing woman who'd taken control of feeding and housing them on that first turbulent day. "You're on supplies and logistics. Every dirtsider supporting us must have a safe place to sleep and food to eat. Set up teams and liaise with the other camps." Another stalwart, her placid acceptance belying the massive scale of what he asked.

"Rathis, step up that records search. We need solid data on every single misappropriation of dirtsider property, every infringement of employment law or business contracts—and whom it was done by." Rathis was another of the an Begum legal clan, a genius at tracking financial dealings. Blind trusts only existed to make life interesting, was his favorite maxim.

On he went, a constant stream of snapped out orders to all the dirtsider leaders crowded into the stark hall. Each one calm, each nodding acceptance although every one of them must have seen the vids from yesterday splashing vitriol onto the divide ripping apart Hathe. Each left with head high and purpose in their stride, until finally he was alone, with only their echoes and the open door to the space he'd purloined for an office. A room that held little. A battered desk, a shaky chair and a holo-field. He set the field to full display and fed in the data from his com unit.

Then let it play, staring intently as the web of conflicting linkages lit up one by one. The complex patterns of political linkage in Hathe, glowing here in bright, ever-crossing lines.

The political system on Hathe was unique, based first and foremost on this myriad of lines connecting each citizen, each region, and local community in an interlocking pattern of affiliations. Jacquel stared at the mass of clashing and braiding lines in every color and shade, head aching and jaw tight.

The Council supreme at the center. Each Hathian linked back to the Council, through the councilors owing affiliation to their family lines. In his case, he looked to old Councilor an Baktish through his birth mother's family, and Sylvan an Castre through his father's. Then came the Senate with elected representatives from each local region. Or that's how it had been before the occupation.

The Senate had been suspended during the war. No role for it, when so many hid up on Mathe and those down here must bow to the dictates of their Terran overlords and Resistance strategists. Now the Senate was back, but in the chaos of the return, elections had been impossible. Somehow, parties had been appointed. By whom, no one seemed to know. It had just happened and few Hathians had the time or energy to worry about it, too busy trying to put their lives back together.

But on a day-to-day basis, it was the local administrations that ran the things that mattered to most. Village elders, town councils, rural boards, whatever the locals decided. Water supplies, transport infrastructure, making sure schools had buildings in good repair that kept their children safe and the teaching supplies they needed. Hathe was a planet of small communities at heart. The City was unique in the size of its population and urban density. He'd grown up here, but even he loved to escape to the plateau. He switched the field's view to add in the physical geography. Lands, islands, and the medium-size continents scattered randomly over the whole face of the planet. Places of small towns, wild communities, and rural gatherings. The City was the nearest Hathe came to the great metropolises of other worlds.

Maybe that's why they had evolved their particular political system. Council membership relied on a curious but universally understood process of each family group putting forward the person best connected, best able, or whatever else seemed important to that family at the time, and most councilors served for many years. It kept things on an even keel, his lecturers had postulated when he'd challenged them about the lack of logic or consistency.

Above all, it worked. Or had, until the Terrans exploded into Hathian space and set their firebrands to the safe, comfortable world of his youth. And now, he had put a foot on a path that risked finishing that conflagration. How to navigate a way through it and bring Hathe safe out the other side? The dirtsiders who had stepped into the fire with him deserved that.

He brushed a hand through those living tracks and slammed off the field. If only he could talk it through with Rheia, hear her cool analysis and unique perspective.

But there was one other. The man who had first taught him about the interlocking strands governing communities.

After he made sure a hero's family received the honor and help due them.

CHAPTER TWENTY-FOUR

The funeral turned out as hellish as expected. The boy's mother crumbled at the first sight of her son's bier, her two younger children standing bewildered beside her. The father had made it after a mad flight from Mathe and stood grimly beside her. Jacquel had read their profile. The dead boy was the child of a teenage affair between two people who lost each other, then found themselves again years down the track. The father had only discovered his son's existence a year before the Terrans invaded and he'd spent the occupation grabbing time away from his duties supporting the Resistance, to create a bond with the boy he'd lost and rebuild a family with the woman he'd found again. The young boy and girl child were born on Mathe.

From the way the small family clung to each other, their efforts had been a success. Jacquel watched the whole bitter display through his com, barred from attending by respect for their grief. Any dirtsider who'd been part of that tragic eviction stayed away, and those dirtsiders who did attend kept well to the back. Hopefully the family never found out that the boy's "pension" came from donations from Jacquel and his squad.

As soon as it was over, Jacquel stalked from his office and up to his private room, to change into the kind of clothes he would have worn if he'd followed the academic pathway that was meant to be his, before the war changed everything. Ras lifted an eyebrow when he caught him on his way out but said nothing, merely tapping his com.

"Yeah, I'll stay in contact," Jacquel promised. A brusque nod from Ras his only reply. So not quite good there yet. But Ras would stand for him, no matter how mad he got. He'd done so all the previous times Jacquel acted like a first-class idiot.

He pulled on a simple hat from the pile in the store cupboard before leaving. Keep a low profile, deln Crantz had warned. The surveillance vids may have been compromised, he guessed that meant. Face hidden, change his walk, do nothing of note, and he became just another civilian taking a late afternoon stroll. He'd done the same many times during the occupation, but then the Resistance had adopted all-enveloping cloaks as normal peasant outerwear, giving them huge freedom. Shrouded in a cloak, one Hathian lowlife scum looked much like another to the Terrans.

He pulled up the reader from his com, wandered down pathways with an abstracted air, took the long way through the City Gardens to avoid the tension in the streets, and finally made it to his goal. The main academic block of City University

Now came the tricky part. His own ID code would send alarms screaming over half the city. A quiet shuffle in a forgotten hallway, a sideways slip and stumble into a group on the stairway, up the steps before anyone noticed, and he slipped into another corridor with a new ID set into his com.

His father's office was out—one place the Senate would be sure to watch. Especially after that unexpected stunt of his father's, turning up at the prison to help him. It still surprised Jacquel—so totally out of character with the man he'd known his whole life—but was the reason he'd thought to come here now. Whatever screwed up feelings lay between them, his father was one of the best political brains on the planet.

Somehow Jacquel had to figure a way out of this mess.

He checked the time on his com. On schedule. Into a quiet room off the main University library. The single door into the room made it a potential trap, one his enemies would expect him to avoid, but he'd been playing in and out of these rooms since babyhood. Inside this room was a small window and on the outside of it, an old falafaux vine sprawled up the wall and dipped over into the courtyard beyond.

As a child, it had been a simple matter to slip through that window and clamber up and down the stalky branchlets of the old plant. That was before he'd grown to his current height. He left a sacrificial scraping of his cheek on the century-old framing and, once out, the vine groaned in shock as he set his weight on its venerable supports.

But it held, and the leaf bracts were in full bloom right now, each cradling the tiny flower-like nodules that sent out their unique scent. The bracts continually shifted in position as the supporting branchlets rotated to meet the oncoming breeze and maximize the spread of the enticing scent. Or that's what a dry horticulturalist had told him once. He preferred to think of this plant as an old friend, moving to welcome and hide him just as it had done when he was a small boy escaping his studies.

Tonight, he moved cautiously through the stalks, climbing over to where a high wall branched off from the main building then easing over the wall into the hidden courtyard beyond, finally shifting to slide under a cluster of flowering bracts as they waved and rotated in their typical random appearing pattern. His foot found the old notch, then the next one and the next one down. Climbing down and down until, close to the ground, he dropped silently behind a rustling shrub in the shadowed edge of the small quadrangle.

"About time, son," said a soft voice. "I've been out here every evening since you started this madness."

His father sat in his favorite chair next to the small, softly lit pond at the center of an exquisite garden. Dressed in his immaculate academic's uniform of tunic, over-jacket and formal trousers, he watched as Jacquel cautiously emerged from the shadows.

A slight lift of those thin lips. "You're safe. Gof has this place under full security, with a clearance level even I don't make. Though I suspect you still have access, despite your latest antics."

"He's been in touch then."

His father nodded. "He thought I might like to know my firstborn was still alive, and well. Though I'm not sure we share the same definition of *well*."

Talking to his father had always been like negotiating a minefield. "I'm well enough."

A lifted eyebrow as his father scanned his face. Jacquel kept still but had no doubt Gauvan de Trurains saw through any kind of front he tried to put on.

"The boy's family?"

Jacquel drew in a breath "…is being provided for. By dirtsider funds. And no, they have no idea of that little gem, so I'd thank you not to advertise it. A refusal to accept our help only hurts them."

"The boy?"

"Solid. Good makings. A loss to us all."

The professor leaned forward and Jacquel caught the hint of a long sigh of release. Then his father looked up and straight into his face. "I wondered, you see. Whether…"

Jacquel suddenly felt adrift. The Pillars knew he'd disappointed his father's expectations for him often enough, but he had never doubted his father's belief in him—until tonight. He didn't want to hear the end of that sentence. Luckily his father stopped, sitting back as if throwing off the thought.

"What have you come for, Jaca?"

Jaca. His old childhood name used by so few now that Bendin and Marthe were gone.

He stepped fully forward into the light. "I need your help," he said simply.

His father pulled up the other chair, the one reserved for his step-mama. "Take a seat. We might as well be comfortable. Given the mess you've made, this is going to take a while."

Jacquel settled into the chair, breathed in the beloved scent of Anhuilla that permeated everything she touched, and suddenly found it was easy. "So how do I fix it?"

The moons were rising high in the sky by the time they had finished. Dromorne shining full and round over the spires of the university. Too bright for Mathe, veiled by the brilliance of its larger partner as usual, but Jacquel knew where to find the lesser moon. A faint shimmer, just beginning to peek over the far corner of the roofline.

He leaned back in his chair and sighed. The talk had ranged much wider than he'd expected, and for the first time in far too long he and his father had found common ground. His step-mama always said they were too alike, and tonight had proven it as they discussed the current political situation, argued over ancient history and came up with, then discarded, strategy after strategy to bring Hathe back to unity, till they finally arrived at a number of possible options "Thanks," he said. He'd needed this: someone to give him a brutally clear analysis, as only his father could.

His father stretched beside him, a creak of bones as he sat up, then settled down again. "Don't thank me too soon. If I hadn't come up with the whole stupid plan to split Hathe in the first place, we wouldn't be where we are now."

"Wha…" Jacquel turned to stare. "The peasant strategy?"

"Yes, that one. Hathe's so brilliant plan to dupe the Terrans into complacency until we were ready to overthrow them."

"You…your plan?"

A grunt, and a rueful twist of his mouth. "Mine," said his father, "and a group of my best students. Your Rheia among them."

"Rheia. Your student." Stringing any more than two words together was beyond him. "She never…Rheia. You."

The professor levered himself forward. "Rheia asn Postrova, yes. The woman has an excellent brain for political tactics. You've met her; you should know that."

Met her. "Yes," was all he said, but there must have been something in his face.

"She's not for you," his father said sharply. "An admirable woman, but too much baggage."

"Her real father, you mean," said Jacquel bitterly.

His father made no pretense of not knowing what he meant. "That, yes. But also because she's ranger bred, not of the City. She has no family support here, no connections to shield her from any fallout. How will she cope when you finally take the place always meant for you?"

"And what place would that be, Father?"

"Here, in the university. Or as a political advisor. Who knows how high you could climb one day."

Except his father's dreams belonged in the past, in a world where the Terrans had never arrived on Hathe. "Rheia asn Forvrad is an extraordinary woman who's been surviving the pitfalls of the diplomatic world for years. I have no doubt she will be able to cope with whatever the future may bring her."

"Nothing's settled then," and Jacquel couldn't miss the relief in his father's voice.

"In her mind, no. In mine, yes. And that's all I wish to say about it."

They stared at each other, each equally stubborn. Then finally, slowly, his father nodded his head, and one more topic tumbled into the silent place between them. "She has become a capable diplomat with a strong bent for the subtleties of political relationships. It's why she was allocated to Mathe, not planet-side with most of the rangers. We weren't about to risk losing her skills to the Terrans."

"Like the rest of us, you mean."

"You were never supposed to stay down here," growled his father. "The Council promised me my family would be safe."

Jacquel stared. He remembered those days before the landing as a mad whirl. When the great plan was announced, it had never occurred to him that he wouldn't be a part of it. Hadn't imagined he would do other than stay on Hathe and fight the Terrans any way he could. Underhanded sneaking and sniveling, spying and frustrating their overlords one step at a time, but never had he wished to be up on the moon base hiding with the rest of his family. "You wanted me to skulk up on Mathe?"

"No, I wanted to keep you safe from being killed down here. You think I was doing nothing but studying old texts up there?"

"You were a chief advisor in the Resistance planning team. I know that."

"Advisor. Hah. I saw every vid, every set of Pillars benighted data. Every time I made a decision, I saw your face, Marthe's, all the students, friends and family down here waiting to become one more in that stack of figures." His father glared at him, leaned forward, hands gripped on his knees. "You weren't supposed to be here, and there was no way I could make you do anything else."

"I was needed here."

"*We* needed you—at home."

Jacquel shook his head. "This is my home. Hathe is my home."

"And you were a very good Resistance agent. I know that. And every time you nearly got killed or found out, it cut a hole in your family's heart."

"I can't...I was no different than any other Resistance agent."

"Hah!" His father leaned back. "Only you and Marthe were captured by the Terrans. Sylvan and I drowned a bottle of very good Antarian whiskey that night. It didn't help one bit."

What could he say. Many Resistance members had family split between Mathe and down here. He picked his words carefully. "You believe we—dirtsiders—think you lived safe up there and ignored what we went through down here." No change on his father's face. "You think that's what this is all about? Revenge for the suffering we went through, without recognition." He shoved a hand through his hair. "You really think we're that petty."

"No, too many dirtsiders have lost out to returning Mathians." Jacquel felt his mouth twist. "The Council and its advisors know the truth of that, and many like Sylvan and Gilda have been warning us about it since the return. There was always just so much work, so much to be restored."

"And we got forgotten."

"No." A glare to match the explosion of that word. Then a sigh of regret. "Lost priority, yes maybe. But you, personally, were never disadvantaged. Why are you so angry?"

Jacquel's mouth dropped open. "They are my people."

"Hathe is not made of two halves. They are our people too. But now, your actions have set us on a path where we could become two. Moonies didn't die. The Mathian-based didn't suffer privation, oppression, injury. But never believe we didn't suffer. All we want is a return to the world we had before all this happened."

"But that's just it," said Jacquel, the endless frustration of this unrecognized truth tearing at him. "Hathe can never be the same. Dirtsiders can't simply forget what happened, or who they became under Terran rule—to which, too many naturally return." He thrust himself out of his chair and swung around, pacing back and forth. His father reached out a hand as if pleading, but he waved it aside. Then swung back, needing to move, needing to walk this off. Needing badly to get his anger under control if he had any chance of explaining his reality to the one man he doubted would ever understand him.

"Can't you see that's the heart of the problem? All dirtsiders. *All* of us are hurt inside in ways from which we may never recover. You poke and push and tell us how we must live—and we have to either fight back or crumble to less than nothing. We will not endure that, not again, but too many dirtsiders were near destroyed by it. It will take a touch only to send them under, and I can't let that happen. I won't lose any more to the Terrans."

A sigh and his father set his hands carefully on the arms of his chair. "You are so like your mother. If she was still alive…I've had had to drag her screaming off-world."

"And you didn't Mama?" He meant Anhuilla, who would always be Mama to him.

"Not quite so undignified. She went into a shell as the doors of the ship closed and said nothing, not one word in that whole long flight. I never want to see her like that again, and that's what will happen if you get killed in this latest madness." His father looked down to his feet, then up again. "Your sisters and me, thank the Pillars, we are her heart, and she lets us know it every single day. But you were the first child she claimed as her own, and to lose you would cut into that heart very badly. Please…"

Once he would have snapped back at his father, cursed him for using his stepmother like that. But now, after Rheia…Every moment he waited to hear of something happening to the woman who had become his own heart. "I'm sorry," was all he said to the father who had finally begun to open up to him. Too late? No, never too late for love, but too late to stop the hell-bent track Jacquel must follow.

"Too many are depending on me. Thank you for your advice," he said. "I think, I hope, maybe now we can find a way out. We have to."

He saw the slump of his father's shoulders and had to turn away. Time to leave, while he still had the strength. Too many depended on him, as he'd said. And one, set on her own dangerous path. If his actions could pull her off that path one moment sooner, he'd do whatever it took. But what if his actions knocked her into the waiting pits…

"Goodbye, Father," he said, as he faded into the shrubs and set his foot on the first cleft in the wall.

"Wait. Jaca, wait."

Not the words, but the urgency of the voice stopped him dead. Had him step down and move back into the light.

"What's happened?"

His father stretched out his com. "Rheia asn Postrova. How much does she mean to you?"

Jacquel reached out his com for the transfer, glanced down, then froze. A message shimmered into space. A message aimed directly at him.

His father shoved a chair forward. "Sit down, Jaca. Now."

"They've taken her."

"And threatened her life if you don't follow her to the plateau. It's out of the question, of course. The thing's a trap and they'll likely kill you."

"I have to go."

His father shot out a hand and grabbed him, holding him tight with fingers clamped down hard like an aerion with prey. Or carrying its young. "No. Your dirtsiders are threatening all their plans. They'll kill you, I tell you."

Jacquel looked down at the hand holding him back. "I have to go."

"Is there nothing I can say to stop you?"

His heart was banging a riot in his chest. He shook off his father's hand. "I don't have time for this. They *will kill* her. She's not important enough for them."

"No…" Any other day, the grief in that single word might have stopped Jacquel in his tracks. Not tonight. A woman's life lay in the balance. Rheia's life.

"Goodbye, Father."

He never remembered much about that trip back through the City streets. Subterfuge was second nature to him, and twice he escaped moonie patrols by luck and ingrained habit as much as by intent.

Then he stumbled through his own guard lines and was safe back in dirtsider streets.

"Cap, we nearly holed you." A too young cadet, manning the perimeters. Jacquel had been wrapped in his fear and forgotten the passcode. A light shone into his face.

"He's hurt. Get him to the med room," said an older woman's voice.

No, not yet. "Cancel that order," he said, and thanked the Pillars for the discipline beaten into all dirtsiders by the occupation. But the woman must have sent through a message to the control center, and suddenly his squad members surrounded him. None of them said a word as they wrapped him in a secure cordon while he strode to the main control room.

He palmed the door and marched up to the console. "Top security level." Then looked around. "Clear the room. Everyone," he added, looking to his squad.

"No can do, Cap. Our clearance level is enough." Ras, eyes blazing at him. They weren't moving, and he didn't have time to make them.

A call sign came through on the tight channel. "Gof," Jacquel said. "They've got her. I'm leaving before sunrise. I need full backup surveillance on me and a deep scan of the plateau region. Concentrate on Hyrvettin. I want everything you have by second moon prime."

For once, Gof made no protest, sitting calmly at his desk and nodding as he listened. "Done. Take your squad."

"Too dangerous. Their faces are known, and it's me they're after. I'll not put my people at risk."

Gof didn't argue. "I'll have a patrol overhead on standby."

"No. Not official."

"You thinking to tell me my job, boy? I know where the leaks are in this department and who they run to. All suspects are under constant monitoring by people and methods I trust. Resistance methods."

But Jacquel had trusted a team member before: the geotech on the plateau mission. Until the man helped a bunch of renegade dirtsiders kidnap him and Rheia. "That patrol. Not overhead—keep it out of their scanner zone, and keep the reason secret."

A scowl this time, but Gof nodded agreement, despite the time it would take any help to get to Jacquel. "What else do you need?"

Jacquel sent him a list. "Release these, I'll arrange the rest." Gof merely glanced at the list of highly classified devices, "And I'm using my backup ID." His most secure identity, known only to Gof, Sylvan and his senior squad members.

"Good," said Gof. "The clearance level on that is still at maximum. Keep in touch, and I want a full report and recording when you get back." Deln Crantz slapped a hand on his com and signed off with a snap. That really had been a growl at the end, and Jacquel felt a small lift in his mood. Nothing better than tweaking his commander, and knowing the man backed him counted for a whole lot. This was the breakthrough Security had been waiting for, but that last growl had felt personal. The kind you could count on.

His night passed in a welter of preparation, checking, organizing, arranging everything to ensure his absence didn't hurt the uprising. In the middle of it all, he made time to call through to Rheia's boss, Myron ven Raden. He didn't know the man well but had heard the respect in Rheia's voice when she spoke of him.

"Young des Trurains. You know what time it is?"

He might snap, but the man was at his office desk and dressed for work.

"You've heard about Rheia, then?" said Jacquel.

"One of my best people is captured while working on a scheme dreamed up by your department. Of course I have."

"I'm on my way at first light to rescue her."

Ven Raden nodded, as if expecting nothing less. "So what did you need from me?"

"Information," said Jacquel baldly. "You know they're taking her back to Hyrvettin?"

"Yes," growled the man.

"Will she survive it?"

Rheia's boss didn't bother asking what he meant. Would the pain of that return be too much for her. "Who knows?" he said. "It was a worry when she was first assigned to that region. Only the possibility she could make a breakthrough there had us agreeing to it. Enduring a visit to the plateau area was bad enough when there was good cause for it. As to someone dragging her out to her home village, let alone putting her through these repeated captivities. I'm the one who had to tell her about her family. I saw what that did to her, and now these scum are forcing her through yet another ordeal that's too much an echo of what happened to her family. Will she come out of that sane and whole, or will it finally break her? I don't know, is the simple answer."

But Jacquel could guess exactly what her captors were counting on. Grimly he returned to his preparations.

Just after mid-prime, when Dromorne rode at full peak in the sky, he sat down and recorded his instructions to the group leaders, passing on the strategies he and his father had thrashed out, and anything else he thought they might need. In case…

He wasn't the only born leader among the dirtsiders. Someone else would step up. They had to.

In the early hours, when Mathe finally escaped the shadow of Dromorne's brilliance, he tried to get some sleep. Fitful and edgy, a parody of rest. Her face mocked all his efforts. Frightened, challenging, defiant, injured and, worst of all, her dead eyes staring blindly back at him.

At last, morning neared and release came. Only Ras saw him go, and only because he'd been waiting outside Jacquel's room, too familiar with his ways.

"Try and bring yourself home," he said.

Jacquel grinned back. "Don't I always?"

"Not as I'd noticed." Then his friend's smile slipped. "Hathe has enough martyrs already. No stupid risks. Not this time."

Ras reached out and grabbed him in a hard hug, and Jacquel hugged him back as hard. "Look after the squad, and don't let Gof commandeer them for his schemes."

Ras gave a half scowl, half choked off laugh, in reply. "Done, boss."

That was it. A short grasp of arms and he slipped into the dark, with com secured and weapons ready—both those which were visible and the others secreted variously about him. Developed by the Resistance during the occupation and protected by shields developed in the field, he hoped to be able to smuggle at least a few through. And if not, he'd just have to find something to use once inside—before the nystat moonies executed him.

He had no illusions that was what they intended. His dirtsiders were walking tall, pushing back against the thieves who'd thought to own peacetime Hathe. Yurin routinely won cases now, and mainstream vidcasters had begun asking serious questions rather than merely showing gratuitous vidcasts of villainous dirtsiders rampaging through the streets.

Jacquel des Trurains had to be stopped. That's all the moonie skuds would be thinking, but his enemies didn't know dirtsiders if they thought his death would finish them. Ras was right: Hathe already had enough martyrs. Creating one more would set off a firestorm the likes of which no moonie grabster could imagine.

The slog through the streets was a nightmare of evasion, concealment and stupid bypasses as he worked to avoid both dirtsider and moonie patrols. The gate of the City Gardens beckoned, and he breathed a sigh of relief. The first test came when he used his cover ID to unlock the security gate, inserting his left hand into the scanner field and dropping his voice a tone as he spoke into the guardhouse sensors. Such simple tricks wouldn't work for a bogus ID, but his had been supplied by the Interior Department, under orders from Security.

The Interior Department that had been run from Mathe throughout the occupation.

Nothing happened. No alarm signaling his intrusion, no door release to let him pass through.

A click. Then a message shimmered slowly into existence above the scanner. He held his breath.

"Non-routine entry request made prior to opening hours. Re-scan required."

He let out a slow breath and did as ordered. Hand under the scanner and concentrate hard to set his voice that precious tone lower. Then waited.

The gate opened. "Welcome, administrator. The gates will lock after you for your security and protection. Please enjoy the gardens." If the impersonal voice had a body, he would happily have strangled it for the delay. But instead he walked through the gates, steps even, unhurried, like any normal staff member entering the precious refuge. The sun lay below the horizon still and the grounds had that eerie half-light; the lingering grasp of the turning season showing up in a faint cold haze hovering over the paths and glades.

All help to him. He moved down the paths, walking steadily now, then slipped into the groves and through the grasses of the plateau garden to the hollow at the far end. Today, he refused to see again the image of Rheia as she fell on top of him from that tussock clump, refused to remember the warm welcome of her body as she slipped onto him.

They would have such days again.

At the hollow, he lifted his com and spoke one soft word. "Show." A shifting of light, a lifting of the haze and a small flyer flickered into view. He quickly threw in his gear bag, strapped down and set the controls to lift off. "Veil," he said, and the familiar feel of a cloaked ship engulfed him, that slightly disconnected feel as the ship reimagined the surrounds and broadcast a projection of the moving space inhabited by the ship.

Up, through the embargoed airspace above the gardens, the ship sending out his high clearance-level ID in a precise beam to the monitoring scanners. The ranking of that signal guaranteed it went unrecorded by anyone but a Council member or deln Crantz.

Hopefully none of the Council members ranged against him thought to look at their monitors. Up went his ship and it quickly settled into full flight mode.

He sat back, coding in the route. Now to endure until they reached the plateau.

CHAPTER TWENTY-FIVE

"Coming up on Hyrvettin, sir."

The pilot's voice broke through the fog engulfing Rheia. She'd heard words, seen images out of nightmares, but the prosaic words of the pilot were the first to make any kind of sense. They did nothing to quell the terror.

A face honed into view, one she recognized. The slimy one from her moonie meetings: Narvin asn Chrostic.

"Ahh, you're awake, madame. Just in time for a first view of home. Let me help you up."

He reached out, and she hastily ordered fuzzy legs and arms to obey, to thrust at the bench beneath her and push up and away from him.

"Why am I here?" she demanded. "And what do you mean by *home*? My home is my apartment in the City. I insist you return me there."

All her outrage brought was an amused chuckle from asn Chrostic. "We'll be landing soon. I'll leave you to recover and prepare to disembark. It's a touch cold on the plateau today, but you will know how to manage that."

He withdrew, and she huddled back against the wall, trying to make sense of her surroundings. She was in a small cabin of the kind found on transcontinental flyers, but nothing about this room said commercial flyer. No premium quality sachets of fine choca beside the bench, no com link to the premiere vid channels, no comfortable robe or fluffy headrests behind her.

The bench seat gave little support, the walls were a scuffed white, and the cleansing unit looked basic in the extreme. Beside her, a small window showed a view of the ground flashing past below. She sat up cautiously, wobbled over to the door and slapped her palm against the control plate.

Locked.

She glared around the room, desperate to find something to give her an advantage over her kidnappers. She had so little time; out the window, she saw asn Chrostic's words confirmed. The rising slopes leading to her home village whistled past below. She caught a glimpse of walls, parts of remembered rooflines, overgrown gardens, and then it was all obscured by a rising dust cloud as they settled on what looked to be the old flyer landing pad.

Her village. Abandoned, but still home, though her own house had been long demolished. She refused to set foot in it looking like a lost outsider. She hastily used the cleansing unit, and checked in the inadequate holoscreen that she looked as presentable as possible. If only she had her own ranger gear instead of this City business suit, but inside she knew who she was.

Footsteps sounded outside her door, followed by the click of locks disengaging, and the door slid open.

Asn Chrostic again, at the head of a squad of overdressed and overfed moonie recruits. Some looked too young to have left school, but the rest had a look about them that set her nerves jangling and her muscles tensed to fight. She'd seen their kind before, in the dark places of too many off-world cities, old in heart and with gazes that wandered over her as if judging the latest livestock. She drew herself up to her full height, lifted her head high and stared down her nose at them.

"If you will follow us, madame," said asn Chrostic. It was no invitation, his men moving into the small space of the room and surrounding her. She could walk out or be carried, said the leers on their faces. She chose to walk, keeping her hands close at her sides and avoiding touching a single one.

Down the ramp, across the bare pad she'd last stood on to say goodbye to her family. If she shut her eyes and tried hard enough, she could see them still. Da, Mama, and Bupha, her young brother saluting as she boarded the flyer taking her away. Yes, he'd been scared, but most of all she remembered his excitement, bouncing in pride at the coming adventure. "We'll slam those Terrans and send them straight back to Earth. You'll see, Sis. You'll be back home before you have time to miss us."

Her parents had put on a brave face, but she still remembered the fear in her mother's eyes and that last tight hug from her father. Too brief, then a gentle push to send her on her way before she gave in to her own fears, and the pride in his face as his arms went around her mother and brother. "Go show those outsiders what a ranger can do."

His last words to her. Transmission had been cut to the planet after the Terrans landed and she had been on one of the last flights out. She could only hope they'd known she was safe.

Now she returned, a prisoner of those same Mathians her family had died to protect. Not one dirtsider had spilled the secret of the Mathian moon bases. Not one had ever told the Terrans of the Hathians hiding just overhead.

She shoved her head up another fraction. "So, what's next in this glorious plan of yours?" she said.

Keeping her locked in a room not even big enough to stand upright, it seemed. They had bundled her across a broken relic of the smooth roadway that should have run up to the pad. A brief but heartbreaking glimpse of the few surviving homes in her village, soft rounded shapes settling into the curves of the landscape, and then they had shoved her inside this alien barrack plonked right on top of the main entrance square. Cheap and temporary, she didn't like the chances of the building standing up to any sort of decent plateau weather, but she wasn't about to tell her captives that. She hoped they got blown away with it when the first of the early winter storms hit.

And you? Won't be here by then, she vowed, taking in the layout of the hut as they shoved her through the door into this cupboard, then locked her in. It was a simple enough building; utilitarian was the best word she could think of for it. A corridor lit by cold white panels running down the center, with doors opening off each side. All locked now, hiding who knew what. In the middle, a short branch off into a side passage and at the end, this horrible little room containing—nothing.

What lay next, it seemed, was waiting. Lots and lots of waiting. She finally gave in and banged loudly on the door.

An irascible face appeared on the security screen beside the door. "Quit that, missy, if you know what's good for you."

"Yeah, and without me, the council gets ownership of this land, not your bosses." Empty threats from an empty head, she reckoned.

"So, what you want?"

"A bit of courtesy, but failing that, I need the personal facilities. Now."

She did a bit of a jiggle to convince him of her urgent need. It wasn't too far from the truth.

The screen blanked, and she did a real jiggle this time. *You're a daughter of ranger dirtsiders. This is nothing.*

Just when it seemed embarrassment couldn't be avoided, the screen came to life again. "Stand back from the door."

She looked around. Took a small step back and felt the wall behind her. Stand back? How did they expect her to do that in a room this small?

The door opened, the same ugly voice snarled at her to lift her hands and another hulking trooper pointed a very capable-looking weapon at her. "On your left," he growled.

She obeyed, needing little talent to act terrified and desperate. Into the unit next door first, her relief paramount. She saw no need to hurry with cleansing and setting herself to rights after and had no doubt a sensor watched everything she did. The growl of the man outside confirmed it shortly after. "That's enough preening. Hurry up in there, unless you want me to come in and get you."

She dropped her head, shaking it miserably. Abject and cowed, she palmed the door release and held out her hands in submission.

"Out, now."

A careful step forward, head still bowed and palms open and up. He waved that weapon at her. Another step forward, a twist as if to go back to her room.

That weapon poked her in the chest. "Other way. Down there."

She stalled, he poked at her again, and her hands whipped out. Grabbed the butt and shoved it back into him. A round swing of her leg and a cuff of fist at the other man stepping forward. Then a punch straight at the gut of her first assailant.

But a third man came around the corner and a patch slammed against her neck. Her legs gave way and her arms flopped uselessly down at her side. Councilor der Greystan had made his entry. He had zapped her with a flummy, a temporary flaccid paralysis that left her fully conscious and totally unable to fight back. Only her voice remained.

"I will escape you, and you will pay for this," she told the man staring arrogantly down at her. "You will not win."

"Oh, but I think we will, madame. And thank you for dispensing with the pretense you're working with us."

She gasped, and he smiled back at her. "We've known for some time you are working with the Security Department," der Greystan said. "It's been a rare pleasure watching you play your tricks."

She stared back, refusing to admit he was correct.

He chuckled. "Such bravery. A worthy opponent, madame, for which I thank you. It means I don't need to waste time explaining the facts of the matter. So tedious."

No, he didn't, not that she would give him the satisfaction of admitting it. Her only value to them lay in her claim to her home village, and once they broadcast her name to the moonie part of Hathe, she could say goodbye to any hope of rescue or support. The dirtsiders may have ignored her so far, thanks to her keeping away from them, but the tales of her father's treachery were too wide spread among all Hathians. Too much hate clung to his name, and her involvement with the desecration of Hyrvettin's village site would have most believing she was just like him. The DIA and Security Department would be forced to publicly disown her.

Der Greystan was watching her face and chuckled again. He gestured to the guard. "Bring her along. Time for the official tests, then we can submit our claim to the ministry and the construction crew can begin. And tomorrow," Councilor der Greystan paused, "tomorrow, madame, you can help us entertain our next visitor."

"Not any visitor of yours."

He smiled, the smile of a killing nystat. "Ah, but I had thought you enjoyed the company of our intrepid hero."

Her heart clunked, stopped, then started again.

A chuckle that left cold bumps rising on her skin. "Master des Trurains appears to be very eager to see you again, madame."

And she was powerless to warn him. Nothing worked, no muscles responded to her urgent need to flee this place. One man slung her over his shoulder and carried her down the corridor and through an open door, plonking her on a chair in the middle of the new room. The smell of it as much as the spare benches and unknown equipment cloaking the far wall, proclaimed its purpose. A laboratory, with sharp chemicals biting her nose and scanning lights raking her body.

A woman stepped forward, the badge of the Central Medical Agency on her lapel. A blasphemous abuse of all those respected officials who had served Hathe for centuries, but no one could deny the credibility of any tests taken by one of their staff. The woman lifted an eyebrow at the man guarding her.

"She's under control," he said. "Can't do a thing till we reverse the charge."

The woman nodded, then inserted a probe into her mouth despite all her useless attempts to refuse the violation. The woman merely got the guard to hold her face tight and tug her lips open to let the medic shove the probe into her mouth then drag it out again. Rheia could taste the blood welling from the cut on her lip. The woman touched her probe to that too, a small smile of satisfaction forming on the thin mouth.

She touched it to her com and looked up at the display. "Definitive, identity confirmed. Rheia asn Forvrad, daughter of Garin an Forvrad and Marya an Pientos. Ranger genome characteristics: 82.386 percent. Samarkan genome: 9.752." She turned to der Greystan. "Do you want the rest of the breakdown?"

He turned that false smile of his on her. "No, that is sufficient," he said to the technician, all the while watching Rheia for any reaction. "That will be all. The proof of identity is incontrovertible. Madame here is most definitely ranger born, a proven member of this village and, in the absence of any other known claimant, the undisputable owner of this village site. Please forward the test results to the Council registrar's office." He clasped his hands as the woman left the room, then all trace of a smile vanished from his face. "The transfer deeds have been drawn up. First thing tomorrow, you will give your consent to the sale of the village site to our company."

"I think not."

"Oh yes, madame. You will." He signaled to the man restraining her still and Rheia was slung back over his shoulder, taken back up the passage and lumped down into the small room again. Another patch slapped onto her shoulder, bringing a ricochet of painful needle pricks rioting over her body as the paralysis lifted, then they left her there.

They had taken her com from her during the flight and turned the lights off in the room. In the dark stuffiness she lost all track of time passing. At some point, a small hatch opened up in the wall beside her and a bowl of gray mush appeared through the light field at the back. Her stomach growled but she shoved it back through the field.

A bang on the wall from the other side and the bowl came back. "Eat. It's safe."

She ignored him but was depressingly relieved to see the hatch stay open. One small source of light to save her sanity. She waited for the screen by the door to fade to black again, then put the bowl on the floor and set about exploring the small niche.

A standard water dispenser; that's all it held. Water she had no reason to trust and from a source she had good reason to reject. Water that taunted her with its presence, making every dry-mouthed swallow seem twice as hard. A long while later, she could hold back no longer. No cup, so she had to make do with dribbling water into her hand and licking it off. A few sips only, the least needed to stave off the raging thirst driving her crazy. She waited, testing her fingers, stretching and touching, her sight, her sense of smell, anything that could be altered by something hidden in the water.

Nothing, just the same. Regardless, she refused to touch the food. Gray, cold, unappetizing, she told her growling stomach. *You won't like it.*

Her belly didn't buy it, growling sadly.

It must be night outside her prison, so morning had to follow, with guards and activity. This darkness would end. Someday, some lifetime it would end. Her eyes clung to the tiny food hatch and its faint glimmer of light. The world existed still, and she had not been abandoned. Not yet.

An impenetrable lifetime later, a sound caught at her ears. A whoosh, a tap. The screen by the door sprung to life again and the guard with the ugly face peered in. Ugly but beautiful, a face in all its contorted humanity.

She lived still.

"Stand back."

She eased away from the door, a grin splitting her face wide open.

The man waved that same lethal weapon at her. "Out," he grunted.

Her hand clung to the door as her legs relearned how to stand straight. A wobble, one hand clutching out fast as the open space above threatened to overwhelm her after so many hours curled up on the floor of her cubbyhole with little water and no food. Then she saw the smirk on his face. A quick grab at the wall, and she thrust her head up, back straight and gave him a sneer back. "What's next in your visitor program?"

He shoved her in the back and laughed when she stumbled. One more thing this man would pay for. One day, after his bosses had paid even more.

But the movement helped, forcing her to stretch her legs and push up to a stand. She tried to shake off the hand holding on to her arm. No use. The guard held firm, an unbreakable hold. He palmed open the conveniences next door then waited again till she had finished. And like yesterday she took her time, making no attempt to leave the clean, shiny and brightly lit room until she had better control of her legs. A quick glance at her holo-image and vain shove at the nest of wayward curls playing a raucous cacophony on her head, and she finally answered the thudding on the door.

He grabbed at her arm again and dragged her along the hallway. Stopped at a door, entered a code, then thrust her inside. She felt the pressure of a restraining field catching at her, holding her body locked in place "Good morning, madame."

The Councilor himself again, sitting at the head of the table filling most of the room. She really wasn't getting out of this, not when the man had so little concern with her seeing him. Sitting on one side of him, his simple and single-minded son, and on the other, the greedy Senator an Kroth. The triumvirate in charge of this merry band, with the Councilor firmly in control. Somehow, one day, she would make him pay for this, and for all the suffering caused by this greedy bunch of traitors.

Seated further down, asn Chrostic sat in all his smug conceit.

She looked down her nose at all of them. Asn Chrostic and an Kroth scowled back, but the Councilor merely looked amused. "Still defiant? Ranger born. Stubborn to the point of stupidity, just like the rest. No wonder there are so few of you left, and none of this village apart from you."

"So you say," she said, "but you haven't convinced me yet."

He shrugged. "It makes no difference. You are here and no other ranger from this village has been found. Your ownership is undisputed and therefore valid."

"Yes, *my* ownership."

"Which you will sign over to us."

"Not going to happen."

He laughed. "You will sign it over to us, madame. But first, I think it's time we welcomed our latest visitor."

He lifted a hand and the guard stepped forward, turning her halfway around to face a wall. In front of it, shimmering into place, a holoscreen of the land beyond the village, rising to a peaked hilltop. One she knew well. She'd played there with her friends or with her brother whenever they could escape chores or schoolwork. That notched rock at the top made a glorious palisade for a fairy tale castle.

Then a flyer appeared above the rock, hovered in place and settled in to land on the flat shelf in front of the peak. It set down, a faint glimmer around it speaking of a defensive shield. Then a man stepped out of the hatch and past that shield—and heart, breath, body seized completely.

Jacquel hovered his flyer on the far side of the ridge leading to Rheia's home. He knew the plateau lands well enough, though had never been in this particular corner. The tragedy of Hyrvettin haunted the soils and hollows, and dirtsiders swore you could hear the tears of lost children searching endlessly for home. Homes these moonies now dared violate.

Scanners monitored his approach. His systems picked up the intrusions as soon as he entered the scan zone. Given the serious credits behind this project, he wasn't surprised and turned off the cloaking system. The stealthy approach was out; his target knew he was coming.

He'd never liked having to hide anyway.

That hill ahead looked to be the most obvious peak. He hovered above it, long enough to make sure their scanners and any human watchers had him square in their sights, then set his flyer down in a cloud of dust. A glance around his control room. "Secure—code full."

All in place. No entry available to any of his systems.

He set the hatch to open, waited another moment, then strode deliberately down the ramp. *Here I am, you Mathian nystats. Come get me.*

They didn't take long. Six flyers winged down on him, one landing and the rest hovering overhead. A voice boomed out from the speakers of the flyer immediately overhead. "We have you under full weapons cover, Colonel. Remove your com patch and raise your hands."

He smiled up at the airborne flyers. His com dropped to the ground and he lifted his hands high, letting his fingers brush against the back of his neck. Security's research wing was as busy now as during the occupation, a fact he hoped these moonies had no idea of.

"High enough?"

A squad of troopers in full Security Department uniform erupted from the grounded flyer and surrounded him. Their leader held out a scanner, passed it showily over him then nodded. "He's clean."

"Of course," said Jacquel. "I know you're new to this business but do try to lift your expectations above those of the playground."

The man almost raised his fists. Jacquel reveled in the clenched hands at the man's side.

"Stand down, squad leader," came from the hovering flyer. "Lower your hands slowly, Colonel, and place them behind your back."

He lifted his head and grinned straight up at the faceless flyer. "Whatever you say." He did as ordered and felt the pinch of security cuffs lock his hands down. The squad leader nodded at the two biggest men in his squad. They stepped forward, grabbed his arms and half walked, half dragged him into their flyer, depositing him into a secured seat right in the middle of the squad section and out of reach of any possible escape through the hatch. He leaned back and crossed his legs as he felt the restraining field catch hold of his body.

"Somewhat excessive, squad leader," he said. "I've made it clear I intend to cooperate."

"Orders," the man snapped at him and moved to take the seat opposite where he could keep Jacquel under constant surveillance.

He kept up the blithe facade all through the trip down to the village site, through the landing, the scurrying and the dragging of his still restrained body through their crass building to a bare inner room holding nothing but a table, chairs and a large screen on one wall They shoved him into a chair on the screen side of the room and set a lock field on his arms and legs again, before ranging themselves against the walls around him.

Then more guards hauled in Rheia.

She stood tall, but her hair curled in a crazy mass of knots, her walk had a stiffness he didn't like and her eyes, the depths of those glorious bronze eyes, were shuttered and flat. Hiding all she felt, all she had suffered.

Everyone in this building had just signed their prison warrant.

Four men followed her into the room: asn Chrostic, Senator an Kroth, Rom der Greystan, and the father himself, Councilor der Greystan wearing a supercilious sneer. Rheia's guards shoved her into a chair opposite him and locked her down, taking up positions behind her. He'd been in a restraining field enough times to recognize the rigid awkwardness of legs and arms held in an overzealous field.

"Councilor. I wish I could say I was surprised to see you."

"The pleasure is mine, Colonel," replied the Councilor, "and thank you for being so predictable. You always did have excellent taste in companions." He glanced at Rheia. "Though there is an element of slumming it, this time. You do know that veneer of polish she wears is slick deep?"

Jacquel refused to answer that. He looked at Rheia instead. "I trust you are well, madame. No permanent injury?"

"Not yet. Nor will there be. You didn't need to bother yourself with my small problems."

Her voice was a whispered crackle, as if ready to fracture, but her head stayed up. He vowed that never again would she be forced to hide behind formality like this, to hide from him. And hoped she meant she hadn't signed any contracts yet. It was the only thing keeping them both alive.

"You're just in time, Colonel," said the Councilor. "Madame asn Postrova – no, we ought to use her true name, since this is a legal matter. Madame asn *Forvrad* was about to join us in an important alliance. A small matter only, then we will leave the both of you to renew your acquaintance."

"Oh?" said Jacquel. "A legal matter, would that be? I don't see any lawyer here representing madame's interests."

"Madame is quite happy with our arrangements—or will be."

"I need her agreement on that," said Jacquel. "We talk in private, without monitoring, or this stops now."

"I don't think so, Colonel."

"If this contract is to hold, you need incontrovertible proof she freely agreed to it. Dirtsiders will be all over it in Council without that, and yes, that is a promise." He deliberately let slip the genial face, let them see the man who had survived the

Terrrans. Jacquel saw the recognition of it in the Councilor's face and in the sudden coldness of eye, but his son ignored it.

"Get the lawyers in and get this signed. I've got contractors waiting," said Rom der Greystan. Two more men came quietly in and took up the remaining seats at the table.

Jacquel lifted an eyebrow. "A fine job you've done in raising this man, Councilor. I assume he takes after his mother's side of the family."

The father glared, then recovered his assurance. "As you say, unfortunately yes."

"I thought so. You, Councilor, would never miss the subtleties, but your son…Such unseemly haste."

A cold smile spread over the Councilor's face. "Thank you, Colonel. It's always a pleasure to be spared unnecessary explanations of the obvious. Now, if we may get on with the contract."

"Ah, but I think I haven't made myself clear enough. A contract made without due representation and followed by the disappearance of any of the parties involved will be disputed in court. There are some rangers left, you see, and all dirtsiders honor the sacrifices they made."

"As do all Hathians," put in asn Chrostic smoothly. "This project will make sure the suffering of those unfortunates is not forgotten."

"As well as making a large addition to the credit balance of the developers," returned Jacquel dryly. "If Madame asn Forvrad, since we're being *honest* here, fails to return to the City immediately following the deposit of the change of ownership, a claim will be lodged to overturn any contract affecting the ownership of Hyrvettin. It is ready for submission now and, failing confirmation in person of her freely given assent to this contract, it will be won."

"You are so certain that the courts and population will excite themselves over the daughter of a known traitor? A woman who has been working to entrap good honest officers of the government into betraying their oaths of office—yes, we know she has been working with your people."

Jacquel's heart and gut joined in a clarion call of alarm. But he had outfaced Terrans, and der Greystan was an amateur compared to them. "According to you," he said in the coolest voice he could manage. "We are addressing points of law here, not soap opera dramatics. That claim is ready to lodge, and will be won. Ask your lawyers," he added, bowing to the two aloof and cloaked newcomers There was enough truth in it to make even the Councilor glare at him, and the lawyers both nodded slowly.

Silence, and a gray scowl on der Greystan junior's face. The Councilor nodded at his guards and Senator an Kroth angrily ordered them to take him and Rheia out.

He let himself be dragged away, let his breath go when he saw the other guards following with Rheia in their midst. They were both dragged into a side room, their hands pulled out in front of them to have cuffs applied and the restraining fields released. Jacquel saw the strain on Rheia's face and glared at their captors, then angrily ordered a seat for her when that failed.

"You want her to pass out before this contract is filed? The one your masters want so badly."

Reluctantly, one of them spoke into his com and a moment later another guard entered the room carrying a chair and shoved Rheia into it. "Now, out," he said.

For a breath it looked to be in the balance. The guards made a show of checking his cuffs, shaking them unnecessarily and creating a few more bruises in the process, but that was all. They left after that.

Jacquel moved over to Rheia, crowding closer and bending down in front of her to keep her face hidden from the scanners he had no doubt watched them.

"How bad?" he said softly.

"I'll survive, for as long as they need me to, but you shouldn't have come."

They'd not beaten the pride out of her, said that quick flare in her voice.

"We're not beaten yet."

"Whatever I promise, whatever I do, they will *kill* you."

"Yes, that's their plan. But not you, not yet, and one thing the Terrans taught dirtsiders is that time can beat anything."

"I will not watch you die. Don't ask me to." Tears touched her lids, tears he was sure their captors had failed to wring from her.

"Don't give up, sweetness. Remember that clump of grass where the dynat hid under the astelia? How brave it was."

Would she understand? She lifted an eyebrow, her eyes dark and the bruises showing clearly on her arms.

"I remember," she said. And lifted her hands to lightly stroke his hair.

That quick flick of fingers against the base of his ear. Unmistakable, the quick staccato of a Resistance code. "Walk, not run," said her coded taps.

He swiftly crouched down, bringing his cuffed hands up to cup her chin as a lover would, stroking his hands slowly down the exquisite line of her neck.

"Be ready," said his taps as his hand drifted down to hold her hands, his fingers pausing and reaching under her wrists. A sudden hard pressure of fingers on skin.

Just as the guards burst back into the room, grabbing them both and dragging them apart before they could do anything more. As if they expected them to be able to break open Security grade cuffs.

"Stay strong," he cried out, the sound of a man in love seeing his precious heart for the last time. And it might come true, if his plans failed. "Stay strong," he whispered as she was bundled out the door and could only watch uselessly as she was dragged back to her captors.

Rheia watched him as long as she could, hope touching her for the first time since she'd been hauled into this nightmare. That soft sweep of fingers had left something behind. She kept her head drooped. No need for the restraining field now, their captors must think. Not for someone as broken as she.

But they hadn't grown up with the scowling winds of the plateau or the biting cold that built resistance into a ranger's soul. She may look beaten, but inside she frantically worked to remember those too brief moments in the gardens when he'd taught her Resistance field codes. "Not standard," he'd said laughing, "but they worked better for us. It drove the support staff up on Mathe frantic as they could never be sure what we were saying about them."

Code shortcuts that only an ex-Resistance agent would know. Had she tapped them right? She wanted so badly to help him, but that night in the cubbyhole had cost her. He couldn't rely on her strength.

If only he would escape without her, but that would never happen. Not the man she had come to know. To love.

They dragged her back into the main room and dumped her into the same chair as before, forcefields locking her legs in place. She held her head up by willpower alone now; but of that, she had bucketloads, thanks to Jacquel.

Hours later, it seemed, the door slid open. Asn Chrostic slithered into the room, this time without his masters.

She scowled at him. "The Councilor feels he can let go of the leash?"

A sharp line across his forehead marked that too smooth face, then an oily smile slid into place. "He has full confidence in me."

She sneered to show her opinion of that but didn't bother pointing out the obvious. Not if the man was too stupid or greedy to realize it. The Council met today and no doubt Councilor der Greystan would figure prominently in its deliberations, his attendance recorded on multiple vidcasts.

"We are wasting time. Please look up, madame. At the holo-field on the far wall."

She could have argued, but the glee in his voice had her looking up sharply.

Jacquel des Trurains, hanging by his arms over a deep ravine and buffeted by the swirling winds. She knew the place well, frighteningly well. He was held in place only by a force field around his cuffed wrists; turn that field off, and the drop to those depths below would kill him.

Asn Chrostic leaned closer, his breath heavy on her neck. "Seal the contract or we release the field holding him up." He touched his com, and Jacquel plummeted down below the cliff edge.

"No!" she screamed, uncaring whether asn Chrostic heard the agony in her voice. "Bring him back."

A creeping hand on her shoulder and the chitbut creep touched his com to activate a screen beside her, then set a scanner on the table. "As you wish, madame. Place your hand on the scanner and agree to the terms in the contract showing on the screen."

She kept her hands in her lap, holding one hand tight with the other to stop it lunging for the scanner. "Bring him back to safety first. Once he is sitting opposite me, I will seal your agreement. Not till then."

Asn Chrostic stared hard at her, that hand heavy on her shoulder and his face leering closer. "Are you quite sure you want to play this game, madame?"

In the holo-field, Jacquel was hoisted up, then released to plunge downward, before the field grabbed hold of his arms and stopped his fall. A hard jolt that must have strained every muscle keeping his arms in their sockets, and his face when they lifted him back looked pale and shocked. But that well-known grin sat on his lips and those blue eyes stared straight at her.

"If I don't, you will let him drop as soon as you have my prints on that deed of transfer," she said.

A chuckle from her tormentor. For long moments, it hung in a balance as lethal and precarious as Jacquel's. She deliberately looked away from the holo-field and straight at asn Chrostic. "Jacquel des Trurains safely opposite me at this table, or you get nothing. Remember, if he dies you have no hold on me."

"Don't be so sure, madame. You are very beautiful, but not irresistible. Such a shame to mar that fine skin of yours."

She held his eyes still. "You need me intact, unharmed, and willing if this contract is to hold. The Council is made up of more than your dear Councilor der Greystan."

Frown lines slashed down those thin lips. Asn Chrostic bent to listen to his com. The frown deepened to a scowl. "You give your word that you will seal the contract if we bring in des Trurains, seal it free and willing?"

She had to trust in Jacquel. "I give my word," she said and held her breath, eyes fixed on that swaying body seen against the far wall. Suddenly, a downwards chop of asn Chrostic's hand. "Bring him in," he said into his com. "That's an order."

Slowly, slowly, that isolated figure moved back from the abyss, swinging always in the vicious air currents swirling up from the canyon below. Field restraints usually left no bruising, but that much movement had to cause visible marks, let alone the agony he must be in. Her captors would be hard-pressed to make anyone believe Jacquel's death accidental with marks like that on his body.

And her heart clenched. No, she must believe that he had a plan. He would know as well as she that their captors had no intention of letting either of them leave the plateau alive, whatever legal threats they might use against them.

If only she knew what Jacquel planned.

CHAPTER TWENTY-SIX

A clatter of footsteps, a bevy of guards, then Jacquel appeared in the doorway and smiled at her. Rheia hadn't let herself believe he was safe, not till she saw him, and a return smile automatically lit her face.

"Hello, sweetness. Miss me?" he said as he was thrust into the chair at the other end of the table and his feet locked down.

"Not a bit. I knew you would be back," she said, uncaring who heard it or saw the mad grin on her face. He was alive. He may have his arms set in his lap, and the careful way he sat told more than any words of the drubbing from that cruel suspension, but his eyes held the spark that said he could move mountains and that cocky lift of head said he was in charge here, no matter how it looked.

Then asn Chrostic thrust his face into hers. "You made a promise."

"What kind of promise?" challenged Jacquel from his end of the table.

Asn Chrostic stood up to his full meager height. "Madame feared for your life."

"And you are a pathetic excuse for a man. Neither fact has any bearing on this matter," said Jacquel. "What promise?"

"A small matter of an exchange of goods."

"I am signing over Hyrvettin," she thrust in swiftly, as asn Chrostic's scowl grew blacker.

"No, you're not," snapped Jacquel. At the same time, a flutter of pulses from the new patch on her arm caught her attention. That pattern, she knew it.

Good, she finally deciphered. She hugged her arms, tracing her fingers to the spot where she remembered his hand pausing. He had taught her so few codes, and right now she heartily wished for the fluent skills of the Resistance dirtsiders. There was a short one she remembered. Two short touches, a quick flick of fingernail and a blink of your eyes. *Acknowledge.*

On her arm, there, it was back. Those same short touches, that quick flick and a blink of those amazing eyes, followed by a wink.

Flirting with her, in the middle of all this? She wanted to cheer out loud at the triumphant defiance of it.

Otherwise, his face never changed from the cold anger directed at asn Chrostic. "You will release Madame asn Forvrad immediately and withdraw your claim to this land."

"Or what? Your dirt scum friends going to fly in here and take on the Senator's entire security squad to save you?"

Jacquel looked at him as if at a bug underfoot. "They will be hunting me. Dirtsiders do not desert their own—unlike moonie traitors. Where's your precious leader now?"

"Councilor der Greystan is a busy man. He has too many projects underway to spend all his time on this one," asn Chrostic said, and Rheia wondered if he realized he'd just labelled the Councilor as the leader of the renegade moonie faction.

Another patter of touches from that patch on her skin. She thought hard. *End*, she finally decided. Or *finished*. Got him, would be a better translation, she reckoned, and sent back a slight dip of eyelids. These dirtsider patches must have a recording function. If only she still had her com with its link to deln Crantz and could broadcast this meeting back to Security Central. But when they were free…

They had to get out of here, somehow.

Jacquel glared at asn Chrostic. "Any contract Madame asn Forvrad seals here is useless. No court would allow it. Not when you're holding her captive."

"We are? Madame, what were those words? The ones you promised in return for saving the colonel. Ah, I remember now. Free and willing."

She glared at him, as if hating the words. Not a hard pretense. "Yes, I promised that. You have the contract?"

Slow, she got now through the concealed patch. Or hoped she did.

Asn Chrostic pointed at the com screen beside her. "It's on there. Read it."

She took it and pulled up the contract he indicated. and set it to scroll, searching for all the red flags to warn of hidden hooks she could think of. An hour later, she was still scrolling and Jacquel had slouched in his seat at the far end.

"Have you done?" asn Chrostic said yet again.

She pulled up a section. "This part here—the one where you cover the actual area involved in this contract. It seems overly generous in its estimation."

Asn Chrostic peered at the holo-map displayed. "There's nothing wrong with that. All land used to support the village activities can be said to be included in the possessions of that village."

"Occasional visits to a place by a hunting party or traveler does not make it part of the village's support area. That zone is wilderness and belongs to the Hathian people, not Hyrvettin."

"Maybe."

"No, truth. Seize that and you buy a fight you can't win with the Council and local administration."

"Your local senator has seen the contract…"

"And made no complaint? Not surprising, since the woman currently holding the Senate chair for this region has never even set foot on the plateau."

Asn Chrostic scowled at her. "She's a duly proclaimed ranger."

"By a dubious marriage to a man long dead in the occupation, in a ceremony that conveniently failed to be recorded due to the break in communications during the early invasion period. And the woman wrangled her way out of danger and up to Mathe as soon as the Resistance found a way to cloak our shuttles from the Terrans."

"Fine." He changed the lines, setting the boundaries back to a zone almost justifiable. "That's it."

He signaled a trooper standing behind Jacquel. The man touched his com, and suddenly the muscles in Jacquel's neck stood out in sharp spasms and beads of sweat dripped from his forehead.

"Stop it! Whatever you're doing to him, stop it!"

Asn Chrostic leaned forward, a cold smile on his lips. "The boundaries, madame. You accept this version?"

She looked to Jacquel, and he slowly shook his head. One taut movement from one side to the other, face red with effort. "I will accept, yes, when you stop torturing the colonel."

Asn Chrostic studied his victim, and for the longest of moments she thought he would refuse. The quirk of lip and stare said he enjoyed watching Jacquel's agony. But finally, he lifted his hand, said, "Enough, soldier," and Jacquel slumped forward, gasping for breath as he fought to recover.

"Have you finished perusing the contract, madame? The colonel appears to be nearing the end of his patience."

"Yes, nearly," she snapped, "and you do not yet have my consent. Nor will you, if the colonel's *patience* is further tested."

A standoff, except she couldn't win this one and all in the room knew it. The door snapped open and Senator an Kroth strode in. "Get on with it. The construction crew are waiting to start work."

She'd always thought him lacking in the subtleties of politics. The man must have no survival instincts if he dared risk being here today. "The Councilor left you in charge?" she said. "Getting desperate, was he?"

An Kroth surged forward, fists clenched, but asn Chrostic held him back. "She's deliberately goading you, Senator. Hoping for a timely rescue, no doubt." He swung around to her. "But that will not happen, madame. We learned a few tricks from the Resistance. Right now, all surveillance records show you as asking to come here, willingly joining us and talking excitedly about the plans for the resort. Only the colonel here came to oppose us; a minor glitch to be dealt with."

"By killing him."

"That depends on you. Are you ready to place your hand to the contract and *willingly* cede ownership to our corporation?"

As he said it, Jacquel lurched forward, clutching his gut, teeth clenched as his muscles spasmed.

"Stop it!"

"Seal the contract."

They weren't going to stop. Not this time. Jacquel's body bent back, further and further, stretched and racked under the force of the field commanding his muscles. How far would they go?

"Stop it!" she cried, trying uselessly to stand up and rush to help him, to pull away from the cruel field locking her in place.

"Seal the contract."

Asn Chrostic thrust the scanner toward her.

"No. I haven't finished reading all the details."

Suddenly, Jacquel slumped forward, his breathing twice as labored this time. "You want a repeat, Colonel?" said asn Chrostic, looking at her. An Kroth hand moved over to his com patch, fingers playing in delight over the control sequence.

"Don't," gasped Jacquel, looking straight at her, open-eyed and pleading. At the same instant, she felt a tingle on that secret patch. *All go.* The code words to start a mission.

An Kroth's lethal fingers plunged down onto his com and Jacquel's body spasmed in a nightmarish dance.

"Stop!" she screamed. "I'll do it." She thrust her hand forward and slapped her hand onto the scanner. It lit up in a brilliant smattering of colors as her DNA synced with the sealing link and locked the shoddy agreement in place.

"You duly swear that this contract is sealed and agreed of your own free will," said asn Chrostic for the recording.

"I do, I do. Just release him."

The scanner changed to a steady white output in response, confirming the acceptance and filing of the contract. The whole filthy exchange was now lodged securely in the central legal vault. Unbreakable without a full court hearing and solid evidence of forced consent.

But Jacquel had slumped back in his chair, and the stark chords of tormented muscles eased in his neck. Harsh, panting breaths as he dropped his head, hiding that beloved face from her and their captors.

Safe, he was safe—for now.

Asn Chrostic and the senator left as soon as she'd sealed their contract, chuckling gleefully about all the credits waiting to be made. Blood-stained credits, earned viciously and without honor, but that didn't lessen their exuberance.

Jacquel slowly regained his breath at the other end of the table. She could do nothing to help him, not while the hated restraint field held her in its grip, despite all her efforts to fight free. She badly needed to touch him, to feel the strength of those lean muscles and hear the lilt of laughter in his voice again rather than that labored gasping.

It's better than silence.

Yet silence was what faced them; of that she had no doubt.

No water or food came into the room. Just the guards at stern attention, waiting for…what?

Then an Kroth briefly returned. A hand signal to the guards. "You have your orders. Make it quick, and quiet."

She surged upwards, defeated by the fields but gaining enough movement to make the senator turn to look at her. "You promised. Jacquel to go free."

"No, madame. You must learn to be more precise. We promised to place des Trurains safely opposite you at this table. But after that…we promised nothing."

"And the court case if I don't return? You will never get control of this village without me. And I won't help you without Jacquel."

"You spread your threats too easily, madame," he said back. "When the issue is a matter of planetary concern, the Council has ultimate power, not the courts. And this will be such a matter. Councilor der Greystan is attending to it as we speak. We have this land now, and we are keeping it. This is only the start."

With a cold chuckle, he left the room and the guards marched over. She surged back, or tried to. She was stuck in this stupid chair and couldn't stand. Could only glare helplessly at the mindless hulks setting their hands on her.

A pulse of beats on her patch.

Stay strong. Was she translating the taps correctly? But Jacquel sat back, set his shoulders straight and that grin said he challenged his captors to do their worst. Strong, yes, he was the embodiment of it, and she could do no less than follow his lead. She squared her shoulders and got another smattering of taps. *Good.*

Two guards for each of them. It wouldn't have been enough without the restraining field. Not for Jacquel, and not for her, not with the anger skirling into a battle cry inside her. *Steal my homelands and threaten my beloved, will you?*

But that nystat field held her in its thrall and only her face could show her feelings.

Her hands were dragged behind her back, and restraining cuffs snapped around them. The kind that left no bruises. They dragged Jacquel from his chair next, less gently and with no care about the bruises they left. They had strengthened the field restraining him, taking in his whole body, and she could see his neck muscles straining to hold his head up. But wasn't surprised to see him succeed, head held high, or at the wicked grin he sent her. "Ready to meet our fate, my darling one?" He winked outrageously, and she could almost have laughed. If she had to die, then she would die in joy.

She had thought they would do it quickly in that room, but instead they were dragged out of the building and loaded into a skimmer. Their captors must have grown complacent by their lack of fight as they sat Jacquel next to her. The soft bump of his shoulder against hers was like a warm wave of courage.

"Any idea what they're planning?" she asked him.

"Leaving us to die of natural causes out here, is my best guess." The light tone of his voice made it sound like they were on a feast day picnic trip. "Difficult with both of our backgrounds, you'd think."

"They need it to look like an accident."

"You certainly, if anyone is to believe you sealed that deed willingly."

"But they need rid of us."

"Oh yes. That they do," and this time there was a touch of grim anger in his voice. "How are you?" he said then, in an even lower voice.

How was she? Terrified, exhausted, and with a thirst little eased by the few drops she'd licked from that tap last night. But happy, in love and fulfilled. Jacquel was not the man to let them die in vain; she forced a smile to show her faith in him, and hoped it was true. Those secret patches must have a record function, and someone as well-known as him would not die unnoticed. Jacquel des Trurains had beat the full force of the Terran invasion; a few greedy moonies would not foil him now.

Then they landed, and her courage faltered. The plateau chose today to display all its riotous willfulness, a biting wind tearing across the grasslands and a murderous rage of black clouds racing over the sky, crashing together in a berserk lament of rain and wind that hit them just as they left the skimmer.

The guards dragged them over to stand on the brow of the same hill they had hung Jacquel from and tethered their feet in place with restraining fields that removed their ability to move but left them to be buffeted like broken dolls by the greedy winds. She knew this place; knew it too well for comfort. A high hill right in the heart of the plateau, topped by a jagged line of rocks looking over a dark chasm of slippery death. A slick haze of mist rose from the depths of the canyon and swirling spasms of rain lurched downwards in ever changing directions, now cutting through her clothes from one side, then another.

She'd been to this place so very recently—a memory of danger and sudden, unexpected delight—and recognized a sick completion in their enemies' choice of setting for their execution. Far below, a fall of water smashed against rocks. A man-made fall; the outlet of the water plant, and the slippery slopes of twisting tussocks hid the entrance to her village crypt. A safe haven and refuge, if only…The entrance lay below, so far below. Too far to save them today.

The guards shoved them up against the edge of the cliff, still held by the stupid fields that stopped any attempt to fight back. Then they pulled at her clothes, at the formal tunic, the silky sheath, the plain shoes she'd chosen so carelessly in her apartment, till she was left shivering in nothing but an undershift and leggings.

Then they did the same to Jacquel, checking each item of clothing carefully—for hidden weapons, she guessed—until he stood in little more than she.

Hypothermia; the silent death, they called it out here. The most common cause of death among those who didn't know this place. But she and Jacquel did.

Then they took his shoes, and banged them against her arms, grabbed his hands and used them to batter her face. Huge slaps, but all she saw was the fury in his eyes.

"No one will believe I would hurt Madame asn Postrova."

"No, but they will believe you did everything in your power to stop the daughter of Garin an Forvrad from destroying the rangers' heritage. The hero of the Resistance letting a soft moonie hurt the memory of the dead?" sneered the leader of the guards.

"Yeah, not the man who shot a kid in cold blood. Killing a woman's nothing to the likes of you," said another, leaning closer to be sure he was heard over the howl of the winds.

Rheia would have liked to claw the man's eyes out, and the icy blue of Jacquel's eyes matched her anger. But the absolute horror of it…Hathians would believe this plot line. And that would destroy the dirtsiders.

The guards closed in, a tight semicircle with no escape. The restraining fields were suddenly lifted, just as a man shoved Jacquel. Shoved him so hard that he fell forward, out and over the edge of that killing cliff. She heard someone scream and realized it was her. Just as a hand rammed into her back and she stumbled forward, straight into the abyss after him. The cold winds embraced her shivering and doomed body as she plunged downwards.

The rain and wind tore at her and fragments of the rocky face flew by in a jagged forerunner of the boulders waiting below. She tried desperately to spread her arms and legs, to gain any sort of buoyancy in the swirling air currents, but it was useless.

Nor could she see or hear Jacquel in the dense haze of rain. Was he already dead?

She would join him soon.

She shut her eyes, then opened them again. She had faced life head on; she would face death the same way.

A gap in the rain, the ground tearing up to meet her.

Coming closer—or was it?

She looked harder, concentrated on arms and legs, her body. The air tore at her, screaming around her body as it fell through the air.

No, as it *glided* through the air. As she moved forward and down, the ground coming closer but not at a killing speed.

Someone, something held her. Something slowed her fall.

She might survive this.

If she could make it to shelter soon enough.

Way above her, their captors must be waiting to hear the thud of landing. Waited in vain, as she drifted slowly now, out of sight, and out of hearing over the howl of the winds and rain. Cold shivers racked her body, but she still lived. Now, she veered away from the pounding waters of the water plant outlet, the waterfall she'd taken Jacquel past that distant first time they'd been taken prisoner. Something she'd had quite enough of.

Then she landed, coming to a crouching halt in a tiny piece of flat land. The unknown, benign force released her, and she stumbled forward, huddling into the shelter of the thrashing tussocks. Squat down, work out your bearings. Old ranger survival lore, drilled into her by her father long years ago.

A tapping on that secret patch. *Find*, she guessed. *Here*, she sent back, trusting the patch had the same directional abilities as normal ones, for she had no idea how to say exactly *where* she was.

It came again, the same patter, and again she sent back the pattern she hoped meant "here." Did it? Who sent it? What if it wasn't Jacquel?

Then his body thrust aside her sheltering grasses, his arms locked around her, and his mouth fastened on hers.

"You're alive," she murmured, long moments later as she huddled into him. "You're alive."

"Of course I am, sweetness, and so are you."

Then a burst of ragged shivers seized her. She clutched hold, and felt the tremors running through him as well.

"For now," she said. He nipped at her lips, and she felt the ice as his fingers touched her cheeks.

"Your hideaway; is it close? I hadn't counted on being stripped bare."

"You planned this?"

A weak chuckle. "Not quite like this. I'll explain later."

Because right now, they both needed shelter, heat, and food, in that order. "That anti-grav field? Someone must have sent it. You have backup on hand?"

She felt more than saw the shake of his head. "Yes, but the command ship had to stay out of zone. It's too big to land here, and its flitters are too small to use in this storm. Those moonie troopers will be down here looking for bodies long before it can rescue us." He hugged her tight. "We need to hide, and that shelter of yours is our best option."

He'd left out so much. Huge clumps of missing information nagging at her curiosity. That gravity assist hadn't been any kind of field she knew of. But they had no time for it now. She lifted her head and peeked out across the grass-covered slopes. They had landed across the stream from the hideout's entrance, and would have to scramble down the slopes, across the slippery rocks then up the other side.

She pointed out the route to him. "Downstream, by that patch of kryptark bushes."

"Yes, I remember them." He looked at her, his mouth tightening as his fingers traced the scratches and swelling on her face where he'd been forced to batter her. His own face was a mess of mottled bruises, lash marks and mismatched lumps from their captors' attentions. "Can you make it?"

"We're alive, we're both alive by some miracle, and we are going to stay that way."

He swooped in for another life-giving kiss. "Well said, my darling. Let's go before this storm dies down."

They hadn't gone far before she had serious doubts about her claim she could make it. She hadn't eaten for more than a day, the icy rain drilled down through her meager layer of clothing, freezing her beyond safety, and her feet bled from a constant carpet of sharp stones, kryptark thorns and slipping on the steep slope.

Then they reached the stream at the bottom. Only today it raged down the hillside in a torrent of storm-swollen fury.

"Is there any place to cross?" said Jacquel.

She lifted one shaking arm, pointing up the far slope. "There's one small dam down further. A pile of rocks under the stream, as long as you know where to look. We can c...cross there."

"Lead on then, sweetness." His arm tugged her close, shielding her from the worst of the weather, but it also let her feel the lethal tremors shaking his body. It didn't stop him. He kept his hold on her as they scrambled down to the bank while far above them, she could just make out the sound of an engine firing. Their captors had begun the hunt for bodies.

"They'll give up in this weather," he murmured.

She wished she could believe him. She was so cold. Shivers racked her, and her hands and feet no longer registered. The glistening, slick rocks of the stream greeted her in a flurry of spume and tumbling debris.

"Here. W…we c…cross here." She put a foot down the bank, reached out with one hand to balance against the current, and slipped off the rock, straight into deep water.

Jacquel watched it happen, powerless and terrified. He lunged forward. A flailing arm. He grabbed wildly for it. Grabbed and caught. Hauled her back to the bank.

She was soaked through, any last vestige of dryness banished. But there was no time to waste on worry. Not with the blanched fright of her cheeks, the dank strands of drowned hair or that heavy shaking tolling her entire body.

He grabbed hold of her and held her tight. "Together. We c…cross here together."

He was so cold, dangerously cold and with muscles barely holding together after their captors' vicious games. They had to make it over the stream and up the bank to the shelter of her hide.

One step then the next, near to crawling and with water sloshing over both of them, tugging madly to demand they join in the wild plunge down the gulley. A nightmare of sharp rocks and slipping stones underfoot. Then up the far bank. He was as good as dragging her by now and had to shake her. Force her to open her eyes and listen.

"The entrance. You need to show me how to get there and how to get in."

"Up."

"Straight.'"

A slight shake of her head. "Right. A b…bit right."

That was all. Neither had energy for anything more than the most basic of words. And still the rain poured down and the wind funneled through the narrow gorge. Above, he could hear the roar of the water falling from the outflow of the plant. A louder roar echoed down from the upper slopes. A flyer, hunting for them even in this weather, and beside him he could feel Rheia failing.

Upwards and on in a hellish scramble for survival. When they first pushed him over that cliff, he'd been concentrating on making his plans work. So much depended on the backups he'd put in place for whatever eventuated. Yet only when he felt the tug of the cluster bots slowing his fall, did he admit to himself he'd begun to fear failure. Tiny, microscopic flyer bots, high-powered products of the Security's secret programs. Designed to travel in all weathers, their combined grappling fields had caught at both of them, bringing them slowly to ground.

At the time, he'd cockily gloated over the storm clouds racing across the plateau with the swirling sheets of thick rain they brought to mask the activity of his tiny devices, but that was before he'd felt the strength of that wind. Now he touched his concealed patch and sent an urgent signal to the bots still fastened to both of them. Rheia stumbled again and he briefly caught a glimpse of her face through the surge of rain and hurling sticks. She couldn't last much longer.

The bots had a limited energy supply, intended only for short-term emergency use. That brief energy burst from the tiny particles had helped them evade the detection of the moonies, but now it could mean death. As soon as he and Rheia had met ground, he'd switched them off to conserve their power but now he signaled all but a small handful back to life and sent his bots over to support Rheia.

Rheia asn Forvrad would not die today. Not if he had a say in it.

Rheia stopped, a gasp as the bots tugged at her and she pulled hard back.

"Don't fight them, sweetness."

"What are they?"

"Force bots. They're trying to help you. Please, my darling one."

For a deadly moment, he thought she couldn't hear him. Or refused to hear him, but then she looked up and those fading eyes caught his. A flare of light, a flash of living bronze, and she nodded back. "Up, nearly there. That bush. Thorns."

He looked, peering desperately through the rain. A bush just at head height, up a steep scramble of bank. It might as well have been on the other side of the planet in the state both of them were in now, exhausted and frozen, near to failure. But he had enough presence still to send another command through his patch to the tiny bot saviors and felt the last spasm of energy as they spent all they had, dragging two human carcasses up the slope through the slashing thorns, past the tussock clumps and depositing them with a splash in the small hidden hollow behind.

High up in the clouds, an engine thrust through the roar of the storm. The moonies, hunting hard. A roar of sound that was coming closer, dropping down. Come to make sure they were good and dead.

Rheia collapsed, head lolling forward. He grabbed at her, shook her with all the meager energy left in his body. "The doorway. You have to open the door for us. We must get out of sight."

For a long moment, he didn't think she'd rally. His heart stopped as she lay crumpled in the cold watery hole. His fingers flickered over his patch, pulling the remaining energy from his tiny bots and activating all but one of those he'd held in reserve. That one he needed. A special type of bot, it had little lifting strength but longer flying range than the others. Yet if he hadn't needed that to send a message to the backup ship once he got her inside, he'd have sacrificed it as well. He shook her hard to wake her, dragged at her arm as he sent a last surge of power through the bots, watching in despair as one by one a tiny flicker in his com field told of their death.

Then a lift of her head, a grunt, and a shoved hand bracing against the muddy ground. She lurched forward to slam her other hand against a nondescript rock in the side of the bank, and a black hole appeared in front of them as a roar of sound blared from right overhead. The clouds hid them from sight, but not from scanners. He shoved, tugged, swore with what breath he had left, and just in time they both fell forward through the flickering shimmer of a security field. No sooner had they rolled past it than the entry slid closed behind them, plunging the space into darkness. A moment only, then lights flicked into action and a warm current welcomed them in.

Safe.

A husky whisper from beside him. "Emergency code, seven nine aerion falls."

So quiet, he doubted it would help them, whatever it meant. But then two med stretchers slid into view from a slot by the door, fields lifted them both up and the stretchers carefully tilted then slipped under them, Jacquel watching closely to see she was held safely.

"Code four, urgent recovery mode," said the stretcher's control unit, and trundled them both down the hallway. Straight into the med bay he'd been in before. A mask came down to cover his face and an infuser pad approached.

"No, must stay awake," he gasped.

Beside him, Rheia turned slightly, saw the approaching pads. "Override," she rasped out. "Ranger code blue," and the infuser pads halted, the stretchers lowering them instead into the warm bath. He moaned in delight at the warm liquid enveloping them both. The life-giving, solution bringing solace to battered muscles and seized limbs.

Another pad lowered down to link to his mask and again he warded it off.

"'S okay," she muttered. "Nutrient infusion. Need it," she managed, before her mask clamped tightly over her face and her body sank deeper into the bath beside him.

Slowly, surely, feeling began to return, and his hand reached out, sought hers. Fingers twined, clasped, and finally he began to believe. *We're going to live.*

Sleep pulled at his eyes, oblivion beckoning, but he fought back. That flyer wouldn't give up. Not if the moonies were prepared to brave a plateau storm. He struggled up through the fluid as soon as feeling returned to all his body.

"Recovery mode still in progress. Lie still," ordered a cool voice.

"Can't," he muttered as soon as he'd fought his way to a sitting position and had pulled off his pad and mask.

Beside him, Rheia struggled to surface as well, pulling off her own mask He put out a hand as she sat up. "Shush, sweetness. You're not ready to leave the bath yet."

"Nor are you," she said, "but it's not stopping you."

He put his hands on the edge to pull himself out. "One of us needs to keep watch. You were more affected by the cold than I was. Stay in and heal fully."

She gave him the look she'd given him the very first day he met her. The one that said he'd thoroughly underestimated her. "And you know how to use the equipment in this place?"

He hoped he did. "Standard Hathian. What's there to know?"

"Hmmph." She hauled herself out, heading for a cleansing unit in a dripping puddle of sticky puddles, with only the slightest of drags of those long legs hinting at her ordeal. "Bet you don't even know the codes to access the main clothing store."

He had to stop dead. He didn't.

Then she gave him a luscious wiggle of that spectacular rear of hers and disappeared into one of the cleansing units opening off the clinic, leaving him grinning stupidly. He hauled himself out of the bath, ignoring the residual pain in his arms, and plopped over to the other cleansing unit. No, he had no idea how to get new clothes if she hadn't already ordered them up but, if it wasn't for that nystat flyer out there, he wouldn't have minded. Not in the least, not with that sexy image waiting him.

By the time he hauled his battered excuse for a body out of that cleansing unit he almost felt human again., as long as he ignored the ache in every muscle in his body. She'd dialed up a pile of new ranger gear for the supply slot of his unit, and the healing bath had repaired his muscles and arm tendons enough that he just might be able to make a run for it. If he had to.

Not possible, not without Rheia.

He looked around for her and panicked when he couldn't find her. Her cleansing unit was empty and she wasn't waiting in the clinic as he half expected. He flicked a *find* command to his patch and breathed a sigh of relief when it latched onto her. For a terrifying moment, he thought she'd figured out how to remove the one he'd hidden on her. After what they'd been through, he needed very badly to be able to track her, to know she was safe and well.

He followed the directions his patch sent through and wasn't surprised to end up in the eating area.

She looked up from her seat at the table, and a flash of warmth lit those beautiful, *alive* eyes. "There you are," she said as if sit set all to rights. She scanned down his length, taking in the ranger clothes. "Not bad."

"Can I pass for a ranger now."

A ripple of laughter lit her up. "Never."

"Oh? I think I look quite the part."

She stood up, bringing a bowl of something that smelled as if it might have come from one of his favorite restaurants in the City. "With your high town looks? We don't do beautiful out here," she said, sauntering up to him and lifting her gorgeous mouth to his. He snagged the bowl, set it on the table, and pulled her into his arms, setting his mouth to hers in a kiss that promised everything he could give and more. He could feel the laughter still on her lips and the answering lilt of it in his heart.

They were safe, whole and together.

"Eat," she said. He obeyed but refused to let her go, tugging her onto his lap and holding her secure with one arm as he ate. At the end, she returned the dishes to the cleaning slot and slid back into his arms.

As if finally accepting she was meant to be there.

An image of her at the end of that enemy table and the fear hidden in her shuttered eyes came back to him. "Never again," he promised. "Never again will I let anything like that happen to you."

She leaned into the weight of his body, let him feel the truth of her presence, and lifted a finger to his lips. "I chose to put myself at risk by being involved in this. I cannot promise I won't make such a choice again. Nor can you."

He hated the truth of her words, while loving her honesty and courage.

"Can you promise me that?" she repeated, and he had to shake his head.

"Not if Hathe needs it." Neither of them could. The spirits of the dead and wounded wouldn't let them. "But for now, we are safe," he said, "and I will get you back to the City."

"And once there, we will crucify these nystat traitors, starting at the top," she said fiercely, and he had to laugh out loud.

"Oh, definitely, my darling. Very definitely. But for now…"

He swooped in again, mouth opening to her warm welcome. After nearly losing her, he very badly needed to feel the strength, the warmth, the slick welcome of her body taking him. He pulled her against his body and walked with her into his bedroom. And there, he made love to her with all the skill, all the courage, all the love and cherishing he possessed. And she matched him, moment by moment, with everything in the wild bravery of her ranger heart.

CHAPTER TWENTY-SEVEN

They slept after that, and Rheia woke to laughter and joy. She had been so long without them.

"This should be wrong."

He sent her a look of mock horror. "Not a bit. Or do we need more practice."

She tried to look stern. Someone had to be the responsible adult here. But one wicked grin, one clever stroke of his hand and she consigned her conscience to the file it deserved.

A long time later, she stretched happily. "We really should be doing something about…"

"What? More food, more practice?"

She laughed up at his wicked face, those intense blue eyes filled with the light of a sparkling sun on her favorite lake. "No, our job. Bringing those nystat losers out there to justice."

He waved his hand. "Plenty of time for that. Let them wear themselves out hunting for us first."

"And what makes you so sure we're safe here?"

He swooped in and stole a kiss. Then leaned back and grinned. "If the Resistance couldn't find this place in all the years we roamed the plateau, those newbies out there haven't a show."

But the niggle of worry had invaded their refuge and wouldn't let her go. She thrust back the cover and swung her legs from the bed.

"Ahh, time for the grown-ups to return," he said.

She turned to hunt for her discarded clothing. Dressed, she felt more secure facing that face and body, and the laughter in those eyes. "You must have a plan, and I need to know what happened back there."

He shoved his own legs off the bed and glanced at her ruefully. "Our miraculous flight?"

"You were searched repeatedly. I can't see or feel the patch you put on me, even though I know where you latched it. Der Greystan is Council; he should know Resistance tricks."

Jacquel stood, carefully stretching out his arms and legs as if suddenly feeling again the battered muscles of the last few days. "Der Greystan may be Council but was never part of the Resistance. He left that to others. Far too much like hard work for him. He preferred to focus on the restoration of Hathe after we'd got rid of the Terrans, not how we got there."

"And dirtsiders have learned not to trust anyone but themselves," she guessed.

"No, too simple. We never forgot how much we depended on the support staff hidden on Mathe. We also kept a very close eye on who up there could be trusted, and who worked only for their own benefit."

A dry chuckle rose inside her. "The Doers and the Takers. That's what we called them."

He grinned back. "Exactly, and der Greystan is definitely in the Taker camp."

"And we should get going. Central needs to know what happened here."

He put out a hand to stop her. "Not yet. Too much risk of being caught. I sent a bot back to my craft."

"It's locked down and secured. That flyer's going nowhere."

"The bot can get in through the air intake and my flyer has a tight beam com that not even der Greystan can break. The bot will have downloaded my message by now and help is on its way," he added with a typical Jacquel flourish of hand and shoulder.

She had to smile. "You are such a showman."

"Does it help?"

Oh yes. The laughter in his eyes made the world safe again, no matter how illogical that sounded. "So they will be here soon and we can leave?"

He shook his head. "Best not. The bot doesn't have the capacity to carry the full recording. Only our patches have that and will need to be direct downloaded. We can't risk recapture." The grim set of his mouth said that Colonel des Trurains was back in charge. "There's a full squadron of Security troops on its way. Until then, they have this whole zone on a comms blackout, Resistance style – messages go out, but not to their intended sender, and we manufacture what comes in."

"But der Greystan? The Council…there's another Council meeting tomorrow."

"One that you and I, my darling one, will be attending— with no forewarning for the estimable Councilor Philos der Greystan." His eyes came to full and sparkling life as his fingers reached across to lift her hand and play a seductive rondo across her palm.

She smiled as the familiar tug began to call to her again. "How long did you say till they get here?"

Another of those wicked smiles and a gentle tug of his hands was her answer. His body might not yet be healed and his movements sometimes caught mid stroke, but the laughter in his eyes, the courage and bravado that she sensed were woven into the weft and warp of his being carried him through and brought them both to a joy she knew she would never forget.

Some time later, the patch she still hadn't managed to see pulsed against her skin, and an answering rustle from Jacquel brought her back to stark reality.

"Time to leave?" she asked.

"Yes," he said, but his eyes said something quite other and one hand lifted and touched her cheek. "You are so beautiful. When this is all finished…"

But a sudden clench inside had her lifting a hasty finger across his lips. "Not yet. Don't say anything. I want no promises, not yet."

Inside, a sad refrain repeated over and over. Never again would she have this. Not when she knew what it would cost him to publicly join with her, a moonie and daughter of an avowed traitor.

Hathe needed its heroes, and Jacquel des Trurains was one of their greatest.

His hand caught hers. "When this is finished," he repeated, his eyes darkening as if he could read her thoughts, "you and I are going to have a very serious talk."

A sharp buzz from her new patch, and Jacquel swore, his fingers reaching over to his wrist. "Hold on, hold on," he muttered darkly. His clever fingers tapped on his arm and he occasionally muttered a word that seemed to have no meaning.

She'd seen the famed Resistance codes in action before, but not like this. Not in full, and despite everything else, she watched in fascination. No wonder the Terrans had never guessed at the constant web of secret communications surrounding them. Even knowing what he did, she wouldn't have picked it as a transmission unless she'd been told.

Then he stopped. "They're nearly here. Time to go."

No time for lingering kisses as he thrust her clothes at her and pulled on his own. "I've said we'll meet them by the outlet falls. I know it's close, but it should still keep this place a secret. Does that work for you?"

She could only nod, between having thrust her tunic over her head and fumbling around for a pair of good outdoor boots. She called up the stores program. "Storm slickers for two. Body measurements as last entered," then passed him the waterproof suit disgorged from the wardrobe slot. "They are waterproof and temperature regulating. They'll keep out the worst of the weather."

"That storm must have passed by now."

She looked up. "I thought you'd worked out here for five years."

His lips quirked in acknowledgement and he took the slicker. In short time, they were exiting the hide and sealing the door behind them. She couldn't resist one last glance back as they stepped through the tussocks and into the covering thorn patch. Would they have a night like that again?

The storm may have lessened enough to let a small flyer brave the air currents but the chill wind slipping up the hills still plucked at any likely entry point on her covering slicker. A constant hail of sticks, small stones and whirling debris forced them to walk head down and leaning into the storm's force.

She'd done this before, many times as a child, and the way of it came back with ease, but her body had spent too long in offices and smart hotel rooms. The brief spell in the healing gel and night's sleep had been barely sufficient to make up for their host's questionable hospitality, and her muscles soon protested in no uncertain terms at the punishment she dished out.

Tough. She had a job to finish. She shoved past a flailing bunch of stringy tussocks, whipping spitefully at her arm, as Jacquel paced beside her, letting her take the lead. The meeting point lay just up the valley, a short walk in normal times. Today, her feet lagged by the time they fought their way up the hill to the roar of the water and Jacquel dug in raggedly beside her. He may have appeared back to his usual blazing self when they left the refuge, but their captors had spared him little, and the brutality of his treatment soon began to take its toll. One night's sleep and a brief healing session could give them a temporary reprieve only.

Finally, they reached the flat hollow at the bottom of the spillway and huddled into the shelter of the rocks tumbled in a pile to escape the spray of the outflow. From the white lines gouged around his mouth, she guessed Jacquel was in a more pain than he let on, the med unit's good work undone by the driving winds and the rough terrain. He collapsed momentarily in a heap by the rocks, then thrust up to a sitting position, rigid bands of muscles telling of the will that drove them. She leaned into him, discreetly wedging him back against the rock face behind them. He allowed it, but softly pulled her back too, until both of them sat propped against the cold surface.

"How long?" she asked.

His eyes focused elsewhere as he checked the transmissions on his personal com display then came back to her. "Nearly here. Coming in low."

The hollow was too small, the rocks around it too sharp for anything big enough to hold them both to land. She hoped they weren't relying on her limited military training to produce some kind of miracle.

"Don't worry, they know what to do," he said, his voice but an echo of the laughing tones that could send a shiver down her spine and charm any room to his will. She leaned over and tucked her head against his.

A flurry of wind. She huddled down, but Jacquel struggled to a stand.

"They're here?" The rain still whirled around them, but she should be able to see a craft big enough to pick them both up.

That precious grin touched his mouth, the briefest of tilts only but it was enough to lift her heart. "Watch," he whispered as if a magician at a child's party.

She waited, and saw a shimmering, that became a shape, that settled into the sleek gray lines of a small flyer hovering just above the ground. Suddenly all the bleak weariness investing her limbs disappeared. She followed Jacquel into the open hatch, taking his hand as he tugged her over the last short gap, helped her settle into a seat, and snapped the restraints down. The hatch slammed shut and they lifted with a whoosh of power.

Safe.

After that, everything passed in a blur. Their flyer shot up and disappeared into the open hatch of a large intercontinental ship, hovering high above the plateau. The command ship, she realized much later, but at the time all she knew were hustling medics, the tramp of soldiers' boots amid brisk orders, a quick trip into yet another med unit and the vast relief of letting someone else take control. She relaxed into an induced haze as she sank into the welcoming depths of a healing tank; warm, safe, and free from pain, worry, fear and the awful pressure to keep going.

A laughing voice woke her.

"Come on, Madame asn Forvrad. We have an appointment in the City."

She struggled, fighting through the gel that enveloped her as thickly as the mush blanketing her brain. "Wha…?"

A strong hand reached to help her up. She emerged from the gel, tugged stupidly at the mask protecting her face and put out a shaky hand to grab the edge of the tank. Finally, she got the mask off. "Wha…"

"Such eloquence, my darling one. Your department has extraordinarily low entry standards."

She looked up into laughing blue eyes caressing every curve and hollow revealed by the goop oozing off her. She chose to ignore the blatant provocation. "Pass me that robe and let me get to the cleanser," she said in as haughty a voice as she could manage when faced with a man she just plain wanted, even in her fuggy, fuddled state. "What appointment?"

"With the Council, of course, madame. You and I have a message to deliver, and there's only so long Security can keep a comms blackout on this area."

She dragged herself out of the tank and seized hold of the robe Jacquel passed her.

"Councilor der Greystan is waiting for us, whether he knows it or not," he said even as his clever fingers reached over and twitched the robe down to let him explore one round globe. "Cleansing unit, now, before I forget why it's so important we hurry."

"The Councilor," she prompted, then disappeared into the cleansing unit with a squeal. Those clever fingers had found at least four spots on her body to stroke *just so*.

They found a few more when she emerged, leaving her both energized and thoroughly frustrated as their ship landed and set out for the Council offices in the waiting Security flitter. She'd worked with the Security forces for months but was amazed anew at their ability to squirrel them through the City bystreets and spirit them right into the back-entrance tunnel used by officials to access the Council building undetected by the public or vidcasters. Her own boss met her in the foyer and reached forward to give her a brief hug. The strongest reaction she'd had from the urbane Myron ven Raden. "Finish the mission, madame. The department is proud of you."

Then, as if caught out in a flagrant breach of protocol, he stepped back and resumed his usual face. Beside him, Commander deln Crantz showed no such reserve, rubbing his hands in gleeful expectation. His eyes sparkled. "Go get those ingrates. Our lawyers are waiting with full briefs to ram down their honeyed throats."

Jacquel gave him a flicked salute and a cocky head tilt. "As you command."

"You are going to have me walking into that chamber in a fit of the giggles," she muttered, and Jacquel gave her an open-eyed look of wounded innocence that nearly did send her into a giggling spasm.

Fortunately, that was his last flourish, but strangely she'd lost the pattering of nerves churning up her guts and walked tall and determined to the door. A man in there, that blatantly self-promoting greedy baron, had done his best to destroy the peace for which Hathe had fought so hard, and she wasn't going to let him get away with it.

A small squad of Gof's troopers escorted them through the security checks and into the main Council Hall. Down the side corridors and through the backways of the vast building, an area she'd never before entered but where Jacquel appeared to be very much at home. They had to leave their shelter and step out into the public areas to reach the formal Council Chamber. Into walkways thronged with people; all those working in Hathe's central offices, as well as the tourists and locals come to gawp at this wonder of soaring spires and vast halls filled with light. A building that told its people you are free again. Hold your heads up and be Hathians.

A promise made with every sweeping curve and stunning decoration. A promise she and Jacquel must ensure was honored.

Then somebody recognized Jacquel.

"It's the traitor."

"Grab him. Lock him up."

"Stop him. That's the dirtsider."

The Security squad closed tightly around them and Jacquel kept walking, refusing to acknowledge the calls and jeers.

A globule of spit landed on his jaw and he lifted a hand to wipe it off, flinging a brief grin at the man who stood jeering still. His squad rushed him on, as another larger squad hurried down the hall behind them.

"Hey, who you shoving? That's the man you want. That dirtsider scum up there, stirring up all this trouble."

If Jacquel heard the shouts, he ignored them.

"Stand back," growled one of the guards behind them. "Nothing to see here. Everything's under control."

"They stole my house," a woman shrieked.

"Child killer," screamed another, and this time Jacquel gave a slight flinch but never slowed. And throughout, that beautiful head of his stayed high.

Then they reached the foyer to the main chamber and came to a halt at the imposing ceremonial doors. Solid, enormous and shut tight to show the Council was in session.

"This is a secured area," said a pompous guard, stepping forward and waving a handpiece at them.

His opposite stepped forward and pointed his blaster straight at the guard. "Stand down, soldier. The colonel is here on planetary business. He has been cleared for entrance by the heads of Security and the DIA."

"But sir, this man is a traitor. The last time he barged in here, he started off that whole rebellion."

"And now I'm going to stop it," said Jacquel.

"With that rabble you're leading, the ones who've taken over half the City?"

A nasty glint in the second soldier's eye. "You mean the dirtsider heroes fighting to protect the well-being of the people who won this planet back for you, *cadet?*"

Ah, the senior man was ex-Resistance. No wonder deln Crantz had been fizzing.

"Stand down, soldier. The council is under no risk from the colonel or Madame asn Postrova."

For an instant only, it looked like the young cadet would ignore the order. Then sanity must have prevailed, and he stepped back, leaving the door free.

Jacquel looked at Rheia and held out his hand. Should she? She looked at the guards, the moonie on one side, the dirtsider on the other, both trying so hard to protect the heart, the honor of Hathe in their own way. Jacquel caught her eye, held it with not a hint of laughter, no lightness in those intense blue eyes and his mouth still and straight. She lifted her hand in reply, reached out and grasped his and stepped close to him.

"Together," he said.

"Together," she agreed.

She took a breath, and took a step, feeling him move smoothly forward beside her. The senior guard hit the door pad, fingers flickering in an ever-changing sequence on the sensor controlling the massive doors of the inner council chamber—doors blazoned with the great seal of Hathe, familiar to every Hathian citizen from birth. The doors that now swung wide and welcomed them in. One look from Jacquel, one glimpse of the metal-bright glitter in those eyes, and they both set their faces forward.

Inside, sudden and sharp silence greeted them. Bodies caught in mid sprawl, mouths still open from the latest debate or taunt, a frozen tableau of political commonplace wrangles. Carved into living statues by their shocking intrusion. Not a word, not a whisper, as they strode forward and placed themselves square in the center of the chamber, right in front of the speaker's rostrum and the table bearing the first settlers' relics and draped with the ancient and ceremonial flag of Hathe. Silver green, with a smoky garland of thymenia surrounding a soaring aerion: the traditional herbage of the first landing sight, and the exultant spirit of Hathe's native fauna—a spirit adopted by those early, hardy settlers. Rheia had seen this place on so many vidcasts, including the one of Jacquel's last, disastrous intrusion.

But she had never been here before. This chamber held the heart of Hathe, held the core of their government that had brought them safe through five years of unimagined peril and restored that most precious of gifts: the freedom for Hathians to be themselves once more.

Now she and Jacquel stood before the table, and before the full Council in session, and the faces of too many said they stood there as a threat.

A shout from the back of the room. "Guards, arrest that man."

Beside her, Jacquel merely lifted his head, barely raising his voice to answer. "Councilor frey Radkish. How nice of you to take time from your latest acquisitions to join us today."

The man spluttered, turned six shades of red, and glared angrily back. "Guards, I demand you throw that traitor out."

The guards stayed at attention at the door. A platoon had arrived as backup. They lined up just outside the door and snapped a full, formal salute toward the table. Then deliberately took one step back, wheeled in formation to set their backs to the door and stood in ceremonial guard over the chamber, preventing any outsiders from entering.

Every one of them had given the subtle flick of fingers she'd come to realize spoke of a Resistance background, the quick flutter of fingers from Jacquel confirming it.

Jacquel strode toward the door, tapped on that hidden patch on his wrist, and reached out a hand to both heavy doors. They swung to his command, each closing to a hand's breadth. He put a hand on both doors and shoved. They shut with an almighty bang that echoed through the room, sending a warning vibration that Rheia swore lifted every hair on her body.

Then he swung around and raked the entire Council with that challenging, bright gaze of his, head high and a look of command on his face. Today, the council faced the hero of the Resistance.

"The councilor brands me a traitor. Anyone else care to add to that?" And he stared directly at Councilor der Greystan lounging in a front-row seat; the one he'd claimed many years ago and had never ceded to anyone since, though Rheia was sure there had been no agreement granting him such seniority.

Der Greystan stared directly back at Jacquel. But she'd been watching the man and had seen the faint movement to escape as she and Jacquel had arrived. He must know they wouldn't have come here without proof of their claims. She'd grant him courage at least.

"You appear to yet again have something urgent to say to us, young man. Please," der Greystan waved an expansive hand, "have your moment, then maybe we can be free to discuss the more serious issues facing the Council."

Jacquel smiled back, and she heard a faintly smothered groan from Councilor Sylvan an Castre, clearly all too familiar with the meaning of that smile.

Jacquel bowed to der Greystan, then lifted his arm high. The one holding the hidden Security patch. He let his sleeve drop back and brought across his other hand. A quick press, a flick of fingers, and he came away with a trace of iridescence coating his fingers. A shimmer he lifted high for all to see.

"A few of you will recognize this—those of you who worked directly with dirtsider Resistance during the war. But many won't, and some won't want to. Some are too busy building a new future to remember the perils of the occupation." He beckoned to the stewards who monitored all Council meetings, and a woman brought forward a comms box. He dropped the shimmer into the cavity, and Rheia suddenly stretched out an arm as if to snatch it back.

"Don't worry." He spoke to her, but his voice lifted to the back of the chamber. "Security and Interplanetary Affairs have taken full copies of the recordings on *both* patches." And with that, he lifted her arm high as well, his hand stroking soothingly up her wrist and gently turning it over. Another press, a patter of finger taps against her skin, and his fingers were coated in another smear of translucence. He dropped this into a second compartment in the comms box.

"What's all this humbug?" said a querulous voice from the front row. Councilor an Baktish, the oldest and most revered member of Council. A clamor of voices rose around him. Other councilors with their own concerns.

Gilda an Rathman rose, lifted a hand, and an uneasy silence fell. "The meaning of this, please, Colonel."

There was no ostentatious bow for Madame an Rathman. A workmanlike nod of the head, and Jacquel placed a hand over the comms box. "This is a record of a recent trip Madame asn Postrova and I made to the plateau country. An *involuntary* trip."

"And what is that supposed to mean, young man?" complained an Baktish. "Anyone would suppose you'd been kidnapped."

A glint in Jacquel's eye, but he kept his face still as he bowed formally to the old man. "That is exactly what happened, Councilor. Madame asn Postrova was taken there against her will, and I followed, hoping to rescue her. Overly dramatic, perhaps, but unfortunately true and these recordings are the proof of it. If I may play them for the Council, you can make up your own minds."

"Can we stop you?" said Councilor asn Jordan, his booming voice echoing through the chamber.

He was one of the undecideds, sitting in the middle of the debate. The group they had to convince.

Councilor der Greystan rose. "Are we really going to let this young ruffian prance in here and coerce the Council into listening to this nonsense? Arrest him, I say, and be rid of him."

"And who is going to do the arresting, Councilor?" said Gilda an Rathman. "This so-called ruffian appears to have the Security forces, the DIA and every dirtsider council guard on his side. We failed to stop him the last time he came in here, and I doubt we would succeed in arresting him today. Or do you want to turn what's happening out there into a real war, but this time waged against our own people."

Sylvan an Castre rose beside her and glared at der Greystan. "Enough. I've already lost two of my children to war. I will not allow anyone to start another, and most definitely not against the heroes who gave us back our home. I have one child left on Hathe and will do whatever it takes to keep her safe."

Der Greystan lifted a brow but didn't back down. "We sacrifice the future of Hathe to misplaced gratitude? We all honor the valiant heroism of those who served on Hathe, but those who lived out the war on Mathe also served. Should they be made to renounce a stake in this planet? Should the Resistance be allowed to keep everything, thanks to some kind of communal survivors' guilt?"

Rheia thought Sylvan an Castre was about to have a heart attack, his color was so high. He opened his mouth to speak, but Gilda reached out a hand and touched him on the shoulder, waiting till Sylvan calmed, gave her a nod of assurance and sat down. Then she swiveled on der Greystan, lounging back in his seat again and wearing a pleased look of satisfaction.

"Councilor, I will assume you speak out of ignorance, having lost no kin of your own during the occupation. But you are out of line." She lifted her voice to address the room. "We will take a vote. Those in favor of the Council viewing these recordings, please register in favor. And those against, register a nay."

Thumbs pressed down on coms, and the balance sheet lit up the wall facing the banked seats. Rheia had to turn to see the result, but beside her Jacquel kept still, staring calmly out at the councilors. She held her breath as the figures materialized.

Then released it. In favor, but a majority of just two. They would listen, but that was all they promised. Der Greystan rose again. "I've had enough of this nonsense," he said, and made as if to leave.

"Ah, but Councilor, this is of particular interest to you. I must insist you stay," said Jacquel.

Gilda had heard the note in Jacquel's voice and stepped forward now too. "I think, Councilor, that I must also insist you stay." She turned to Jacquel. "The main doors?"

"Are secured," he said. "My apologies to the esteemed members, but the Security Department has locked the outer doors—to protect the Council from the current disturbances."

"Disturbances created by this rabble-rouser," growled der Greystan.

Jacquel did not deny the charge, but merely looked to Gilda and Sylvan an Castre.

Unexpectedly, support came from square in the middle benches. "Since we're going nowhere at present, we might as well view these recordings," said the quiet voice of Councilor an Heurain, and a chorus of murmurs rose in agreement. Rheia had heard of an Heurain; a self-contained man who said little in public. Then suddenly remembered Myron ven Raden's appraisal. *Don't underestimate an Heurain. The man has huge influence. If you want to know which way the council will vote, he's the one to watch.*

Right now, she would have said he was firmly on the fence, watching and deciding.

In the front row, der Greystan took his seat again, bowing sardonically to Gilda as she settled herself back into her own seat but Rheia could see the tension in the man even as he gave another of those sweeping hand waves. "If we must endure this stupid charade, get on with it."

She allowed herself a small smile of victory, then stood back and let Jacquel begin the recordings.

He set them both to play simultaneously in the holofield filling the empty space on the floor of the chamber, interspersing the differing points of view to let the incidents play in a continuous sequence. Now from Jacquel's view of her when she was brought into the interrogation room after her night of misery in that cramped cell, and his view of being dragged out and strung up, then switching back to her horrific view of it in that interrogation room and the damning words of Narvin asn Chrostic. The ones that exposed Councilor der Greystan as the leader and instigator of the whole grubby plot.

A gasp came up as her true name was spoken and she cringed inside, seeing the rejection on the faces of too many around her.

Stand firm, my daughter. Yes, Da, she promised the memory of the man who had raised her in love and honor, and set her shoulders back.

Finally, the whole wound to an end. Seen from both recorders, their injuries and near-death exhaustion was obvious. Just as was the vicious stripping and attempted murder when they'd been rammed off that cliff face and plummeted down to the abyss below. Only Jacquel's hidden cluster bots had saved them—and revealed the degree of Security help he'd had all along.

The recordings stopped. No longer was the room filled with the whoosh and thunder of a plateau storm, the whipping lash of the grasses and the sight of the wild stream as they set out for cover. Nor was it filled with voices. Rheia looked carefully around the room and saw the pinched mouths and wide-eyed horror on the faces. In the front row, der Greystan seemed to have shrunk, slinking down into his seat. He'd recover and try to bluster his way out, but right now, she knew the sweet joy of victory.

Jacquel touched the comms box. "These same recordings have been broadcast across the vid channels in every part of Hathe. In homes, public ways, offices and farms. All Hathians know what was done to us, and by whom."

Gilda an Rathman rose slowly to her feet, walked to the front of the room and faced them both. "Hathe thanks you for your service. I understand you have both only just been released by the medics. The Council will now consider this information. You may leave it with us."

"Very affecting," said a booming voice from the middle "It doesn't change the rebellion this man has lead against the proper authorities of Hathe. Doesn't bring back the parts of this city held by his dirtsider allies, restore the homes of the citizens they drove out, or bring the young cadet back to life who was merely trying to defend his home from their thievery."

Councilor an Jordan stood tall and waited for their response. In the front row, der Greystan swelled in confidence before her eyes, but Rheia held her breath and tried to sense the currents in the room. An Jordan either fully backed the moonie dissenters, or hadn't yet decided where he stood. Would he back them, or fight them?

Beside her, Jacquel lifted his head. "No, Councilor, it will not bring back the life of that young cadet, a true servant of Hathe. Nor would it have brought back the life of my squad member if that young cadet had succeeded in stabbing her. Both of us had good reason for our actions, but that doesn't justify what happened. *Nothing* justifies what we've had to do these last years. Wars should never happen, and they always have consequences."

Rheia saw the tension in his shoulders, but he let none of it enter his voice. "We now have peace, a peace for which every Hathian has paid. But," and the harsh bite of broken gravel coated his voice, "never forget that dirtsiders paid a different price for that peace. Dirtsiders paid with their lives, with five years of living in fear, never feeling safe, with a constant diet of bitter endurance and thin hope. All we ask in return is a fair part in modern Hathe, with a full chance to return to the kind of lives we were promised. Some of us will never fully recover— and Hathe *owes* those brave Unsung the dignity of the best life they can now manage. Yes, we seized the City, yes, I killed a fine young man, and that I will regret to the end of my days. But not anything else. All of it I would do again if it meant just one dirtsider can find a real future."

He stepped back and cast his eyes right around the room. "You have seen the evidence. Your coms now hold a list of names of the people responsible for our capture, for conspiracy to steal the lands and wealth of Hathe for themselves, for torture and using inexcusable pressure in gaining the consent of Madame asn Postrova to the illegal sale of a ranger village."

A hateful smile coated der Greystan's arrogant face. "You forgot to mention which ranger village we are dealing with. Hyrvettin, her home village. One she had every right to sell as the sole remaining ranger inhabitant. Isn't that right, Madame asn *Forvrad*."

Der Greystan stared at her, challenging her to deny the words clearly heard in the vid. To deny her name and explain her legacy. The evidence of the recordings couldn't be denied, but without public confession of her true name and family, the contract meant nothing. Not now it was clear their DNA sample had been taken under duress.

"Is it true?" demanded Councilor an Baktish. "Are you related to that traitor?"

"If you mean my father, Garin an Forvrad, then yes, I am very definitely related to him. My father was a fine man and will always be a hero to me. As will my deceased mother and young brother."

"He was only a boy when that man let him die," said an Baktish. "How can you defend the man—unless you support what he did."

Rheia glared back at him, feeling a volcano of anger storming to life inside her. Jacquel's hand shot out, touched her on the arm but she shook it off and marched right up to where an Baktish sat so pompously in the front row. She didn't care how old he was, or how respected.

"My father," she said, leaning right over the man and poking a finger at him, "was a true ranger and the best father I could have wished for. You talk of him *letting* his family die. They didn't just die. They were tortured to death by the Terrans, all of them. That's why my father gave up his secrets; to try to save his family, and no, he should never have trusted the Terrans to keep their word." She took a deep breath, a ragged gulp of air. "I've seen my father's postmortem results, and the recordings of the deaths of my mother and brother. No one…*no one* has the right to say anything to me about the deaths of *my family*. Not you, not that piece of excrement masquerading as a councilor over there who dares to use my family's name against me, and certainly not anyone else on Hathe."

She stood tall and looked straight at every single member of Council. "Yes, my name is asn Forvrad. I am the daughter of Garin an Forvrad and Marya an Pientos, and the sister of Bucephalis asn Forvrad, all of whom were murdered slowly and painfully by the Terrans. And I am here today to demand justice for their memories, and for the memories of all the others of my home village—and of too many more no longer with us, thanks to the Terrans. Their bones deserve better than to be granted a polite ceremonial courtesy then consigned to the graveyard of history, while those with no conscience plunder today's Hathe for their own enrichment."

She had to pull deep, gasping for breath as the pain of her loss hit her again. "Colonel des Trurains demands legal redress for the actions of Philos der Greystan and his cohorts, their arrest and trial to answer for their crimes against us these last days. I demand justice for those who are no longer with us to demand it."

Another deep breath, a clench of fists and tightening of back muscles. She had to finish this. "I demand justice for the murder of my entire family. I demand that you give back to all Hathians the life they deserve." Back forced upright, she glared at the Council.

"I demand that this Council do its job."

CHAPTER TWENTY-EIGHT

With a crash, the doors behind them suddenly swung open. The Security guards stood to attention as a full squad marched in, headed by Gof deln Crantz. Then Rheia recognized the woman on one side of him, and the man on the other.

Advocate Generals Maritsa ven Bradden and Ventnor deln Croasch.

The two most senior members of the Hathian Planetary Prosecutions Service. Not even a Councilor could claim immunity from their deliberations.

Der Greystan crashed to his feet. One mighty "Humph," a growled, "I've had enough of this nonsense," and he marched to the door and made to push past the ceremonial guard.

The new troopers surrounded him, forcing him to halt. Advocate ven Bradden lifted her hand, displaying the holo-shield of her department above a formal proclamation. "Councilor Philos der Greystan. You are hereby detained for questioning on the following charges: unlawful imprisonment of two Hathian citizens; using coercion and physical threats to obtain a financially beneficial contractual agreement; real estate fraud; and treason under the emergency laws promulgated during the recent occupation of Hathe and not yet rescinded by Council. You are to be transferred to a secure location pending trial on these charges."

Der Greystan opened his mouth, but Advocate deln Croasch spoke before he could say anything. "You will have plenty of time at your trial to speak in your defense, Councilor."

With that, the guards seized hold of the man and forcibly marched him across the chamber and through the staff doors at the other side.

"And the rest of us? Are you going to put the whole Council under arrest as well for daring to disagree with these young louts?" said an Baktish.

The advocate bowed to the old man. "You have seen the recording, Councilor. Only der Greystan was implicated. We thank the Council for its patience during this painful incident and will leave you to your deliberations."

"And those two?" a voice shouted from the back of the chamber. "What about those two? Barging in here, interrupting the Council in its important work. And that man des Trurains has singlehandedly lead a rebellion that has spread right across the planet."

"Do you mean Colonel des Trurains and Madame asn Postrova? Do not concern yourself with their fate, Councilor," said Advocate ven Bradden, stepping forward as a protesting der Greystan was dragged away. "The Security Department and the Prosecutions Service have reviewed every single action of Colonel des Trurains and Madame asn Postrova, born Forvrad, along with the context of those actions, and will in due course release their findings. The current discussion centers on which honor is to be granted them. But for now," she turned and bowed deeply to Jacquel and Rheia, creating a storm of muttering from der Greystan's neighbors but silence only in the middle benches. "I have been informed by the medical staff that both of you are to return immediately to the medical wards. Your doctors feel that this afternoon's excitement has been quite sufficient given your condition at the time of your rescue."

That wasn't what Rheia had planned and opened her mouth to say so, but felt a squeeze of her hand, as Jacquel gave that superlative upper-crust bow of his. "Thank you, Madame Advocate General. We will do as ordered. With the Council's permission…"

He pulled on her hand, as Gilda an Rathman lifted her hand in assent.

Jacquel knew it wasn't the end, of course. Not while they had a city in rebellion and a planet divided, and as soon as he was pronounced fit, he had a question to ask one very brave woman.

"A med unit can hasten healing; it can't create miracles, young man," said Doctor an Mathson to him when he tried to convince her he was ready to be discharged from hospital. "Pulling off that all-conquering wonder-boy charade for the Council doesn't mean your body is back to normal. You've been running on empty for too long and those muscles of yours were badly torn up thanks to those thugs of der Greystan. All your readings are still below par. Get back in that bed immediately and give your body a chance to mend properly."

He'd been ignoring Doctor an Mathson's advice for years and saw no reason to change now. "I have people out there who need me."

"And I'm coming with you," said Rheia from the bed beside his.

"Your readings are nearly as bad as his, young lady."

"Meaning?" he demanded of the doctor. He could see too clearly still the bruises mottling her face and the blue smudges under those stunning eyes.

"If she doesn't rest and follow orders, she's going to have a serious relapse and will be spending a long time in here to recover properly. As will you."

He'd learned to read Rheia's face and saw the stubbornness setting in. If he left, she would follow. He had no choice. "You win," he said to the doctor.

But if he couldn't go to his people, they could come to him. Doctor an Mathson tried to limit it, her voice the cold blast of authority the day she walked into his room to find it crowded with dirtsiders arguing madly over the best way to resolve the current impasse as he tried to get them to listen to the solutions he and his father had hammered out that night. When his supporters nearly came to blows with a group of passing visitors who'd been turfed out of their homes by the dirtsider uprising, Doctor an Mathson turned dictator, ordering deln Crantz to send in a full squad of Security staff and stationed them square in his doorway to stop any more unauthorized visitors arriving.

Which left him with only family and those whose security pass was too high for even the good doctor to keep out. Although he had a feeling she'd tried, from the twitch on deln Crantz's face.

"You've got to get me out of this place," he said to his commander as soon as the door shut behind him.

"Out of the question. How can we get anyone to believe the truth of what happened to you both if you waltz out of here almost as soon as you're admitted?"

"I have work to do," said Jacquel, frustration riding him hard. No one would tell him what was happening out there.

"Have they set a date for der Greystan's trial yet, or has he got those twisted lawyers of his conniving his way out of this?"

Deln Crantz looked pointedly across at Rheia in her bed, currently sleeping in that fitful way that had Jacquel worried.

"Whatever you have to say to me can be said in front of Rheia. She's more than paid her dues to Hathe," he said, glaring at deln Crantz.

"She doesn't have your security clearance, and likely never will."

"Because of her father?" he said bitterly, fists clenching despite himself.

"No, you young idiot. Because she hasn't got your connections or history. Like it or not, Hathe is a stratified society and you've been trained since the cradle in what it takes to work close to the core of government. Most importantly, she's not Resistance. You earned that clearance; she hasn't."

"Then Hathe will have to change," was Jacquel's curt answer. "Now tell me what's going on. When will the Council make their decision public?"

"When they make one," growled deln Crantz, looking as frustrated as Jacquel.

He'd been stuck in here for days and the Council was still considering? The dirtsiders had given them all they had asked for: screeds of legal filings; reports on real estate skullduggery that left valiant heroes homeless; the daily struggles of dirtsiders to get jobs, decent houses and treatment for the stress disorders so heartbreakingly common among the survivors.

"At least tell me der Greystan and all his cronies are locked up tight."

"Of course they are. Not even those puling cowards investing the Council benches have the nerve to release them.

All his so-called friends are racing each other to pledge support for the brave heroes of the Resistance and selling off property so fast there's going to be a massive crash soon if someone doesn't step in with some common sense."

"Good," said Jacquel. "Maybe dirtsiders can buy back their homes."

Deln Crantz made little effort to hide the smile lurking at the corner of his mouth, but that was all he said on the matter.

His family came too. An awkward silence fell between them, and Rheia excused herself, despite his hasty demand she stay.

"When's the wedding?" said his father sourly, to an elbow in the ribs from his stepmother.

"I like her," said Anhuilla with a big hug. His half-sisters' mouths dropped open and they scrambled up on the bed.

"Can we be her attendants?" said one.

"Since she hasn't got anyone else," blurted out the other.

"Baby!" cried his stepmother, to a scowl from the youngest member of the family who hated the word.

"But she hasn't, and I know exactly what I want to wear."

"I haven't asked her yet," he said quickly before a full-scale war broke out between the two girls, and for a second time their mouths dropped open.

At the back, his father stayed silent. Soon after, his stepmother quirked a brow at her husband, and herded the girls out of the room, telling them that their brother was still recovering, and they could bother him when he was home again.

His father cleared his throat.

Jacquel did the same. "I have to thank you for telling me of Rheia's capture," he said.

"It nearly got you killed—again," his father growled back. "Nor will it be the last time. I taught you your duty too well—or maybe the asn Castre twins did that."

Jacquel shrugged. His friendship with the twins was something he refused to discuss with his father.

Then his father shocked him.

"I came today to apologize," he said. "You have grown into a fine man. Something I haven't told you enough. Your mother, your birth mother… She would have been very proud of you, too. It wasn't easy watching you grow up, seeing all I had lost brought back to life again, but you have the best of her and for that I am so very grateful."

Jacquel's mouth dropped open, and a fleeting spasm of pain crossed his father's face. "You have her expressions too."

His father stretched out a hand, palm open and waited for Jacquel to accept the clasp. "Whatever you need to help your people, it's yours. That's a promise. Just please…ask me."

Jacquel looked at the outstretched palm, remembering all the times he'd needed a father's hand, then thrust the petty thought aside. Today was for the future. He put out his hand to take his father's, and was even more shocked when his self-contained father pulled him in for a hug, telling him what he'd always known deep in his heart but too often doubted. This man loved him, and Jacquel would not forget it again.

His father left and Rheia returned, quietly, as if belonging only to the shadows of his life. What happened to the virago who had marched into that first plateau briefing, the champion who'd challenged all of Hathe to honor her family's name only days ago?

"We need to talk," he said, and the look of sheer panic on her face confirmed how overdue this was.

She put up a hand as if to ward him off, but he caught it, tugged her toward him and tilted her chin up to let his mouth claim hers. That hadn't changed at least. Her mouth opened and welcomed him as always, and he felt the thrum of passion in her body. But he could sense how much she kept back as he broke the kiss and cradled her face in the palm of his hands.

"You know what I want to ask you."

"No." She thrust a palm against his lips, lifting it when he closed his mouth again. "Don't say it. Please. Let's just carry on like we are."

"With you pretending you're nobody to me, that there is nothing between us."

"It's for the best."

"For who?" But her face remained stubbornly closed and she refused to answer. He tugged her closer. "Please, will you marry me, my darling one? I've missed you so badly these last months."

She tugged hard, pulled back and stood by the far wall with a face as pale as he'd seen it. "No."

She swung about as if trying to leave. He slammed the door shut with his com, watching her as she scrabbled to open it as if desperate to escape.

"Why not?"

One more scrabble at the control panel and she had the lock phased to open. His heart plummeted, as if thrust into the deepest chasm. She was escaping, and he could do nothing to stop her—had no right to.

But then she turned back. "Why not? Because you cannot do the work you must if I'm standing beside you. A moonie, and the daughter of a man dirtsiders believe betrayed them? My father let the Terrans break him and my whole village died because of it."

"You are no traitor."

"I am his daughter, and that would make it impossible for you to do the work you were made for. Not now it's been made so public who I am."

"A hero, that's who you are. A woman who worked as hard as any Hathian in the occupation and gave all of herself to this world. You've seen the vidcast of your speech in Council and heard the cheers of the crowd outside."

She ignored him and turned away again. Turned to leave.

"Rheia, please. I need you." It was truth, pure and simple. He needed her good sense, her ability to read people and soothe the burred strands of his dealings with them. And he just plain needed her.

"No," she said, her voice a whisper. Her hand touched the door pad again. Touched and held for the longest of moments. His heart beat tight every second of that long interval.

Then she took her hand off the door pad and turned back to him, her face blanched and mouth gripped tight. "I will not marry you. But I will work with you, be part of your support team, as long as I can stay behind the scenes."

It was something, if desperately short of what he hoped for. He should accept but found his mouth opening. "And us. What about us? I love you."

"Pillars help me, I love you too. Which is why I refuse to do anything to hurt you—and marrying me would do that."

All he had left was abject pleading. All pride gone, he lifted a hand to her, desperate for anything. "Reject the public hero, but what about the man behind the hero? Can you be with me in private?"

A tear dripped onto her lips and her eyes clung to his. "Yes," she whispered. "In private, I am yours and ever will be. In public, no."

And like a sledgehammer, he suddenly knew if he accepted such a bargain, he would lose her. To live a half-life, exist as a ghost of herself. How could he agree to that when it would destroy her?

He had one option only and felt as if about to lose his heart's blood.

He shook his head…

A man burst through the door, barreling into the room with all the energy in his rotund body. Commander deln Crantz, completely ignoring the dark riptides buffeting the room.

"They've decided," he said jovially. "That wily pack of nystat prevaricators have finally made a judgement."

"What?" said Rheia, shaking her head as if as stunned as he.

"Ah, madame, you're still here. Good—saves me a trip. They've seen sense," he said, rubbing his hands gleefully, "and will take no action against any dirtsider rebel. Further, they have appointed a panel to oversee the reintegration of dirtsiders into full participation in the new Hathe, with restoration of any properties lost through duress or double-dealing, and a panel of enquiry to look into those exploiting the postwar situation on Hathe for personal enrichment. Your friend Yurin an Begum is to lead that one. And you…" Jacquel waited, as the man paused dramatically. "You, you young rabble-rouser, are to lead the reintegration panel, with at least half of the members to be made up of your fellow officers from the recent rising."

A brief pause for a breath, that brilliant smile splitting his face. "We've won, boy. This time, we've really won."

"If I can deliver," said Jacquel, still watching Rheia's face.

But deln Crantz waved his hand at that. "Of course you will. With that twisty brain of yours, and the help of the good madame's diplomatic training here, who can beat you?"

"Just what I've been trying to tell Rheia. She feels our marriage would not be a good idea at present."

Nothing could dampen deln Crantz's spirits, it seemed. "Quite right, too," he said, to Jacquel's dismay. "Far too provocative—but chief assistant, no one will object to that."

And to Rheia's consternation, that is exactly what happened after they were both released and declared fit for duty, despite her insistence it would be too public a role and a myriad of pleadings and protestations from Jacquel for the opposite reason. He did threaten to walk unless she was appointed co-leader with him or returned to the interplanetary duties to which she was so well suited, but deln Crantz rightly ignored that and Jacquel stormed out of the meeting. To return to the Security headquarters two days later with a drawn face and the shadows of dissipation hollowing out his eyes.

What did he expect from her, and why? She could never be Marthe, his first love, never be acceptable to the public if he was to take up the position in Hathe he was born for. Yet he gave no sign of relenting. Marriage or nothing, was his ultimatum, and Pillars help her, she found she couldn't bear the thought of being left with nothing. To never see him again? All pride gone, she begged him to reconsider, and only when she burst into tears, as much a surprise to her as it was to him, did he relent.

"Just know that to me you are a hero, a true Unsung, and I will never allow anyone to treat you as less than that," he said, a scowl on his face.

But that night he came to her apartment, and she had no strength to deny him. She took him to bed, and he showed her all the gentleness, all the passion and honor in his body, leaving all her worthy resolutions defeated. He was trying so hard. If only she could leave him, could know that in time he would forget her.

But that was not possible. He was needed, and so, she came to see over the following days and weeks, was she. They had work to do, together, work too important to be set aside for her vexed sorrows.

She had him in private at least, even knowing that it couldn't last. She was not made for living a half-life of stealth, and neither was he. Too often she saw the lines of it on his face or felt the sudden clench of his muscles as she withdrew from him and faded into the background. It couldn't last, but for now she grasped at what little she had. There would be plenty of time to wallow in misery in the long, lonely nights when Hathe was fully restored and he took his rightful place in their world. She certainly had enough to do to keep her brain off its tired treadmill. For if Rheia thought her work during the war had been hard, it was nothing to her workload on this recovery phase.

After the first hundred cases, she had the convoluted legal phrases down pat. Whatever the strains of their private life, in public they fell easily into a smoothly operating team. She served notice on the moonie grabsters and he did the same for any dirtsiders with an overdeveloped sense of entitlement. When hours of talking only produced more arguments and the way ahead seem more convoluted than ever, they stood together. As they did on those rare and special days, when suddenly two sides became one and a room became filled with

Hathians rather than dirtsiders or moonies. Slowly, slowly, she became an accepted part of Jacquel's team. Not in the fore, but solidly at the core. A place where she could stand tall and do the work she knew best.

And they had wins. The day the camp in the Avenue could be abandoned and dirtsiders and moonies return to living next door to each other. The protestors marched out in triumph, singing songs from Hathe's past and raucous ballads composed during the long nights of the occupation, tears and smiles mingling in equal measure on the faces of marchers and watchers alike. The partying in the streets that night carried on till well into the dawn of the new day.

Both Jacquel and Rheia avidly followed every recorded instant of der Greystan's trial, reviewing the highlights each night curled up together in their sleeper, cheering madly at each point won by the prosecutors and growling at the nystat snivelings of the defense lawyers. All Jacquel's squad joined them on the day the former Councilor was found guilty and sentenced to a life working as a minor administrator in a far off and very isolated corner of Hathe, where he would hopefully learn the true meaning of service to his planet. Rheia unashamedly reveled in the vids of his new quarters: primitive, utilitarian and lacking all the ostentatious luxury to which the man had grown far too accustomed. As for her personal nemesis, asn Chrostic, Rheia felt personally vindicated when it turned out the sniveling little offsider had been the main instigator of the clique's plans. The man would be enjoying the inside of a prison for many years to come, along with every one of the troopers who had captured and mistreated her and Jacquel so badly.

A promise kept, and both she and Jacquel grinned when the final list of the guilty was released.

Most precious of all the wins though, came the day Jacquel walked in her door with a smile as wide as the plateau on his face. "We've found them."

She had to shake her head. "Found who?"

He grabbed her and swung her around her too small room, the merriment in his eyes contagious. "You are a madman," she cried between gulps of laughter. "Found who?" she gasped again.

"Your family of course, my darling one. Or where they lie now, at least."

And that stopped all her laughter. She stood, rooted to the spot, and could only stare. "Are you sure? Their bodies…?"

The laughter had died, but not his glint of triumph. "No, but the place they lie, along with most of your village. There's not much left," he added, suddenly too solemn. "But Gilda tells me they can lift the soil and rescue the essence of those who sleep there. You can bring them home, all the lost ones, and put them where they belong."

Tears dripped down her cheeks, and she grabbed blindly at him and flung her arms around him. "I've drenched you," she muttered some time later. Then lifted her gaze to that beautiful, so beloved face. "Thank you. I…This means so much. Thank you."

When the time came, he stood beside her as she placed her village's urn inside their cavern. In pride of place near the front, on a special plinth inscribed with all their names, all the lost ones come home. Then he held her close all the way back to the City and refused to leave her that night, blocking off his com for the first time since she'd known him.

They had kept their apartments separate until then, but after that day, Jacquel refused to tolerate it any more, making it plain how much he hated it. He found an apartment in a mundane and totally unremarkable block overlooking the City Gardens.

"What do you think?" he said, after tugging her inside.

She couldn't speak, eyes turning all around. Nothing on the outside had led her to expect this. A large window at the far end bathed the whole living area in a spectrum of light, and laid out below in an ever-changing panorama lay the plants and walkways of the City Gardens. "How?"

"It used to belong to a friend of mine, before a growing family called for something bigger."

It was beautiful. "It's you," she said, taking in the furniture and the stylish interiors.

He shook his head. "We can change that. Between us. This place is for both of us. No more one of us having to staying at the other's."

She didn't argue, having come to hate the constant changing of where she slept. Sometimes at his; or he would come to her. And worst of all, those times when they must stay separate to stop discovery of being together. He hid it well, but she knew he hated that most of all, making her feel guilty every time.

But still she refused to marry him, however many times he asked. Jacquel des Trurains must not be bound to a tainted moonie. The dirtsiders may have cheered her speech, but the story of her father's infamy was too deeply ingrained in the story of the war.

"Give them time," Jacquel told her, but she suspected not even time could fix this.

Alone among the dirtsiders, Jacquel's squad welcomed her in as they had from the start, treating her as a mixture of mascot and proxy aunt to the younger ones. They alone knew of the secret apartment and it became a gathering point to escape the continuing tensions outside.

One day, Jacquel crashed through the door and his squad erupted in tight-lipped formation behind him. Rheia leaped off her seat.

"What's happened?"

"That Pillars thrice-damned deln Crantz. He's gone and made me a commander."

She turned to Ras, even more tight-lipped and holding one arm awkwardly. "That's all?" she said.

"No, it's not all," said Jacquel's second-in-command and most trusted remaining friend. "A young idiot on the avenue, carrying a C-390 under his robe. Luckily he was a useless shot as he got a burst in."

"Before you killed him?"

"No, we do not kill children," said Jacquel, glaring at her, then at his entire squad. "Not usually, and not when they are a front for a group of stupid so-called dirtsider patriots refusing to admit the war's over."

Rheia looked to Ras for an answer. Both of them had become long resigned to Jacquel ignoring the threats against him if they interfered with his work. She knew of at least two previous assassination attempts, not to mention three failed political coups.

"The boy was a front," agreed Ras. "The attack a feint for an ambush on the way back from Council. They had a squad planted in front of Jacquel's apartment building—the one where vidcom addicts and idiots think he spends his time flagrantly enjoying the peace." The old vidtapes from when Jacquel had haunted the bars to track down moonie grabsters had taken on a life of their own, endlessly recycled through the worst of the vid channels.

"If it keeps them from fighting each other, and if I don't mind, no one else has any right to object—except Rheia. And she's got more sense than that."

She hated all those scurrilous vidcasts, and so did he. But he was right. She grabbed Jacquel, turning him around. "Are you hurt too?"

"Pretty boy there hasn't got a scratch on him," said Ras in disgust. "While I…"

"Have one slight sprain of a shoulder from grabbing the kid the wrong way," said Dreya, on Jacquel's other side.

They had smiles on their faces and their verbal sparring had the usual cutting edge to it, but the rest of the squad had spread out through the room to check windows, doors and any possible intrusions. She and Jacquel were herded into the central seating area, waiting there till Ras answered a comms signal. He listened in, sending the call through to the rest of the squad and Rheia's com.

"Security has them under wraps. All safe now. Stand down, you lot," said Jacquel pugnaciously.

They snapped to attention.

"Sir, yes sir, Commander."

"And that is quite enough of that. The next nystat idiot who *sirs* me gets stuck on foot patrols for a month. Now, help me drown my sorrows over this Pillars-plagued promotion."

The squad had been at war long enough to never need a second invitation to party. In no time, they had organized drinks, food and shoved back the seats to create a dance floor. It wasn't till much later in the evening that Rheia managed to get Ras aside and find out the true story of the latest attack.

"They're getting less frequent though," said Ras, in some misguided attempt to make her feel better. "This is the first in months."

"Oh good, and when the day comes that someone manages to pull it off successfully, I'll at least know the man I love died after a 'less frequent' attack on him. That will really help."

Ras gave that big-bellied laugh of his. "So that's what it takes to make you admit it."

She looked at him mystified.

"You and Jacquel. The Cap's told me time and again, but this is the first time I've ever heard you admit it out loud. So when's the wedding?"

"Don't be silly," she said crossly. "He can't marry me."

"Why not?" said Ras.

"I'm a moonie, and a nobody with a questionable background."

Ras looked stunned. "You still believe that nonsense?"

"So many dirtsiders have bad memories. They don't need to have their leader shoving me down their throats as well."

"A moonie and daughter of a ranger traitor," said Ras in a mock squeaky tone, copying the worst of the gossip channels, before dropping back to his own in disgust. "Everyone knows who you really are—even you use asn Forvrad as much as asn Postrova now."

It was true, despite the looks it still brought, and she had to admit Jacquel may have been right there as the horrified glances had grown less frequent

"So how about you start trusting us miserable dirtsiders. Don't you know that speech you gave to the Council is treasured by dirtsiders everywhere? Or do you think yourself too good for us?"

"Of course not," she said, shocked to her core he should think that.

Then Ras grinned back. "So next time he asks you, think about answering *yes*. He deserves a happy ending," added Ras softly, "and so do you."

She considered Ras's words often after that. Yet when the council met in formal session and welcomed in all the leaders of the dirtsiders' rising and gave them a formal apology for their treatment after the end of the war, she held tight to her position as Jacquel's chief assistant. A working relationship only. Dreya called her a first-class idiot, but she still refused the seat beside Jacquel at the banquet, staying home and watching it avidly instead. The vidcasters had pounced on him as he'd arrived.

"Commander, and who are you escorting this evening?" one flossy broadcaster had asked. "Someone special, dare we ask?"

"Not tonight, Varinya. She's busy working." And he'd walked alone and single into the hall, with that wicked grin firmly in place and ignoring the rising chorus of yells to know more. Playing the aristo, Ras would call it, and Rheia fumed at the sight. But when he arrived home later, she pointedly said nothing and welcomed him back with open arms and a dress she'd ordered for this night. One the equal of any other woman's at the banquet and that she knew flattered every curve and line of her body. Or so the couturier promised. He burst out laughing at the sight of her, a gleeful grin on his face, and proceeded to take full advantage, but there had been a moment when he'd walked in—a briefly glimpsed flash of sorrow in those bright eyes. They had both been hurt by the night.

Next morning, after he'd left, she realized they couldn't continue like this. She cancelled all her appointments that day to indulge in a fit of weeping. It changed nothing, though. She needed help, but not the kind she could get from Ras or Jacquel. Her mother was gone, and she didn't know Jacquel's mother well enough, but there was one trooper she had come to trust as much as Ras. Time to visit Dreya.

She knocked on the door and was surprised to hear the shriek of childish laughter from the other side. Next moment, a very disheveled and laughing man opened the door.

"Oh, I was told… Is Dreya… is this her home?"

The man turned and called out to someone inside. "Drey, honey, it's the Cap's lady for you." He turned back with a grin on his face. "Come in, come in. Sorry about the mess. We weren't expecting company and our two terrors were letting loose.

Rheia stepped back. "No, sorry, I shouldn't have intruded. My apologies. I'll catch up with Dreya at work."

A head appeared behind him, the usually immaculate trooper wearing an equally mad cap grin as she elbowed the man aside. "You'll do no such thing. Frithan, stop frightening Madame.

Then two boys stuck their heads into view as well, pushing madly at each other until one stuck his tongue out at the other, then grinned triumphantly at his brother as he wriggled to the front.

Rheia gasped and turned to flee. Dreya caught up with her halfway down the hallway, hauling Rheia around to face her. "What's wrong with my boys. You don't like children or something?".

She could only shake her head in denial.

Dreya glared at her. But then her flush faded and she stepped back from Rheia, that cool gaze of hers studying her. "Now I come to think of it," she said. "I've never seen you around children. Do they not fit your lifestyle, madame? Or is it something else?"

Dreya waited and Rheia had to pull up all her courage to answer. Nothing but the hard truth would suffice here. "I had a brother. We called him Bupha." She swallowed, her mouth as dry as a plateau rock bed. "He would poke his tongue out at me then grin in triumph, just like your son." She breathed in, pulling away from the woman. "I'm sorry, I have to go."

But Dreya's hand reached out to hold her, grasping onto her arm, and her voice was the one Rheia had heard often before. Cool and filled with professional calm. "How long since you've allowed yourself to be around children?"

"I see some. A colleague had a little girl."

"But not boys. Not ones who remind you of your brother." Dreya's hand released her but she still stood in the way of her escape, though her voice softened. "Come back in. Come and meet them properly. You have to do it one day."

She shook her head. "What must they think of me?"

"That you are as broken by your past as any dirtsider."

She could think of no argument, nothing that would get her out of this, but her heart hammered as she walked back to the apartment and a hot flush swamped her as she met Dreya's husband again. The family had been talking in Resistance field codes. She was learning to notice the slight flick of fingers and body, and his eyes looked warmly at her, a lopsided smile of sympathy on his mouth.

"Come on in and meet the scamps, madame. They have been warned to behave."

"Thank you," she managed to get out. "I apologize again for my lack of manners."

"We all saw your speech and viewed your father's record when the Council released it. No apologies are ever needed, not to one of us."

And so she followed him in, and the two boys smiled politely at her and bid her welcome, with no echo of that cheeky grin that had brought back Bupha so suddenly and catastrophically. Soon after, their father diplomatically suggested he take them to the park and she was left alone with Dreya. The woman moved to sit beside her.

"Right, out with it. What brought you here?"

"Your husband, he called me the Cap's lady," she countered.

"And so you are." Dreya said flatly.

Rheia looked down, twisted her fingers together, then took a breath and lifted her head again. "How well did you know Marthe an Castre?"

"Ah, so that's the problem." A wicked grin lit Dreya's face. "I didn't meet her till the second year of the occupation. She was as mad, as brave and as brilliantly pig headed as any of the reports say. But also hurt badly, deep inside." The grin vanished from Dreya's face and she leaned back, staring into space. "One of our team got into a tangle with a bunch of Terrans and ended up with a patchwork of nasty gashes where they kicked him for being too slow. They needed sealing. Simple field work; any of us could do it, especially Marthe. She was a physician by training, you see, which was why she was so flat out busy that first year, especially when she got assigned to the mines.

Dreya looked across, nodded when she saw Rheia was listening. "She was good too, near as good as she was at undercover work. But this day, she walked away. I went to see where she'd got too, and found her in a back room, tears streaming down her cheeks. She couldn't face it, you see, not doctoring. Not after what she'd been through that first year. The patients she'd lost again and again. She got her courage back later and went on to treat most of us at some time or other, but she was never the same again."

Rheia didn't know what to say. They were all broken, the heroes most of all. She kept silent for a moment, giving honor where it was due. But there was still one question she badly needed answering. "Jacquel. It's said they were expected to marry?"

Dreya burst out laughing. "Don't tell me you think he's pining because he lost the love of his life?" She took Rheia's hand, turned up the palm and studied the lines scored there, then lifted her head and looked her in the eye. "Yes, he loved Marthe, always will, but not in that way. And also, yes, they probably would have married—and it would have been the worst mistake either could have made. She's his oldest and closest friend, a sister in all but name, and there's a part of him she will always own.

But the love of his life? That's the women who strode into a meeting room and knocked him sideways. That's you, Rheia asn Forvrad."

She came home, not yet convinced but knowing she must find her courage and decide, one way or the other. And it had to be soon. Jacquel said nothing when he came home that night, but his searching look said he'd seen the burden of the day on her face and day by day she saw the shadows grow in his eyes when he thought she wasn't looking.

Then came the day he arrived home with eyes dark with grief. She held her arms out and he walked straight into them. A long time later, he lifted his head. "Marthe. She's leaving, really leaving. The Terran," he never used Hamon an Radcliff's name, "he's been made head of the colonizing mission to Annan IV. And Marthe is Chief Medical Officer."

Annan IV. An untouched paradise, the farthest planet to be colonized yet. Two years minimum transit time. It would be years before any of the settlers could return. She tightened her arms and gently brought his head to the cradle of her shoulder. Dreya had been right in what she'd told her. Marthe an Castre would always hold a special place in Jacquel's heart. Sister, childhood friend, a part of him that Rheia could never own. Then a thought. Could the rest of what she'd said be true? Marthe may hold his past but did Rheia hold his future?

She went with Jacquel the next day to visit the grave of Bendin asn Castre. The fleet pilots had become semi-mythical legends in postwar Hathe, their images marching at the head of the remembrance parades held each year on the anniversary of the Zenith of Mathe, the day of liberation. But now Jacquel told her of the man behind the legend. The golden-haired, laughing and brash young man, cut down when barely out of his youth. The big, bluff leader of an unholy trio of bright young things who had both terrorized and entranced prewar City society.

"I never knew if he was serious when he came up with an idea," said Jacquel. "Except when it was totally outrageous. Then I knew he meant it, and we were heading for trouble again." He grinned briefly, then glanced up at the pristine memorial block. "Mathe, how he'd have hated this place."

In the months before the Annan IV colonizing mission left, Jacquel haunted the vidcasts for every single snippet of news. Sylvan an Castre headed the Council panel in charge of the preparations, and through him they learned the details of the settlers choosing to leave Hathe to go to Annan IV.

"Dirtsiders. Those we failed," Jacquel said bitterly. "Those who can't find a home on their own planet anymore."

She didn't try to soften the blow of it. There were moonie names there too. Not many, but some lost souls. She could sympathize. Without Jacquel, she may have been among them. The Terrans had much to pay for.

But it wasn't only Hathians on the list. Settlers came from all over the federated worlds. Men, women and children hungry for new hope.

"Those are Terran names," she said, shocked by the latest list. And saw by the grim look on his face that Jacquel had already heard of it.

"That should keep their new leader happy," he said bitterly.

They watched the vidcast of the first meeting of all the proposed settlers, curled up on the sleeper in their apartment, clutching hands as they avidly studied the crowded hall. Friends, enemies, strangers. The lost castoffs of every settled world.

"How can they make it?" she wondered.

"Look at their faces," said Jacquel, and she heard the reluctant acceptance in his voice. Then saw what he meant. The open eyes, the tentative lift of head, the subtle straightening of shoulders as they faced their new leaders standing on the podium at the front.

Sylvan an Castre stepped forward to introduce Hamon an Radcliff and his wife, Marthe an Castre. She and Jacquel listened as Radcliff spoke, and that deep voice filled the room. Rheia watched the heads of the settlers lift higher and their backs straighten. Eyes wide, mouths set and determined, they drank in his words.

"He's got them," said Rheia. The man was a born leader.

Jacquel said nothing, and she nudged him with an elbow.

"All right, he's good," he conceded.

The faces in the crowd weren't the only ones she watched. Marthe an Castre stood beside her husband, and Rheia watched her face as she looked at Hamon an Radcliff. Saw her lean in toward the Terran. Then saw the man's hand touch hers as he eased her forward. The bond between them couldn't be missed.

"That's real. The love between them."

"Yes," said Jacquel gruffly. "And I better not see my sisters looking like that at a man as wrong for them."

She swiveled, open-mouthed. "Marthe an Castre is not your sister."

"Near enough to," he said grudgingly. "And yes, I know you've read my file. Deln Crantz told me," as she opened her mouth to demand how he knew.

"After Bendin's death. The vidcasts all said …"

"We'd marry? Only good thing the Terran ever did was stop Marthe and I going through with that nonsense."

She had to smile at the annoyed scowl on his face. Then turned back to watch the vidcast again. "I do believe they can do it," she said.

Jacquel stayed stubbornly silent, but he pulled her close as he broodingly watched the rest of it. And that night, he made love to her with a desperation that would have once had her questioning. Now, after what she'd seen on his best friend's face…And she thanked Dreya anew, for making her see the truth. Marthe was his friend. Not his lover; not like her and Jacquel.

Months later, he came to her one afternoon. "Marthe's ship leaves soon. It's my last chance to say goodbye."

She clenched her hands and forced herself to smile and wish him a good journey. *All right, maybe she wasn't so mature about his very beautiful childhood friend.*

Then he surprised her.

"Will you come with me?" he asked. "You can stay on board. You don't need to meet anyone you don't want to. But…" He raked his hands through his hair. "I've said goodbye to too many people. This one…"

"Yes, I'll come."

It was that simple.

Jacquel heard the door of Marthe's station quarters clang shut behind him as he headed back to his vessel. She had been happy, a touch sad, but…Content, yes, that was the word. Content. A bit scared of the future, the kernels of grief lodged inside still, just as they were for all Hathians who had lost homes or family in the war, but in general—content. And the mad child he'd grown up with was still there, curled up happily inside her. Just as his own wild child lay still in him, he suddenly realized, that smart-mouthed grin he'd given her giving his heart a gleeful kick.

She was going to make it, and so was he.

He walked briskly to the station transporter and sat impatiently as it whisked him back to his own ship, the military-class shuttle he'd shameless requisitioned for this trip. He barely waited for the transporter to release him before striding toward the shuttle lock. Punch in his code, curse as the inner lock ponderously opened, then he was inside.

And waiting for him was Rheia asn Forvrad. He flung out his arms, and she stepped into them, holding him tight and setting his world near to right again.

"You had a question you wanted to ask me," she said, smiling up into his face.

"I've been asking you that question for a very long time," he said suspiciously. "I don't want a pity *yes*."

She laughed, those gorgeous bronze eyes sparkling to life. "Have you looked at yourself in all those celebrity channel vidcasts?" She reached up, and softly touched her lips to his. "Ask me," she said.

He whispered the words he had said to her so often before.

And this time she said Yes.

ACKNOWLEDGEMENTS

A big vote of thanks goes to all those who have helped me bring "Aftermath" to reality. Firstly to my editor, Linda Kimpton, for her patience, wisdom and amazing talent for detail and continuity issues. To Fiona Jayde for all the lovely Hathe covers. And to my fellow writers at SpecFicNZ, RWNZ and RWA, particularly the Auckland specficers and RWNZers: thank you for your generosity, your never-ending support, the laughter and the mutual moans, but most of all for helping me to believe I can do this!

Biggest thanks of all go to my family. To my parents, for raising me in a house full of books, taking us to libraries and taking it for granted that we would all get an education and be able to think for ourselves. To my sons, without whom I don't think this book would ever have been finished. For a birthday present, they gave me a holiday in New Zealand's beautiful lake district, just when I was really bogged down in writing the first draft, and that time out gave me the break I needed to find the story and finish the book. Most of all to my husband who is always there for me, even though I'm far away in my own world more often than not. Thank you all for your acceptance, for everything you've taught me over the years, and for the smiles on your faces when I really need them.

www.ingramcontent.com/pod-product-compliance
Lightning Source LLC
Chambersburg PA
CBHW020906110726
47900CB00001B/31